BLOOD ROSE

RACHAEL VAUGHN

This is a work of fiction. Names, characters, places, and incidents either are the product of the author's imagination or are used fictitiously. Any resemblance to actual persons, living or dead, events, or locales is entirely coincidental.

Copyright © 2019 by Rachael Vaughn

All rights reserved. No part of this book may be reproduced or used in any manner without written permission of the copyright owner except for the use of quotations in a book review. For more information, address: rachaelvaughnauthor@gmail.com

First paperback edition November 2019

Cover image by Johnny Hazard

ISBN 978-1-7337827-3-9 (paperback)
ISBN 978-1-7337827-2-2 (ebook)

www.rachaelvaughn.com

1

ROSE

The window over the sofa in Rose Micenko's living room was stuck.

She shoved hard at the rail and groaned. She wasn't sure why she was surprised; every other day it seemed something in her apartment broke or popped out of alignment or melted or *stuck*—she heaved again—and in her less optimistic moments, she was starting to believe that maybe it wasn't just her apartment that was miserable, but that maybe Indiana was actually an entire miserable state. After three months of living here, Rose was coming to the conclusion that her cross-country move-on-a-whim may have been a mistake.

But today was not the day to think about that. Today was a day to keep her head up, stay busy, and not let her mind wander to what might have been, or what could never be. Today she was going to relax on her worn and slightly lumpy sofa with a tall glass of deliciously cold iced tea and a brand new mystery novel that should take exactly zero brain cells to read, and enjoy the gentle breeze that wafted through the *goddamned open window.*

She heaved again, pressing her shoulder against the glass and leaning her weight into it. For a fleeting moment she considered that if the pane sprung open with no warning, she might just topple through. But considering she was on the first story of the apartment building, the fall would probably be less than four feet. Though god knew what she would land on, considering the complex's less-than-savory location. Broken beer bottles? Dirty needles? Abruptly, Rose eased her weight off the window. Maybe it had actually been sealed for her benefit.

She slid back down onto the sofa in a smooth motion, where she landed with a soft bounce on the worn springs, and considered her options.

She could call the landlord, of course. For the—what—sixteenth time this week? With the heat outside climbing up past ninety degrees, and the air conditioner's dramatic Academy Award-worthy death upon her return from work the day before—no one had answered her calls to repair *that*, either—staying inside and slowly roasting to death didn't seem like the most favorable choice. Why had no one told her that Indiana got so damned *hot* in the summer? *Because there's no one left to tell you anything.* She steered her mind firmly away from this thought.

Okay, so it was late August. And sure, this was probably what she deserved for throwing a dart at a map of the country in a drunken haze and blindly following its trajectory into the unknown. But how was she supposed to know the unknown was this hot, sticky, mosquito-infested hellhole? She was used to the cool, rainy summers of the Pacific Northwest. Ninety-degree heat was not even fathomable.

Rose sighed, shrugging off the creeping fingers of self-pity. There was only one thing to do then. With a groan, she pushed herself off the couch and got to her feet. Grabbing an insulated thermos from the dimly-lit kitchen, she poured in the rest of her tea and sealed the lid. She then retrieved her novel from the floor by the couch, pulled on her shoes, and headed out the door without a backward glance.

∽

Outside, the breeze fooled her into thinking maybe the humid air was actually cooler than the stagnant interior of her apartment. Unfortunately, the sun was doing its best to counter that feeling by blazing down onto the black asphalt as if single-mindedly determined to set the whole complex ablaze.

Rose ducked her head to shield the pale skin of her face against the angry inferno and walked quickly toward the edge of the parking lot, where the hot pavement gradually gave way to scraggly brown tufts of grass, and then finally the cool, lush green that grew in the shade of the forest.

While the thoughtlessly thrown dart had directed her to this godforsaken state, it was actually this forest that had led her to choose this town, and even this apartment complex in particular. Rose could overlook broken air conditioners, sealed windows, and leaky faucets. She could overlook mice. Most of the time. Hell, she could even overlook neighbors shouting drunkenly through paper-thin walls in the dark hours of the night, and smashed car windows—not hers, not yet, anyway—if it meant that she could be near the forest. And here she was not just near it, but practically on top of it.

It was her one concession to home. Growing up amidst the rainy haze of the Cascade Mountains, forests were her refuge and sanctuary. Trips into the woods had been a weekend staple in her family: hiking, camping, searching out new waterfalls...and as much as she had needed to get away from that painful landscape and make a new start, she knew she wouldn't be able to live far from towering trees and creeping undergrowth.

Still, the Hoosier National Forest was a far cry from what she was used to. An unexpected blessing, maybe, as it evoked fewer memories. Here, the gently rolling hills stretching under the low canopy of maples, ashes, and elms was a drastic change from the sharp peaks and towering canopies of Douglas firs and Western hemlocks that blanketed the forests at home. And she had to admit, the decreased likelihood of stumbling across a bear was a welcome change. But in the end, a forest was a forest, and as Rose stepped out of the glare of the sun and into the welcome shade of the trees, a sense of peace that she rarely found anywhere else blanketed her, making her feel—at least momentarily—safe.

Rose wasn't sure how her apartment complex had come to be located in this unlikely spot, but a thin trail meandered out from the trees and opened into one corner of the back parking lot. If you skirted the buildings around to the other side, the trail picked up again and wandered back into the woods toward the west.

It was this first path Rose chose to take, the narrow trail that led straight east for a ways before meeting up with one of the larger hiking trails that carried the Midwest's "outdoor enthusiasts" through the forest. She took a deep breath, letting the cooler air under the canopy fill her lungs and clear her head. She felt her shoulders drop slightly as she walked, the tension that seemed to accumulate through each day at work starting to melt away as her muscles relaxed.

Before her sudden move across the country, Rose had

never worked a day of retail in her life—discounting a two-day stint as a restaurant server during high school, which she mostly pretended had never actually happened—and so the last three months as low man on the totem pole at the local sporting goods store had been an eye-opening experience. She had initially been excited to land a position without too much difficulty at a store that sold things of actual interest to her, but it hadn't taken more than one shift for her to discover that rude customers were a universal phenomenon, seemingly unrelated to the type of goods a store sold.

She had been astonished to discover just how entitled customers could be, as well as dismayed to find out just how little management cared about her treatment by said customers, or her wellbeing in general. Her coworkers had offered little in the way of support or comfort, instead laughing or rolling their eyes at her naivety.

Her sister, Lily, had always said that everybody should have to work at least one retail job in their life, if only so they would learn how to treat the employees. Rose was beginning to suspect none of the citizens of Indiana had ever worked in retail, or if they had, they certainly hadn't learned any lessons from it. And so, as the days passed and began to blur together, the stress took up permanent residence in her neck and shoulders, and her attitude grew more jaded and bitter with each unpleasant interaction. That wasn't who she was, and it certainly wasn't who she wanted to be, but Rose was having a hard time remembering the carefree girl she'd been just half a year ago.

It was Monday, a day she should have been at work, had she not called in sick. Or rather, "sick." But she'd picked up the phone without a second thought, because it was also the nineteenth of August. It was the day that she—that previous version of herself, the one that, in another life, had graduated with honors and had her whole life stretching out in front of her—was supposed to be starting her first day in the prestigious internship she had worked her ass off to win.

It was decidedly *not* a day for a solid nine hours of listening to customers patronizingly inform her that the casual fashion sneakers they had chosen would be "just fine for marathon training." No, that wouldn't do. But if she couldn't have her old life back, at least she could spend the day out in the woods, escaping her memories in the pages of a novel as the leaves rustled around her.

∽

After arriving in the great, flat Midwest, Rose hadn't wasted a day before exploring the path leading out from her apartment. She soon made the delightful discovery that by turning to the north about a mile before the path joined the main trail, and then briefly following a narrow curving deer path, eventually the forest opened into a small circular clearing dotted with tall grasses and wildflowers. Even better, situated just on the eastern edge of this clearing was the most wonderful tree she could ever remember encountering, tall and thick and extraordinarily old, with a forked trunk that formed a seat that matched the exact dimensions of her behind.

Rose sometimes liked to imagine that she had sat down on this tree when it had been a young sapling, and stayed still and motionless for so long that the tree grew around her, molding itself to her shape. There were moments she could almost convince herself that she and the tree were one being, taking the forms of two different species, never truly whole without each other.

And so it was to this tree that Rose escaped whenever the memories became too much, and it was to this tree she headed now, book and thermos of tea firmly in hand.

The deer path was hard to find, a nearly invisible parting of the undergrowth, but Rose had followed it so many times over the past three months she thought she could likely find it blindfolded. She took the turn and altered her course northward, weaving between the trees and vines that crowded thick and leafy in the height of the summer.

The foliage was so dense Rose didn't notice the clearing until it opened up abruptly in front of her, and she was so lost in her thoughts that she was nearly out of the woods before her brain caught up with her eyes and registered what was right in front of her.

It was a house, sitting smack in the middle of the clearing like it owned the place, despite the fact that Rose knew with complete certainty that it had never, ever been there before.

2

ROSE

Rose took in the sight before her, feet rooted to the spot. The house was small, more of a cottage really, with light-colored brick rising up to meet the steep pitch of an A-frame roof. Stone steps led up to the front door, which was framed by a pair of wooden trellises that grew thick with bright purple blossoms and creeping vines. Sunlight glinted off the windows, giving the entire place a warm, cheery look.

At first, Rose thought there must be a rational explanation. She was probably in the wrong meadow. She was pretty sure she had followed her normal path, but she had been distracted; maybe she'd taken a wrong turn?

Keeping to the tree line, she carefully skirted the meadow until she reached the opposite side, watching the house out of the corner of her eye as if it might be a mirage that would suddenly disappear. She turned her gaze and felt a jolt. There it was. Her tree, standing thick and gnarled against the backdrop of the forest, its forked trunk and heavy branches waiting just where they always were.

Eyes wide, Rose turned back to face the house, her

thoughts racing furiously. When was the last time she had been here? Four, maybe five days? Was it even possible to build a house in less than a week? Rose assumed the forest was owned by the state, but she had no idea if there were private residences located on state land.

She continued around the edge of the clearing, ending back where she'd started with a clear view of the front door. Those vining flowers were huge; they didn't grow there in four days. Besides, there was no construction debris, no freshly overturned earth, no utility markings.

The grass grew thickly up to the foundation of the little cottage, wildflowers blooming profusely, the cottage perched in the midst of them, as solid and real as Rose herself.

An unexplainable emotion welled up inside her. Without conscious thought, Rose's feet carried her slowly toward the front door, where she hesitantly climbed the two stone steps and laid her hand upon the sun-warmed wood. Before she could stop and think about what she was doing, she balled her hand into a fist and knocked sharply against the door.

A moment passed, but no response came. She tried the handle, but the door was firmly locked. She took a quick step back, then another, nearly tripping over the steps as she backed down into the grass. What the hell was she *doing*?

What if someone had answered the door, you idiot? she silently berated herself. She could just imagine how that conversation would go: "Yes, hello, I don't need anything, I'm just here to trespass on your property and tell you I'm pretty sure your house didn't exist last week. Have a nice day!" *Brilliant.*

She was backing away through the grass when something above the house caught her eye. Glancing up, she saw a thick square stone chimney rising jauntily out of the center of the cottage's roof, a plume of smoke drifting out lazily and dissipating into the cloudless sky.

So someone *was* in there. But who the hell had a fire going in this million-degree heat?

Edging back into the cool cover of the trees, Rose felt torn. She knew she should leave. She couldn't imagine what kind of circumstances led to this house existing here in what had last week *clearly* been an empty meadow. The only sane answer was that she had somehow gotten lost and mistakenly found her way to a similar but completely different meadow.

W*ith an identical tree?* She pushed the thought away. Either way, the smart thing to do was to get the hell out of here. If the cottage was occupied, which its smoking chimney suggested to be the case, then she was trespassing and shouldn't linger here.

And yet, Rose was feeling unaccountably stubborn. She had been here first. It was *her* meadow, *her* tree, and she hadn't come all this way, on today of all days when she actually *needed* the comforting solace of that damn tree, to be chased away by a strange house that shouldn't even be there! Besides, her tree was on the far side of the meadow. If someone *was* in the house, they probably wouldn't even notice she was there.

Making up her mind, she resolutely marched back behind the house, keeping a wary eye out as she went. If someone came out and told her to leave, she would. Otherwise, this was public land—as far as she knew—and she would sit in a tree if she damn well pleased. Besides, if she considered the situation logically, it *had* to be a different meadow. Either that or she'd gone crazy, in which case it didn't matter anyway.

The tree was just where she'd left it, and she hauled herself up onto the low branch by the forking trunk, settling into the familiar curved space that seemed to have been made just for her. She stretched her legs out in front of her, feeling the rough, warm bark against the back of her jeans, and heaved a sigh. Deliberately ignoring the house standing not a hundred paces away, she took a long drink of her iced tea and flipped open her book, losing herself in the story until her eyelids grew heavy.

∼

Rose didn't realize she had dozed off until the harsh screaming call of a barn owl jolted her awake, heart pounding and palms sweaty where they still held the book against her chest. She took a moment to catch her breath, letting the disorienting fog of sleep lift as she remembered where she was and what she was doing.

She glanced down at her watch. After nine o'clock. Had she really managed to lose most of the evening? Her jaw cracked in a yawn. It wasn't that surprising. Long days on her feet at work left her exhausted, and between the warm sun and gentle breeze, she hadn't stood a chance. She swung her feet over the edge and hoisted herself to sit upright against the trunk.

Dusk had fallen as she'd napped, and was quickly edging its way into full dark. The meadow was thick with the sounds of frogs and crickets, the brief pulsing light of fireflies flashing against the silhouettes of the trees.

The house was still there, she was surprised to see. She'd half convinced herself it was a dream. Soft light filtered out through the curtained windows, giving it a feeling of welcoming coziness against the growing dark.

Her stomach gave a plaintive growl and Rose was reminded that she had missed dinner. *Time to head back*, she thought, dropping the short distance out of the tree to land in the soft grass. She fumbled in her pocket for her phone, intending to use the flashlight to light the path. It wasn't full dark yet, but it would be soon, and despite her earlier thought that she could find the path blindfolded, she really didn't want to test that theory.

Patting each of her pockets in turn, Rose quickly came to the disheartening realization that she hadn't brought her phone. She thought back and could picture it sitting on the kitchen table, right where she'd left it. It was often impossible to get a signal out in the woods, so she never made too much of a point to bring it unless she planned to go far.

She cursed her stupidity. She knew better, she really did. Her parents had drilled into both their children from an early age that you never went hiking in the woods without letting someone know where you were, and bringing a phone for emergencies. But she'd grown lazy since her move, sadness and depression overcoming her common sense. She kicked herself for it now.

For a second, she contemplated just stumbling back in the dark, but she could practically see her father's raised eyebrow and skeptical expression, so with great reluctance she sighed and turned toward the house. It was still possible she was going crazy, but someone clearly appeared to be home. She would just borrow a flashlight and go.

~

Rose gathered up her empty thermos and tucked her book under her arm, making her way over to the house. The field was growing darker with each passing moment, so she crept closer around the side of the brick wall where the glow from the windows shed enough light for her to see. She wondered what kind of person would live in a house in the middle of a state forest, nervously speculating that knocking on the door may perhaps be even less safe than wandering home in the dark.

Quite suddenly and without any warning, there was a flurry of movement at Rose's feet. The creature she had inadvertently startled burst out of the tall grass and dashed away into the night. With a stifled scream, Rose jumped, stumbling over her own feet. Her thermos went flying from her grip as she reached out a hand to catch herself against the side of the house, but instead of the smooth wood of the windowsill she expected, she felt a searing pain as a protruding nail scored a deep gash into the flesh of her palm.

Cursing loudly, Rose stumbled another step before stopping and bracing herself against the brick wall. She leaned there for a moment to catch her breath and slow her pounding heart, dropping her book and grabbing the hem of her shirt to wrap the fabric around her injured palm.

After a moment she straightened, tentatively opening her clenched fingers to view the gash in her hand. The blood welled from the wound, thick and black in the darkness, and it was difficult to see the extent of the damage. The blood was smeared over both hands now, and though her hand stung fiercely she could see that it was already clotting. Not too bad then, though she found herself wondering how long it had been since she'd last had a tetanus shot.

Holding her injured hand out to keep the blood from further staining her clothes, she crouched and felt around in the grass with her good hand for her book and thermos. When her search turned up nothing but prickly grasses, she muttered under her breath and decided that further searching would be better left to the light of day, or at least the light of a flashlight. Frustrated, she stomped around to the front of the house. She could see the lights on inside, and with the racket she'd made she couldn't believe no one had come out to investigate. They'd better answer the door.

A light encased in a bell-shaped wrought iron fixture hung high on the wall by the door, casting a warm yellow glow over the front porch. Rose hadn't thought to look earlier, but there didn't appear to be a doorbell, so she once again knocked hard against the wooden doorframe, calling out a forced but friendly, "Hello?" in case the occupants were alarmed by their late-night visitor.

As she'd half-expected, there was no answer, so she knocked again, louder. Still nothing. A handful of minutes and an array of knocks and shouted greetings later, the door still remained resolutely shut, not a trace of movement showing through the muted light beyond the curtained window.

"Oh, come *on,*" Rose muttered, holding tight to her irritation to fend off the panic she could feel creeping in around the edges.

With one last thump on the door, her gaze slid down to the handle. She knew it would still be locked, as it was earlier, but nevertheless she let her hand settle nervously on the latch. What on earth was she going to do now? Full dark had fallen, and she was just beginning to consider the possibility of spending the night in her spot in the old tree when she felt a stab of pain and realized that she'd inadvertently reached out with her injured hand. But before she had time to react, the strangest thing happened.

A faint glimmering light caught her eye and she glanced down, gasping softly. The skin of her hand was *glowing.* It was faint, just a slight iridescent shimmer, but it was decidedly, undeniably *there*. She released the handle as if burned and raised her hand in front of her face. The light faded almost immediately.

Rose stared hard at the offending limb, wondering if, in her panicked and injured state, she'd begun to hallucinate. The wound throbbed in her palm, but there was no light emanating from it. Eyeing the lamp above the door, she decided that it clearly had been a reflection of the light in the shiny metal surface of the handle. What else could it have been? Before she could think too hard about it, she stretched out her injured hand and placed it gingerly back on the handle.

Feeling as if nothing could surprise her after this day, she nonetheless inhaled sharply as a shimmering glow flared to life, seeming to radiate from where her hand met the handle. With a start, she noticed that her *other* hand was glowing as well. No, not her hand, Rose realized, her heartbeat quickening—it was her *blood*. It was there on her shirt as well, a faint luminescence emanating from the dark spots where the blood had stained the fabric.

The next second all thought of the curious light fled her mind as the latch moved with an audible *click* and the door swung open in front of her.

3

ROSE

The door made no sound as it swung open. Hesitantly, Rose poked her head through the opening, keeping her eyes cast down at the floor.

"Hello?" Her voice was tentative. She cleared her throat and tried again. "I was hoping to borrow a flashlight!"

There was no response from the interior of the small cottage, so with a deep, steadying breath, she stepped across the threshold and let the door swing shut behind her.

"Is anyone here? I just—" Her voice broke off in an audible gasp as her eyes adjusted to the dim light, and she registered the sight in front of her.

The entryway was...grand. There was no other word for it. Her feet carried her forward involuntarily, and her mouth gaped open; it was almost too much to take in.

The floor was marble, inlaid with an elaborate mosaic constructed of tiny reflective glass pieces. A sweeping staircase rose to both the right and left, curving up in a huge arc to meet in the back of the enormous foyer. A plush-looking carpet ran up the center of the stairs, and the bannister on the railing was carved to form elaborate, interlocking shapes. The ceiling soared high overhead in a series of sweeping arches reminiscent of a gothic cathedral, and an enormous chandelier hung suspended from the apex, seemingly hundreds of tiny lights shimmering in their carved holders and casting a warm flickering glow on the richly painted walls.

Against the back wall, underneath where the staircases met on the second floor, hung an enormous tapestry, its woven threads depicting what appeared to be a creature set against a forest scene, but both creature and forest were unlike anything Rose had ever seen before.

As Rose's eyes widened to drink in the elaborate scene in front of her, frantic alarm bells sounded in her head. This was *not* the interior of a cozy cottage. The cottage could have fit three times over in this entryway alone, and who knew how far the space extended down numerous hallways and out of sight. No, this was the interior of a freaking *castle*, and she didn't know what the hell was going on, but it was time to clear out and run home as fast as her legs could carry her, dark or no dark. Nothing about this place had made sense since the second she'd laid eyes on it, and it was time to stop making excuses and get the hell out of here.

She began slowly inching backward toward the door, and she had almost reached it when a soft voice stopped her in her tracks.

"Wait—don't go."

It was masculine, but also not. Low and melodious, velvety smooth yet with a strange, almost otherworldly resonance. But it wasn't the beauty of the strange voice that made her pause, it was the tone, hesitant, but with a noticeable undercurrent of desperation. Rose turned toward the source of the sound, and saw the tapestry against the back wall ripple and then lift from the corner, revealing a tall figure. He stepped around the heavy folds of draping fabric, and moved toward her into the center of the room, where he was illuminated by the flickering light cast by the chandelier.

Rose's mouth, which had opened to voice her request for a flashlight, fell closed as the words died in her throat.

The creature was clearly a man—or male, anyway. He was tall, with broad shoulders and a strong jaw, his form lithe but masculine. Beyond that, Rose had no idea what to make of the figure that stood before her. Her eyes fell first on his hair, clearly his most striking feature. It was pure white, long and silky, falling loose past his shoulders and down his back in a shining curtain. Despite the white hair, his skin—which appeared to have a pale blue cast in the light from the chandelier—was smooth and unlined, and he had an aura of agelessness about him. His dark eyes had a slight upward tilt to them that reminded Rose of a cat as they studied her as intently as she did him.

And dear lord, his *clothes*. She had never seen such a bizarre assortment outside of a theater's costume department. She had no knowledge of historical garb, but he wore what she could only describe as a frock coat. It hung open, long and black nearly to his knees, with a row of carved wooden buttons running up the front and along the cuffs. A spill of lace fell from the cuffs, covering the tops of his hands. Beneath the coat he wore what appeared to be a white shirt with nearly invisible pale gray stripes, as well as black pants tucked into tall black boots with a line of shiny silver buckles running down the sides.

His eyes on her were dark and penetrating, and he met her gaze with a searching look that Rose couldn't quite interpret.

The stranger pulled himself together first, gesturing at

Rose's hand. "You're bleeding," he said, drawing her attention back to the injury that had completely fled her mind in the wake of all these strange new developments. His voice still had that strange resonant quality, as if it were coming from both within him and *around* him at the same time.

She looked down at her palm. The flow of blood had almost completely stopped, only a thin trickle still oozing from the gash. With the blood smeared on both hands though, it looked worse than it was.

"I cut my hand on a nail on the side of the house," she said, leaving out the embarrassing scare from what was likely just a squirrel or a mouse. She felt unbalanced with his eyes on her.

"May I?" He nodded at her outstretched palm, and Rose nodded wordlessly. The panic she had felt just moments before was still there, but it felt muted somehow, like she was trapped in a dream where everything felt both completely foreign and completely familiar at the same time.

The stranger stepped forward slowly, cautiously, and Rose almost felt like he was trying not to spook her. When he was close enough that she could make out his features clearly in the soft light, she drew in a breath. His slanted eyes were a deep lustrous purple, fringed with long dark lashes, and they contrasted startlingly against his skin, which Rose could now see actually *was* a pale blue. Most alarming of all though, were the curving lines of silver filigree she could see etched faintly into his skin. When he stood still the lines were nearly invisible, but when he moved, they seemed to shift and swirl, skittering over the surface of his skin to form new patterns.

Dreamlike or not, her brain had reached its maximum weirdness capacity and, unable to process anything more, proceeded to shut down. She didn't flinch or ask any questions when he reached her side and gently lifted her hand into his own. Idly, she noticed that his fingers were long and smooth, his skin soft on hers as he turned her palm to catch the light.

"This needs to be cleaned, and you need a bandage," he said, then looked at her questioningly. "Will you wait?" he asked, and Rose got the impression he thought she might bolt if he left the room. She wasn't sure she wouldn't, but she nodded anyway.

He turned and she watched the silver patterns swirl across his skin as he strode across the room toward the tapestry, pushing one edge aside and disappearing behind it.

Rose blew out a breath. She wasn't sure how long she'd been holding it, but she felt somewhat lightheaded. She considered doing the smart thing and running straight out the door, but something held her in place. For one thing, if she left now, she'd be right back where she started, out in the dark with no way to find the path back to her apartment. For another, if she was really being honest with herself, the actual reason she didn't run was plain curiosity. She had to see this through, had to get some answers, or she wouldn't be able to stop wondering.

The stranger was back before long, and Rose didn't miss the flash of relief on his face when he saw her standing where he had left her. He carried with him a bowl of water, steam rising in tendrils from the surface, and an assortment of other supplies. When he reached her he continued on past, beckoning her to follow, and Rose turned to see him heading toward a small seating area near the door. A low, backless sofa ran along the wall, each end lifting to curl in a tight spiral. An equally low table stood in front of the sofa, and two matching chairs framed either side.

After a moment of hesitation, Rose took a seat on the sofa, and the stranger placed the bowl and supplies on the table before lowering himself hesitantly to sit beside her. He gave her a questioning glance as if asking for permission, and Rose offered her wounded palm. She kept quiet, not wanting her barrage of questions to break the trance she felt from his calming influence. The man chose a soft cloth from the pile on the table, dipped it in the warm water and began to gently wash the blood from her hand. She winced when the water stung the cut, and the man grimaced in apology.

As he worked, the lace cuff fell back from his left hand and the sleeve of his jacket rode up slightly. Rose caught a glimpse of something thick and dark winding around his arm. It appeared to have the texture of an old scar, thick and ridged, but jet black and stark against his pale blue skin. It grew thinner the further down it reached, tapering out into thin tendrils at his wrist, leaving the skin of his hand smooth and untainted. Rose felt his hands falter in their movements against hers, and she looked up to see him following her gaze to his wrist. He self-consciously pulled the cuff back down into place, covering the black lines, and Rose hastily looked away.

"Sorry," she mumbled. He didn't respond, only retrieved the cloth and began wiping blood from her other hand. Once both were clean, he let the cloth fall into the now pink-tinged water, and took a bandage from the table. He paused for a moment, before setting the bandage back down unopened.

"You must have a lot of questions," he said softly, not quite meeting her eyes.

A startled laugh escaped Rose's throat. That was the

understatement of the century. He gave a soft chuckle and she realized she had voiced the thought aloud.

"Yes, I imagine that must be true." He turned to face her directly, and his eyes met hers. She was alarmed at the intensity in their purple depths, and his voice was urgent when he spoke again, the words coming fast.

"Listen, I'll explain everything, I promise. But you're not safe here, and I need you to trust me."

Rose opened her mouth, but he continued before she could respond.

"I know we've only just met, but I *promise* I won't let any harm come to you. There's so much you need to know, and so little time, and I—" he paused, seeming to exert quite a bit of effort to gather himself. He took a deep breath and lifted his eyes to hers. "Will you trust me?"

His gaze bored into her, and without the slightest idea why, Rose found herself nodding. Anything to get that look of desperation off his face.

He seemed to wilt, relief coloring his features, and he held out his hand for hers again. She placed her wounded hand in his, and he flipped it over, palm up. Lifting his other hand, he gently placed his index finger against the gash in her palm, and without warning, a burst of light emanated out of his fingertip where it met her skin.

Rose felt strangely detached, as if she were watching this happen instead of actually experiencing it. She felt no pain, only a bright, comforting warmth that grew to encompass her whole hand. He traced his finger slowly down the length of the wound, the bright light following the path of his finger, and Rose watched in surprise as the line of her blood began to glow bright, the same iridescent glimmer she had noticed when she'd touched the handle of the door what seemed like ages ago.

Rose watched in wonder as the stranger lifted his hand, the light fading. The shimmer faded from her palm as well, the wound sealing in its wake.

"There," he said, releasing her hand. His voice sounded faint, its resonance muted. Rose looked up, sensing something was off, and found his face pale, nearly white, the silver lines practically nonexistent.

"Are you okay?" she asked, suddenly worried for this man—creature—she didn't know, but he simply nodded and waved off her concern. She looked down at her palm again in amazement, a thin faded line all that remained of the red gash.

"What *was* that?" she asked, "How did you—" But her attention was caught quite suddenly by his hands, which were clutched tightly in his lap. He held his right hand wrapped protectively around the left, but past his grip Rose could see the black lines moving on his skin, creeping slowly beyond the edge of his cuff and onto the back of his hand, tendrils snaking across the pale flesh there.

She looked back up at him in horror and found him leaning back against the wall, his face pale and his dark eyes unfocused. "You're not okay at all," she said, hastily reaching to support him before he slumped over. "What can I do? Tell me what you—"

"What is your name?" His voice was barely a whisper, and she could see the monumental effort it took him to focus his eyes on her face.

Her voice was sharp and panicked. "Rose. How do—"

"Rose." Her name on his lips was a resonant whisper that spiraled away into the dark of the night. Then his eyes drifted shut, and a moment later he slumped over, his weight more than Rose could support as he slid off the couch and down to the floor.

4

ROSE

Rose crouched over the limp form lying sprawled on the floor by the couch. Was he *dead?* She reached her fingertips to his throat, feeling for a pulse. Would he have one? Was he even *human?* But there it was, strong and steady against her fingers, and she blew out a relieved breath.

She rocked back on her heels, trying hard to keep calm and think logically. A wave of panic rose in her chest like a wave, and she fought it back. Freaking out now would do no good. She had to figure out what to do. Call for help? Yes, that seemed like what a reasonable person might do.

Cursing herself yet again for leaving her cell phone back in the apartment—you really never knew when you'd need to call an ambulance for a potentially inhuman magical creature—Rose heaved herself to her feet. She bent and slid a pillow from the couch under the unconscious stranger's head, smoothing the long white strands of hair out of his eyes, then went in search of a phone.

Twenty minutes later she found herself back in the foyer where she had started, frustrated and befuddled but very aware of two things: first, this cottage, house, castle, whatever it was, was *enormous*, and second, the man who lived here apparently either didn't believe in telephones or was unaware of their existence.

She checked on him again and found him still unconscious, his breathing even and his heartbeat strong. She braved a peek at his hand and found the black tendrils had stopped twisting and writhing, but had definitely crept lower on his hand than they had been when she'd first glimpsed them.

Well what now? She couldn't just *leave* him like this. Should she go for help? For all she knew, he'd wake up in five minutes completely recovered. But then again, who was to say he didn't desperately need a doctor? What on earth would a doctor even make of this bizarre creature? Rose ran her hands roughly through her disheveled black hair, tugging on a few loose strands as she tried to think.

Go for help. Yes, that was the thing to do. Better safe than sorry. She hated the thought of leaving him here to wake up—or not—on his own, but she couldn't think of any alternative. At any rate, she wasn't all that far from her apartment, and if she hurried, she could be back home in half an hour or so, assuming she could somehow navigate the dark of the forest. She had no idea how anyone was going to get an ambulance out to a random clearing in the Hoosier National Forest with no road access in the pitch dark, but that would be someone else's challenge. Her task was to get to a phone.

Rose hovered over the stranger a moment longer, feeling helpless as she crouched down and checked him over once again. There was nothing she could do for him here. She got to her feet and headed for the door, but when she reached the entrance, she froze in place.

Where the door she'd entered had stood, there were now *two* doors. Rose shook her head, thinking she'd finally lost it, but both doors remained, identical from their filigreed wood down to their gleaming handles.

I don't have time *for more craziness,* Rose thought with an exasperated huff. She refused to be sidetracked by yet more of the sheer nonsense this day was doling out. Choosing a door at random, she grabbed the handle and yanked it open. The fleeting thought that she *still* didn't have a flashlight crossed her mind just as the door opened wide, bright sunlight pouring through the gap.

Had she been there all *night*? No, that surely wasn't possible. Rose stepped through the opening, blinking against the bright light of midday as she tried to get her bearings, but when her eyes adjusted and she took in the scene in front of her, she realized that bearings were the least of her concerns. Whatever secret pride she may have had in her ability to take these bizarre events in stride, she saw now that she was well and truly out of her depth—or out of her mind. When a *house* had appeared—out of nowhere—in her meadow, she'd managed to accept it. When the house turned out to be impossibly larger on the inside than the outside, she'd not said a word. And when the strangest man she'd ever laid eyes on, with symbols moving on his freaking *blue skin* had done God knew what to her hand, she hadn't run screaming. But this—*this* was too much.

A sweeping stone veranda spread out from the door in a semicircle, enclosed by an ornate wrought-iron railing. Without waiting for permission from her brain, her feet carried her to the railing and she looked out over the breathtaking vista. A long flight of stone steps led downward, meeting at the bottom with a path that led through a clearing that was, on the surface, similar to the one she'd expected to see. But while the shapes and general layout were the same, everything else that met her eyes was...*wrong.*

The forest grew close, swallowing the path with towering trees, hundreds of feet taller than they should have been, with a sweeping canopy of iridescent leaves in every color and shade except what they were *supposed* to be. Shining swathes of rich blues and shadowy purples glinted in the sunlight and rustled in the breeze, which, Rose noticed, was actually rather chilly, cutting through her thin t-shirt and raising goosebumps on her arms.

The melodious call of birdsong echoed through the clearing, but even that sounded different in a way Rose couldn't quite put her finger on. It was as if the birds were singing in a minor key, their song eerie and haunting instead of cheerful.

Wrong door.

The thought caught Rose by surprise, and she suppressed a slightly hysterical laugh as she turned back to the house, which she was unsurprised to see bore no resemblance to the simple cottage she had originally entered. *This* structure was all soaring expanses of stone, balconies and porches, turrets and towers cobbled together into what she could only describe as a castle. *Or maybe a fortress*, she thought, eyeing the crenellations on the highest peaks. She forced her attention back down to the door—it was only one door now—that she hadn't noticed had closed behind her as she'd stood taking in the scene, and gripped the handle with a sense of wary fatalism.

It didn't budge. It was locked. Of *course* it was. Why the hell had she expected anything else? Rose leaned her forehead against the cool wood of the door and took a couple of deep breaths, fighting the wave of nausea that accompanied the panic coursing through her. What *was* this place? What was *happening*?

She closed her eyes and concentrated on the feeling of air filling her lungs, stubbornly willing her mind to calm and clear. She'd already moved across the country on a whim, left everything she'd ever known to start fresh in a new place. What was this but a new adventure?

When at last her heartbeat was slow and her hands steady, Rose pushed herself off the door and turned. With a feeling of resigned acceptance, she made her way down the long flight of stairs and followed the path into the forest.

5

ROSE

Rose's first reaction once she had been engulfed by the towering trees was one of sheer awe and amazement. The leaves that blanketed the forest floor were enormous, the size of dinner plates and oddly shaped, some with jagged saw-tooth edges, others with giant star-shaped holes, and their colors ranged from the palest lavender to bright piercing cobalt blue. They were beautiful. The bird song was louder there too, haunting melodies echoing through the canopy, and every so often Rose caught sight of odd furry animals with unfamiliar markings scuttling through the undergrowth or clinging to tree trunks.

She had to remind herself not to get distracted; she was there to find help for the unconscious stranger, and everything else could wait. Then she would go back to the castle, he would wake up and tell her what the hell was going on here, and how to get home, and she would leave this completely bizarre situation behind. *And go back to your exciting retail job?* Best not to think too hard about that at the moment. Just focus on the task at hand.

But though the novel sights and sounds overwhelmed her senses and stole her attention, as she trudged along the forest path, she became uncomfortably aware that she was both very, very hungry, and very, very cold. She tried to think back to when she had last eaten, and vaguely remembered a granola bar and an apple from—was it the day before? Did this still count as night? A glance at her watch indicated that it had stopped entirely at eleven forty-two. She had no idea what that meant, or how to reconcile whatever time shift may have taken place. Suffice it to say she hadn't eaten in a long while, and she was famished.

The temperature, too, seemed to have dropped nearly thirty degrees. Rose wouldn't necessarily call it *cold*, but it was a harsh contrast to the ninety-degree heat and midwestern humidity she had left behind, and the flimsy T-shirt she wore offered no protection from the breeze that gusted through the trees as she walked.

On the plus side, Rose realized she wasn't tired. Between her long afternoon nap and the adrenaline that coursed through her system as her brain tried in vain to search for explanations for her current situation, she felt highly alert. Which was just as well since she had no idea how far she may have to go before she encountered another human who could help.

Her mind wandered as she marched briskly along the path, rubbing her arms to keep from shivering, and her eyes darted from tree to tree, taking in the strange sights all around her. She thought back to her first walk in the woods in Indiana, how she had found the forest there to be such a drastic change from what she was used to at home in the Pacific Northwest. The thought made her chuckle. No matter how strange the different species of trees had been, no matter how flat the land was when she was used to mountainous ridges, none of the trees in Indiana had been *blue.* Or covered with thick furry moss the consistency of 70s shag carpet with colors to match.

She smiled again, watching a small, fuzzy, rodent-like creature with bold stripes scamper up the side of one of the trees at the edge of the path. This was certainly not the kind of woods she ever imagined she'd be walking in, but it had the same comforting familiarity she seemed to find in all forests. She couldn't put her finger on what it was exactly. A particular smell, perhaps, or the familiar sounds of leaves crunching underfoot and the sigh of the breeze through the branches? Or maybe just a feeling that was ubiquitous to forests everywhere? A feeling of peace and calm, of safety and distance, as if her life was muted while she was here and her worries were left behind, waiting for her to pick them back up on the other side. She'd always had that feeling in the woods, ever since she was a small child in the forests at home.

Her smile faded as she thought about home. Abruptly, she realized that while she wasn't sure what day or time it was, it certainly wasn't Monday anymore. She had made it through the day. Somewhere, across the country or in another world, the internship she had worked so hard for had started without her. Another lucky recent graduate had probably been called in to take her place, and the world had moved on like she'd never even existed. No one was left there to miss her. Even at her new home in Indiana, she doubted she was missed. She wondered how long it would take her job to replace her. Would they even wait for her to come back? Retail workers were a dime a dozen, and Rose doubted it would take more than a day or two to fill her position with another nameless warm body.

Suddenly, Rose felt very alone. She missed her parents

and her sister fiercely, with an ache in her heart that felt like a real, throbbing wound. Without them, she felt infinitely replaceable, like there was no one in the world who cared about *her*, specifically, when another person could just as easily fill her shoes.

The melancholy thoughts swirled in her mind like the funnel cloud of a forming tornado, feeding off each other and escalating, and Rose felt her steps begin to slow as the wave of hopelessness grew large enough to engulf her.

It was at that moment that the wind shifted and she heard, very faintly, a sound quite unlike anything she had ever heard before. She stopped and cocked her head to the side, her troubles suddenly forgotten. She listened hard. What *was* that?

The sound seemed to fade as she stood still, so she cautiously began to move again, careful to keep her footsteps quiet as she moved down the path. Yes, it was definitely growing louder. It was ahead of her, then, and moving as well. It sounded almost like the wheels of a cart or a wagon—perhaps more than one—crunching through leaves and bumping over rocks, but different somehow.

Quite suddenly the vision of the stranger's face filled her head, his eyes closed and his skin pale, his white hair fanned out around him as he lay deathly still on the floor, black tendrils creeping around his wrist. She gave herself a shake, angry that she had let her troubled thoughts distract her. She had no time for self-pity. If there was someone up ahead, maybe they could help. Rose broke into a jog, following the path as it twisted and turned through the trees, listening intently as the strange rumbling sounds grew louder.

It took about five minutes before Rose followed the path

around a tight curve and came upon them from behind. When she saw what was ahead of her, she skidded to a halt.

She had been right, she thought with bemused amazement. It *was* a bunch of wagons. A whole caravan, really, and it looked to Rose almost exactly like the pictures she remembered depicting convoys of early American settlers crossing the plains to settle in the west. She counted twelve wagons altogether, although these ones were brightly painted and covered with odd symbols Rose didn't recognize. But the strangest part of all, she noted with wide, disbelieving eyes, was that the tallest of these wagons reached no higher than Rose's waist.

The caravan of wagons rumbled forward, and after a moment, she hurried to keep up. They were moving rather slowly, and Rose looked around but couldn't see anyone accompanying the group as it bumped along the forest floor. Hesitantly, she stepped off the path into the underbrush and hurried forward toward the front of the wagon train. Turning to peek inside as she passed, Rose's jaw dropped as she caught sight of what exactly was perched on the seats of the wagons. Each wagon boasted a pair of what appeared to be mice—much larger than the mice she was familiar with, and with oddly colored fur—but mice nonetheless, with large ears and long thin tails. Their small pink hands gripped tightly to a set of reins, which were attached to harnesses wrapped around pairs of odd, insect-like creatures about the size of raccoons that clicked their jaws as they skittered forward, pulling the wagons in their wake.

From closer up, Rose could see groups of the bizarre mice sitting inside the wagons as well, and a few walking alongside. Their strangely-colored fur gave the impression of a patchwork quilt—a brown arm with a grey body, black legs with a brown head. It almost looked like each mouse had been cobbled together from the mismatched parts of other mice, and the overall effect put her vaguely in mind of Frankenstein's monster.

The Frankenmice ignored her as she passed by, and Rose wondered for a brief moment if there were any actual *people* in this strange place. Should she try asking the mice for help? The thought made her feel a bit silly, considering that they were mice, but then again, they *were* riding in wagons. Who was to say they didn't speak English?

Feeling foolish, Rose stepped back onto the path and addressed the pair of Frankenmice perched on the seat of the lead wagon, matching their pace as she walked alongside.

"Um, excuse me?" The mouse holding the reins looked her way, which she took as an encouraging sign.

"My name is Rose, and I'm not from around here, but I need your help." The mouse did not respond, but continued to look at her expectantly. "There's a castle a ways back, and the...uh...person there is hurt, and I think he needs help, and—" Rose broke off as the mouse directed its attention back to its fellow on the wagon bench.

"I...excuse me?" Feeling ridiculous, Rose tried again to capture the mouse's attention, going so far as to bend and wave, but it did not look up again.

Cheeks flaming red, Rose muttered under her breath and turned away. How ridiculous that she should feel embarrassed right now. What she should be doing is questioning her sanity.

Facing forward again, Rose considered the fact that the bizarre Frankenmice were clearly leading their caravan *somewhere*, and therefore if she kept following the trail, hopefully it would lead her to that somewhere as well. *And hopefully not to a town full of Frankenmice,* she thought with a scowl. Heaving a breath, she picked up her pace again, quickly leaving the mice behind as she pushed onwards.

6

THE MA'AR

The sun sat high in the sky, shining its blistering rays down on what had once been the magnificent city of Trelissar, capital of the glorious kingdom of High Trelis.

The cloaked figure ducked out of the blinding afternoon light and into the musty damp interior of what had once been the Trelissar cathedral, his face twisted in a contemptuous sneer that only faded once the sunlight was swallowed by the gloom inside.

Cautiously, he checked his surroundings to be sure he wasn't seen. It was unlikely; the cathedral had long since been abandoned to the Rot, which had crept in subtly at first, black tendrils reaching tentatively from under the pews and snaking down the leaded lines in the soaring stained-glass windows.

Time, though, had not been kind to Trelissar. By the time the forward momentum of the Rot was halted, the entire second story of the cathedral had already been consumed. Now, it coated the altar in a thick black mass, dripping down the chandeliers that hung from the arched ceiling. Even those beautiful stained-glass windows were broken and blackened now, jagged pieces of glass framing gaping holes. The cool afternoon breeze filtered in and blew the subtle stench of the Rot through the windows. The odor wafted into the figure's sensitive nose, which wrinkled in disgust.

No one else seemed to be able to smell the sickly scent. Though of course, no one else was overly concerned with the presence of the Rot. Not anymore. And that was largely thanks to him. He worked hard to keep it that way, and due expressly to his efforts, Trelissar was now one of the safest places to live in the whole kingdom. Possibly the whole world. For the moment, at any rate.

There wasn't a lot of Rot left in Trelissar now, but it seemed to cling stubbornly in the places where it had managed to keep its hold, and no matter how hard he tried, it never seemed to budge from the cathedral.

Moving silently, the cloaked figure slid around the corner through one of the few remaining rooms untouched by the Rot—a small library at one time, he thought—and took the dark stone steps that led down to the catacombs that ran the length of the cathedral deep underground.

Dark, dank, cold, and musty—but blessedly free from Rot.

So far.

It was only when the soles of his boots met with the hard stone floor of the catacombs that he released the breath he had been holding. The torches that lined the walls in deep-set sconces were still lit from earlier, and their flickering light chased away at least some of the shadows.

Heaving a relieved sigh, the figure pulled off his cloak and tall black hat and draped them carefully over a nearby tomb. He hated that hat—always made his head itch—but he fancied it gave him an air of respectable authority when dealing with his citizens. One had to keep up appearances, after all.

Today in particular had been a long day of public appearances. It seemed the petty squabbles of the Trelissar's citizens had no end. Not that he would ever consider relinquishing his position, no matter how tedious. He was the *Ma'ar*. He'd worked hard for his status, just one step beneath the king—*and what a small step it was,* he thought with a snort—and if the price he had to pay for that authority was mindless hours of arbitrating petty disputes and listening to the pointless concerns of small-minded citizens, then so be it. People were so easily manipulated, anyway. Look the part, tell them what they wanted to hear, and they never asked any questions.

Lucky for him, the citizens of Trelissar had no idea the kind of trouble they were actually in. And once the day was over, once he had passed the time in his gilded offices, smoothing ruffled feathers, promising to bring the citizens' 'pressing concerns' before the king, then he could escape down here, to the catacombs. Where the real work of running a city took place. The dirty work.

And unfortunately, tonight was going to be a long night of dirty work.

The Ma'ar leaned back against the stone wall of a tomb and slid down to sit on the floor. He pulled off one boot and then the other, wriggling his toes inside his socks. Reaching up, he snagged a corner of his cloak from where it lay draped over the stone above, and pulled it down over him, wadding one corner behind his head for a makeshift pillow. He slumped further against the hard stone. He had a few hours to kill before dark, and a cat nap would pass the time efficiently. He briefly considered making his way deeper into the catacombs to where the pallet he normally slept upon was laid in a dark alcove, but he didn't want to risk sleeping too long. There was much to do this night.

～

When the Ma'ar awoke, the torches were guttering low and his neck was stiff. He'd managed to slide fully down onto the floor as he slept, and his back complained noisily as he pulled himself up to sit.

Many layers of earth and stone separated the catacombs from the city above, and thus no natural light penetrated the gloom. The Ma'ar hoped he had not overslept. Tonight's task was long overdue; it had been well over a month since he'd last performed the ritual—if you could call it that—and he knew the effects of his negligence would soon be visible if they were not already.

He pulled his discarded boots back on before heaving himself to his feet with a grunt, swinging his cloak back over his shoulders as he rose. The hat he left on the tomb where it lay. A pair of dark gloves and a scarf completed his look. No need to put on appearances tonight.

Moving down the passageway, the Ma'ar ducked through a low doorway into a small room where a single crumbling tomb sat on a low slab in the center. The carvings on the side of the stone had long since worn away, and the Ma'ar had no idea who had once been given the dubious honor of this secluded burial. No matter. Whoever it was, anything he had left behind—from spirit to bones—was long gone.

With a practiced motion, the Ma'ar slid the tips of his gloved fingers under the lip of the lid, and with a grunt of effort, hoisted the lid of the tomb back before peering inside. His cache of bones was dwindling rapidly, he noticed with mild alarm. It wouldn't be long before he would have to make the dangerous journey to obtain more, a task he did not relish the thought of. And who knew how many were left at the source? He didn't think it was very many.

The Ma'ar shook his head. Nothing to be done about any of that now. These were concerns for another day. Reaching into the depths of the tomb, he selected the longest and heaviest of the remaining options. It was lighter in his hands than it should have been, and discolored, the bright white transformed to mottled yellow with age. Another worry. These older bones didn't have the power of the more recent ones. And with no newer ones to come by, how long before their power wasn't enough?

Resolutely, the Ma'ar stuck the bone into the deep pocket of his cloak and hauled the lid of the tomb back into place. It would have to do. He made his way back along the corridor, up the stairs, and with a quick glance each way, out into the darkness of the streets above.

∽

The tallest building in Trelissar was the old city museum. It, like many other fixtures of the old city, had been abandoned in the early days of the Rot, when the sudden and drastic decrease in population had made the extravagant building impossible to maintain. The building itself was relatively free of Rot though, thanks to his efforts, and despite its crumbling facade it was easy enough to gain access to the roof.

The Ma'ar was used to blending into shadows, and he passed through the city like a wraith, creeping down alleyways and around corners before finding his way into the dank interior of the old museum. The elevator was far beyond repair, and the Ma'ar eyed it with longing as he always did before he began trudging up the seemingly endless flights of stairs toward the roof.

His breath came in panting gasps as he finally ascended the last few stairs and stumbled through the heavy metal door. Despite the bold warnings etched into the metal of the door, no alarm bells sounded, and the night was silent aside from his wheezing breaths as he staggered out onto the rooftop and doubled over, hands planted on his wobbling knees.

The things I do for this city, he thought irritably as he caught his breath. Of course, at the end of the day, he was really doing it for himself, but there was nothing wrong with that. When he served himself, everyone benefited. Usually.

When his breathing had finally evened out and his thundering heartbeat slowed, the Ma'ar made his way along the roof to the pile of stones he'd laid in the center. Any ashes left from previous nights had long since blown away, but the wood remained, and it wasn't long before he was able to reignite the kindling and coax it into a robust blaze.

He crouched near it for a moment, warming his hands in the chill night air, before drawing the long bone from its place in the pocket of his cloak. He paused for a moment, examining the pocked surface of the bone—a very old one; he hoped it had enough power left—before laying it gently on the fire and stepping back.

It didn't take long. The iridescent shimmer was bright even through the roaring fire as the bone caught. It glowed, bright and pulsing for a moment, before smoke, thick and blue-black, began to pour from it, rising high into the sky to form a dense cloud over the former museum.

The Ma'ar lowered himself down onto the cold roof of the building and settled in. He would wait there until the fire burned out, its thick smoke rising to blanket the city, and he prayed it would be enough to push back the Rot a little further.

7

NEKUTHAEDRIS

Nekuthaedris awoke sprawled out on the floor with a pounding headache and a vague sense of confusion about how he had gotten there. For a moment, his circumstances were so similar to the last time he had found himself in this situation, nearly ninety years ago, that his heart began to pound and he felt the panic rising in his throat.

Trembling, Neku fought down his fear and concentrated hard, trying to remember what had happened. But this time, instead of the blank space in his memory that had taken years to recover—and even now he wasn't sure he had all his memories back—this time it all flooded back in a rush.

The girl!

Neku shot to his feet. His heart, which had begun to slow as the panic faded, leaped again as her face flashed in his mind. His head throbbed at the sudden movement, and he sank down on the sofa, his eyes drifting to the basin of pink-tinged water on the low table in front of him and the bandages and bloody strips of cloth spread out around it. So, it wasn't a dream. She was real.

He squeezed his eyes shut. A *planeswalker*. Here. For the first time in nearly a century. And he'd let her get away.

He rubbed his temples with his fingers in an attempt to dull the ache. When he opened his eyes and caught sight of his wrist under the fall of lace he paused, pulling back his cuff to examine the flesh there. The thick black lines appeared carved into his wrist like old scars, ridged and puckered and ugly. Tentatively, he ran a finger over the skin, feeling the texture there. It was definitely lower now, further down on his wrist and creeping towards his hand. He should have known better than to use magic. But what other choice did he have? He shuddered, pulling his sleeve down to hide the marks.

What in the world was he supposed to do now?

Suddenly, another hazy memory rose to the surface. Rose. Her name was Rose. He could picture her perfectly, long black hair escaping from the braid down her back, eyes the turbulent gray of a stormy sky. Her clothing seemed strange, but he assumed it must be typical of the other world, the sister world, a place he sorely missed but dared not enter. He could see the look on her face, warily cautious but brave as she agreed to trust him and let him seal the magic in her blood. He remembered the bold challenge in her eyes, as if daring him not to be worthy of her trust.

Frustrated, Neku ran his hand through his tangled hair. In all his years of imagining what would happen if a planeswalker were to walk through the door, he'd never actually believed it would happen. And now that it had, nothing had gone right. He'd meant to explain everything, to ask for her help—beg if need be—not let her wander out into a dangerous and foreign world with no knowledge or protection. At least he'd managed to cast the spell before she left.

Neku trembled. Would he ever see her again? His head and the marks on his left arm pulsed painfully in unison. Would he live that long? Would any of them?

Rising, Neku crossed to the window overlooking the stairs that led down to the dense forest surrounding the castle. He threw back the heavy curtains and gazed out through the thick glass panes. The sun was beginning to set, rays of light limning the trees, making it appear as if the leaves were tiny individual tongues of flame. He had seen this scene often, stared out of this window so many times he knew the shape of each tree.

He could see no sign of the girl, nothing to suggest which way she had gone, and yet he could feel the barest pull of the magic he had sealed in her blood. It was faint, and yet its presence, somewhere off to the north and east, let him know which door she had exited through. She was still in this world.

Following this thought to its logical conclusion, he gripped the windowsill until his knuckles turned white. He hadn't left his castle for eighty-seven years. Not since that night. At first, he couldn't, lost in the dark spaces of his mind. When his sanity finally returned, he dared not leave, focusing all his time and attention on the protection of the gate. And now...well. He still told himself that his place was here, guarding and watching and protecting. What reason was there to leave? And yet...part of him knew that it was only fear and cowardice that kept him here. He didn't really want to see what the world had become after that night. He didn't want to know how many people had been harmed by his mistakes. It was easier to remain here. Safer. Or it had been. Until now.

But with a planeswalker loose in the world, hiding in his castle was no longer a choice. He had to get her back.

∼

Nekuthaedris had assumed the first step would be the hardest, but he was wrong. After pulling open the heavy door, he had stood on the wide porch, waiting for the panic to rise and engulf him. But nothing had happened. Slightly bolstered, he'd started down the steps, the movement so familiar and yet so foreign, his boots ringing against the stone.

It was only when he reached the bottom and felt the first gust of wind upon his face, wind he hadn't felt in nearly a century, that his pulse spiked and he had to clench his fists to keep them from trembling. He turned back to face the high stone walls behind him, hoping the sight would calm him enough to press on, but instead his gaze was drawn as if by a magnet to the dark opening in the stone that led beneath his castle.

The memories stirred, and before he could stop himself, he found his feet moving, drawing him unerringly toward the entrance to the Ossuary. The steps were still lit by the lowering rays of the sun, and he took them down, as he had so many times before, feeling the air around him grow cooler as he passed under the high stone archway and descended deeper into the earth.

Despite the horror and tragedy that had occurred the last time he had been here, his memories of the Ossuary were primarily happy ones. It was a holy place, and he remembered how it had looked during the Rebirth Ceremonies, when the entrance was decorated with garlands of flowers and the citizens of High Trelis turned out in droves to celebrate long into the night.

Neku could picture the bright lanterns that had lined the walls, decorative patterns carved into their sides to cast bright dancing shapes upon the stairs as the citizens cheered and drank wine and waited for the Drani'shadara to be reborn, the magical creature rising from the seed planted amongst the bones of its previous incarnation to climb the stairs, trailing its magic back out into the world. What fine days those had been.

But that was a long time ago. The lanterns were dark and rusted now, the flowers long gone as Neku continued down the stairs that led into the Ossuary.

Each time the Drani'shadara was reborn, it left its bones here in this holy place, and the room was filled with them, covering every surface. There were the bright new bones from recent rebirths, so white they practically glowed, the brittle yellow bones from years long past, so delicate they crumbled to dust with a touch, and everything in between. Neku wondered what the most recent bones looked like now, almost ninety long years later.

The moment he cleared the bottom step he knew something was terribly wrong. The room should have been bursting with magic—he should be able to feel it.

Oh no.

Rounding the corner, Neku burst into the Ossuary and felt all the blood drain from his face. *No...oh no, no.* He turned in a tight circle, his eyes frantically scanning the surfaces, the floor, the ledges, all of which had been piled high with bones. All of which were now empty.

His breath seized in his lungs, and he hurried toward the altar at the far back of the room. A small pile of bones remained there, pitted and yellowed with age. His hand automatically reached out toward them, but stopped short, hovering in the air above the pile. He could feel the faint pulse of magic, all that was left of the Drani'shadara.

Abruptly his despair turned to anger, blazing through

him like an inferno. This was his fault. If he had not been so caught up in self-pity and fear, he would have felt the change in the magic, would have been protecting this place as he was supposed to. How could he have let this happen?

Enough self-pity.

Neku turned again and began to blindly make his way back up the stairs. He had enough self-loathing and regret to last for the rest of eternity. It was his bad decisions that had got them into this mess in the first place, and his negligence that had robbed the Ossuary of its magic. But if through some trick of fate an untainted planeswalker was going to wander into his world right as the final curtain began to fall, he'd be *damned* if he was going to let her get away. He wouldn't mess this up again.

Cresting the top step, Neku aimed for the woods and broke into a run, leaving the ruins of the Ossuary behind without a second glance.

8

ROSE

Rose hadn't been in the forest for more than a couple of hours, but already it was sorely trying her patience. She was cold, she was hungry, she was growing tired, and through the dense canopy she could see the sun was beginning to set. The light hadn't yet begun to fade, but the idea of being trapped here after dark made her jumpy. She briefly considered turning around and heading back to the castle, but couldn't see how that would improve her situation. There, she knew what she would find: a locked door and a cold, hungry night on a stone porch. At least she didn't know what lay ahead, questionable comfort though that may be.

She was lost in thought as she rounded a bend and pulled up short. Something was blocking the path ahead, something large and suspiciously familiar looking. Starting forward again cautiously, Rose was astonished to see what appeared to be a goose sitting inconveniently in the center of the path, its beady black eye trained on her as she approached.

Everything she had come upon so far had been so

completely outside the bounds of reality, that Rose almost felt it more unnerving to be faced with something so strangely familiar. As she drew near, the goose rose to its feet and faced her.

By its coloring, Rose recognized it immediately as a Canada goose. She chuckled quietly to herself. She'd seen plenty of those both at her home in the northwest as well as her new residence in Indiana. If there was one animal that would be so overpopulated that it spilled over into nonsensical worlds like this, it *would* be Canada geese.

Her steps slowed as she approached, because if there was one thing everyone knew about geese, it was that they were *mean,* and she had no desire to be attacked in the middle of the forest by an ill-tempered goose. She had just made to step off the path and duck through the trees to give it a wide berth, when the goose's head swiveled toward her. It stepped forward, its beak opening. But instead of a hiss or a honk or any expected goose-like sound, what emanated from the goose's beak took Rose completely by surprise.

"TOLL."

Rose was so caught off-guard, she actually responded. "What?"

"TOLL."

The goose stepped forward again, threateningly, and Rose backed up a step. Suddenly, a glint of reflected light caught her eye, and as the goose moved aside she caught sight of a small pile of...something, sitting in the dirt. Keeping one eye on the creature, Rose squinted at the pile, trying to make it out. It appeared to be a collection of random objects. She could make out a small cache of ribbons, some coins, and what appeared to be a yo-yo. What had caught the light...was that a *toaster?*

She looked again at the goose, who stared back impassively. *Surely it doesn't mean...*

"TOLL."

Feeling quite ridiculous, Rose dug into the pockets of her jeans. She could picture her wallet sitting next to her phone back in her apartment, and knew she was going to come up empty. Just lint in the left, and from the right, she pulled out the wrapper from a stick of gum.

"Look, I don't—" she started, but the goose's small black eye had fastened on the shiny wrapper in her hand. She held it out in front of her cautiously.

"TOLL," the goose bellowed again, but moved slightly to the side. Edging forward, Rose sidestepped around the creature, moving slowly and keeping her eyes alert in case of attack. When nothing happened, she deposited her shiny offering on the pile of assembled objects before straightening and moving back quickly. The goose waddled forward, its attention focused once again on its horde, and Rose took the opportunity to make a quick getaway.

She stumbled forward, trotting down the path and away, mumbling under her breath as she went.

"Mouse caravans. Toll geese. This is the stupidest, most ridiculous—"

Looking back over her shoulder to where the goose had settled itself on the path again and was calmly grooming its feathers, she didn't see someone standing in front of her until they collided.

Rose stumbled and fell, landing painfully on her tailbone with a muffled curse. The figure she had struck from behind had stumbled as well, a worn leather bag dropping from her shoulder and spilling its contents onto the packed dirt of the path. She caught herself before falling though, and Rose looked up to see—to her astonishment—a real human woman, her back to Rose as she regained her balance.

Her profound relief at having actually encountered another person was cut short as the woman straightened and turned to face her, and it took every ounce of Rose's self-control to keep from recoiling in horror.

The woman was tall and thin, with long, wild black hair that seemed to explode out of her head and fall down past her waist in a mass of tangled waves. She wore a bizarre collection of mismatched, old-fashioned clothing. A long, full black skirt belled out in a style Rose could picture being at home in a nineteenth-century ballroom. The skirt was gathered in pleats at the bottom to reveal what appeared to be layers of petticoats beneath, once dark red perhaps, but now streaked with the brown dirt of the forest. Above this she wore a black t-shirt advertising what appeared to be a band Rose had never heard of. Elbow-length red silk gloves, torn and stained, completed the ensemble.

But it was her face that made Rose start in alarm. The woman's skin was pale and smooth, nearly translucent in the fading light of the forest, except for a slash of dark, ridged scar tissue, black as night where it crawled up out of the collar of her T-shirt, over her jawline to bisect her face before disappearing into her hair. It was the same puckered black tendrils that she had seen on the arm of the stranger in the castle, only magnified a thousandfold. Rose could see that the face under the black marks must have been quite beautiful once, and she found herself unable to assign an age to the strange woman.

Her eyes were possibly the most disconcerting part; the left one was an opaque milky white, contrasting starkly against the puckered black skin around it. The iris of the other eye was a piercing blood red, and it swiveled down to focus on Rose where she still sat stunned on the forest floor. The woman extended a gloved hand toward Rose, her brow creasing in concern.

"I'm so sorry, miss! Are you quite alright?"

The voice was high-pitched and bell-like, its musical quality so incongruous with the figure itself that Rose blinked at her mutely for a moment before the meaning of the words penetrated her brain.

"Oh!" Rose accepted the hand and the woman hauled her up with surprising strength. "Yes, I'm fine. Please don't apologize; I ran into you!" Rose brushed the dirt off her jeans before bending to retrieve the woman's fallen bag. The leather knapsack was heavier than she expected, and was full of large, lumpy round shapes. She handed it back to the woman, who gazed at Rose with her eerily red eye as she accepted the bag without comment and slung it over her shoulder.

"You...you're not from around here, are you?" The phrasing of the words seemed to Rose like a statement of the obvious, but the woman's tone suggested that she really wanted to know the answer to the question.

Rose shook her head. "No, I—" How on earth to answer that? "I'm not," she finished rather lamely. "My name's Rose. I'm looking for help."

The woman cocked her head. "Looking for help? Are you hurt?"

"No, not for me. There's a castle back through the woods," Rose said, gesturing back the way she had come, "and there's a...person there who...he...well he passed out, and he's got..." Rose trailed off into awkward silence, unsure what to say, and feeling thoroughly unsettled by the woman's strange red gaze. The woman didn't answer for a long moment, just examined Rose's face with discomforting intensity, her head cocked to the side like a bird.

"Have we met before?" the woman asked suddenly.

Did she hear anything I said? Rose wondered. "No, we haven't. But the man in the castle, he—"

The woman cut her off abruptly. "Ydenda," she said, thrusting a hand forward.

"Excuse me?"

"Ydenda. That's my name. It's so nice to meet you, Rose."

Baffled, Rose accepted the proffered hand and shook it. Ydenda had a strong grip.

"Yes, it's nice to meet you too. Did you hear what I said? The man in the castle needs help."

A look of sorrow flashed across Ydenda's face, then morphed to one of confusion. Ydenda cocked her head again, like an inquisitive bird, and suddenly her expression cleared, her eye shining as she looked at Rose with interest.

"If you're not from around here, do you have a place to stay? Where are you going?" She looked Rose up and down and continued on before Rose had a chance to respond. "Oh, you poor thing, you must be freezing! It's settled then. You must come with me. You can tell me everything back at the cottage. It's warm there, and I'll make dinner. Not safe to stay out in the woods after dark you know. You might lose your way. Come, help me gather my heads."

Feeling thoroughly overwhelmed, Rose let the matter drop for the moment, choosing to focus instead on the tantalizing promise of warmth and food. She followed suit when the woman crouched down and opened the drawstring on her worn knapsack before reaching to collect her —"Wait, what?"

Ydenda's words caught up to her just as her eyes fell to the open knapsack, which was indeed filled with the lumpy shapes of human heads. She recoiled in horror, but Ydenda didn't notice, gathering the pair of heads that had rolled into the brush by the far side of the path.

After a moment, Ydenda noticed that she hadn't moved, and looked up. "Could you grab the one over there?" She gestured to an indentation in the ground by a nearby tree where a lone head had rolled. "We should hurry back."

They're not real. It's probably just clay or something.

Gingerly, Rose reached out a hand and gripped the nearby head by the hair. The eyes glared sightlessly up at her out of the grimacing face. It definitely looked and felt real, or at least, how she would assume a decapitated human head might look and feel. Stifling a squeak, Rose held her breath and heaved the head into the bag before wiping her hand reflexively on the hem of her shirt.

Pulling the cord tight, Ydenda rose and slung the large bag over her shoulder as if it weighed nothing, then turned and began to make her way down the path, gesturing eagerly at Rose to join her.

Rose fell into step beside the strange woman.

"The village isn't far up ahead, just a short walk. Do you have any warmer clothes? If not, I can find something that will fit you. Oh, how fun! It's been so long since I've had company."

Ydenda continued to talk, happily describing the village and her cottage, seemingly content to carry the conversation without assistance.

Rose kept pace at her side, silently questioning the wisdom of this decision. If her father would have been disapproving of her careless choice to take off into the woods without a phone, he definitely wouldn't approve of her following a scarred stranger of questionable sanity with a bag full of human heads back to her home. *This is how you get murdered,* she told herself. Nothing about this was a good idea. Besides, those heads had to come from somewhere. She glanced at the knapsack. Who was to say it wouldn't soon be her head rolling on the forest floor?

As if reading her thoughts, Ydenda gave her a sideways glance and a conspiratorial wink. "Don't worry," she said in her musical voice, "I'm not going to steal your head. These are just for selling." As if that explained everything. Rose eyed her askance. That's probably just what a murderer would say, right before they murdered you.

And yet, while logically she knew she should be suspicious, Rose felt nothing malicious from the woman. There were no misgivings, no twisting in her gut to alert her that there was something wrong. Ydenda was decidedly odd, that was certain. She jumped from topic to topic mid-sentence with no apparent notice that she was doing so, and while Rose got the distinct impression that maybe Ydenda had more than a few screws loose, she seemed much more like a guileless child than a hardened killer. As Ydenda chattered on, happily filling the silence, Rose could feel nothing from the woman but warmth and the excitement of having made a new friend.

Nothing could make this day stranger than it had already been, she decided. And if there was food and warmth and maybe even sleep at the end of this bizarre road, then by God she was going to follow where it led.

9

ROSE

Where it led, it turned out, was to a quaint, charming village, just as Ydenda had described, with tiny oddly-shaped cottages clustered in rows around a central square. The trees grew sparse as the path led out of the forest, then merged with the central road that led into town from the south. Ydenda led the way through the growing darkness to a small, cheery cottage with a bright red roof. The wooden door leading into the cottage was aged and weathered. New panels had been nailed on top of worn sections over time, creating a haphazard patchwork, and when Ydenda produced a key from the depths of her skirt pocket and fitted it into the lock, the door swung open to reveal a house in a similar state of chaos.

Rose moved toward the threshold, but Ydenda stopped her in the doorway.

"Don't step on the purple planks," the woman instructed soberly, indicating a wide floorboard that stretched across the entryway, painted in a cheerful purple hue. Bright splashes of color adorned other floorboards as well, so the purple ones didn't look out of place. Ydenda hopped easily over the board before gesturing Rose to follow. "There are three of them," she added, pointing out the offending floorboards.

Rose noted their positions before looking back to Ydenda with a raised eyebrow. "Do I even want to know?" she asked, half to herself, but the woman just winked at her before turning away.

Rose followed suit, giving the purple plank a wide berth as she stepped into the room. Her eyes were wide as she took in her surroundings. The door opened directly into the kitchen and the room was tidy and clean, but Rose got the impression that nothing broken had ever been replaced, just patched over. Not one thing in the entire place matched; everything from light fixtures to individual table legs was unique in shape and size and material. Even the paint on the walls was a mismatched jumble of color, and despite the sensory overload, Rose found the whole effect quite charming. The house suited its owner, Rose thought, as Ydenda swung the door shut and deposited her lumpy bag on the floor in the corner, before stripping off her long red silk gloves and placing them on the table.

The sight of Ydenda's bare arms made Rose gape. Both arms were thick with the shiny black scars, which wound in ridged ropes of puckered skin out of her shirt sleeves and down onto her forearms. They stopped above the wrist on her right arm, but on the left her entire hand was black, smooth pale skin only showing through in small sections. Rose remembered how the man in the castle had reacted to her seeing his arm, and she quickly smoothed her expression back to neutral, but Ydenda didn't seem to notice.

Bending to retrieve the bag of heads, the woman turned and opened a side door Rose hadn't noticed. "Better get these into the cellar where they can stay cool until tomorrow," she said pragmatically before disappearing down a hidden staircase and into the darkness. Rose shuddered, but when Ydenda returned, the bag was thankfully absent.

"Here, come with me," she instructed, her voice firm. "I'll show you to a room where you can stay tonight. You can freshen up, and there are clothes in the closet there; help yourself. You'll want to dress warm; the weather's turning colder every day. When you're ready, come on down. I'll have dinner ready, and you can tell me everything."

The events of the day had left Rose too overwhelmed to protest, so she followed Ydenda without complaint out of the kitchen and up a narrow flight of stairs to the second floor. Three closed doors bracketed the landing, and Ydenda identified them as her own room, a bathroom, and, to the left, Rose's room. "Take your time and please help yourself to anything in the bathroom," she said cheerfully before disappearing back down the stairs.

The cottage had no attic, so the second floor rooms were tucked tight under the roof, and the ceiling sloped drastically in Rose's room, lending it an air of coziness. It was furnished in the same haphazard style as the kitchen: a twin-sized bed with mismatched posts stood under the window, which was framed with patched curtains. A closet door was tucked under the sloped section of ceiling, and a garish, yellow-painted dresser stood in the opposite corner. The floor was made of wide planks of wood, with a floral-patterned throw rug in the center. The whole effect was charmingly confused.

Rose collapsed on the bed, her mind so overwhelmed that it was curiously blank, as if it had taken so much in that it had opted to shut down entirely rather than attempt to process it all. She yawned and stretched her arms up over her head before forcing herself to sit up again. If she let herself relax, she would be asleep in minutes, and she was far too hungry to let that happen.

When Ydenda had said she was making dinner, Rose had been concerned about what exactly that might entail. Who knew what they ate here. From all she had seen so far, she wouldn't have been surprised if Ydenda planned to serve a concoction of tree bark and eyeballs. Or maybe heads. But the savory aroma that was beginning to waft up the stairs was so appealing that Rose thought she might be willing to eat eyeballs if they tasted the way this smelled.

Making her way into the bathroom, Rose was pleased to find it similar to what she might expect from a bathroom at home—though she was learning not to make assumptions.

She stooped to look in the cabinet under the sink, where she found a plethora of comfortingly familiar supplies. She helped herself to an unused toothbrush, setting it on the counter, and then a bottle of shampoo that claimed to be scented with "bogberry and borlus root"—whatever those were. The shower stall was cramped, but when Rose stripped off her dirt- and blood-stained clothes and stepped into the warm spray, it felt like the tension immediately seeped out of her muscles and ran down the drain.

As she took an experimental sniff of the shampoo—which smelled vaguely citrusy and not at all unpleasant—the thought occurred to her that she was feeling surprisingly comfortable for being so entirely out of her element. Trapped in a place that made little sense with no obvious path home and an uncertain future, she didn't have so much as a hairbrush or a change of clothes, no money, no identification, no idea where she was going or what she was doing. And yet, she realized with surprise, today had been so bizarre and confusing that she'd barely thought of her family since that first moment in the woods. Usually that crushing weight was with her always; she had grown accustomed to it lurking in the shadows, waiting to spring out and engulf her any time a familiar voice or a photo or even a scent brought the memory of her parents or sister rushing to the surface.

Rose had thought the change of scenery in Indiana, the complete lack of connection to anything she had known before, would help her cope with the loss. Building an entirely new life away from anything familiar seemed like an effective way to keep the memories from overwhelming her. But instead, she had just found herself adrift, lonely and directionless in a pointless, dead-end job, living in a crappy apartment, surrounded by people who didn't care about her any more than she cared about them.

But here she was, in a stranger's house in what could only be an entirely different world, feeling more at home than she ever had in her run-down apartment. Everything was so foreign here; it made her home seem a million miles away. The colors of the forest, the shapes of the houses in the village, even the people. Especially the people.

She closed her eyes, letting the hot water rinse the soap from her skin, and again her mind went back to the stranger in the castle. She could see his face clearly in her mind's eye, his deep purple eyes pleading with her to trust him. And she had. She didn't know why, but she had.

She still had to help him. But it was becoming clear she had no idea how. Was he still on the floor of his castle, unconscious? If so, anything she could do would be too little, too late. But...he'd been breathing, his pulse solid. Besides, she didn't even know if he was human. Could she make the same assumptions of him she would of a normal person? Hadn't she just prided herself on not making assumptions?

Turning off the tap, Rose held up her palm and examined the place where he had traced his finger, remembering the line of glowing iridescence that had followed his touch. It wasn't glowing now; only a pale white line remained of her wound, the blood staining her shirt, which now lay crumpled on the floor, the only remaining evidence that she had been injured at all. She traced the faded line and wondered—was he awake, was he alright? Did he have any idea where she had gone? He had seemed concerned for her safety. Was he looking for her? And what *was* that black stuff marking his body?

Well, Ydenda would know the answer to at least one of those questions.

Snapping out of her reverie, Rose lifted a fuzzy towel off a hook on the back of the door and wrapped it around herself before gathering her discarded clothes and crossing back into her bedroom. A quick search through the closet revealed a huge selection of bizarre clothing, but the yellow dresser was stocked with cozier options. She felt a little awkward wearing the woman's clothing, but eventually chose a pair of soft black leggings with horizontal green stripes, and an equally soft long-sleeved grey shirt. Ydenda was taller than Rose, but they had similar builds, and her clothing fit quite well.

After making quick work of her hair with a comb she found lying on the dresser, Rose made her way down the stairs to join Ydenda in the kitchen, careful to step gingerly over the purple floorboards as she entered the room.

"Perfect timing!" the woman exclaimed, ushering her to take a seat at the table, where steaming dishes had been laid out. Rose's stomach growled loudly in response, and Ydenda laughed before handing her a chipped plate with a scalloped edge and joining her at the table. "Eat, eat!" She said, waving her hands enthusiastically toward the food.

Feeling overwhelmed by the amazing smells and the woman's kindness and hospitality, Rose obeyed without question, following Ydenda's example to ladle food onto her plate. She hadn't the faintest idea what she was eating, and it seemed somehow impolite to ask, but whatever it was, it was delicious. Some kind of stewed vegetables, perhaps, and a meat dish that tasted a little like chicken but had a bit of a lavender tinge to it.

Ydenda kept up a steady stream of friendly chatter between bites, and at the end of the meal she brought over a steaming pot of what she identified as Corlis root tea. It was a faint reddish color, though it tasted an awful lot like chamomile. With a happy sigh at the comforting familiarity, Rose eagerly accepted the mug Ydenda offered her and wrapped her fingers around the porcelain, letting the warmth seep into her hands.

Once they were both settled at the table again, Ydenda's feet tucked up under her skirts and her own mug gripped in her hands, she leveled her shrewd red gaze on Rose and said, quite bluntly, "Are you from the sister world, then?"

It was a phrase Rose had never heard before—"sister world"—and yet without a doubt she knew the answer. "Yes, I suppose I am," she said. "I'm not sure how I got here though…"

Ydenda nodded sagely and took a long sip of her tea. "You got here the same way planeswalkers always do. Your blood let you in."

"My blood?" Startled, Rose raised her palm again and stared at the faint line. Ydenda reached across the table and gently took Rose's hand, bending her head to examine the mark there. When she raised her head, her expression was unreadable. "You've got a spell on you."

Rose grew unaccountably nervous. "Yes, I thought so. The man in the castle..." She broke off when a flash of confusion crossed Ydenda's face.

"What castle?"

Rose stared. "The castle through the woods. I told you. He was hurt, and I came for help."

Expressions seemed to flit in quick succession across Ydenda's ravaged face. Confusion gave way to suspicion, then fear, then something Rose couldn't interpret before her face cleared like a slate being abruptly wiped clean. Rose started slightly at the blank expression.

"I'm sorry," Ydenda said after a moment, "what were we talking about? Would you like another cup of tea?" She gestured at Rose's untouched mug.

Unwilling to give up, Rose tried another angle. "You said 'planeswalker.' What's a planeswalker?"

"Oh," Ydenda smiled. "A planeswalker is a person that can pass between the gates to the two worlds. Their blood has a magical quality that activates the gate." She heaved a wistful sigh. "I remember when they used to come through regularly enough. They're rare, you know, but I used to see them passing through on their way to Trelissar."

"What's Trelissar?"

"It's the capital city," Ydenda explained. "You have to pass through there to see the King."

Rose wasn't sure if she was making headway or just deepening the mystery of the place. Deciding the king could wait, she pressed on with her original line of questioning.

"So, you think I'm one of these planeswalkers?"

Ydenda gave a startled laugh. "What? Don't be ridiculous. We haven't seen a planeswalker here in decades. I'm not sure there *are* any more of them."

Rose gave her head a shake. No, she definitely wasn't making any headway. Desperate, she gave it one last try.

"What are the black marks on your skin?" The words were out before Rose could stop them, and she was appalled at her own lack of tact. "I'm so sorry; I didn't mean to be rude," she tried to backpedal, but Ydenda didn't seem offended. Looking up from her mug, she met Rose's eyes directly, and the vague abstraction that had been there passed as she focused on Rose with a piercing intensity.

"It's Rot," she said softly, and Rose could hear the emphasis she put on the word. She found herself holding her breath as she looked into Ydenda's face, her gaze drawn to the milky white eye surrounded by the slashing lines of shiny black. Unsettled, she shifted her focus to the other eye, but the intensity of the red gaze was equally unnerving.

"It's Rot," Ydenda repeated, her sharp gaze lucid and her voice barely above a whisper, "and it's spreading. And if you really are a planeswalker, you must never let it touch you."

10

ROSE

The words echoed in Rose's head as she lay in bed that night. The bed in Ydenda's guest room was soft, the quilt warm around her, but Rose's head was too full for sleep. Every time she closed her eyes, the face of the stranger in the castle swam in her vision, his expression pleading, and Ydenda's voice echoed through her skull. "*It's Rot.*"

What the hell did that *mean* anyway? And planeswalkers? Rose didn't know what exactly that meant either, but it seemed incredibly unlikely that she just happened to be possessed of magical blood that let her travel between worlds. What a ridiculous concept. Frustrated, Rose turned on her side and squeezed her eyes shut, stubbornly attempting to clear her mind. She needed sleep if she was going to deal with another day like this one.

After Ydenda's unnerving comment about Rot, her gaze had turned abstracted again, and she had started cheerfully talking about Rose's plans for the next day. Rose wasn't aware that she *had* plans for the following morning, but Ydenda automatically assumed that she would be pressing on to the capital and from there to visit the King, and would not be deterred, despite any arguments Rose attempted. Not that Rose had tried hard to dissuade her—she had no better idea, save backtracking to the castle and seeing if the stranger had recovered on his own and was willing to open the door.

"Whatever your problems may be, the King can help you," Ydenda promised, and in the face of her cheerful certainty, Rose eventually decided to trust that in this, the bizarre woman probably knew best.

Rose spent the remainder of the night in a kind of fitful doze where each time she woke she was not entirely sure if she had been to sleep at all. And yet the sun was streaming through the window over the bed when Rose was startled awake by a knock on the door and a chipper call of, "Breakfast in half an hour!"

She stretched her arms above her head, feeling surprisingly alert despite the long night, which she took as a good omen for the day ahead. With the sunlight shining onto her quilts and the distance of sleep putting the previous day in perspective, Rose was feeling decidedly optimistic. She had a plan. Simple and straightforward. She would go see the King, he would help the man in the castle—and maybe Ydenda, too—and then Rose would go home and...figure out what to do from there.

Not return to her retail job, that was for sure. Maybe she had been too hasty in her sudden move across the country. Maybe running away wasn't the solution to all her problems as she had hoped. She chose not to dwell on this thought, determined not to spoil her good mood. *One thing at a time.*

Despite the bright sunshine, the air outside her cocoon of blankets had a definite bite of chill, and Rose decided to take another shower. Who knew when she would have the opportunity again, after all. She stepped out of the hot spray smelling of bogberry and borlus root, and then, returning to her room, she braced herself and flung open the closet door, fully prepared to look ridiculous in Ydenda's borrowed clothes.

In the end, while it certainly wasn't a look Rose would have chosen on her own, she didn't think she looked half bad. She had managed to find a pair of jeans—only slightly too long—that seemed rather ordinary aside from their vibrant turquoise color, and a black fitted t-shirt similar to the one Ydenda had worn the day before. The shirt had a picture of a large white bird with a hooked beak on it, and the word 'Albatrocity' was emblazoned across the top. She had no idea what the image was meant to convey, but the material was soft and it fit well. Over top she layered a warm black hoodie with a series of symbols on the back that she couldn't read, and, feeling slightly self-conscious of the scar on her palm after Ydenda's reaction the night before, a pair of black and grey striped fingerless gloves.

When she had straightened her room and headed downstairs, Ydenda met her with a wide smile. "Good morning! Did you sleep well? Breakfast is almost ready." Catching sight of Rose's clothes, her smile widened. "How did you know those went together?"

At Rose's confused look, she laughed and gestured at the shirt and hoodie. "Albatrocity. Everyone's going to think you're a big fan." Rose realized the symbols on the back of the hoodie must spell out the same word as on the shirt. "Oh! Should I change it?"

"No, no, they look good together. Besides, it's a great band."

Rose wondered what kind of a band had an albatross as their logo. Considering her surroundings, she thought the chances were high that the large white bird was actually *in* the band. Chuckling to herself, she went to help Ydenda with the food, but the other woman shooed her over to the table, following moments later with a plate piled high with what looked like small, blood-red pancakes.

Deciding to follow the trend she had started the night before of not questioning the food, Rose followed Ydenda's example and helped herself to three of the pancakes, slathering them with a clear, lumpy-textured jelly from a small bowl on the table. The consistency of the jelly was rather like the eyeballs she had feared they would be eating the night before, but the pancakes were delicious, slightly sweet with a faint cinnamon flavor.

She ate as many as her stomach could hold, unsure of where her next meal would come from, but Ydenda seemed to have anticipated her concerns, and after breakfast had been cleared away, she presented Rose with a worn backpack that had been stuffed with all the essentials she could think of. Rose felt tears prick behind her eyes as Ydenda opened the bag and spilled the contents onto the table, eagerly showing her what supplies had been included. There was a small bag of toiletries, a change of clothes, several wrapped sandwiches that looked strange but not too scary, bottles of water and a purse filled with an assortment of coins, each stamped with the profile of a very bizarre-looking creature that Rose thought looked vaguely familiar.

Rose, feeling overwhelmed, tried to refuse the coins, but Ydenda would have none of it.

"Take them, I insist. You have nothing, and it's not a short distance to the King."

"But you've done so much," Rose protested. "You've given me your clothes, and fed me, and let me stay the night, and I've given you nothing in return."

Ydenda gripped her by the shoulders and pulled her into a tight embrace. "You come back here anytime, you understand? *Anytime.*" She pulled back and wiped surreptitiously at her own eyes. "I would walk you into town, but I need to get those heads taken care of before they start to rot, so here's what you do. Follow the road to the center of town; you can't miss it, all the roads spread out from there in spokes. The Millipede station is on the corner of the central square, and you can take the Millipede all the way to Trelissar." She pressed a token into Rose's palm. "This should get you there. From Trelissar, ask for directions to the King. Anyone there can tell you the way."

Millipede station?

Deciding it was wiser not to ask, Rose zipped the bag closed and they made their way out onto the front porch, both women stepping carefully over the purple floorboard near the entryway. She looked at Ydenda, whose face at first glance had nearly made her recoil in horror, but whose kindness and generosity had outmatched anyone she had ever known, and felt her heart overflow. "Thank you so much," she said, meeting the woman's warm red gaze and squeezing her hand tight. "For everything."

Ydenda smiled at her gently. "You're welcome, my dear. Don't worry, I'm sure we'll meet again before the end of the world."

Rose looked at her in surprise, but with those unsettling words, Ydenda had turned back into the house and closed the door, and she found herself staring in consternation at the colorful patched wood of the door. *What on earth was that supposed to mean?*

Before she could turn away, the door opened again, and Ydenda poked her head through the gap. "I meant what I said before," the woman said, her voice serious and her red eye piercing. *"Don't touch the Rot."* The door closed again swiftly.

Rose stood on the stoop for a moment, eyeing the door uncertainly, before turning to face the road. Hoisting the backpack onto her shoulders, she made her way down the sidewalk, then turned and headed toward the central square of the tiny town. Her mind replayed Ydenda's words briefly, turning them over in her head before mentally shrugging and adding them to the growing pile of things that made no sense in this world.

Ydenda was right, the center of town was a straight shot down the road and easy to find. The main square was just that, a block of shops and offices, the brightly painted signs above the storefronts labeled in a mix of English and the same bizarre curly-shaped symbols that Rose sported on the back of her borrowed hoodie. Any concern she had over locating the 'Millipede station,' whatever that might be, was laid to rest when she stopped under a large sign stating just that, in both symbols and English. The sign stretched across the front of a large brick building, and with a sense of mingled trepidation and excitement at the thought of a new adventure, she blew out a breath and pushed through the revolving glass doors.

The interior was large and brightly lit with tall windows and an ornately decorated ceiling, and immediately put her in mind of the train station in Seattle her family had sometimes visited when she'd been a child. Turning in a circle, she was relieved to see that it really did appear to just be a train station. With any luck, this journey wouldn't be too difficult to navigate after all. The space was much smaller than the train station of her memory, but still seemed too large for a village of this size, and Rose wondered if the town had at one time been larger.

To her consternation, all of the signs inside the station were written only in symbols, with no English to be seen anywhere. It looked like asking for help was unavoidable. The ticket counter was easy to find however, and to her immense relief the place seemed to run exactly as she might expect.

The small, portly man at the ticket counter didn't bat an eye at her, accepting her token and exchanging it for a ticket without comment before directing her to, "Platform Green, out through the doors there, all the way to the left. Stay on 'til the end; Trelissar is the last stop. You can buy lunch onboard if you like. Next Millipede in," he checked his watch, "ten minutes. You'd better hurry."

Thanking the man profusely, Rose left through the back doors in a rush and made her way to the left across the platforms all the way to the end. All of the tracks were empty, so she settled on a bench to wait.

Staring down at the tracks, she noticed with surprise that they weren't actually tracks at all, or any kind of rail lines she was familiar with. They were really nothing more than wide unpaved paths, each one planted with different colors of what appeared to be grass, growing thickly in a lush carpet. The grass on the path below her was green, the same green grass she was familiar with from home, but a glance at the other platforms revealed a rainbow of grassy trails leading out away from the station in a profusion of color. No rails though; perhaps they were actually buses instead of trains?

She didn't have to wonder long, as the vehicle in question approached the station and lurched to a stop in front of her. An audible gasp escaped her mouth as she gazed up at it. It was...well, it was a millipede. As wide and half again as tall as a subway car, with a finely segmented body in dark brown and gold, a pair of jointed legs protruding from each segment. She could see the head from where she sat, and she stared in fascination as a young attendant appeared through a door she hadn't noticed, forking a mass of decaying leaves into the space where the creature waited. A shiver ran down her spine as she watched the millipede's massive jaws working to devour the food, its small antennae twitching as it ate.

Having spent a considerable portion of her life in the forest, Rose was not one to be squeamish around what her sister had always referred to as "creepy-crawlies." And yet coming face to face with a millipede the size of a bus was quite another story altogether, and she found herself leaning back into the bench and away from the enormous arthropod with its grinding mandibles. Surely there was another way to reach the capital.

A soft whooshing sound reached her ears, and Rose turned to see a series of ropes sliding down over the rounded sides of the millipede in intervals. With a muted *plop*, they hit the grass and resolved into ladders, and a moment later a figure leaned out over the side, peering down from the top of one segmented section.

"Green Line! All aboard!" the figure called out, pitching his voice to carry down the line.

Rose took a deep breath and forced herself to her feet, not allowing herself the opportunity to consider what she was doing before her hands found the sides of the rope ladder. She screwed her eyes shut and entertained a brief fantasy of returning to Ydenda's house, or better yet, back to the castle and the stranger's enigmatic purple eyes.

"Up you come, Miss," the voice encouraged, and praying for strength and fortitude and whatever other qualities a person might need to survive a ride on a fourteen foot tall millipede, Rose heaved herself up.

The figure extended a hand down as she neared the top and helped guide her off the ladder and onto the hard surface of the millipede itself. Up close, the carapace resembled overlapping plates of armor, and felt hard and sturdy under her feet. The helpful figure turned out to be a boy, a few years younger than Rose herself, with a wide grin revealing a chipped front tooth. His smile was infectious and put Rose immediately at ease despite her surroundings.

"Looks like you'll have this section of Millie all to yourself for now, Miss," he said cheerfully, taking her ticket. "Have a seat anywhere you like." The boy read the symbols on her ticket. "Trelissar, huh? Well, you'll be here a while then. There's food up at the front by the head if you didn't pack a lunch, and we'll probably get in to the capital around..." he checked his watch, "four o'clock I'd guess. Oh! Up you come, mister!" The boy turned away to help guide another passenger up the ladder, and Rose turned to survey her options.

A narrow path ran the length of the millipede, with a low platform and rows of seats bordering the aisle, two on each side. Further up Rose could see another rope ladder and attendant leaning over the side. She chose a seat somewhere squarely in the middle of her section, setting her backpack on the seat next to her and firmly securing the seatbelt over her lap before leaning to peer over the side. Metal braces rose in intervals, looking like giant staples set in a line down the back of the creature, and a thick canvas canopy stretched between the braces to offer shade from the bright sunlight. Still, Rose thought this might not be an enjoyable journey in the rain.

Glancing down at her watch, Rose remembered that it

had stopped running the previous day after crossing through the castle door. She was surprised to see the second hand was moving again, though the time was clearly wrong. She flagged down the attendant to ask for the correct time and reset her watch. Ten fifty-eight. If his estimate was correct, she was looking at a roughly five-hour trip to the capital.

Three other people had joined her on top of the millipede by the time a loud chime sounded from the station below. One, a tall mustached man, had his head buried in a newspaper covered in blocks of print made up of the squiggly symbols, while the other two, a pair of elderly looking ladies, kept their heads bent together in low conversation.

"Green Line, Broken City to Trelissar, leaving the station!" the boy attendant bellowed over the edge. Rose blinked in surprise. Broken City? Is that where she was? She hadn't thought to ask Ydenda.

But her thoughts were scattered as, with a mighty lurch, the millipede swung into motion, its feet skittering forward over the grass as they moved away from the station and out into the rolling hills beyond. The gentle rocking movement of the creature was surprisingly soothing, and despite Rose's initial wish that she'd had her unfinished mystery novel with her, she soon found that the impressive view from the top of the millipede was more than enough to hold her attention.

Sweeping hills of soft grasslands provided an impressive panorama, and Rose goggled at the strange creatures they passed, herds of large, giraffe-like animals covered in overlapping scales, and birds of every size and shape imaginable swooping through the cloudless sky, trilling out their discordant songs. It was like nothing she had ever imagined, and any trepidation or fear she may have felt was swallowed up by the wonder she felt now with the warm sun on her face and gentle wind ruffling her hair.

From the instant she had lost her family she'd been surviving moment to moment, day by day. Each day she made it through without being swallowed by despair was an accomplishment, and she had grown used to approaching her life that way, existing without too much thought or planning. But what had started out as a coping mechanism, she realized now had grown into a useful tool. She would approach this adventure the same way. She would not worry about where she would sleep that night, or what she would eat when her sandwiches were gone, or how she would find the King and what he would say. No, instead she would focus on the moment, as she had been for months, except instead of using each moment to hold back the darkness, she now found herself focusing on the light. And as the bright hills rolled past with their profusion of flowers and clusters of grazing creatures, she felt the wind on her face and saw a pair of deep purple eyes in her mind, a question in their depths, "Will you trust me?" And with the sun warming her face, Rose closed her eyes, and felt at peace.

11

THE MA'AR

The Ma'ar's head was itching under his tall black hat, and he wanted nothing more than to rip it off and throw it across the room. He was nothing if not patient though, and he had never lacked in self-control, so he took a deep breath and turned his attention back to the room in front of him. It was large and elaborate, with detailed carvings on the fluted columns and gold scrollwork on the arched ceiling. Never mind that the building was a relic from years past when the population had been large enough to support such grandeur. It was a room befitting his station, and so the Ma'ar made sure it was kept in good repair, heedless of the cost.

Shifting his weight on the dais to relieve the pressure on his aching feet, he consulted the papers resting on the podium in front of him.

Only one more case this morning, he saw in relief. One more case before he could return to his office and take off this blasted hat and eat his lunch in peace. Raising his voice to carry over the hum of conversation from the spectators in the room—how did they not have anything better to do?—he announced, "Griswell versus the Blotheed Caravan. Please come to the front."

Out of the mass of milling people that filled the gallery ringing the ornate room, a handful of creatures stepped forward and approached the wide table set for their use beneath the dais. There were no chairs there—this process was not intended to be *comfortable*—and so they formed a line behind the table. To one end stood an unnaturally tall man, bald but with bushy eyebrows and sagging features. Mr. Griswell, the Ma'ar noted. He had removed his cap and held it awkwardly in front of his body. The Ma'ar noticed this sign of deference and respect to his position, and filed the information away for later use.

Toward the other end of the table stood a cluster of Klistfolk, their heads barely poking over the top of the table as they chittered amongst themselves, their long pink tails lashing angrily. Their short stature was magnified even further by Mr. Griswell's height. This must be the Blotheed Caravan, then.

The Ma'ar sighed inwardly. With the weather growing colder, the Klistfolk caravans would soon begin filling the cities in greater numbers, seeking long-term accommodations to wait out the winter before resuming their travels in the spring. The odd creatures were generally bad tempered, and the number of disputes always rose with their presence. If they were here already, it was going to be a long winter.

"Mr. Blotheed, would you care to start?" The Ma'ar addressed his invitation to the oldest member of the gathered Klistfolk, his large ears sporting big brown tufts that twitched as he spoke.

The chittering stopped as Mr. Blotheed switched effortlessly to English, his voice high-pitched and squeaky.

"Yes, your lordship. My caravan and I had secured lodgings at the Griswell Campgrounds for the duration of the winter, and yet when we arrived yesterday, we found that the spaces we had reserved were already occupied. We paid in advance for the space, and Mr. Griswell refused to refund our money!"

Angry chittering broke out amongst his companions, and the Ma'ar summoned his best glower and directed it at the Klistfolk. He was pleased when the chatter ceased abruptly. Straightening his coat—it was gold brocade with thick golden buttons worn over a black vest and black trousers; one did have to keep up appearances in this position—the Ma'ar turned his attention to the tall man at the other end of the table. Best to keep this moving along, lest his break get cut short and he lose the chance to take off this damnable hat.

"Mr. Griswell?" he prompted.

Mr. Griswell clutched his hat tightly to his chest.

"Your honor. Yes, I did refuse to refund their money. They were a day late, with no notice given. So, I let their space to another group. How was I to know they were coming at all?"

The Ma'ar turned to the Klistfolk.

"Our schedules are not set in stone," Mr. Blotheed said angrily in his squeaky voice. "We cannot control the weather or broken wheels. We were in the forest, and unable to send word ahead."

The Ma'ar turned his long-suffering glance to Mr. Griswell. "Surely you deal with the Klistfolk every year in your campground? You must know that their arrival times are variable? And if you managed to lease out the space, you have not lost any money. Was there a reason you did not refund their money?"

Mr. Griswell's brow furrowed, his eyebrows resembling two caterpillars drawing together for warmth. "Well, I did offer them another space, your excellency. It's on the other side of the grounds, but of the same quality. They stayed there last night."

The fact that the Ma'ar was able to keep his temper in the face of this egregious waste of his time was a testament to his self-control. He closed his eyes briefly and rolled them heavenward, before turning his attention back to the caravan representatives.

"You took a different space at Mr. Griswell's campground, and yet you are still here demanding he return your money?" The Ma'ar's voice was quite level, and he mentally patted himself on the back for this accomplishment.

Mr. Blotheed's ear tufts twitched in annoyance. "Well, it wasn't the space we *paid* for initially," he declared. Then, sensing he was fighting a losing battle, he added, "Besides, he didn't *apologize* for the inconvenience." There was more chittering.

Mr. Griswell looked quite put upon. "Well, neither did *you.*"

The Ma'ar lifted the heavy wooden gavel and banged it loudly on the podium in front of him. Everyone behind the table jumped as the sound echoed through the large room, and the Ma'ar smiled inwardly. He loved doing that when they were least expecting it.

Taking a deep breath, the Ma'ar summoned his most authoritative voice. "The Blotheed Caravan can continue to occupy the alternate campsite for the duration of their reservation. Mr. Griswell is not required to refund any money, and both parties will honor the terms of their original contract."

He banged the gavel again with emphasis, and without waiting for a response, the Ma'ar strode to the door set to the side of the dais and disappeared down the hallway toward his office. The muted sound of angry chittering was audible through the door, but he ignored it, closing the door to his office firmly before lifting the cursed hat from his head and hurling it across the room. Dropping into a chair behind the ornately carved desk, he scratched at his head and gave a deep sigh of satisfaction.

Leaning forward, the Ma'ar pulled off his heavy brocade coat and rolled his shirtsleeves up his forearms. The coat landed in a heap on the rich carpet, and with a grimace he leaned down and retrieved it, smoothing it out and laying it over his desk. He couldn't afford to appear rumpled. Then he leaned back and propped his booted feet up on his desk.

Such a waste of time. It was all such a waste of time. And yet he needed the power, the respect and notoriety, or he wouldn't be able to perform the tasks that really mattered.

He sighed and tipped his head back, closing his eyes briefly. It had been a long morning, and the afternoon promised to be equally irritating. As he laced his fingers together over his stomach, the Ma'ar felt a slight twinge in his bones and shifted in his chair to relieve the discomfort. He may have held on to the good looks of his youth, but he was starting to feel his age. It looked like it would be another late night of ritual performance.

For a moment he pondered whether his hour would be better spent eating or napping, but a sudden knock on the door brought his chair upright and his feet to the floor. He scrambled back into his brocade coat, straightening the lapels, and peered around the desk, eventually giving his hat up for lost. He smoothed his hair into place and sat up straight, a mask of confidence and competent authority falling over his features as he called, "Yes, come in."

The Ma'ar had a lot of practice maintaining his composure and not letting his thoughts show on his features, but despite his best efforts to keep his expression neutral, his eyes widened when he saw the figure in the doorway.

"What are you doing here? Come in, quick—before someone sees you!" His voice was a hiss and the figure scurried into the room and closed the door behind him.

"Lock it," the Ma'ar commanded. The other man did so, before turning back and removing his hat, holding it in front of his chest in a motion that reminded the Ma'ar unfavorably of Mr. Griswell.

"What are you doing here?" the Ma'ar demanded again, his irritation clear. He did not bother to offer the man a seat; he had no illusions to maintain here. "You know you are never to come here. This couldn't wait until I returned to the Catacombs?"

The other man clutched his hat tightly, his knuckles white on the brim, but despite his apparent nervousness, his eyes met the Ma'ar's directly. When he spoke, his voice was thickly accented. "Sir, this couldn't wait. There's news from the gate."

At this, the Ma'ar's mouth snapped shut and his irritation dissipated as if a plug had been pulled, all annoyance draining away as the entire weight of his attention fixated on the man in front of him.

The man was nondescript, neither tall nor short, attractive nor ugly, thin nor fat. His clothing was simple: plain and brown, yet clean and well-tailored. Like all the men in the Ma'ar's employ—men he privately referred to with amusement as his hired goons—this man had been carefully selected and trained not to be memorable in any way. To be sure, he had other skills as well, and the Ma'ar desperately hoped that those skills were the reason the man was here at his office, a place the Ma'ar kept rigidly separate from his… less savory activities.

The Ma'ar thought this hired goon's name was Yven, but was not quite certain enough of this fact to actually call him by name. Fortunately, seeing that his statement had grabbed the Ma'ar's attention, the man continued without prompting.

"I been stationed in the Broken City, an' yesterday I got word from Gann, the man you got watchin' the gate."

The man spoke in a slow drawl, dragging out his words and slurring them together in the manner of those raised in the Eastern Provinces. The Ma'ar didn't want to appear impatient, but he couldn't keep the words from spilling out. "What happened?"

"Said 'e saw a girl leavin' the gatekeeper's castle. He's sure 'e didn't see 'er go in."

A long slow breath escaped from the Ma'ar, like air leaking from a balloon. How long he had waited for this moment. But he must not get ahead of himself.

"Did he see any sign of Nekuthaedris himself?" The Ma'ar kept his voice level.

The-goon-who-might-be-named-Yven shook his head. "Yer honor, no one's seen Neku in years. We woulda told you right away."

"So, what happened to this girl once she left the castle?"

"Gann followed 'er through the forest. Said it looked like she was lost. Then she ran into that crazy lady that lives in the Broken City, ya know? The one you have us watch sometimes?"

The Ma'ar closed his eyes briefly, struggling to maintain his composure and let the man continue at his own pace.

The girl had run into *Ydenda?* Gann was the one he really needed to be talking to.

"Anyways, the girl stayed the night at that lady's house, and Gann's still there watchin' 'er, but 'e sent me on t'tell you. Said I shouldn't wait, no matter what you were doin'. He said t'tell you 'e was pretty sure she'd be takin' the Millipede into the city, but 'e didn't know when. 'E's gonna follow her, but 'e wanted you t'know before she got in."

"Did you see the girl?" The Ma'ar leaned forward intently.

"No sir. She was at the crazy lady's house when I left."

"So, you don't know what she looks like?"

"Well, Gann described 'er, sir. I think she'd be hard to miss."

The Ma'ar didn't doubt that was true. Especially if you knew what to look for. Which he did.

"Okay. I have a new task for you," the Ma'ar said, leveling a commanding gaze on the man. "As soon as you leave here, I want you down at the Millipede station. You stay there until she arrives, and then come let me know immediately. If Gann arrives, send him to me as well."

"You want I should just bring 'er here?"

"No! Don't touch her, don't speak to her, don't call attention to yourself in any way. Just find out where she goes, and come tell me *immediately.* Do you understand?"

The man-who-really-probably-was-named-Yven nodded. "Yessir, as you say."

"You may go," the Ma'ar waved a hand in clear dismissal, but probably-Yven hesitated, turning his hat over in his hands.

"What is it?"

"Do you think...is there a chance she could be..." The man trailed off, unwilling or unable to say it, and the Ma'ar was abruptly reminded that the man was, despite his horrible accent and lazy way of speaking, far from stupid. He may not know all the details, but he knew what was at stake.

He met the man's gaze and answered honestly. "I don't know. But I *will* find out."

12

ROSE

Rose noticed a few things as the Millipede drew closer to the capital city of Trelissar. The first thing that caught her eye after the miles of seemingly uninhabited wilderness was the presence of small villages, at first tiny and widely spaced, a few farmhouses dotting the gently rolling hills of the countryside before growing more clustered together, eventually giving way to little towns laid out much the same as Ydenda's village. She was so taken with the idyllic pastoral scene, quaint and charming as viewed from her high perch on the scuttling arthropod, that it wasn't until they had passed down the main street of the second village that Rose began to notice that something was off.

It took her a minute to figure out what it was that had drawn her attention, but as they came upon the third village, larger and more impressive than the two preceding it, she realized what she'd been missing. It was the sounds that she noticed first, or more specifically, the lack of them. No voices, no birds singing, none of the myriad noises that accompany human occupation. It was a strange, unnatural silence.

Leaning cautiously over the side, Rose peered down to confirm her suspicions. There was not a single person or creature of any kind to be seen anywhere in the town. No movement in any store front or house. The buildings themselves didn't look particularly run down, but on closer inspection, they were clearly abandoned.

They were two villages further down the track before Rose saw the Rot. It caught her eye as just a slim patch of darkness in her peripheral vision, and when she turned to look she just caught a brief glimpse of the thick black tendrils snaking up the side of a house before the Millipede was past, the bright red house fading in the distance as Rose twisted in her seat to stare behind her.

Was that...

It was. Once she started paying attention, she began to notice it everywhere: a mass coating the side of a barn, swallowing the stripes of a candy-cane colored barber pole, encircling the base of a thick-trunked tree, whose leaves had turned dark at its tips. Had there been more along the way that she had missed?

Feeling suddenly chilly, Rose pulled her gloved hands inside the sleeves of her hoodie and wrapped her arms around herself. When she'd seen the black marks on Ydenda and the stranger in the castle, she'd assumed they were old scars, or maybe some kind of disease. She'd never expected to see it out here in the world, on buildings and trees. What *was* it?

And it looked different here, too. The marks on Ydenda and the stranger had looked like old scars, black but dull, puckering their skin. But here the Rot looked fresher, blacker, somehow. It didn't seem to be moving, but it lay heavy, shiny like thick tar, so dark it seemed to swallow the light around it.

By the time the attendant had wandered down the aisle, calling "Next stop, Trelissar, twenty minutes!" Rose was seeing it everywhere. There was no doubt at all that it was growing denser the closer they drew to the capital. Entire trees were engulfed here, their great leafless branches black and twisted against the bright afternoon sky. Buildings towered dark and decaying, crumbling on the streets surrounding them, like scenes from a nightmare, and Rose observed that when they came upon areas where the Rot had spread too closely to the roads they followed, new paths had been cleared for the Millipede, sidestepping the tainted villages.

As they'd made their long journey, the Millipede had stopped on multiple occasions to take on new passengers. The mustached man and elderly ladies were still on board —the latter propped against each other and snoring loudly —but they had now been joined by a rather harried looking couple with four young children in tow, and a quiet, rather unremarkable looking man of average height and appearance, dressed plainly in a brown suit. He had taken the seat two rows directly behind Rose, then pulled his hat down over his eyes and appeared to have spent the majority of the trip asleep.

None of the passengers looked even remotely concerned with the vacant buildings or the increasing quantity of shiny black tar-like tendrils, which stood motionless, twining around trees and up the sides of buildings as though they had been painted on with viscous black paint. But Rose had no trouble imagining how they might move, their sinuous forms creeping forward and wrapping tighter until they devoured everything in their path, the way they'd crept up the stranger's arm in the castle after he'd cast his spell. She drew comfort from the other passengers' unconcern, but still felt the need to pull the hood of her sweatshirt up to cover her hair, burrowing deep into the warmth of the soft fleece.

All things considered, the trip had been an uneventful one, and Rose had never lacked for things to stare at. The sandwiches that Ydenda had packed her—strange in texture, but like all the other food she'd tried so far, wonderful in taste—had kept her stomach from growling, and she hadn't had to brave the food stand at the front of the Millipede, situated uncomfortably close to the waving antennae.

The Millipede began to slow as they crested the last hill and the wall of the city swept into view on the horizon. Rose drew in a surprised breath. The city was enormous; much larger than she had expected based on the sizes of the small settlements they had passed through so far.

The wall was tall and seemingly constructed of huge rough-hewn stones. The stones themselves were oddly shaped, all jagged edges and varying sizes, but ranged in color from the dark gray of stormy skies to pale lavender with veins of pink running through them. The effect of the multicolored stones stacked together and glinting in the sunlight was quite beautiful. The stones she could see, that was. Because for every stone visible on the wall, two more were coated thickly with Rot. It almost looked more like it was the spaces *between* the stones that were covered with Rot, as if it had somehow been pushed through the wall to the outside. Like the Rot was the only thing holding the last vestiges of stone together.

Her attention was quickly diverted again though, because beyond the wall rose spires and domes on par with any city Rose may have seen before, a sea of roofs sweeping the breadth of her vision.

She didn't have long to gape before the wall was closing in on them, and, craning forward in her seat to take in as much of the view as possible, she caught sight of the tunnel cutting right through the wall only moments before they were in it, the Millipede skittering forward into the dark. Rose instinctively ducked down in her seat as they passed into the tunnel, even though logically she knew the roof was far above them.

It took a minute for her eyes to adjust to the dim light of the tunnel, and moments later they were out again, the Millipede slowing to a crawl as they entered a huge open station. They pulled to a halt by the edge of a platform crowded with people.

She barely had time to look around her before the attendant was crouching down and unfurling the rope ladder, reminding them to, "Check and be sure you have all your belongings. Anything left behind we feed to Millie!"

Rose stood slowly and took her time pulling on her backpack, letting the other passengers work their way down the ladder as she got her bearings. The nondescript man in brown gestured to the ladder, but she shook her head and waved him on, and with a shrug he disappeared over the edge.

"Have a lovely time in Trelissar, Miss," the attendant said cheerily as he helped her onto the ladder, and then she was down as well, hastily stepping clear of the Millipede's feet as the throng of people on the platform enveloped her.

Rose couldn't imagine she looked like anything but a tourist as she gaped at her surroundings. Her comparison of the station back in the Broken City to the train station in Seattle suddenly seemed silly when compared to this. The massive building bore a striking resemblance to the King Street Station of her memory, from the chandelier hanging from the high plastered ceiling right down to the compass rose set in marble tiles on the floor. The press of people moved like a current around her, and for a moment she felt like a child again, and had to stop herself from trying to search out her parents in the crowd.

Giving her head a shake, she pushed through the melee and out of the rotating glass doors into the crisp fresh air. While it was definitely cooler and less frantic out of the press of people in the station, she found that the large square extending out from the entrance was also packed.

Feeling slightly claustrophobic, Rose jostled her way through the bustle and found a shadowed corner against the wall of the train station where she could pause. She swung her backpack off of her shoulder and rummaged through before extracting a bottle of water and taking a long sip.

Now that she was out of the throng, Rose could see the crowd more clearly. The square was packed with people, all wearing brightly colored clothes, some with elaborate hats, and yet, she realized that none of them were *doing* anything. No one appeared to be going anywhere, they were all just milling about in groups, talking over each other and—she saw as she peered into the mass of bodies—watching something.

Replacing the cap on her water and tucking it away into her bag, she zipped the backpack and swung it onto her shoulder before rising onto her toes to try to see what the commotion was all about. It was no use. She was of average height, but no one could compete with those hats.

She glanced around surreptitiously, before realizing that obviously no one knew her here, so it surely didn't matter if she made a fool of herself. She jumped, launching herself as high as possible, craning her head to catch a glimpse of whatever was causing all the fuss in the square. What she saw left her even more confused than before. Beyond the great mass of people, all she could see was a giant, red… something. It was huge and shiny, like vinyl.

A momentary hush fell over the crowd, and then a great cheer went up, a group of women in front of Rose squealing excitedly. She winced and stepped back against the wall. When the noise settled back into the hum of conversation, another sound caught Rose's ear. It was a low hiss, growing louder with each passing second, until it nearly drowned out the noise from the crowd.

Eyebrows furrowed in bewilderment, Rose jumped again. The red vinyl appeared to be growing now, slowing rising in a mass of billowing fabric, and she was suddenly put in mind of the bouncy castles she'd seen at kids' birthday parties. *What the—*

"You're not from here, are you?"

The voice came from Rose's left, startling her, and she jumped as she turned, knocking her shoulder hard against the wall.

"I'm sorry, I didn't mean to scare you." It was the man from the Millipede, Rose saw with relief, the one in the brown suit. He had removed his hat—a simple brown derby hat, nothing as elaborate as the women in the crowd were wearing—and held it by his side.

"No, that's okay," Rose assured him, rubbing at her bruised shoulder. "I was just trying to see what all the commotion is about."

The man smiled, revealing a dimple in his left cheek, which made his forgettable face appear younger. His eyes, also brown, were bright and alert on her face. Rose guessed he was in his mid-forties.

"That's why I figured you weren't from around here," the man went on cheerfully. "It's Inflation Day. Everyone in the city is either here to watch the spectacle or as far away as they can be to avoid the crowd. No one from Trelissar accidentally shows up in Central Square on Inflation Day."

At Rose's blank stare, the man chuckled. "It's the Trelissar Inflatable Opera House. It goes up once a year and the performances run for two weeks before they take it down again. Where are you from, anyway?"

Avoiding his question, Rose managed to find her tongue, if only to parrot the man's words back at him. "It's an *inflatable* opera house."

He nodded.

"An opera house. Like…a theater. That *inflates.*"

The man laughed, but his eyes were sharp and she got the impression he had noticed her evasion of his question. "You should see a show if you're staying in town. Performances start tomorrow evening. Posters with the schedule are up all over the city."

At Rose's continued blank stare, the man shook his head and extended his hand. "I'm sorry, my name is Gann."

Rose eyed his outstretched hand for a moment, her childhood admonition from her parents to "never talk to strangers," welling up inside her for just a moment before she grimaced, feeling silly. She had talked to Ydenda, and where would she be now without her help?

"Rose," she said, accepting his handshake.

"I only came over because you looked a bit lost, and I wondered if you needed any help with directions."

Rose let out her breath with a whoosh of relief. Yes, that

was exactly what she needed. Directions, not to be standing around foolishly watching this nonsensical spectacle.

"Yes, thank you," she said with sincerity. "I need to see the King, and I was told that anyone in the city could point me in the right direction."

Gann raised an eyebrow, but he didn't look surprised at this statement, Rose was glad to see. Hopefully that meant gaining an audience with the King was not a difficult task.

"The King, you say? That's...quite a dangerous journey." He eyed her and Rose shifted uncomfortably, certain he was measuring her up, but unsure what he was looking for. After a moment he went on. "I can certainly give you directions, but it'll take you quite a while to get there, and it's pushing five o'clock," Gann said with a glance at his wrist. "Your best bet is to spend the night in the city and go tomorrow." He offered her another dimpled smile. "Or catch an opera tomorrow and go the next day."

Rose considered his words with an internal sigh. She had hoped not to prolong her visit here. She still felt drawn back toward the castle, worried about the strange inhabitant there. It was almost as if she could feel an invisible cord stretching between herself and the castle in the woods, pulling taut the further away she traveled. Surreptitiously she closed her hand into a loose fist, rubbing the mark on her palm with her fingers through the fingerless gloves she wore. She wondered if whatever the stranger had done to her hand was making her feel this way, or if it was something about the man himself. Either way, she wanted to be on her way. But on the other hand, Gann was right. It was growing late, her stomach was starting to growl again, and if she couldn't make it to the King tonight then she would need to find somewhere to sleep. All things considered, she would just as soon not sleep on the streets in a city surrounded by masses of black Rot.

Suddenly, she wondered if it was in the city as well. She hadn't seen any since she'd left the Millipede, but then again, she'd barely left the station, and she hadn't exactly been looking, either. Ydenda's words from that morning echoed in her head.

"*Don't touch the Rot.*"

She remembered the tendrils coating the sides of buildings in the abandoned villages they had passed through on the Millipede and suppressed a shiver, wondering just how safe this city really was.

"Rose?"

Her attention returned to the man in front of her and found him looking intently at her hand where her fingers rubbed against her palm. She forced her hand into stillness, uncomfortable with his attention even though she knew he couldn't possibly suspect anything. She shook her head and smiled. "I'm sorry, I was just thinking. Yes, I would love a suggestion of a place to stay if you have one."

He smiled back, seemingly unperturbed by her wandering attention. "Of course. I can think of four hotels within walking distance of the Millipede Station if you don't have transportation? Right," he said as she shook her head in response. "Lots of people are in town for the Inflation, but if you don't mind a bit of a walk, you can probably still find a room at the Trelissar Tree or down the road at the Arms Hotel. Would you like me to show you the way?"

Rose shook her head hastily. "No, that's alright. If you just give me directions I can find my way."

She was worried that he would insist out of some sense of gentlemanly duty. As friendly and helpful as Gann was, his sharp gaze was unnerving and Rose very much wanted to be alone so she could process the day's events. She was beginning to feel overwhelmed again, and the last thing she wanted was another half hour of small talk.

Fortunately Gann didn't press the issue, and was content to give her detailed directions to the two hotels and leave it at that.

"The staff at the hotel can help you find your way when you are ready to see the King," Gann said, placing his hat back on his head.

"Thank you," she said sincerely. "I really appreciate the help."

"Anytime," he responded with a smile, and then he was gone, disappearing into the crowd.

Rose watched him leave and was surprised by how his brown suit was instantly swallowed up by the mass of bright colors.

She shrugged her shoulders, hitching the backpack further up onto her back, and repeated Gann's directions over in her head so she wouldn't forget them. Then, steeling herself against the imminent press of bodies and sound, she pushed off of the wall and made her own way out into the sea of people.

The tall, stately woman with a thick mass of bright red hair behind the concierge desk was not the older gentleman who had checked her into her room last night, but they both had the same friendly, welcoming demeanor that put Rose at ease.

"Good morning!" the woman said cheerfully, checking the register she had behind the counter. "Rose, right? I just called up to your room."

"Oh, that was you. Sorry I didn't answer; I only just got up."

"Ah, sorry to wake you, dear." The woman crouched down, fishing for something under her desk. She continued talking, her voice muffled behind the wood. "A man stopped by for you this morning. He left you an invitation. I've got it here somewhere."

A man? An *invitation*? The only men she'd met were Gann and the stranger in the castle. And only one of them knew she was here. Her heart sank.

"Aha!" The red head bobbed back into view as the woman came up, waving an envelope triumphantly. "It's an invitation from *the Ma'ar*." Her voice changed as she said the last words, falling into a hushed tone of utmost respect, and her gaze on Rose's face was awed. She handed the envelope over with reverence.

"The...who?" Rose raised an eyebrow.

"The *Ma'ar*," the woman repeated, her expression changing to incredulity. "Where in the world are you from, girl? He practically runs the whole city. Second only to the King."

Rose was abruptly reminded of her purpose. "Speaking of the King, that's why I'm here. I need directions to his... uh..." His what? Castle? Tower? Fortress? It had never occurred to her to ask. "To...him," she amended lamely. "I was told you could help me find my way?"

The woman's eyes narrowed in dismay. "You're going to see the *King?* That's...a dangerous journey."

That was what Gann had said. "What do you mean?" Rose asked.

"It's just...well, the bridge that leads to the King is *dangerous*." The woman lowered her voice conspiratorially and leaned in. "They say anyone who crosses the bridge loses their sanity." She gave a nod for emphasis, then straightened up and returned her voice to normal. "Most people take their troubles to the Ma'ar. He decides when he needs to take things to the King."

Rose raised an eyebrow. "So, the Ma'ar crosses this bridge? How does he keep from going insane?"

The woman looked at her blankly. "He's the *Ma'ar.* Now, aren't you going to open that?"

"What? Oh, right," Rose followed her gaze down to the envelope. It was heavy paper, ivory, with her name written elegantly in silver ink across the front. Flipping it over, Rose was surprised to see a blob of red wax over the seam where the flap was sealed, an ornate letter "M" pressed deep into the wax. Good lord, a letter actually sealed with sealing wax? What was this, the sixteenth century?

Glancing up to see the woman behind the desk watching, her rapt gaze fixed on the envelope, Rose sighed and pried her thumb under the edge of the flap, tearing across without breaking the seal. She pulled out a thick sheet of stationary, ivory to match the envelope, and unfolded it to see a message written in silver ink, the same elegant script as on the envelope.

"Rose," it read, "It has come to my attention that you are new to Trelissar and wish to beg an audience with the King.

I would be delighted to assist you with this matter, and can provide papers to expedite the process. If it pleases you, I would be most honored if you would accompany me to the opening presentation of this year's opera season, this evening at seven o'clock. We can speak more of the matter then, while introducing to you the finest entertainment our grand city has to offer. I will send someone to collect you at your hotel at half past six, and I look forward to meeting you this evening." It was signed simply, "Your servant, The Ma'ar."

Rose looked up, completely bewildered. Who was the Ma'ar? How did he know she was here, and what her plans were? And why on earth did he care? It also didn't escape her notice that the invitation was not framed as a question.

The red-headed woman was looking at her eagerly, trying to remain professional but completely failing to contain her curiosity. With a shrug, Rose handed the letter across to her.

The woman actually squealed. "He wants to take you to the opera! On opening night!" She fanned herself with her hand as Rose looked on in bemusement. The woman caught sight of Rose's face and her expression turned stern. "You have no idea what an honor this is," she lectured. "You have to go; you simply *have* to."

"Can't you just give me directions and I can head out now?" Rose asked. "I don't have any reason to stick around all day, and I really do need to see the King."

The woman looked horrified. "You can't possibly be thinking about refusing this invitation." She waved the paper in Rose's face. "Besides, he said he could help you. I told you, it's *dangerous* to see the King. Most people don't survive the bridge. And if they do, I've heard it can take days to get an audience. *Weeks!*"

Rose frowned. She hadn't known that. She didn't have weeks to wait. Or even days. She still felt that pull back toward the castle. And while she wasn't exactly concerned about losing what passed for her sanity, she wasn't excited about discovering what the people of this world classified as "dangerous." Besides, she was already wearing her only change of clothes, and who knew how long Ydenda's money would hold out. Not long if she had to keep paying for food and lodging. Maybe this Ma'ar could help her after all.

"Okay, okay," she said, taking the paper back from the woman, who beamed at her. A thought suddenly occurred to her, and she looked down at her ripped jeans and long-sleeved t-shirt, this one sporting the image of a giant yellow slug. She looked back up at the woman behind the counter with a plea in her eyes.

"What does one wear to opening night at the opera?"

14

ROSE

It seemed that formal attire was one of the few things this world had in common with Rose's own. More or less.

At six-twenty she found herself fed, showered, dressed, and standing again in the hotel lobby. Thanks to a hurried shopping trip and the eager assistance of the red-headed concierge—whose name turned out to be Anae—she had traded in her torn jeans and t-shirt for what had swiftly become Rose's new favorite article of clothing. Not that she currently had much to choose from.

The dress had two layers; the outer layer was as black as her hair, with long sleeves and a hem that draped nearly to the floor. The fabric turned sheer in a slow gradient just past her thighs and partway down her arms, revealing the under-layer, a silky fabric in deep purple with patterns of silver filigree twining up her legs and arms until they disappeared under the outer layer. The neckline was cut low, a bit more revealing than Rose typically was comfortable with, but the dress was wonderfully soft and silky, and she couldn't remember ever having owned something so fancy in her life.

Soft black slippers covered her feet, and a black lace shawl draped over her shoulders for warmth. Anae had insisted on helping Rose with her hair, which was coiled down her back in an intricate braid that Rose was sure she would never be able to replicate. Her jewelry belonged to Anae: a glittering necklace in the shape of an exotic-looking bird, with matching earrings styled as feathers.

The dress appeared to be the height of current fashion in Trelissar, and Anae had tried to convince Rose that she should also allow her to apply makeup according to the current trends. But when Rose discovered what exactly that meant—something involving stripes that put her in mind of war paint, she politely but firmly declined, and Anae, clucking her tongue in resigned disappointment, contented herself with a subtle touch of shadow around Rose's eyes and a wine-red stain to her lips.

In the end, Rose felt gorgeous—and entirely out of her element.

She also felt broke, since the outfit had cost a large chunk of her remaining money. She had enough left, assuming she was counting correctly, to pay for one more night at the hotel and breakfast the following morning, so she dearly hoped that her visit to the King, if that still proved necessary, would be both short and productive.

"Stop fidgeting," Anae scolded her, smoothing the front of the dress where Rose had been plucking at the fabric nervously.

Rose subsided, and began picking at her fingernails instead. "Oh!" she exclaimed suddenly. "I never thought to ask. What is the show tonight?"

Anae retreated behind the desk and consulted a poster that hung on the wall. The same poster was plastered all over town, but it hadn't crossed Rose's mind to actually *read* it.

"'The Gibbering Winds,'" Anae announced, beaming as she turned back to Rose. "That's a good one."

Rose eyed her askance. "Sounds ominous."

"Oh no, it's a comedy. They always start the season off on a lighter note. Then they can end with something really dark like, 'The Necromancer's Folly,'" or..." She trailed off as she consulted the poster again, running her finger down the list. "Ahh, yes. '*Toad*.' That one's quite the tragedy. Beautiful music though," she added wistfully.

The chimes over the front door sounded as the door swung open, and both Rose and Anae turned to see a man step into the lobby.

"Gann!" Rose exclaimed, taking in the man's brown suit and hat, before settling on the face that, while vaguely similar to the man she had met the previous day, actually belonged to a completely different person.

"Oh, I'm sorry," she began, feeling slightly embarrassed, "I thought—"

"Miss Rose?" The man removed his brown hat to reveal carefully combed hair and gave her a slight bow. "My name is Yven. The Ma'ar's sent me t'collect you for the opera." He transferred his hat into his other hand, which held an umbrella despite the late afternoon sun, and held out his arm toward her.

Rose's initial relief that the man was not Gann was short-lived, as she noted that the brown suit was not the only thing the two men had in common. Yven, too, had the same disconcerting gaze and air of watchfulness. He did not stare or do anything that Rose could pinpoint as the source of her discomfort, but his eyes made Rose feel as if she were under a microscope, as if her every word or gesture was being noted and mentally catalogued.

She looked to Anae for help, but the concierge was looking toward Yven with a wide, star-struck gaze, and Rose mentally rolled her eyes, writing the red-headed woman off as a lost cause. Well. The sooner she got this over with, the sooner she could have help for the man in the castle. Plastering a pleasant smile on her face, she crossed the small space and tucked her hand into the man's proffered elbow.

Casting a farewell wave back over her shoulder to Anae and promising that she would have a good time, she pulled the shawl tight over her shoulders and followed as Yven guided her out the door and down to the sidewalk. They set off toward the bizarre shape of the opera house, which loomed high in the distance, its fully-inflated red walls shiny in the late afternoon sun.

To Rose's immense relief, Yven did not attempt to make small talk as they walked, and though she got the distinct impression that his watchful focus never wavered from her, she also felt that perhaps he was as awkwardly uncomfortable as she was. She felt overdressed in her finery next to Yven's plain suit, and as they walked in silence Rose wondered again why exactly she had agreed to this.

Finally, they approached the wide green expanse of the central square, with the Millipede station rising to their left, and the shiny red opera house filling her vision to the right. Up close and fully inflated it looked even more ridiculous, like an enormous bouncy castle, and Rose had to stifle a giggle as they joined the throng of opera-goers milling around outside the entryway. She was relieved to see that her clothing was no longer out of place in this crowd; in fact, if anything *she* was the one who was underdressed here. The men wore suits in various jewel-bright colors, and the women were in lavish gowns and sparkling jewelry. Anae had been right, and bold black streaks of makeup adorned the faces of men and women alike, though Rose was relieved to see that she was not the only person who had chosen to forego the warpaint for a more understated look.

To the side, near the front of the theater, was a small booth with a sign stretching overhead. Beneath a row of curving symbols read a small English translation: Shoe Check. Rose raised her eyebrows, watching as a line began to form behind the group of people clustered there, each removing their shoes and exchanging them for tickets.

There was a subtle tug on her arm, and Rose turned to follow Yven as he led her smoothly through the crowd, which seemed to part and flow around them seamlessly. Rose thought that if anyone should feel out of place and underdressed, it was Yven, but no one seemed to notice him at all, nor her either as she kept her hold on his elbow. Even as he moved through the crowd, Yven's eyes were watchful on her, and Rose began to look forward to meeting the Ma'ar, if only to escape Yven's company. If the Ma'ar turned out to be a sharp-gazed man in a brown suit, she was leaving.

When they finally drew toward the front of the crowd, a man stepped out of the entrance to the opera house, and it became immediately apparent that the Ma'ar was not, in fact, another brown-suited man. He was easily identifiable by the brief hush that ran through the crowd, followed by the babble of adoring voices that rose to fill the silence.

The Ma'ar was a tall man with broad shoulders and an ageless quality about him. He wore black pants and shiny black shoes, and the most elaborate coat Rose had ever seen: black as well but embroidered with metallic filigree, long tails in the back, wide cuffs over his wrists, and row upon row of silver buttons marching down the front and along the cuffs. On his head over neat, silver-streaked hair, was perched a matching top hat in black with a wide filigree band in the same metallic thread. Pristine white gloves covered his hands. Clothing aside, the man had a presence about him, and his face was handsome with thick silver brows over twinkling blue eyes and a charismatic smile above a neatly-trimmed goatee.

He nodded to the crowd, offering gracious smiles and winks but ignoring the questions and other fawning attention directed his way, and turned to Rose. He removed his hat and swept into a deep bow, which Rose, unsure of proper etiquette, returned in the form of an awkward, wobbling curtsy. Setting his hat back on top of his head, he offered her his arm in the same motion Yven had made. Suddenly reminded, Rose turned to offer polite thanks to the strange brown-suited man, only to find that he had vanished, presumably slipping invisibly back into the crowd while her attention had been on the Ma'ar.

Shrugging, Rose took the Ma'ar's arm and allowed him to escort her into the theater.

"My dear," he began, his deep voice rich and pleasant, "Thank you so much for agreeing to accompany me tonight. Opening night at the opera is my favorite night of the entire year, and it is such a delight to have a lovely new acquaintance to share the experience with. Tell me, have you ever been to the Trelissar opera before?"

Rose felt certain he already knew the answer, but she shook her head anyway as the Ma'ar guided her over the raised entryway. Despite the reservations she'd had, she immediately liked the man, his effortless charm and charisma putting her at ease. "No, I've never even been to the city before."

"Ah," the Ma'ar said with a wide smile. "Then you are in for a treat. 'The Gibbering Winds' is one of my favorites. And," he added with a wink in her direction, "we have the best seats in the house."

The interior of the opera house looked, confusingly enough, exactly as Rose had expected. It was a study in contradictions, glowing chandeliers hanging from bulging vinyl ceilings; ornate carpets laid over a floor that bounced unsteadily underfoot. For one slightly hysterical moment Rose was glad she was not wearing heels, and the booth outside suddenly made sense as she imagined a stiletto puncturing the floor with a careless step and the entire structure collapsing around her amidst the hiss of leaking air and the screams of trapped patrons.

Rose gripped tight to the Ma'ar's arm as they proceeded through the lobby, not just for politeness' sake, but also to keep her balance as she wobbled unsteadily across the air-filled floor. The Ma'ar, who seemed more practiced in his movements, chuckled and patted her hand where it lay on his arm. "Don't worry, my dear, you'll get used to it quickly."

There was a long line at the ticket counter, but the Ma'ar neatly sidestepped the queue and led her toward the stairs. Between his arm and the railing set into the wall, Rose was able to keep her balance enough to slowly ascend the richly carpeted air-filled steps, and they eventually came out onto the first balcony level. The Ma'ar guided her past the entrances to the theater, where uniformed ushers stood ready with programs, and around to a narrow hallway where a series of alcoves lay concealed behind heavy curtains. The Ma'ar released her arm and swept back the curtain from the first alcove with a flourish, then bowed and allowed Rose to wobble past him into the space.

Inside, she found a private balcony, with a row of comfortable-looking chairs and an impressive view of the stage. She looked to the Ma'ar, who entered after her, letting the heavy curtain fall back into place, and gestured to her to choose a seat. "You weren't kidding; these *are* the best seats in the house."

The Ma'ar smiled widely. "Being the Ma'ar does have its privileges. Can I get you anything to drink? Cloudy Mable? Perhaps a glass of Fizz?" There was the barest glint of humor in the Ma'ar's eye, and for a brief moment Rose thought perhaps he was testing her, to see if she was familiar with any of his offerings. She quickly dismissed the thought. She had no idea if those drinks were local to Trelissar or common throughout the world, but the Ma'ar knew she wasn't from the city and had no reason to suspect anything further.

Politeness warred with curiosity for a moment, but after a brief pause she declined with a shake of her head, thanking him for the offer, and chose one of the thickly padded seats, sinking into its comfortable warmth. With a wink, the Ma'ar ducked back around the curtain and Rose could hear him speaking with the nearest usher, ordering himself a glass of 'Fizz,' before rejoining her and settling himself in the seat next to her. The seats, like the structure itself, were filled with air, but here in the Ma'ar's private alcove they were covered with thick plush cushions and were quite comfortable.

The Ma'ar settled back and his friendly smile fell on her. "So, my dear, what do you think of our city so far?"

Rose hesitantly smiled back. "I only arrived yesterday evening, but from what I've seen so far, it's quite nice." She paused, wanting to ask how he'd found her and why he'd invited her here, but unsure whether it would seem rude or ungrateful. Eventually, she gathered her nerve, choosing her words carefully. "Do you often invite newcomers to the opera? I wasn't aware my presence in the city would be of any interest."

The Ma'ar laughed, a deep jovial booming sound. "I know Trelissar seems like a big city, but to me, it's just a friendly little town. We don't get visitors as often as you might think, or at least, not ones whose acquaintances I've not already met. It's a great task, maintaining a city like Trelissar, and I like to offer assistance where I may. It is simply a fortunate coincidence that your arrival coincided with the opening of our esteemed opera season."

He hadn't answered her real question, how he'd known she was here and why, but she couldn't bring herself to ask more directly. She was also afraid that he might ask her point-blank where she came from, and she wasn't sure how she would answer. She paused, trying to formulate another question, but the Ma'ar beat her to it.

"So, what brings you to our lovely city?" As he spoke, the curtain behind them opened and the usher stepped in, delivering a tall glass of what looked to be a viscous, bubbly drink in a shocking turquoise hue. The Ma'ar accepted the drink and thanked the usher before taking a long sip and giving a contented sigh. "Do let me know if you change your mind," he said, indicating the glass as he sat it down on the low table in front of them. "They have the best Fizz in the city here."

Rose smiled faintly but demurred, and the Ma'ar looked at her expectantly, awaiting an answer to his previous question. Rose was pretty sure the Ma'ar already knew what brought her to Trelissar—hadn't he mentioned it in his invitation? But she answered anyway.

"I'm here to request an audience with the King."

"Ah, yes," said the Ma'ar, as if he had forgotten. "The King is not an easy man to see; I'm sure you have heard the rumors. Is there perhaps anything I may personally help you with?"

Rose hesitated, but as she took in his open, friendly face, and considered that he might well be in a position to help her, she decided to give him an abbreviated version of the story.

"I was…visiting with a man who lives in a castle in the forest far from here," she began, unsure of which details to provide and which to hold back. "Near the Broken City. He…got sick while I was there, and I went looking for help."

"He was ill?" The Ma'ar's gaze was interested. "Was a healer unable to help?"

Rose felt entirely out of her depth, suddenly aware of how ridiculous her story sounded but unsure of what to say. "I—it was suggested to me that the King may be able to help."

"Indeed?" The Ma'ar raised an eyebrow. "I don't deny that the King might be of assistance, but that seems a rather, ah, unorthodox use of his time."

Rose felt incredibly foolish. Why *was* she going to see the King? Only because Ydenda had seemed so convinced that she should. She mentally kicked herself. She should have gone straight back to that castle, instead of floundering around aimlessly in a world she was woefully unequipped to handle. She glanced down at her lap. What was she *doing?* She had spent her last remaining money—money that had been given to her as charity—on a dress, so she could sit here making small talk at a fancy event instead of dealing with the problem and getting herself home. She was wasting time.

She should just ask the Ma'ar for help. She should tell him where she came from, and explain about the stranger, and the Rot. And yet she couldn't seem to force the words past her lips.

The Ma'ar must have sensed her internal struggle, because he reached over and gently patted her hand. "I'm sorry, my dear, that was unkind. I don't know what is wrong with your friend, but we have excellent healers here in Trelissar, and if you do have need of the King, he can be found outside of the western city gate, across the Mist Bridge. I can provide documents to expedite your visit, should you need them."

Before Rose had a chance to respond, the house lights dimmed, and the Ma'ar turned expectantly toward the front of the theater. "Ah, here we go," he said, smiling widely. "We can talk more during intermission."

∼

The next hour and a half flew by. Rose had been fully prepared to endure something bizarre and nonsensical, in keeping with the theme of her journey so far, but she was surprised to find that the production was not only easy to follow, but highly entertaining.

Their seats were, without a doubt, the best in the house, the stage stretched out wide beneath them, and the opera was a spectacle unlike any she had ever seen. It was indeed a comedy; the plot itself was actually rather silly, but the costumes were spectacular, all shimmering jewels and elaborate headdresses, and the music was achingly beautiful. Five minutes into the first act, Rose could understand why half the city had turned out with excitement to see the Inflation take place. Most surprising of all, Rose thought, was how good the acoustics were for what was essentially the inside of a balloon. She wasn't sure how it was possible, but the music seemed to fill the air, the strains of the orchestra coming from every direction at once, and she was hard-pressed to keep tears from her eyes as the two singers' duet rose to a crescendo at the culmination of the first act.

When the lights came back up Rose turned to catch the Ma'ar surreptitiously wiping the corners of his own eyes before turning to face her. "So, my dear, what did you think?" The expression on his face was endearingly hopeful and just for a second he reminded her of a child who had just shared a precious drawing and was eager for her approval.

Rose laughed, searching for the appropriate word. "It was magnificent. I had no idea what to expect, and it was..."

The Ma'ar grinned as words failed her. "It certainly was, wasn't it?" He stretched and rose to his feet. "I believe I am going to get a refill," he said, indicating his empty glass. "Can I interest you in anything? Not to seem pushy, but the Fizz really is marvelous here."

Rose laughed and nodded. "If it's as good as you say, how can I refuse?"

After the Ma'ar had ducked behind the curtain, Rose pushed to her feet and stretched, walking around the little alcove and peering down at the audience below. From her high vantage point, it was a sea of bright colors, painted faces and elaborate clothing, and Rose marveled at the beauty of it all. She was no longer upset that she had come, no longer felt that she was wasting her time.

She looked forward to the second act of the opera, as well as another night in the warm bed at The Trelissar Tree.

Tomorrow she would set out to find the King. She could easily understand how it might seem silly to the Ma'ar that she sought the King's aid only to help with what he must assume was a friend's minor illness, but Rose knew it was something more than that. Besides, she needed the King's help to find her way back to her world, and she just didn't feel that was information she should share. Regardless though, tonight was a night for enjoying herself. Her problems would still be there in the morning.

A moment later, the Ma'ar reentered the alcove, two tall glasses of the turquoise liquid held in his gloved hands. He offered one to Rose before they both returned to their seats. Rose eyed the viscous liquid for a moment before taking a hesitant sip. The drink was thick, the consistency of syrup, and bubbles rose in her mouth, bursting against her tongue. She gave a surprised laugh, and the Ma'ar smiled widely, his eyes twinkling. The flavor was surprisingly delicate, and unlike anything she had tasted before.

"That's delicious," she said, then raised her glass to clink it against the Ma'ar's where he held it aloft. "To new friends," he commented, and they both drank.

She sat back comfortably in her chair as the Ma'ar turned to her, apparently ready to resume their conversation in the few remaining minutes of intermission. "So, tell me more about this friend of yours in the castle," he began conversationally. "Did you mention it was near the Broken City? I believe I may know of where you mean."

"Yes," Rose nodded, "somewhere in the forest not too far from there. He's," she paused, unsure of what to say, "Well, I don't know him that well. I'd hurt my hand and he helped me bandage it."

The Ma'ar's gaze fell to her hands, seeking out the faint

white line that ran the length of her palm. "May I?" He held out his hand.

Rose suddenly wished she hadn't mentioned her wound. With her attention focused on it, she could again feel the slight tingle there, almost like a connection, pulling her back toward the castle. She felt exposed and had a sudden urge to sit on her hand to hide it from sight, but instead she forced herself to hold her hand out to the Ma'ar.

"It's nothing," she said uncomfortably, "just a little cut. It's healed now."

The Ma'ar's gaze seemed sharper now, focused on her hand. "When did you cut it, did you say? Two days ago?"

She hadn't said. She wanted to pull her hand back, but didn't want to be rude.

The Ma'ar peered closer, lifting his other hand, but stopping shy of touching the faded scar, seeming to realize what he was doing. He released her hand, turning his once again charming smile back to her face. "I'm so glad you weren't seriously hurt. It seems to have healed well."

Rose nodded and drew her arm back, smiling a trifle unsteadily. "Yes, it's fine now." There was a brief silence.

When the Ma'ar moved again, it was much faster than Rose would have expected from a man of his age or size. Quick as a viper, his hand shot to his hat, where he drew something out that had been tucked underneath the wide band, hidden from view. The light winked off the metal edge and Rose barely had time to register that it was a small, flat dagger, before the Ma'ar lunged forward, gripping Rose's closest hand. In one smooth motion, the Ma'ar dragged the sharp edge of the blade across her skin, scoring a deep gash into the back of her hand.

Rose was too shocked to scream as pain lanced through her, just gaped dumbly as the Ma'ar gripped her with bruising force and they both stared at her hand. The gash burned fiercely, but no blood flowed out. Instead, a shimmering iridescence glowed from the cut, bright and luminous, before the wound sealed itself, the skin flowing back together along the length of the gash until only a thin white line remained.

Rose's instincts finally overrode her shock and she wrenched her hand out of the Ma'ar's tight grip, lurching out of her seat. The dagger dropped from the Ma'ar's grasp as he stared at her, his expression twisted with a kind of stunned elation.

"*I was right.*" His voice came in a whisper, and Rose took a step back.

"Don't move or I'll scream," she said, her voice shaking.

The Ma'ar didn't so much as blink. "Go ahead. Who do you think they'll believe?"

Suddenly he lunged again, both arms reaching out to grab for her, and Rose tripped, colliding with the low table in front of their chairs as she twisted out of his reach. One of the two glasses overturned, sending vivid blue liquid splashing all over the floor and onto the front of her dress. She fell hard on the carpeted floor, which bounced softly under her weight, and she scrambled to her feet, the hem of her dress snagging on the table as she hauled herself up, a tearing sound filling her ears as she pulled free.

The Ma'ar was on his feet by then too, the dagger back in his grip, though he held it positioned to threaten, not to cut. "*Planeswalker,*" he whispered, his fervent expression seeming to make his eyes glow as he stepped between her and the curtain separating their alcove from the corridor.

Without pausing for thought, Rose crouched, grabbing the second glass of Fizz. She threw the contents of the nearly-full glass into the Ma'ar's face before sweeping his legs out from under him. He gave a curse as he fell, his heavy body bouncing hard on the inflatable floor, but Rose stepped back before his flailing arms could pull her down with him. Ducking around to the other side of the table, she scrambled for the curtains, wrenching them aside and stumbling out to the corridor. The lights began to dim, signaling the start of the second act, as Rose lurched toward the stairs, her legs wobbly on the unsteady floor.

She heard a shout behind her and her heart leapt. There was no one to be seen in the corridor or the stairwell, no ushers, no patrons returning to their seats. No one to help her. But what would she have said anyway? *He's the Ma'ar,* she thought hysterically. *What was happening?*

Gripping the railing, she threw herself down the stairs as fast as she could, cursing the unsteadiness of her legs. A blur of movement caught her eye from further up the stairwell, and she redoubled her efforts, launching herself into the lobby and across the empty space, just as the faint sound of music resumed from inside the theater.

When she finally stumbled out of the main doors, the firmness of the ground beneath her feet nearly made her cry with joy. It was growing dark now, the sun setting and the shadows growing longer, but there were still people out in the square, exiting the Millipede station and milling around the opera house. She rounded the side of the theater and paused, leaning against the wall as she tried to catch her breath. She didn't think the Ma'ar would pursue her out here. His reputation seemed very important to him, and she didn't think he would want to make more of a scene.

Still, she didn't dare stay long. As soon as her heartbeat finally slowed, she turned and began to head purposefully up the road toward her hotel. She tried to calm her racing thoughts and took inventory of herself. Other than the back of her hand, which still stung slightly but was marked only by a thin white line identical to the one on the other palm, she wasn't injured. Terrified, but not injured. Her shawl was still in the theater, and her dress was torn up one side and splattered with bright teal droplets. She kept her head down and hoped no one would notice her state of disarray.

She tried to organize her thoughts enough to formulate a plan. She would go back to the hotel, lock the door, and wait until morning. Then she would immediately go to the King. Yes, surely she would be safe at the hotel. Even though the Ma'ar knew where she was staying, surely she would be safe with other people around. And yet the Ma'ar was powerful. Rose had no doubt that he would need only to smile and tip his hat at Anae and she would let him in without question. Her stomach twisted and she felt sick. She had no idea what to do.

Despite her preoccupation, Rose hadn't gone more than a couple of blocks before she realized she was being followed. Spinning to look behind her, it didn't take long before she recognized the brown suit and bowler hat. She couldn't see his face, couldn't tell if it was Gann or Yven or someone else entirely, but he strolled nearly a block behind her, not hurrying to catch up but clearly in pursuit. Heart leaping into her throat again, Rose picked up her pace, making a beeline for the hotel.

She was nearly running when the building came into view, and so it took a few steps for her to skid to a halt, her eyes instantly picking out the two brown-suited men against the backdrop of crumbling brick that framed the hotel's front door. She stood frozen on the sidewalk, two brown suits blocking her route to safety ahead and another one slowly sauntering up the street behind her. She felt like she was a lone sheep being carefully herded by a group of well-organized wolves.

Before she could figure out what to do, the two men in the doorway saw her and turned as one, pushing off the side of the building to move toward her at that same unhurried pace. Panic welled within her, shutting out rational thought, and she turned frantically, abandoning the hotel. She spun in a circle, picking a new direction at random, and without a glance behind her, fled into the night.

15

ROSE

Rose ran. She ran until her lungs strained and burned and her heart felt like it might explode. She ducked around corners and down alleys until the adrenaline that fueled her began to fade, and her frantic sprint slowed to a stumbling jog and finally to a limping stagger. When she couldn't move another step, she chose a dark corner where two buildings met and slumped against the wall, sliding down until she crumpled into a heap against the cold bricks.

It was dark in the city, the moon periodically hidden by passing wisps of clouds, and Rose huddled back into the corner, letting the shadows envelop her even though there was no one around to see. To her dismay, her watch had stopped working again, but the unmoving hands read four minutes past eleven, so she knew it had to be very late. With a sigh, she tilted her head back against the bricks and closed her eyes. She was so exhausted she thought she could sleep here.

But now that she had stopped moving, it wasn't long before the worry began to creep in. Opening her eyes, she looked down at where both of her hands lay propped on her legs, her pale skin faintly illuminated in the moonlight. Flipping one over, she looked at the two matching scars. If she concentrated, she could feel the faint, tingling pull from both hands now. She had so many questions that they filled her head to bursting, toppling over one another as they circled in her mind like vultures.

What had the Ma'ar been *doing?* And what exactly had the stranger in the castle done to her? Given her magical healing powers? Stopped her from bleeding? Turned her blood into some kind of glowing iridescent liquid? And *why?* The Ma'ar had said that he was right. Right about what? He'd cut her like he'd expected the results he got. Had he known about the spell?

She thought then about what else he'd said. He'd called her a planeswalker. Just as Ydenda had. But what did that *mean?*

Frustrated, Rose let her head drop back against the wall. This was ridiculous. Speculation was getting her nowhere.

After a moment, Rose became aware that the trembling she had attributed to shock had not subsided, and had in fact increased to full-on shivering. It had been chilly when she'd fled the opera house, the flimsy fabric of her torn gown offering little protection against the night air without the extra layer of her shawl. But now with the sun entirely gone and the chill of the bricks seeping into her back, she began to realize that she was in no state to spend the night outdoors. She lamented the loss of her backpack, with Ydenda's warm Albatrocity hoodie and money enough to find one more night of lodging. She wondered what Anae would think when she didn't return to the hotel.

As her shivering grew worse, Rose heaved a sigh and tiredly levered herself to her feet. She had to keep moving so she didn't freeze. Glancing up toward the sky, she fervently hoped this world had enough in common with her own that the celestial bodies moved the same way. She waited a moment for the moon to appear from behind the clouds, then turned to get her bearings, trying hard to remember what the Ma'ar had said. West, she was pretty sure. The King was outside the western city gate, across the Mist Bridge. She would figure out what that meant when she got there. And west was...that way?

She turned to face what she desperately hoped was west, hoping also that her panicked flight hadn't led her too far off course, when suddenly the bank of clouds cleared. A bright beam of moonlight shone down on the wall near the corner where she had been hiding, and she saw it. With a gasp, she jumped away from the wall. The black tendrils that snaked down from the eaves seemed to quiver slightly, like at any second they might leap toward her. They weren't as thick as those she'd seen outside the city, but they were still unmistakable. *Rot.*

She lurched back another step, the ground cold and hard through her thin slippers, and frantically checked herself over. She couldn't see anything on her skin or clothes, and a check of the wall showed that there was nothing in the spot where she had been sitting, but suddenly she felt even more exposed and vulnerable. She'd assumed the Rot was contained outside the city, but it seemed nowhere was safe from the creeping blackness. *All the more reason to get out of here as quickly as possible.*

Facing the west, Rose glanced around one more time, but she was alone here, not another soul to be seen. *Just me and the Rot,* she thought darkly, and with her arms wrapped around her torso for warmth, she set off again into the night.

∽

The minutes and hours seemed to drag on forever as Rose made her slow way toward the west. She was afraid to keep to the shadows, loathe to get too close to any hidden patches of Rot. Yet she was equally afraid to stay in the more well-lit areas of the city, lest she catch the attention of one of the seemingly ubiquitous brown-suited men. The fact that she hadn't actually seen any of what she assumed to be the Ma'ar's henchmen since she'd fled her hotel didn't actually do much to soothe her paranoia. Instead, she pushed through the city in a state of constant tense alertness, vacillating between sidewalks lit by streetlights and shadowed alleyways, muscles clenched tight against the cold but still unable to prevent the shivering spasms that ran through her intermittently.

The city seemed largely deserted, and despite the lateness of the hour, Rose began to get the impression that the population was actually much smaller than what one would assume from a city of this size. Small vehicles rumbled past intermittently, each time causing Rose to jump toward the shadows, where she stood pressed against a wall or in an alcove, heart pounding as she waited for the road to clear again. At first glance, from a distance, Rose took the vehicles to be some strangely shaped variation on a car—small and boxy, gleaming metallic in the moonlight—but a closer inspection revealed that they were not vehicles at all, but some sort of strange insect-like creature, similar to what she had seen pulling the frankenmice's wagons in the forest. Each had a hard, shiny carapace and some sort of ridged, bony protuberance toward the front, behind which each rider sat, gripping reins that connected to a bit in the creature's mouth much as one would use on a horse. Dark spots low on the creatures' sides mimicked the shape of wheels at first glance, but were in fact just colored markings resting over the spot where multitudes of legs moved in unison to propel the strange creatures down the road. Each time, Rose waited for the creature and its rider to pass, before stepping cautiously out from the shadows and continuing westward again.

At first it seemed her mind spun in circles, incessantly turning over and over the events of the night, the events since she'd first arrived in this place, replaying every conversation and searching futilely for answers to questions that kept piling up. But as the night progressed, as she lost track of time and how far she'd walked, as her fingers and toes grew nerveless with the cold and her brain foggy with weariness, her mind finally began to settle, until eventually the entirety of her attention was focused on simply putting one foot in front of the other. She glanced at the sky periodically, adjusting her direction, as the hours ticked slowly by. Eventually the sky began to lighten, almost imperceptibly at first, and then slowly signs of life began to reappear, the odd person out walking a dog or collecting a newspaper.

At the first sidelong glance and raised eyebrow, Rose altered her course, shifting away from the residential neighborhood and skirting around the uninhabited commercial district. A small, still-functioning part of her brain was aware of how she must look in her finery, her torn, stained dress, makeup streaked and hair wild around her head from the wind, frozen half to death and not a possession to her name. The last thing she wanted was to be picked up by whatever excuse this city had for law enforcement.

As she exited a shopping plaza and began to trudge through what appeared to be some kind of warehouse district, Rose for the first time began to wonder just how big this city was. Could it even be traversed by foot? The thought, however, felt wooden and hollow inside her head, simply a passing curiosity. Because in truth, it didn't matter. She had no other options. Nowhere to go, no one she knew, no money or clothes. She would keep walking west, until she found the King or fell off the edge of the world, whichever came first. *Or until you freeze to death*, her numb mind reminded her. That would likely come first. Still, she carried on. One step at a time. One foot in front of the other.

By the time Rose reached the western edge of the city, she had stopped caring entirely about what happened to her. The Ma'ar could appear in the street in front of her, knife in hand, and if he promised she wouldn't feel cold anymore she'd let him slit her throat. She'd been passing through an endless industrial area for what felt like hours, stumbling past rows of low metal warehouses and skirting around enormous piles of what appeared to be quarried stone.

The sun was high in the sky when she crested a low rise and finally saw the long, stone bulk of the city wall rise up ahead of her. It was the same patchwork amalgamation of stone she had ridden through on the Millipede, but no Rot was visible on the interior of the wall, and the relief she felt upon seeing it was so muted it felt as if it belonged to another person entirely. She forced her leaden feet forward, passing by the last of the warehouses until she stepped onto the soft grass beyond. The ground sloped down away from the metal warehouse, the wall set into the base of the small hill, and Rose stumbled down the incline, her feet tripping over each other in the grass until she reached the wall.

She collapsed against it, sliding down and wavering there for a moment, propped against the stones, before finally giving in and sliding listlessly down into the soft green carpet below. The chill inside her was bone-deep, even though the day had warmed considerably since the sun had reappeared. Rose realized, distantly, that she had finally stopped shivering. With the last of her energy she raised her arm, pillowing it under her head, before rolling back into the depression formed where the sloping hill met the wall. She was asleep in seconds.

16

YDENDA

Ydenda was confused. That in and of itself was nothing new; it seemed she spent a great deal of time being confused and had grown rather used to it. But something was different this time. It was like something had changed, but she had no idea what that something was.

It had to do with Rose; she knew that much. Ever since the girl had left, Ydenda had the sneaking suspicion there was something she was missing. She'd been so sure that sending Rose to see the King was the solution to whatever the girl's problem had been, but now she wasn't so sure. She was missing some important piece of the puzzle.

The uneasy feeling persisted as she went about her daily routine. The consistent cool temperature of the cellar had kept the heads well preserved, and so she returned home with her purse newly filled with coins, large and small—and more large than small this time—and all stamped with the likeness of the Drani'shadara, its noble profile striking against the shiny metal. Ydenda's brow furrowed as she turned one of the coins over in her hand. She hadn't seen the Drani'shadara around in quite some time now, come to think of it. That was odd too.

There were so many unanswered questions. Ydenda was used to living with unanswered questions. She had grown accustomed to the feeling that there were pieces of the past that she couldn't reconstruct and important memories missing. But never before had she felt this sense of sinister *wrongness,* like she had missed some important cue or opportunity, and if she didn't right that wrong then something horrible was going to happen.

Back at home, errand complete and coin purse tucked neatly into a kitchen drawer, Ydenda stood in the middle of the room, her head cocked to one side, weighing her options. Lacking the comfort of being able to make rational decisions based on real information, she had grown used to relying on instinct instead. She knew that it made her seem impulsive and paranoid and strange to others, and sometimes she did or said things that didn't make any sense, even to herself, but her instincts hadn't steered her wrong yet.

Unfortunately, her instincts were currently steering her in two separate directions. Part of her wanted to go after Rose. To do what, she wasn't sure. Bring her back? Watch over her and keep her safe? She knew she had misstepped in sending the girl to see the King, but she didn't know how.

But another large part of her warned her to stay here; she had no need to chase after trouble because trouble would soon be coming to her. She blew out a breath, causing a tangled lock of her thick hair to fan away from her face.

Stay, she decided on impulse. She had to stay. Trouble was coming; she could feel it. She didn't know what the trouble was or what form it would take, but if it came to her maybe she could keep it away from Rose.

Crossing to the stove, Ydenda filled the kettle and put it on to boil before heading up the narrow stairs to the second floor. With the heads disposed of, she had no further reason to leave the house, and suddenly it seemed like a good day for taking extra precautions.

At the top of the stairs, the door to the spare room caught her eye, the light from the window there spilling through to brighten the landing. She stepped into the small room and stood still, her eyes closing as the faint scent of bogberry and borlus root filled her nose. Sometimes the memories seemed so close, as if they were just on the other side of a sheer veil and if she could just reach out and pull it back, she would remember everything. At other times, she barely knew there was anything missing at all. Today was not one of those times. As she sank to her knees on the rug in Rose's room, it wasn't the memories but the emotions that overwhelmed her. Sadness that seemed to have no cause. Fear of an unknown threat. And a deep, wrenching sense of loss for something she wasn't sure she ever had.

Ydenda allowed herself a moment to wallow in the baseless emotions that swirled inside her, before gathering herself and rising to her feet. She strode across the small landing and into her own bedroom, where she opened the closet and stood on her tiptoes, stretching up to reach the top shelf. She let her fingertips slide along the wall until they met the lip of a small panel hidden there. With a careful press in the right place, the panel swung open, and she stretched further, reaching into the cavity. When her fingertips met the smooth wood of the box shoved back into the recess there, she breathed a sigh of relief before hooking her fingers around the edge and hauling it forward. She pulled it out into the light and stepped back, lowering herself to the floor with the box in front of her.

A thick layer of dust had settled on the lid, obscuring the carved design there, and Ydenda absently wiped it off with her sleeve, watching the ridges of the carving take shape. The box was a relic from the days before the Art Mines, back when the finest works of art were created by real artistic prodigies, not by slaves. In those days, artists mixed pigments formed of the Drani'shadara's tears, imbuing the paint with magic that made the finished paintings dance and swirl on their canvases.

This box, while carved, not painted, was still one of the most beautiful pieces she had ever seen. It was small, no more than six inches square, and the intricately carved lid depicted a scene of the Drani'shadara, young and spritely, frolicking through a meadow of wildflowers. Many different varieties of wood had been laminated together to depict the brightly colored flowers, and the detail the artist had been able to capture in the Drani'shadara's flowing tail and the ridges of its horns was incredible.

It was heartbreaking what had been lost in the years since...well. Ydenda wasn't sure *what* exactly had been lost, or when, or how, even. Her memories of how she had obtained the box were muddled, residing in the gray area of the past where the memories came and went and blurred together into a confusing jumble. But she knew somehow, *knew,* that there wasn't another box like this in all the world, and never would be again. And the contents...well, those were to be protected at all costs. She ran her fingers lightly over the lid, feeling the ridges of the carving with the fingertips of her undamaged hand, before springing the latch. The lid folded back on silent hinges, and carefully, Ydenda lifted out the object nestled inside.

She wasn't quite sure what it was, or what it was for. It was a small glass vial, thin and clear, with a shimmering liquid inside. The cap of the vial was wrought out of gleaming silver, and formed into the shape of a twisting vine with tiny delicate silver leaves that sprouted forth from the silver vine as it twined around the body of the glass tube.

Ydenda lifted the vial toward the light in a familiar motion. In years past, barely a week would pass that she didn't retrieve the box from its hiding place in her closet, running her fingers over the delicate carving before lifting the vial out of its velvet nest and holding it up to the light. She'd admire the way the sunlight made the liquid sparkle and tip it from side to side, the viscous liquid flowing thickly inside its glass encasement. As time passed, she retrieved the vial less and less often, but a part of her was always aware of its presence there, drawing her like a beacon.

It had been years now since she'd last taken it out, but the sparkling liquid had not changed, its gleam undiminished in the bright sunlight. As with every other time she held it, she wondered what it was for, feeling the importance of the vial but not knowing how to use it. She'd long since stopped trying to wrack her brain for answers, stopped berating herself for not remembering something so important. If the answers were in there, they weren't coming out, and all she could do was hope she would know what to do with the vial and how to protect it—because she felt sure she was meant to do that—when the time came.

Rather than return the vial to the box as she always had before, she hesitated for a moment, feeling the weight of the glass in her hand, surprisingly heavier than it appeared. Her uncertainty lasted for only a moment, before she decided that now was not the time to stop following her instincts. In one smooth movement, she slipped the glass vial into the deep pocket of her skirt, then decisively closed the lid of the box before rising and returning it to its home behind the hidden panel in her closet.

As she made her way down the stairs, Ydenda could feel the weight of the vial as it brushed against her leg through the fabric of her skirt. She may not know what it was, but she knew, beyond a shadow of a doubt, that she would need it when the trouble came.

∼

In the end, trouble came far sooner than Ydenda expected. It came in the early evening, just as the sun had begun to set, in the wholly unexpected form of a very polite but unremarkable gentleman in a brown suit. He had a matching brown derby hat perched jauntily on his head, which he removed respectfully when Ydenda opened the door.

"Good evenin', Miss," the man said, his slow drawl and slurred words marking him as a native of the Eastern Provinces.

Ydenda blinked in surprise, cocking her head to the side. "Can I help you, sir?"

"Yes'm." His voice was friendly. "My name is Flerend, and I represent the Ma'ar of Trelissar. He is...well. There is a delicate situation, and 'e believes that you might be...ah... uniquely positioned t'aid him in this matter."

The man's words seemed at odds with his way of speaking, but Ydenda knew better than to assume the man was slow simply because of his speech patterns. Trelissar, the man had said.

Rose.

Alarm bells sounded in her head, and Ydenda acted without thinking. "Please, do come in, and tell me what your

Ma'ar thinks I can do for him." She flashed her biggest and friendliest smile, hoping the piercing red of her working eye didn't appear too unsettling. The man smiled back, seemingly unperturbed.

Ydenda took a large step back, doing her best to appear charmingly innocent as she held the door open for the man to enter. He was friendly but watchful, his eyes taking her in and scanning the room as he stepped across the threshold—his weight falling directly on the wide purple floorboard.

The click was audible only if you were listening for it.

Ydenda had never before had the opportunity to see her traps in action, but to her immense relief the plank shifted seamlessly, the panel set into the wall at knee level springing open in the blink of an eye. The trio of darts fired out, and had pierced the man's trousers and penetrated deep into his leg before he'd even had a chance to shift his weight to the next step. Ydenda watched in unabashed pride and amazement as the man dropped like a lead weight, his bulk hitting the floor with a muted *thunk*.

It had worked! It better have; it had taken an obscene number of the finest quality heads and quite a few less savory items in trade to obtain that poison. Not to mention the trouble she'd had designing and installing the mechanics.

Feeling it wiser to celebrate after she had dealt with the issue at hand, Ydenda tore her gaze from the unconscious form on her floor. She didn't know exactly how long the poison would last. She thought she should have at least a few hours' head start, but there was no time to waste. Stepping over the prone body, she grabbed the purse from the kitchen drawer and threw a shawl over her shoulders before heading out the front door, glancing around before locking it securely behind her.

She'd made it nearly all the way to the Millipede station before the other brown-suited figure stepped out from the shadows. This time it was Ydenda who didn't have time to react, her body hitting the ground before she could register the pain blossoming at the back of her skull.

17

ROSE

Rose woke confused, disoriented and sore. She levered herself up to sit against the wall, rubbing sleep from her eyes and pulling brambles from her hair. Her flight through the city seemed distant and hazy, as if the memories of the previous night were actually weeks old and had been filtered through multiple glasses of wine.

She wasn't sure how much time had passed; it could have been an hour or a day, but she felt only slightly more alert for having slept. Her fingers and toes still felt painfully cold and her stomach uncomfortably empty, but she braced herself against the wall anyway and, with a monumental effort, hauled herself up to stand. Her legs were wobbly and her head still cloudy with a mixture of fatigue and fear, but she forced herself to stay calm and take stock of her surroundings.

The wall towered high overhead and stretched away in an unbroken line to the north and south. If she concentrated, Rose could hear the faint sound of rushing water on the other side of the thick stones. Was that a river? She shaded her eyes and glanced up at the sky, seeking out the sun that peeked out periodically from behind the slow-moving clouds. It wasn't straight overhead, but not close to the horizon either. Mid-afternoon, then. With luck she could find her way out of the city and reach the King before she was forced to spend another freezing night outdoors.

Rose spun in a slow circle, weighing her options as she looked up and down the wall. She was loathe to climb back up the hill to where the rows of warehouses were situated, but she also knew that a narrow winding road had run through the center of the industrial area. Yesterday she had avoided the road in fear of being seen, but she wondered now if following it was her best chance of finding the western city gate. With a grimace, she began the slow trek back up the hill. It was the best chance she had, and to be fair, she hadn't seen any signs of the Ma'ar or his men since fleeing her hotel the night before.

Nevertheless, Rose felt exposed and conspicuous as she ducked through the maze of warehouses, doing her best to keep out of view of the workers that swarmed in and around the structures, until the thin paved road came back into view. Traffic on the road was steady, but not heavy, with groups of creatures passing intermittently. These creatures were similar to the ones she had seen the previous night, but longer, with hard flat shells upon which crates and other transport containers had been piled and securely fastened. In the brightness of the day their metallic shells gleamed and their waving antennae and protruding pincers were visible. How had she ever mistaken them for cars?

Rose waited for a break in the traffic before stepping out toward the road. Turning to the west, she breathed a huge sigh of relief. From this vantage point the city gate was obvious, just to the north where the road through the warehouses met with a larger thoroughfare before winding out of the city. Not far at all.

With a quick glance around, she stepped back off the road into the sparse cover of brush near the warehouse walls, and began to follow the curve of the wall. The journey took longer than she expected. Her progress was slow on her aching feet, and it was obvious that her thin slippers hadn't been made for such rough treatment. The left one had large worn patches on the sole, and the right one had a long rip on the side where the seam was, allowing sharp rocks and debris to tear at her feet. Her dress was only in marginally better shape: dirt and grass stains joined the streaks of Fizz, and various rips and tears let the cold wind billow through the thin fabric.

Rose was past caring about her appearance though; her only thought was to reach the King.

At long last, the thin winding industrial path joined with the broad straight road leading out from the city, a well-kept sidewalk running alongside the pavement. Rose gave up any pretense of concealment and headed straight for the place where the road cut through the city wall. Traffic here, too, was sparse, and to her relief no one slowed or spared Rose much more than a glance as she trudged down the narrow sidewalk.

'Gate' appeared to be a misnomer. It was actually more of a tunnel, the road disappearing into the wall with no barrier of any kind to prevent or monitor access into or out of the city. A feeling of immense relief washed over Rose as she stepped into the darkness of the tunnel, lit only barely by dim lights set at too-great intervals. It seemed like the first real emotion she had felt in hours, everything else muted by exhaustion, hunger, and cold.

With that, it was like the dam she had been holding in

place broke, and she was suddenly flooded with the emotions she had been repressing. What on earth was she *doing?* The tunnel seemed to stretch on forever, every sound echoing loudly against the thick stone walls. Pushing forward in the darkness, Rose began to second-guess herself. How many mistakes had she made already? What if she hadn't gone to meet the Ma'ar? What if she hadn't gone to Trelissar at all? What if she'd stayed with the stranger in his castle? Would he have woken up? Could she have avoided all of this?

Her breathing accelerated, and Rose could feel her hands growing clammy. She sensed the panic pushing in at the edges of her awareness, and she paused for a moment, leaning against the tunnel wall. She took deep breaths, trying to wrestle her emotions back under control.

Finally she started moving again. There was no point to this game. She could play it forever. What if she'd never entered the little cottage in the woods? Then she'd still be stuck in her dead-end job in a life she barely recognized as her own. Was this really any worse? More dangerous, definitely. More unanswered questions, certainly. But worse?

Her thoughts spiraled backwards, time stretching out in the dark of the tunnel. She thought back to the last time she could remember being truly happy. It was her graduation day. She'd climbed out of bed with her future stretched bright and exciting ahead of her. She'd finally made it through her exams, her parents and sister were coming to watch the ceremony, and she'd just received word that she'd actually gotten the prestigious internship she'd applied for. She hadn't even told her parents yet, and she couldn't wait to see their faces. The summer stretched out in front of her with plans no more stressful than planning a beach vacation with her sister and eating as much of her mom's cooking as possible before her internship started in the fall. She'd been invincible that morning, on top of the world.

But then her family hadn't arrived. And she'd spent the afternoon at the hospital instead of her graduation ceremony. The memories rushed in, eclipsing those of the happiness she'd felt before. If she closed her eyes, she could still hear the flat unbroken beep of the monitor, smell the antiseptic odor of the hospital. The vague sense of suspended reality as she avoided friends who offered condolences. And then between planning funerals and an impulsive decision to pack a suitcase and drive into the night toward the east, following a carelessly thrown dart across the country to Indiana, suddenly her life had changed so drastically that her current surroundings seemed just as foreign as the ones she'd left behind when she stepped out of the Hoosier National Forest and into a new world.

Tears pricked behind Rose's eyelids. *Keep moving forward,* she told herself. That was all she could do. It didn't matter which of her decisions had been mistakes. It didn't matter that she felt adrift or aimless, or that she didn't know how to cope, here or in Indiana. She would keep moving forward. Ydenda had been adamant that the King would help her—help her with what, she wasn't even sure—and so she would put her trust in the crazy one-eyed woman with the bag of heads, and she would go see the King, and he would help her. She couldn't end up any worse off than she was now.

Rose felt marginally bolstered by these thoughts as the tunnel finally ended, giving way to blue skies and piercing sunlight. The cloud cover seemed to have thinned, and Rose's steps slowed as she took in the view. She'd been right, there *was* a river bordering the city on this side, and the rush of water was loud in her ears after the muted silence of the tunnel. The river seemed enormous as it stretched out before her, the sparkling water flowing by in a rush.

The road she had been following ended in an intersection not fifty paces out, a large signpost set into the corner.

It was labeled clearly, bold arrows pointing each direction. To the left, where the wide, paved road turned and followed the curve of the city wall out of sight, it read, "Low Trelis Woods," in a clear, precise script.

Straight ahead, the road was narrower. The dark, paved roadway slowly transitioned into a bright path as it stretched out over the rushing water of the river, its surface made of a bright indeterminable material that gleamed in the sunlight. Before Rose's eyes could follow the path more than fifty feet into the distance it disappeared, swallowed by a cloud of thick, swirling mist. She didn't even need to see the words on the signpost to know what they said.

"The Mist Bridge."

She swallowed, resolve straightening her spine. She had come this far; she would not turn back now.

∽

It was hard to gauge the passage of time without a functioning watch, even harder still with the sun shrouded by the swirling mist. But judging solely by the weariness of her bones and the pain in her feet, Rose guessed she had been on the bridge for at least an hour already.

Which made no sense. She had long since passed the point where it should have met with the opposite shore of the river, and yet the path never rose or fell or changed in any way, it just marched on into oblivion. She tamped down her unease. If it wasn't so clearly obvious that she was in the right place, she would have assumed she'd taken a wrong turn at some point.

But there hadn't been any turns to take. The bridge ran straight and true, too narrow for anything other than foot traffic, the path bordered by ornate scrollwork railings made out of the same unidentifiable material as the bridge itself. Beyond the railings she could see nothing but mist.

It had occurred to her early on that she had only the Ma'ar's word that this actually *was* the way to reach the King, and he had not proven himself to be the most reliable of individuals. But on the other hand, she had no other options, and at this point, she certainly didn't have the strength or stamina to turn back and try anything else. So she followed the path into the mist.

At one point she stopped and looked over the edge, gripping tight to the railing as she leaned forward, but the mist swirled below as well as forward and behind, obscuring anything that might have existed outside of her limited field of vision. It was like walking through a cloud. Sound was deadened; the rush of the river was gone, and even her own footsteps were muted. Strangely, temperature was as well. The cold that had permeated her bones over the past night and day had begun to leach away, and while it wasn't cold here, it wasn't warm either, just a kind of still nothingness. While it was certainly better than freezing, it made Rose feel decidedly unsettled.

She hadn't passed another soul since she'd left the city, and the bridge proved no different. With the mist pressing in around her she felt like the only person in the world.

Anae's warning echoed in her head. *They say anyone who crosses the bridge loses their sanity.* Rose's chest felt tight, the mist claustrophobic.

Time stretched out and lost all meaning as she moved

through the mist like a wraith, and after a time the sole of her left slipper wore through entirely. She paused long enough to remove the battered shoes, and after a moment of indecision, dropped them over the railing. No sound met her ears as they fell and quickly disappeared from sight. Even beneath her newly bare feet, she could detect no temperature difference between her feet and the bridge, and it gave her the bizarre feeling that she was walking on nothing at all.

It was then, as she stood at the railing letting the discomfort of her muted senses wash over her, that she saw the dark shape ahead of her. With her visibility so limited, she had little warning. The figure simply wasn't there one moment and was the next, materializing in front of her in a billow of dark fabric, feet bare like hers and the hood of its cloak pulled up so its features were hidden in shadow. The figure glided by in one swift movement and was gone, swallowed by the mist before Rose could think to react.

"Wait, I—"

She hesitated, the hairs rising along the backs of her arms. Should she go after the person? Keep moving forward? Who knew how long this blasted bridge was, anyway? It clearly defied any semblance of logic.

Anger and fear warred in her. The mist swirled close despite the lack of any breeze. Stubbornly, Rose tamped the emotions down and started forward again, her pace slightly faster.

She hadn't gone a hundred paces before it happened again. The figure was identical: dark hood, bare feet, there and gone in the blink of an eye. She felt the brush of its cloak against her leg as it passed and she jumped, breath coming fast and shallow. The mist swirled closer, until her visibility ended where her feet met the surface of the bridge.

By the time the figure passed a third time, Rose had already broken into a run.

She kept it up, feet pelting soundlessly on the invisible bridge, panic clawing its way up in her chest despite her best efforts to fight it back, until the mist cleared abruptly between one step and the next, the world rushing back in a cacophony of sights and sounds.

Rose skidded to a halt, her senses overloaded as they tried to catch up after so much time spent straining in the void. In front of her, rising from the mist that still swirled below, stood a tall windmill, its thin body stretching up to tower overhead. High above, its four massive blades swooped in a wide arc with a great swooshing sound, their tips disappearing into the mist above at the apex of their arc. The bridge she stood upon led up three steps and ended at the front door.

18

ROSE

Any reticence Rose might have had about entering the looming windmill was erased by her desire to get away from the mist. Cautiously, she approached the door—a surprisingly small, simple, wooden door—and gave it an experimental push. With a creak of rusty hinges, it swung open.

Rose was starting to learn that expectations were meaningless. Her previous experience with royalty was limited to a family trip to London as a child, where they had toured Buckingham Palace. While she hadn't exactly expected to find a full complement of guards in red livery guarding an elaborate palace flying a royal standard overhead, still, she had certainly expected something more...*kingly*...than this. Pushing her misgivings aside, she stepped into the gloomy interior of the windmill.

The darkly paneled walls made the space seem dim and confining, the only light filtering through a pair of windows as narrow as arrow-slits set high into the side of the circular tower. A rickety-looking spiral staircase rose in the center of the room, dominating the small space as it climbed the height of the tower. There was nowhere else to go.

With a glance upward, Rose began to climb on shaky legs. There were no landings, no breaks in the stairs as they led higher and higher. She tried not to glance down over the railing to where the floor dwindled below, just resolutely concentrated on putting one foot on the next step and then the next, until finally, legs wobbling and breath coming in pants, she stepped up onto the landing at the top of the windmill.

Even with no expectations, what she saw left Rose feeling bewildered and mildly harassed, as if it was someone's idea of a great joke that each new challenge left her even more lost and confused.

The top level of the windmill consisted of a wide platform made of thick wooden planks. A series of heavy wooden gears were mounted on the wall and jutted out in an elaborate interlocking mechanism. The gears creaked loudly as they spun slowly, their motion driven by a thick wooden handle that protruded from the bottom-most gear. And turning the handle, his whole weight leaned into the task, stood the strangest creature Rose had ever encountered. And considering her experiences of the past few days, that was saying something.

The creature was shaped like a man, but with some rather jarring differences. He—it?—was wrapped from head to toe in trailing strips of cloth, resembling nothing so much as a child dressed up as a Halloween mummy. Even the hand that gripped the handle was wrapped, no skin showing through on the wrist or between the fingers. One wrapped foot stood planted firmly on the floor, but the other two limbs ended short in trailing strips of cloth, no flesh to be seen, only empty air where the cloth spiraled down from the elbow and knee. On the head, the strips were wide and overlapping, no features visible beneath the wrappings save a single protruding eye, which swiveled to lock on Rose as she determinedly forced herself to approach.

She had come this far—she would not be scared away now by some disturbing ragman from a children's ghost story.

The creature's attention was already on her, but she cleared her throat anyway before delving in awkwardly.

"Excuse me, my name is Rose..." The eye stared at her unblinking as the hand continued to turn the crank.

Her voice was hoarse and she cleared her throat again before continuing in a tone that sounded much braver than she felt. "I'm looking for the King." She felt completely ridiculous. What on earth did she expect the creature to say? There was nowhere else to go from here. Her eyes drifted up to the creaking gears. They didn't appear to be connected to anything, just spinning aimlessly as the handle turned.

Rose's attention was wrenched back to the Ragman as, to her surprise, he began to speak.

"You are looking for the King." The voice that repeated her words was as dry and creaky as the wooden gears, and it seemed not to come directly from the creature in front of her, but from the air around her, from the mist itself.

Rose shuddered even as hope swelled within her. She nodded, holding her breath. Was he going to help her? Was something finally going to make sense?

"Then you have come a long, long way to be greeted with disappointment."

Her breath left her lungs in a rush, her hopes flowing out alongside the air. She scrambled for clarification, knowing it was futile, her voice growing desperate. "Is the

King not here? Can you tell me where he is? How do I find him?"

The Ragman cocked his head to the side in a motion that reminded Rose of Ydenda. "No..." the word coalesced in the air around her, a long creaking wheeze, and Rose wasn't sure at first which of her questions he was answering. "The King is not here anymore."

"Where—" she started, but her words were cut off.

"There has not been a King here in a long time. A long, long time."

The gears creaked as they slowly turned, the interlocking teeth clicking into place.

No. Rose gritted her teeth. She had not come all this way for nothing. She tried to keep her voice even. "Are you telling me there *is* no King? Or that he simply is not here?"

Without lifting his hand from the crank, the Ragman turned to face her fully, his unblinking eye meeting hers directly, and with a gasp Rose saw the familiar black lines of Rot that peeked between the gaping strips of cloth that covered the other side of his face. Suddenly the mist began to rise again, swirling slowly around Rose's feet, clouding the air between them. His eye stared out from between the wrappings, boring into her.

The voice, when it came again, was harsh, loud in the confined space, and the words echoed in her skull as if they'd been spoken directly into her head.

"There is nothing for you here, planeswalker."

∾

Rose was halfway down the winding staircase before she even realized she was moving. The mist rose and drifted as she fled, coiling around her like a spring. Her throat felt tight, her heart hammering in her chest, all thoughts eclipsed but one. *Get out of here.*

She made quick work of the stairs, bare feet thudding on the wooden planks, and when she reached the bottom, she flung the door open and pelted through it, picking up speed as she entered the open nothingness of the bridge.

She ran. Her eyes squeezed into slits against the tears she held back. How stupid could she be? Why had she thought there would be anyone to help her? Why had she assumed the Ma'ar would tell her the truth?

The mist was dense around her, her footsteps silent as her feet met the barely visible surface of the bridge beneath her. What was she going to do *now?* She felt hopeless, lost and confused and betrayed, and finally she let the tears go, streaming down her cheeks as the thoughts swirled in her mind to match the mist that surrounded her.

She ran until her body refused to let her continue, then walked, limping, her limbs and her mind both throbbing painfully in unison. When the mist grew impossibly heavier and her panic rose, she ran again, tripping painfully as she stumbled out of weariness, blisters on her feet cracking, and at some point the thin white matching lines on her palm and the back of her opposite hand began to throb as well, keeping time with her heartbeat.

Head down, breath labored, she pushed on, until her tears had dried and her mind was blank, and then slowly, almost imperceptibly, the mist began to thin. It was growing dark, she saw with surprise, the sun beginning to set. Small, blurry shapes began to form in the distance as her vision cleared, and the rush of water from the river became audible once again. Her steps began to slow, her panic starting to ebb, and the adrenaline that fueled her flowed out alongside it, leaving her feeling hollow and empty.

Weariness flowed in to fill the void. Her head ached and her feet ached and her palms throbbed.

Finally, the mist dissipated completely and the path ahead of her swam into view. The forked path lay ahead in the distance, where it met with the paved road that ran across the river to the city. She lifted her bleary eyes to the signpost that stood at the intersection, trying to decide if it was wiser to cross into the forest or head back toward the city before she collapsed, but when the small dark shapes at the fork grew closer and she took in the rest of the scene that awaited her there, her footsteps faltered and she fell heavily to her knees.

It was over.

The Ma'ar stood at the fork, not two hundred paces off, his expression smooth and calm, hands tucked comfortably into his pockets as if he had all the time in the world to wait for her to reappear out of the mist. Men stood to either side of him, tall men in brown suits and hats, their faces blurring together. So many men; how did the Ma'ar have so many men? She realized belatedly that the whole mob wasn't made up of brown-suited men, but other people as well, other creatures. She saw in muted surprise a group of what she had dubbed 'Frankenmice,' their beady black eyes turned her way. There were others too, in plain clothes with dark hats shielding their eyes. Were they helping the Ma'ar or just here to witness the spectacle?

The cuts on her hands seared like fire. She glanced down. The lines were no longer white and smooth, but red and slightly raised, angry looking welts. She looked back up. The Ma'ar gave her a lazy smile and removed a hand from his pocket long enough to gesture forward. The brown-suited men stepped out onto the Mist Bridge.

Rose couldn't move. She was too tired, and anyway, there

was nowhere to go. Back into the mist? Never. She had no fight left in her, and so she stayed there, on her knees, hands burning, and watched with heavy-lidded eyes as the men in brown closed in.

When a shout came from the crowd, it didn't register at first, until another voice joined in. Hazily, Rose tried to focus on the distant figures, hands raised to shield their eyes against the dying rays of the setting sun, fingers pointed up toward the sky. The brown-suited men didn't pause in their advance, but the Ma'ar turned to follow the direction of the pointing fingers, a frown creasing his brow. Rose followed his gaze and immediately saw the object of their attention. It was a dark speck on the horizon, growing larger as it passed over the densely packed trees of the forest. A curt word from the Ma'ar, and the men in brown began to run.

The pain in her hands grew sharper, and she began to feel dizzy, wobbling on her knees for a moment before her strength gave out and she crumpled to the side. She leaned against the railing and closed her eyes as the world tilted alarmingly. The shouts from the crowd grew, and she could hear the Ma'ar's voice rise above the rabble, but she barely had it in her to care what was happening until she felt a rough hand grab her arm.

The men in brown had reached her. Hands encircled her upper arms, hauling her to sit upright. She opened her eyes, searching deep for a last burst of strength with which to fight them off, despairing when there was no strength to be found.

Abruptly, she realized the hands on her arms didn't belong to the Ma'ar's men. The brown-suited men were still paces away, closing in fast, but the hands that gripped her were familiar, pale blue with the faintest hint of silver filigree swirling through the skin, the eyes that bored into hers slanted and purple.

Before Rose had a chance to react, great translucent wings unfurled, silver filigree crawling upon them in ever-shifting patterns.

"You said you'd trust me, do you remember?" His voice was as she'd remembered, a resonant echo. She nodded mutely and wrapped her arms around his neck.

Without another word, he lifted her effortlessly, his wings gave a thunderous beat, and they rose together into the sky, the grasping hands of the men in brown missing her torn feet by centimeters.

19

ROSE

Rose could only assume she had passed out, because there was a gaping hole in her memory that stretched from the moment of their narrow escape from the Mist Bridge to when she awoke, blinking confusedly in unfamiliar surroundings.

She gave a tentative stretch, feeling the soreness in her arms and legs as she straightened them and sat up. She flexed her still-aching feet against the bedclothes, disrupting a pile of bandages and other first-aid supplies she hadn't noticed were stacked by her side. Surprised, she looked down at her hands. They were both bandaged now, strips of white gauze wrapped around each palm, and while they ached mildly, it was nothing compared to the searing pain she'd felt before. She wondered what the state of her hands was under their wrappings, unsure if she really wanted to know. Tearing her eyes away from the bandages, she straightened further and looked around.

Rose sat, still in her ripped and stained clothes, on top of the coverlet of an enormous bed. The room was elaborate in its furnishings: the carved wooden posts of the bed reached all the way to the high ceiling, and there was a matching dresser and vanity set under the large window. Light streamed in, further brightening the warm blue-gray walls and gleaming off of the parquet floor.

Glancing out of the window, from her vantage point on the bed Rose could see the familiar view of the lawn stretching far below toward the edge of the woods. The brightly colored leaves of the densely-packed trees glinted in the sunlight, confirming her suspicions. She was back in the castle.

Suddenly her stomach gave a loud growl, drawing her attention to the dull ache that had been with her through the entirety of the previous day. Her head felt light as well, off-balance. Sliding her feet to the floor, she cautiously put weight on them, grimacing as her sore muscles protested. With her attention focused on her myriad aches and pains, Rose didn't notice the body slumped on the floor of the room until she tripped over it, sending herself sprawling forward to land in an unceremonious heap half on top of the unconscious form of her host.

Wincing and rubbing at her elbow—a new bruise to add to her collection—she scrabbled off to the side, rolling her rescuer's limp body onto his back as she went.

"Oh no, not again," she muttered as she knelt over his prone form, giving his shoulders a shake to be sure he wasn't simply asleep. When there was no response, she sat back on her heels, looking him over. He definitely looked worse for wear, almost in as bad shape as she herself was. He wore the same clothes he had when she'd seen him last, and they were disheveled and stained. Dark circles ringed his eyes. There was a scrape on his cheek and a livid bruise rising on his chin.

Her eyes ran down his body, and when her gaze fell on

his left hand she had to stifle a gasp. The black tendrils of Rot were still there, but there was no doubt that they'd spread. They wrapped down the hand now, twining around his fingers where they lay still on the floor. Tracing her eyes up his arm to where it disappeared under his shirtsleeve, she could see the black marks under a rip in the fabric that covered his shoulder, and now that she looked closer she noticed the edge of the blackness peeked out over the collar of his shirt as well, just barely beginning to snake up the side of his neck. She definitely didn't remember seeing that before.

She reached a hand out toward him before hesitating, unsure if the Rot could spread from another person through a touch. Instead, she reached for the opposite side of his neck and pressed her fingertips against the warm skin there. There it was, his heartbeat, pulsing slow and strong.

What to do? Not leave this time, that was for sure. She thought ruefully that a lot of grief could have been avoided if she'd just stayed put the last time she'd been here. She watched the body before her, his chest rising and falling under the torn coat. Well. She couldn't help anyone in her current state. Her best option was to find something to eat and wait. He had obviously awoken once before, surely he would again. Surely.

She pulled the coverlet and one of the pillows down off the bed and tried to make the man as comfortable as possible, arranging his flowing white hair over the pillow and tucking the blanket tight around him. Then she stood on shaky legs, and went off in search of food.

~

The castle was enormous, the sort of place Rose imagined

would require an entire support staff to keep running. Yet as she hobbled through the empty rooms, finding a much needed bathroom before arriving at last in the kitchen, not a single maid, housekeeper, or butler was to be seen. No cluster of cooks in the kitchen, no team of gardeners outside the windows. Initially, she was surprised to find the two of them alone in the massive place, but after making a full circuit of the castle, poking her head into room after room, backtracking when she found herself running into dead ends down winding hallways, she began to realize that only a small fraction of the rooms were kept in any kind of a presentable state.

The room she'd awoken in had been in flawless order, as was a nearby bathroom, the entry foyer, the kitchen, and one or two other rooms Rose could not immediately identify. Beyond those few spaces however, the remainder of the castle looked as if it hadn't been entered in years. Decades, even. Thick layers of dust had settled on the furniture, light sockets were empty, whole corridors were unheated. Was the strange man really the only one who lived here in this enormous castle?

By the time Rose's winding and circuitous exploration led her to the kitchen, she was so turned around that she questioned her ability to retrace her steps to the upstairs bedroom. For the moment though, her primary focus was food. After seeing the abandoned state of the majority of the castle, she had been slightly concerned that the kitchen would be similarly empty.

The kitchen was no less impressive than the rest of the castle, with long stretches of shining countertops, endless cabinets and gleaming appliances. It seemed large enough to prepare food for a whole banquet hall. On the far side of the space, next to a large window that overlooked the forest, sat an enormous solid wood table, with heavy carved legs and matching chairs.

Fortunately, her fears that the kitchen would be abandoned were unfounded. In the adjacent pantry, the shelves were stocked high, albeit with unrecognizable foods. She didn't put too much effort into trying to identify anything, and contented herself with grabbing some packages off a high shelf whose labels were brightly colored and bore the unfamiliar symbols that she had been encountering throughout her journey. Anything prepackaged, she told herself as she sat at the kitchen table and tore into the wrapping, was likely meant to be eaten without preparation, and she hoped she was not about to find she had chosen this world's equivalent of uncooked spaghetti noodles or something equally unpalatable.

Admittedly, her current standards for enjoyable or even edible food were low, but to her delight the contents of the package—pale green, square shaped blocks of something slightly chewy—were surprisingly good. They reminded her vaguely of Rice Krispie treats. She wolfed them down, then the rest of the box, before returning to the pantry and decimating most of the contents of an entire shelf. Aside from a couple of boxes whose contents were decidedly *not* meant to be eaten, everything was, if not good, at least edible. By the time her stomach was full she was feeling drowsy again, and she laid her head down on the table for a brief moment to contemplate what to do next. Should she bring food or water back up to the unconscious man? Who knew what state he would be in when he awoke. And who knew how long that might take. Should she try again to wake him? Maybe attempt a shower? Try to find clothes?

Her eyelids grew heavy. Maybe she would just rest here for a moment. Her thoughts still swirled with unanswered questions, and her concern for the strange man was still present at the forefront of her mind—though the knowledge that he'd woken on his own the last time did help somewhat to soothe her fears. But for the first time in days she had a full stomach and a roof over her head, and she felt the need to lie still and really experience how wonderful that was. She felt as though her priorities had shifted, and she considered how having things like food and shelter, and safety—things she had always taken for granted—suddenly removed, could really change one's perspective. Especially when she had already lost everything she thought there was to lose.

But now, a full stomach and a still body felt like a miracle, and so she closed her eyes and relaxed into the sensation, and was asleep again a minute later.

20

NEKUTHAEDRIS

When Neku awoke, it was to the same dull, throbbing headache as before, and a wave of nausea rose within him. The skin on his left arm felt tight, and as he laid there, waiting for the pounding in his skull to abate and his stomach to settle, he examined the limb. The Rot had spread, as he'd known it would. It seemed his whole arm was affected now, the tendrils curling around his fingers. An exploratory touch above his shirt collar indicated that it had begun to crawl upward as well, the puckered ridges now likely visible on the side of his neck. Well, there was nothing to be done for that. He'd known what would happen if he used his magic again. But there had been no other choice.

After a long moment the pounding in his head finally began to lessen, and with it the nausea began to fade as well. With a groan he levered himself up to sit, turning immediately to look at the bed. His heart surged in alarm. It was empty. *Not again.*

Judging by the spilled piles of bandages, it seemed he'd been in the middle of treating her hands when he'd fallen.

He felt the rumpled sheets; they were cold. How long had he been unconscious? Suddenly he became aware of the blanket still tucked around his legs, and saw the pillow his head had been propped on. The barest hint of a smile crossed his lips. Even in the state she'd been in, and she saw to his comfort? Well, that was better than the terror he feared would be her primary emotion when she awoke. He had tried hard to fight the pain and dizziness, hoping to at least keep it at bay until she woke up, but judging from the state of things he'd succumbed rather quickly after all.

But where had she gone? With the spell gone from her blood, he could no longer sense her direction. If she'd left the castle, and all her struggles and his own had been in vain...

He rose cautiously to his feet, using the edge of the bed to push himself up. His head swam as the blood rushed out of it, and he held still for a moment as he regained his equilibrium. But the moment his vision cleared he was out the door, checking each room as he made his way down the stairs. His panic rose with each empty room, but he forced it down. *Please, let her still be here.*

When, at last, he stumbled into the kitchen, he was so surprised by the scene that confronted him that a laugh escaped his mouth before he could stop it. She was there, torn dress, mud-stained skin and all, with her head facedown on the kitchen table, pillowed on her bandaged hands. Her dark hair spread out from her head in a tangled mess, and around her, like a halo, lay a huge assemblage of empty boxes and torn wrappers. It looked as though she'd eaten her way through half of the pantry, with a focus on sugary snacks. It occurred to him then that she couldn't read the package labels and likely wasn't familiar with any of these foods. She must have just picked a shelf and dove in.

Her head lay tilted to the side with her mouth open, and she was snoring softly, and between the amusing scene and the overwhelming relief of seeing she was still there, another laugh bubbled up out of him.

At this, the girl mumbled softly and then came awake, jolting upright with wide eyes that immediately met his own. A candy wrapper was stuck in her hair, and her expression was so comical that while he was able to suppress another laugh, he couldn't stop the wide smile that crossed his face.

She flushed beet red, her expression darkening as she attempted to smooth her hair and straighten her clothes, removing the offending wrapper as she did so.

"Well, I'm glad you find the situation so amusing." Her tone was acerbic.

His smile faded, but to his own surprise, he was unable to remove it completely. How long had it been since he'd had anything to smile at? Just the sight of another person in the castle after all this time was almost more than he could believe.

He approached her cautiously, still a little afraid she would run, and gestured questioningly at the chair across from her. She looked surprised for a moment before nodding at him. "Of course, it's your house, you don't need my permission."

He sank gratefully into the chair and helped himself to one of the appropriately named Sugar Blasts left in the nearly empty box. He chewed the candy slowly, using it as an excuse to let the silence stretch. Good lord, what to tell her? Where to start?

Her dark eyes were steady on his face, and she seemed to know what he was thinking, because she said gently, "How about your name?"

He cleared his throat. "Yes, I'm sorry. My name is Nekuthaedris." At her alarmed expression he smiled faintly. "You can call me Neku. Everybody does. Or at least, they used to." The smile faded.

Awkwardly, he ran a hand through his dirty white hair and met her eyes. "Rose," he said somberly, her name strange and weighty on his tongue. "I'm very sorry about... well. About everything. I can't imagine the past few days have been easy for you, and I want to explain. There's so much you need to know. But the story is a long one, and the situation is complicated. I scarcely know where to begin."

There was a long pause, and he shifted uncomfortably under her gaze until she finally sighed and took pity on him.

"Look. I have so many questions I barely have room in my head for anything else, and I very much want to hear your explanation. But, at the moment, what I'd like even more than that, is a shower." She looked down at herself, a rueful smile crossing her lips. "You know, this was the fanciest dress I've ever owned. Maybe this is the universe's way of telling me to stick to jeans." She looked back up. "Any chance you have any women's clothes around this place?"

Her dress was torn in a dozen places, and stained with substances he couldn't even identify, but enough of the sheer fabric and its deep purple underlayer remained that Neku could imagine how it must have looked when it was whole. She would have been stunning. But why on earth was she wearing a dress in the first place? It certainly wasn't what she'd been wearing when she left his castle. What had she gotten up to in the intervening days? Anxiously, he checked her over, but he didn't see any traces of Rot, on either her skin or clothes. The spell must have worked.

Blowing out a breath, he pulled himself back to the present. "Yes, of course you'd like to clean up. Let me show you where to go." He pushed back from the table and rose to his feet, and she followed suit. He led her down the hallway to the stairs that led up toward the bedroom he'd brought her to when they'd arrived. It was his room, one of the few in the castle he'd bothered to maintain all these years. He would have to do something about that.

"Everything you need should be in there. Please, take as long as you like," he instructed as they walked down the darkly paneled hallway. "I may be able to scrounge up some clothes that will fit you, but I warn you, they haven't been worn in nearly a century. They'll likely be out of date." He threw her an apologetic glance, but she laughed. The sound startled him; it was a sound he hadn't heard in a long time.

"If they're warm and dry, I won't care if I have to wear a corset and bustle," she assured him.

He just nodded, unsure how to respond. When they arrived at the bathroom, he opened the door and stepped back so she could enter.

"I'll leave the clothes for you outside the door. I'm going to clean up as well, and when you're finished, if you would join me in the kitchen, I can make us something to eat and then we can talk."

She gave him a grateful smile before disappearing behind the heavy door.

∽

There were no working lights in the room, only the thin rays of sunlight that filtered in through the small window to illuminate the dust motes that floated in the air. Neku stepped gingerly, but still the dust rose in clouds as he crossed to the closet. The door hadn't been opened in nearly ninety years, and the hinges creaked noisily as he pulled it open.

Neku was extremely grateful that he'd never bothered to throw out Ysenderia's clothes after the Event.

His heart twisted at the thought of her. She'd been his dearest friend once. Of all the people in this world and its sister, only the planeswalkers had a lifespan to rival his own, due to the magical properties of their blood. He'd known many in his long life, but never one he'd cared for as much as Ysenderia. But she was long gone now. He'd lost so much that day.

After the Event was over, once his memories had returned alongside his sanity, he'd come to his senses only to find the castle deserted and himself unable to deal with the aftermath of his catastrophic decisions. He'd withdrawn into himself, shutting off all but a few rooms and ceasing to leave the castle under any circumstances. He hadn't wanted to deal with whatever the world looked like now.

In the old days, when he'd had a full staff that maintained the castle, members of the nearby village would visit monthly to bring donations of food and other supplies. It was part of the honor and privilege of being gatekeeper. After the Event, the donations had ceased, and Neku would have been content to wither away until one day, a few months later when his supplies had dwindled and he could barely find it within himself to care, one of the old donation wagons had unexpectedly shown up outside of his door. He had no idea who in the village remembered him, or why they even believed he was still alive, but since that day he'd found the wagon placed there faithfully, once each month, enabling him to stay alive in order to guard the gate. And wallow in his guilt.

The hope had always been there, much trampled but still present, that a planeswalker would one day come. But as time passed the hope shifted until it was more of a pleasant fantasy that he knew would never come true.

Until it did.

And now, faced with this least likely of scenarios, with a planeswalker in his shower and the looming obstacle of how to explain the situation without scaring her right back through the gate, he scarcely knew what to do. It was a delicate situation, and here he was with ninety years of no human interaction. He was hardly the best candidate for the job. And yet he was the only candidate.

One step at a time, he told himself. *Just find clothes.* Yes, that much he could do.

Ysenderia used to keep clothes here in the castle, as did many of the other planeswalkers, options suitable for each side of the gate so they could pass through without drawing attention to themselves. A small shelf at the back still held some of William's clothes too, but Neku avoided those, moving the hangers that held Ysenderia's clothing to block the view. Her wardrobes from both worlds were now decades out of date, and Neku hesitated, unsure which option would seem the least odd to Rose. The clothing from Rose's own world was what he vaguely remembered women wearing the last time he had been able to cross over, and seemed to consist primarily of skirts and dresses with puffy sleeves and wide collars, some with elaborate embellishments and fancy matching hats. They didn't look anything like the clothes Rose had been wearing when she first came through. He fingered the edge of a floral print dress. He didn't know Rose well, but it didn't seem like something she might choose. Besides, she'd probably freeze if she wore it here at this time of the year. What had she said? Warm and dry.

Turning to the other end of the closet, he considered the

clothing from his current world. Styles from that period seemed more concerned with comfort than anything else: fabrics were soft and flowing, shapes were simple and straightforward. That seemed like the best bet. He chose a pair of pants in black that seemed like they would be comfortable, and a few shirts and sweaters that didn't seem too outlandish. Best to let her choose, he thought. In the tight space of the closet, they seemed to have avoided most of the dust, and were in fairly good condition as he pulled them out and folded them in a pile.

Good. One step at a time. Maybe he could do this after all.

21

ROSE

Nothing had ever felt as good as this shower. Rose nudged the tap until the water that streamed out was just shy of scalding, and after she'd rinsed all evidence of the last few days from her hair and body, she just stood there, reveling in the heat as clouds of steam billowed out to fill the room.

Eventually, she felt suitably scoured clean, in both her body and mind—and besides, she'd been in here way longer than was probably appropriate—and she reluctantly turned off the spray. The towels were soft and she was beginning to feel slightly human again as she opened the door to find a neatly stacked pile of clothes right outside, just as Neku had promised.

What a strange character he was, she mused, as she brought the clothes in and shut the door again. He seemed more nervous of her than she was of him, which was saying something. She flipped through the stack of clothes he'd left her. They were definitely odd, but the fabrics were wonderful, and it felt amazing to be dressed in real clothing again. She slid her legs into the black pants, made of a strange somewhat fleecy material. They were narrow and fitted, and while they were a bit long, they otherwise fit her surprisingly well.

Setting aside an oddly shaped sweater with a huge cowl neck and sleeves that seemed at least a foot too long, she chose a thick forest green sweater from the pile. Actually, it seemed that many of the shirts had abnormally long sleeves, some trailing down practically to her knees, and many had loops hanging down from the cuffs, the purpose of which was a mystery. Logic suggested that the loops were for tying the sleeves up somehow, but there didn't seem to be anything to attach them to. The green one at least seemed to be a relatively normal shape, with sleeves that only hung just past her fingertips and could easily be rolled up. It was fitted in the torso and long in length as well, falling past her hips, but its strangest feature was the row of pockets that ran down the seam on either side, over her ribs and down her sides all the way to the hem. The pockets increased in size as they went down, each one fastened with a gleaming silver button, and while she couldn't imagine a less convenient place to store things, the effect of the design was still surprisingly flattering. But more importantly, it was warm and soft.

He'd also left her a pair of black slipper-like shoes, similar to what she'd worn to the opera, and she slipped them on her feet. As she ran a comb from the bathroom vanity through her damp hair, Rose wondered where all the clothes had come from. Did someone else live here after all? She added the questions to her ever-growing mental list, hoping that she would get answers to at least some of them.

Her stomach began to growl again as she finished up, reminding her that boxes of sugar weren't exactly a good replacement for all the food she had missed over the last few days. Leaving her hair to dry on its own, she began to make her way back down to the kitchen, feeling like she was finally ready to get some answers.

∼

The food had been delicious. So far, Rose had to admit, she'd been rather impressed with the food in this world. Most of it had been unrecognizable, as she'd expected, but after dinner Neku had put a bowl of fruit on the table, and she'd been delighted to find what appeared to be an ordinary apple resting on top. It had tasted like an apple too, crisp and juicy, and Neku had smiled at her reaction when she bit into it.

He was handsome when he smiled, Rose thought. It softened his serious expression, creasing his face into laugh lines that looked like they hadn't been used in a long time. He looked better as well, cleaned up from whatever adventures he'd had over the past few days. He was dressed strangely again, but he seemed comfortable in a loose pair of dark gray pants and an oddly cut shirt of deep blue that was striking against his white hair and vibrant purple eyes. His hair was clean again and lay shining and straight as it fell down his back. He had it pulled forward over one shoulder though, and Rose wondered if it was intentional, to hide the creeping darkness she knew was visible on his neck.

Aside from the apple, the other commonality between the worlds appeared to be tea, and once the table had been cleared Neku produced a gleaming silver teapot and poured her a cup. She wasn't sure exactly what the tea was, but the taste was delicate and floral and delicious, the flavor slightly milder than the Corlis root tea she'd had at Ydenda's house. She sighed contentedly, leaning back in her chair.

"Thank you, it was all wonderful."

Neku smiled a little awkwardly. "Thank *you*." The faint resonant quality of his voice was muted when he spoke softly. "Thousands of years of practice, though I admit it's been a while since I cooked for anyone else."

Rose stared across the table at him. *Thousands of years.* Her list of questions grew ever longer.

Dinner had been mostly silent, both of them concentrating more on eating than making conversation, but now it seemed the time for talk had come. She sat up straighter, holding her teacup between her palms. She had eaten everything he had placed before her, but rather than feeling overfull or lethargic, she was actually feeling more awake and energized. She leveled her gaze on him.

"So."

He sat up straighter as well, and Rose could see the emotions play across his features—fear, anxiety, was that desperation?—before he smoothed his expression with an obvious effort and took a deep breath.

"Ever since the moment you first walked through my door," he began softly, looking down at his teacup rather than meeting her eyes, "I've been trying to think of how I would explain everything to you. It's so overwhelming, and especially to someone from the other world...well." He finally looked up at her. "Then I collapsed, and you left, and I was terrified that I'd lost the chance."

She didn't respond, just looked at him levelly, and he shook his head. "But now that you're back, I realize how I say it isn't important. Just as long as I can help you understand. So please, feel free to interrupt, ask questions, and I'll do my best."

Rose nodded, the questions rising within her, but she forced herself to remain silent and give him a chance to think. The swirling patterns on his skin were now motionless as she waited for him to start. And after a moment, he did.

"I don't know what they teach in your world. So much has changed since I was last there, so I apologize if you already know much of this." He took a breath, then dove in. "All the universe is made up of worlds, and all the worlds exist in bonded pairs. We call them sister worlds. The world you live in is the sister to this one. They are separate worlds, but they share the same magical energy, and this binds them together."

Rose caught her breath. She already knew this was going to take some processing.

"Each of the two sister worlds is unique and separate, but there are three things that they share in common and can move freely between them," Neku went on. "First: there is a gate that separates the worlds, which is guarded and protected by a gatekeeper. The gatekeeper can pass through the gate and move freely on either side. He or she generally stays close to the gate though, and is able to use the magical energy that flows through both worlds."

Rose raised an eyebrow. "So, what, is it like an elected position?"

"No, the gatekeeper is...um, created for the position. He exists as long as the worlds are bound together."

"And the gatekeeper for these worlds is..." She already knew the answer.

Neku cleared his throat. "Me."

"Right." Rose blinked. He was as old as the *world?* She didn't know what to do with that information. Best to file it away to deal with later. "Go on."

Neku eyed her warily, as if uncertain if the conversation was going well or not. "Okay. Well, the second element. There are people who have magical properties in their blood that allow them to pass through the gate and dwell on either side. They're born into one world or the other, but they can move freely in either world. We call them planeswalkers."

"Are there many planeswalkers?" Rose asked.

"No. They are very rare. Although they're rather long-lived."

Really. She wondered what exactly that meant. They'd have to come back to that. A thought occurred to her. "Are planeswalkers able to use this...magic?"

Neku tipped his head to the side, considering. "Well, their magical blood opens the gate, so yes, in a way. But no, not in the way the gatekeeper can. They can use the magic for one other thing, in order to...well. I'm getting ahead of myself."

Rose leaned back in her seat and took a sip of her tea. "Sorry, go on."

"Okay, the third element is the Drani'shadara."

"The what?"

Neku smiled slightly. "It's actually a who. The Drani'shadara is a magical being, essentially the lifeblood of the two worlds. It's a creature that can pass between both worlds, and maintains the balance of magic that flows between them."

"So, the..."

"Drani'shadara. Drani', if you like."

"Drani'," Rose said carefully, "is also as old as the world?"

Neku looked into his tea with a thoughtful expression.

"Well, yes and no. Are you familiar with the myth of the phoenix? I think that's what it's called in your world."

"You mean the bird that dies and is born again from its own ashes?" Rose asked. "That phoenix?"

Neku nodded. "The Drani'shadara is kind of like that. The Drani' is born from a seed—"

"From a *seed?*" Rose broke in before she could stop herself. This just got stranger and stranger. "Like a plant?"

Neku smiled again, his slanted eyes twinkling. "Yes, it's a pretty unique creature. It's not really a plant or an animal, but has attributes of both. Anyway, it's born from a seed, and grows, and lives for a time. Then when it gets old and weak, it dies, leaving a new seed behind in its bones."

Rose continued to stare.

"That's the other important role of the planeswalker," Neku went on, shifting uncomfortably under Rose's stare. "At the Rebirth Ceremony, the planeswalker takes the seed, and waters it with their magical blood. Then the seed can grow again."

"Into a new Drani'shadara?"

"No, there is only one. It's reborn."

Rose sat still, attempting to process all this outlandish information. She wasn't sure if Neku was answering her questions or just creating new ones.

"You know none of this makes *any* sense, right?"

Neku's face fell. "I was afraid of that."

Rose felt a surprising pang at his crestfallen expression. "I mean...it's not that it doesn't make sense, it's just that..." She searched for the words, not sure why she felt the need to reassure him. "I mean...linked worlds? Immortal creatures? *Magic?* It's not that I don't believe you," Rose assured him quickly, though she wasn't sure if that was entirely true. "It's just that a couple of days ago I was pretty sure I lived in the only world there was. There were no gates, or magical creatures, and everything made sense. It's just a lot to deal with."

Neku's expression was apologetic. "I'm sorry. I can't imagine having all of this thrown at you all at once. There was a time that you would have already known everything."

Rose looked up at this. "Really?"

"Well, sure. The magic is in your world as well. The Drani'shadara spends just as much time there as it does here. There was a time when it would have been unthinkable that a planeswalker didn't know what she was."

"So, it's true then," Rose said softly. "I'm a planeswalker."

Neku nodded, looking at her. "This isn't the first time you've heard that word," he observed, the question clear in his eyes.

"Ydenda called me that. And the Ma'ar. And the...King?" Rose said with a shrug.

Neku's eyes grew wide. "You'll have to tell me what happened to you over the past few days."

Rose nodded, but her mind was still turning over his previous words. "But I've never seen this Drani'shadara," she protested, the unfamiliar name awkward on her tongue. "And there's no magic in my world. No one there uses *magic*. And I've never even *heard* of a planeswalker before."

"No, no one actually uses magic except the Drani'shadara, and the gatekeeper," Neku clarified. "And the planeswalkers only use it to cross the gate or during the Rebirth Ceremony. Most people here are just like people in your world. Just normal people, going about their business, living their lives. But the magic is still there, all through the world. The world would die without it. The world would die without any of those three elements: the Drani'shadara, the planeswalkers, or the gatekeeper."

Rose's brow furrowed. "Okay, but why have I never heard of any of this? Why have I never seen the Drani'shadara? Why hasn't anyone ever seen it?"

Neku was silent for a moment, his face turned down toward the teacup in his hands, but his gaze was far away. His hair still covered the marks on his neck, but he made no effort to cover the black ridges that crawled out of his sleeve and wound around his fingers. They were dark against the white porcelain of the teacup. When he finally looked up and met her gaze again, Rose's breath caught at his expression.

"Because," he said, his voice barely above a whisper, "the Drani'shadara is dead."

22

ROSE

"Dead," Rose repeated. "Like ready to be reborn?"

"No, just dead." Neku rose from his chair and turned to stand in front of the large window that looked out over the forest. The lawn that separated the towering trees from the castle was wide on this side, stretching far enough out to allow the sun to shine through the window, casting dappled shadows on the floor where he stood. Rose thought it looked to be about mid-afternoon, but it was hard to tell. Was it really just yesterday that she had been down the Mist Bridge? How had so much happened in less than a week?

Neku faced the window for a long moment, his hair falling in a shining curtain down his back. Rose waited patiently. As confusing as all this new information was to her, she could see that he was struggling as well. His grief seemed so close to the surface.

After a long pause, he turned back to face her, but his eyes looked off into the middle distance, as if his attention was focused somewhere far from here.

"Now you understand how the worlds are supposed to work," he said in a quiet voice. "But they haven't actually worked that way in a while now. Everything is falling apart," he said, his eyes refocusing on hers, "and it's largely my fault."

His expression was pained, and Rose felt the urge to go to him at the window. To do what, she didn't know. Hug him? Take his hand? She barely knew him, but she felt a strong desire to offer some kind of reassurance. Uncertain what to do with these feelings or this new information, she forced herself to remain seated. After a minute, he returned to the table and slumped back into the chair across from her.

She gave him a minute to continue, but when the silence stretched on, she prompted him gently, "What happened?"

He took a deep breath and seemed to steel himself to continue. "William happened."

"William?"

"He was a planeswalker."

"From my world, then, with a name like that."

Neku nodded. "Yes, originally. Most planeswalkers tend to end up spending a lot of time on both sides. Like I said before, planeswalkers tend to live very long lives. But they are not immortal. William was very old, nearing the end of his life, and that didn't sit well with him. He decided he deserved immortality, and came up with a scheme that he thought would get it."

"What scheme?"

Neku lifted a shoulder in a kind of half-shrug. "Kill the gatekeeper."

Rose raised a hand to her mouth to stifle a gasp.

Neku met her eyes. "He thought if he killed me, he could take over my role, gain access to my magic and live forever."

"Would that actually work?" Rose asked, her eyes wide.

He gave a full shrug this time. "Who knows? I doubt it though. I don't think it can work that way."

"So, what happened? Obviously, he didn't succeed."

Neku's lips curved up in a wry smile, but his face was hard and it didn't reach his eyes. "No, he didn't succeed. He attacked me, stabbed me with a knife imbued with the Drani'shadara's magic, and knocked me out. When I woke up, there was blood everywhere, and William was dead. I don't know what exactly happened while I was unconscious; it's possible the magic killed him. I'm not sure even William knew exactly what he was doing."

Rose felt her eyes go wide like saucers over the hand she still held to her mouth. "What did you do?"

Neku grimaced. "I'd lost a lot of blood. It took me a while to recover. It wasn't until some time had passed that I realized there was a side effect of William's attack. I'm not sure what he did, and I don't think it was intentional, but somehow, he'd sealed the gate. It might have happened by itself, as some kind of safety precaution, I'm not sure. But by the time I realized what had happened, and opened the gate again, it was too late."

"Too late for what? What does that mean, sealed the gate?"

"You remember how I told you that the magic permeates both worlds?"

Rose nodded.

"Well, just like anything else that wants to pass between the worlds, it has to flow through the gate. The gate is the only thing that ties the worlds together, and it's always open, at least enough so the magic can flow back and forth. When William sealed it, it stopped the flow of magic between the worlds. And the magic...well, stagnated, for lack of a better word. It began to...Rot."

Rose drew in a breath at the way he emphasized the word, the same way Ydenda had. Was that...did that mean... "Is that what the black stuff is?"

Neku looked down at where his hand lay upon the table, fingers twisted with black. He nodded. "It's Rot. Rotted magic. Impurities exist in the magic, but usually they get filtered out when it passes through the gate. With the gate closed, those impurities had nowhere to go, and they began to pile up, and stagnate. And then it began to spread. By the time I realized what had happened, it was too late."

Rising abruptly from the table, Neku crossed to the sink and dumped out the cold remains of his tea. He then poured himself a fresh cup and returned to the table, wrapping his hands around the now steaming mug. He made no move to drink it though, and Rose wondered if he just wanted the comfort of the heat.

"So, what did you do?" she asked hesitantly.

He sighed. "Well, the first thing I did was open the gate. But as the magic began to flow again, I realized that the Rot was flowing through with it, so I slowed down the flow, and started to pull the magic back and filter it, keeping the Rot on this side so it wouldn't pass through and infect your world."

"What would happen if it did pass through? What does the Rot do?"

"It kills." Neku's voice was soft. "All living things are permeated with magic. The Rot is magic, but deadly now. It spreads fast, and it engulfs anything it touches. It's killing our world."

Rose was silent at this, letting the words sink in and turning everything over in her head.

"Wait, you said earlier that all of this was your fault. I don't see how any of this is your fault," she protested. "And besides, I've seen the Rot. It doesn't look like it's spreading at all. Isn't there a way to hold it back?"

"We thought there was. We thought we could fix everything." Neku's gaze was focused on the tendrils of steam rising from the cup still firmly clenched between his hands.

Rose's brow furrowed further. "We? And what does the Drani'shadara have to do with any of this? Didn't you say the Drani' is a magical creature? Can't it get rid of the Rot somehow?"

At that, Neku looked up at her, rueful surprise evident on his face. "Yes, that's exactly what Ysenderia thought. Must be a planeswalker thing."

"Ysen...what? Who is that?"

Neku seemed to pull himself together, sitting upright and giving his head a shake. "Yes, I'm sorry. Let me explain.

"Ysenderia was another planeswalker. She..." he paused, and Rose could see him struggling with the words. When they came, they were so quiet she could barely hear him. "She was a very dear friend. Once I realized what had happened, she came to help. She also suggested that the Drani'shadara might be the key to getting rid of the Rot. Together, we came up with a plan." He broke off again.

"And? What happened?"

Neku's voice was flat and emotionless. "It didn't work."

23

NEKUTHAEDRIS

87 YEARS EARLIER

Nekuthaedris hated waiting. It occurred to him that impatience was rather uncharacteristic of a being that had been alive as long as he had, but the passage of time had never seemed quite so threatening as it did now. Every second that passed seemed to pick up speed, hurtling him forward at a rate he couldn't control.

Darkness fell outside as he paced the grand foyer of the castle, listening to the seconds tick by on the elaborate grandfather clock that stood at the base of the stairs. His footsteps matched its pace, his boots clicking on the marble mosaic with every step, and the silver patterns etched into his skin swirled and shifted as he moved. It was dark inside as well, with the lamps unlit to suit his mood and no moonlight filtering in the tall windows. The clouds were heavy and thick as they scudded across the sky, and the wind lashed fiercely. There was no rain though, just a thick, oppressive humidity to the air, as if the whole world held its breath to await the outcome of this night. Neku held his breath as well.

But he ignored the heaviness in the air. He ignored the blowing wind that rattled the window panes, and he ignored the insistent reminder of the ticking clock that time was still passing. He paced, and he waited.

In the end it was Ysenderia that arrived first, the wind practically blowing the heavy door out of her hands as she slipped through and closed it firmly behind her. Her black hair was tousled, the wind outside pulling strands free from the elaborate design she had it pinned in.

Despite the gravity of the situation, her musical voice was as warm and lively as ever as she came to a stop in the middle of the room with her hands braced on her hips.

"Come now, Neku," she chided, "you couldn't even light the lamps?" Not bothering to wait for an answer, she marched around the circumference of the room, twisting the knobs on the lamps in the wall sconces until a cheerful, if artificial, glow lit the entry hall. Then she turned her attention to him.

"And you can stop glowering. It'll all be over soon." She glanced around. "Where is everyone?"

Neku heaved a sigh and came to a halt in front of her. "I sent the staff away. I don't want anyone to get hurt if our plan doesn't work. Better it just be the three of us."

Ysenderia looked up at his face, her normally dancing eyes sympathetic. She wrapped her arms around him and gave him a tight squeeze before stepping back and taking his arm to drag him over to the low couch by the door.

"It will work," she said firmly, sitting him down and settling in beside him. "It has to."

A sudden burst of wind gusted against the door, and

Ysenderia glanced out the window into the darkness beyond. "I assume the Drani'shadara isn't here yet?"

Neku followed her gaze, but he could see nothing in the window but their reflections. He shook his head. "It shouldn't be long though. I summoned you both at the same time, though I don't know where it was when I sent the summons."

One of the benefits of being gatekeeper was that the magic gave him a link to the other magical beings inhabiting the sister worlds. It didn't work with normal people, but if he needed to summon a planeswalker or the Drani'shadara, a magical kind of tug through their bond would alert the other party that they were needed. He couldn't transmit anything else; no words or emotions would accompany the summons, but he could only hope the Drani'shadara would come quickly.

If the Drani' was in this world, then surely it had already seen the devastation and would have known it would be needed. But if it was in the sister world, it might be wholly unaware of what was happening across the gate.

Ysenderia cast a glance his way. "You look terrible, Neku." Her tone was gentler than her words. "When was the last time you slept?"

He gave a wan smile in response and shook his head. "I don't remember. It takes everything I have to filter the Rot out at the gate. I barely have time or energy to eat, let alone sleep. I haven't left the castle since this began." He hesitated, wanting to ask but unsure if he wanted to hear the answer. "How bad is it out there?"

Ysenderia hesitated too, as if trying to decide how honest she should be, but eventually she let out a breath and met his gaze. "It's bad," she said softly. "The Rot is...well, it's everywhere, and it's spreading fast. Too fast. Some of the villages have been evacuated, and people are gathering in the untouched districts of the major cities, but it's really just a matter of time. I think...well, I think it's good that we're doing this tonight."

Glancing over at his face, she added under her breath, "And it doesn't look like you'll hold out much longer, anyway."

He reached down and took her hand, wrapping her small fingers in his and giving them a squeeze. "I'll be okay. As long as the Drani'shadara gets here soon."

~

Nearly two hours had passed before heavy footsteps outside the door brought Neku out of his increasingly worried thoughts. He and Ysenderia had long since lapsed into silence, and questions spiraled in his head like a cyclone. What if the Drani'shadara didn't get there in time? What if it didn't receive his summons? Ysenderia had taken up Neku's original role of pacing the floor, but she pulled up short when she heard the sound outside, and they both hurried over.

When the door opened, it was the one to the left, and bright daylight spilled in from the sister world. He'd been right, then; the Drani'shadara hadn't been in their world. Did it even know what had happened here? He held the door open and stepped to the side, allowing the creature to enter.

Neku's breath caught in relief as the Drani'shadara moved ponderously through the door. The creature was large; on all fours it rose nearly to his shoulder, and its thick fur was a rich bright jewel green, twined through with vines and blooming flowers. The horns that protruded from its head were large and curved. A full adult then. It had not yet begun to change color or diminish in size, and its flowers had not started to wilt, so it was nowhere near ready for a Rebirth Ceremony. Oh, well. Nothing to be done about that.

As it walked, seeds dropped and sprouted, plants rising from the floor where it stepped, growing and flowering and wilting and decaying, a process of months or years reduced to seconds before disappearing in the creature's wake.

Finally, the Drani'shadara came to a halt in the center of the large room, and turned to face the two. The sense of a question being asked filled Neku's mind, an inquisitive sending from the Drani'shadara. Magic was the creature's primary means of communication, as it did not speak. It was able to read, and write, after a fashion, but did so rarely, choosing instead to communicate with planeswalkers and the gatekeeper through magical sendings that often took the form of emotions and sensations rather than words.

Since all of Neku's magical ability was currently engaged in filtering the magic that passed through the gate, he did not attempt to respond in kind. Instead, he simply gestured to the other door, the one the Drani' had not entered through, and asked, "Have you seen?"

He knew even before he received the negative impression from the creature that it had not. He bowed his head.

Ysenderia had been waiting silently by the door, but at his hesitation, she spoke up. "Let me show you, and explain," she said to the Drani'shadara, then glanced briefly at Neku. "You should stay at the gate until the time comes to perform the Ceremony."

Neku didn't argue. He didn't know how much of an additional strain it would be to filter the gate from a distance, and he didn't want to risk it. He could feel the

Drani'shadara's inquisitive probing, and he knew the creature was able to sense what he was doing, just not why.

Ysenderia moved to the door on the right and held it open for the Drani'shadara to pass. The blowing wind scattered fallen leaves over the entrance in the moment it took them to exit and close the door behind them.

Again, Neku stood alone in the foyer, but this time he felt too tired to pace. The magical strain, coupled with the lack of food and sleep was wearing him down quickly now, his vision beginning to blur. He hoped they would hurry. He could have simply explained the situation to the Drani'shadara, told the creature of William's betrayal and the horrific aftermath, but better it should see the Rot firsthand and understand the true gravity of the situation. They would not have to go far; the Rot was thick in the forest surrounding the castle, where the magic had first started to stagnate. He hoped they would be careful; it was a miracle Ysenderia had made it through without becoming infected.

As predicted, they were back within minutes, moving a bit more quickly this time as the wind blew them in the door. Neku could immediately tell from the Drani'shadara's face that it understood the severity of the situation. The swirling colors of the creature's eye fastened on him, and he could see the sorrow in its unfathomable depths.

"Did Ysenderia explain what we want to do?" he asked.

An affirmative sending, at the same moment as Ysenderia nodded, and then another sending, this time of haste, immediate action.

Neku nearly collapsed in relief. "So, you consent?"

Another affirmative sending.

Neku nodded with more authority than he felt. "Let's go."

The Ossuary was located deep beneath the castle, accessible by a large cave-like opening featuring a high stone archway and a set of wide stone steps that led down into the darkness. Symbols were carved into the arch overhead, but they were invisible now, the only light coming from the lantern Neku held close to his body to shelter it from the gusting wind.

It felt strange to descend the stairs cloaked in darkness and secrecy. Rebirth Ceremonies were a time of great festivity, and never before had one happened under these circumstances, in the middle of the night, with the wall lanterns dark, not a single other person around to celebrate. He fervently hoped it would never be like this again.

Finally, they all ducked inside the shelter of the stairwell and Neku was able to raise the lantern and light their path. There were no signs of Rot inside the Ossuary itself. With the sheer amount of clean magic that permeated the place, he imagined it would be the last place to succumb. It was only a small comfort.

Neku hurried down the stairs ahead of the group and into the large main cavern of the Ossuary, where he used his lantern to light the others that were set into alcoves around the stone walls. He'd been right; it *was* harder to maintain control over the magic at the gate from a distance, and even though he'd barely left the castle, he could feel the strain. He prayed he could hold on long enough.

Ysenderia entered behind him, and they wasted no time moving to the altar and gathering the bones that still sat there, leftover from the last Rebirth Ceremony, moving them to join the piles of bones that already rested on a nearby raised stone platform. Neku could feel the hum of magic in the bones as he held them, and the air practically vibrated with magic around him. Every surface was covered with bones in every state of preservation, from every Rebirth Ceremony stretching back through time beyond memory.

The Drani'shadara entered the Ossuary just as they cleared the last of the bones from the altar, and its slow, heavy footsteps sounded throughout the cavern as it made its way up to the newly empty space. Plants flowered and died in its wake, and the Drani'shadara put its front feet on the edge of the altar and smoothly jumped up onto the stone surface.

Lantern light flickered against the stone, and Neku shivered in the dank heaviness of the air. There was no procession. No revelers lining the passageway. No songs, no merriment. No onlookers dressed in finery, holding candles high.

He wondered what the Drani'shadara thought about their present circumstances. He knew the situation wasn't technically his fault; no one could have predicted William's betrayal, or what would happen in the aftermath, but he still felt a sense of responsibility. If he had just noticed earlier that the gate was sealed...if he had been able to do more to stop the Rot...if there was any other way that didn't require the Drani'shadara to sacrifice a life before it was time. If, if, if. It all somehow felt like he had personally failed.

But this plan would work. It *had* to work.

Ysenderia put a hand on his arm, drawing his attention back to the moment. They were all in place. There was no time to waste. He turned to where the Drani'shadara sat, perched on the altar. "Are you ready?"

An affirmative sending, then a cautionary follow up. *Stay back, out of the way.*

Neku grabbed Ysenderia's arm and pulled her back against the far wall, well away from both the altar and the stairs.

The Drani'shadara waited until they were pressed back into the stone, safely out of the way, before closing its eyes, the heavy lids falling to cover the bottomless depths within. It didn't waste another moment, and Neku felt the power in the room increase in a sudden burst. He gasped involuntarily, and felt Ysenderia draw her breath in sharply as well, their hands fumbling against the wall to clasp together between them.

The Drani'shadara *pulled.*

For a long moment, the magic continued to increase, as the Drani'shadara seemed to gather it in, pulling from every corner of the world. The scattered bones that covered every surface began to vibrate with energy, slowly starting to rise into the air. Neku gritted his teeth as it continued to flow, surging into the creature that sat so still and calm on the altar.

It didn't take long before the first traces of Rot began to creep in, flowing down the stairs and across the room as they were swept along on the invisible tide of magic. He felt Ysenderia flatten herself back against the wall, but he couldn't pull his eyes away from the river of magic that flooded toward the altar and into the Drani'shadara. It was an impossible amount, more than Neku could even imagine holding without being torn apart.

And yet the river continued to flow, the Rot coming faster now, in thick black clumps, and then it was like the floodgates burst and a great deluge of darkness rolled down the stairs, putrid and gleaming in the lantern-light. The Drani'shadara took it all in, pulling it into its body with scarcely an effort. It was rare to get a display of just how powerful the creature really was, and Neku looked on in awe as the river of decaying magic continued to flow. For the first time, he allowed the seeds of hope to take root.

As the thick ropes of Rot flowed in, the strain Neku had been feeling from his own task of filtering magic through the gate began to ease. Tears sprung to his eyes, and he chanced a glance over at Ysenderia. Her eyes were shining and her lips were parted as she watched the spectacle before them. When she saw him looking at her, she gave his hand a squeeze as if to say, "I told you this would work."

Neku had no sense of how much time had passed, minutes or hours, as he stood still against the wall with his eyes trained on the Drani'shadara. He saw the moment the creature began to fatigue, a slight trembling of its legs, the barest darkening of its rich green fur as the Rot filled it. *Hold on*, he thought desperately. *Just a little longer.*

The Drani'shadara was shaking noticeably by the time the influx of Rot began to slow. The thick blackness began to thin imperceptibly, a moment before it began to break up into thick globs, like clumps of sod rushing down a river that had overflowed its banks. The globs grew smaller, further apart, dwindling until finally they disappeared entirely and the river of magic ran clear again. Neku loosed a breath he didn't know he'd been holding.

Another minute later, and the river thinned, slowed, and then finally reversed, bright clear *clean* magic flowing out of the Drani'shadara and up the stairs to disappear into the darkness. Neku could feel the tingle of magic on his skin as it rushed past, and he felt the relief rush through him as powerfully as the river of magic. It had *worked*! He hadn't been certain the Drani'shadara would be able to hold it all, would be able to filter it completely, but the magic that flowed past was perfectly clear, not a drop of Rot in sight.

The hard part was over. All they had to do now was enact the Rebirth Ceremony. Once they sacrificed the current Drani'shadara, the Rot would die with it, and the new creature that was reborn from the seed would help restore order to their suffering world.

Ysenderia gripped his hand, squeezing tightly, and when he met her eyes, they were bright with unshed tears.

"I thought you weren't worried," he teased her softly, his voice thick, and she gave a choked laugh in response, squeezing even tighter.

He watched the torrent of magic until it eventually slowed, thinning until it was a mere stream, then ceasing entirely. He waited for a moment to be sure it was over, then released Ysenderia's hand.

"It's time."

He stepped away from the wall and his gaze landed on the Drani'shadara. Shock flooded his system.

The creature was a mere husk of its former self. Its fur had darkened to a lank, grimy shade of green, and the skin around its face and legs was wrinkled and sagging, pitted and marked. Its breathing was labored, and tremors racked its body as it lay on the altar, no longer able to support its own weight.

A gasp sounded from beside him, and Neku knew Ysenderia had just taken notice as well. He hesitated, waiting for a sending from the creature, some kind of reassurance or indication that it was ready to proceed, but nothing came.

"We have to do it now, Neku," Ysenderia said in a shaky voice as they both stepped up to the altar.

He nodded and pushed up onto his toes, fumbling on the wall above the altar to retrieve the ceremonial dagger that hung there.

Under normal circumstances the Drani'shadara could initiate the rebirth process itself if it was close to the end of a life cycle. But as a healthy adult, it would require assistance to begin the process, in the form of a magically-imbued dagger that was kept above the altar. The dagger was traditionally used during Rebirth Ceremonies by the planeswalker, to water the new seed with his or her own magical blood and thus give rise to the new incarnation of the Drani'shadara. It also happened to be the same blade that William had used on Neku himself, and he gave a slight shudder as his fingers met with the cool metal handle.

The weapon was more decorative than anything, the hilt ornately carved with designs that pulsed with light from the magic held inside it. It was always a nice showpiece during traditional Rebirth Ceremonies. But as Neku brought it down and held it reverently in his hands, he could feel the sharp edge of both the blade and its magic, and knew it was as functional as it was beautiful.

And that was just as well, because tonight the dagger would be used for its secondary purpose, for the first time in history: to sacrifice a healthy Drani'shadara and bring on the resurrection before its time. Though with a glance down at the shivering creature, Neku thought grimly that "healthy" was not the first word that came to mind.

The dagger shook as his hands trembled, and he glanced to where Ysenderia stood beside him. "You remember what to do, right? I'll initiate the sacrifice, then once it's over and the seed appears, you take the blade and give the seed your blood."

Ysenderia had performed the Ceremony more than once before, and knew quite well what to do, and it was a testament to how anxious she must be that she did not snap at him or make some snide comment. Instead she nodded mutely, her gaze fixed on the shuddering form before them. It was a ghost of the creature it had been not an hour earlier.

"Do it," she whispered, not tearing her eyes away.

It took all of Neku's effort to keep his hands from trembling as he reached out and tentatively touched the Drani'shadara. Its body was cold, colder than he had expected in the dank air, and the skin around its face had a kind of waxy quality that made him instantly want to snatch his hand away, but he forced himself to push forward. He gripped the heavy head, which lolled limply on the neck, eyes still closed and breathing unsteady, and lifted it.

It was almost over.

There was no specific action needed to begin the ritual; he only had to be sure that the blade pierced deep enough to create a killing wound, and the magic would take care of the rest. Best to be sure the first strike was effective then. With his fingers gripped tightly in the creature's fur—no longer soft and silky, but now strangely coarse, the strands dull and lank in his grip—Neku pulled the Drani'shadara's head back. He drew in a breath, and in one smooth motion he sliced across the creature's throat, deep and sure.

The result was instantaneous. Instead of the magically-imbued blood he expected to flow from the wound, there was a concussive blow like a detonated bomb. The force of the blast threw him back, and he fell hard, landing on his tailbone as all but two of the lanterns were extinguished. The form of the Drani'shadara crumpled like a puppet whose strings had been cut and thick, black ropy strands of Rot exploded outward, spewing forth from the empty husk. It was an impossible amount, shiny black twisting tendrils disappearing up the stairs and out of the Ossuary like a foul river, even as more coated both himself and the walls in a thick, dripping layer.

He'd lost sight of Ysenderia, but she had been standing to his side, fully in front of where the Rot had burst forth. Where was she?

Particles of Rot filled the air in a greasy miasma and Neku struggled to breathe, choking and gasping as he dragged himself back, heedless of the bones that crunched and broke under his feet as he scrabbled at the ground in an effort to get away from the altar.

The Rot coated him, dark and thick, and with the force of the blow Neku began to gasp and shudder, feeling the first spiderweb cracks begin to fracture along the surface of his sanity.

Panicked, he reached mentally, grasping blindly for the magic the Drani'shadara had released into the world, the *clean* magic, pulling it into himself and holding tight. He barely had the presence of mind to reach mentally toward the gate, filtering the magic again. He would *not* let the Rot pass through.

His thoughts were muddled, his brain foggy. *He couldn't —the gate—the Rot—*His vision began to blur, and he held onto the clean magic within him, too confused to do more than cling to it like a lifeline in a raging tempest.

Vaguely, as if from a great distance, he could hear Ysenderia coughing, great wet, hacking coughs. With a ragged gasp she caught her breath, and then she began to scream, a great rasping shriek that seemed to reverberate through the interior of the cave.

The sound was sharp and piercing and for just a moment it shocked Neku to alertness. His wild eyes settled on the altar, where there, amidst the foul pool of blackness that had replaced the withered body of the Drani'shadara, sat a single, gleaming seed. It was the size of a large egg, oblong and smooth with a delicate swirling pattern that appeared to be etched into the hard outer shell. It had a pale green sheen that flickered in the light from the remaining lanterns, shifting between colors like forest shadows. Fingers of Rot coiled blindly around the altar, but the seed remained, for the moment, perfectly clean and untouched.

With a gasp, Neku lunged toward the altar, tripping in his haste, and he snatched the pristine seed out from its bed of decay and poison.

He couldn't think clearly, all his thoughts eclipsed by others as soon as they were formed. *Ysenderia, is she*—-the screaming had stopped—*Have to get the seed to safety*—*the Drani'shadara*—Darkness lapped at the edges of his mind. He could see the Rot creeping down his arm, thick and black as it moved against his skin.

Focus. Get the seed to safety.

Clutching the seed to his chest, and tamping down the rising panic, Neku leaped for the stairs, scaling them in a rush and hurtling out into the night. The oppressive heat still hung thick in the air around him like a blanket, but the wind had died, utter stillness taking its place. But Neku didn't notice the lack of wind. He didn't notice that the silence around him was absolute—not a single bird call or insect song to break the stillness. He didn't notice the devastation all around him as he fled blindly into the forest, carrying the seed to safety.

24

ROSE

The silence at the table stretched as Rose sat on her hands to keep them from trembling. At some point during the story, Neku had slumped forward, his head cradled in his hands as he spoke. His voice had been muffled, but Rose had heard every word. He sat there still, head propped on hands, hair falling like a curtain over his face. His shoulders had shaken as he'd described his frantic, half-mad flight through the forest, desperately trying to filter the magic at the gate and deal with the seed while clinging to the shreds of his sanity, but he was still now, his body as motionless as if it had been carved of stone.

Rose gave him a moment, needing the time herself to sort through her jumbled thoughts and emotions, but as the silence in the kitchen grew, she gathered her courage and asked softly, "Ysenderia?"

After a long moment, Neku finally raised his head and straightened. His face held the answer to her question even before he shook his head. "She took the brunt of the Rot. No one could have survived it."

"I'm sorry." Rose felt the words were inadequate, but she didn't know what else to say. They lapsed into silence again.

Late afternoon had turned to evening as they spoke, and the dying light of the sun cast the trees in long shadows that danced on the floor of the kitchen. The tea sat cold and abandoned between them. After another long moment, Neku pushed back his chair and rose, moving to the entrance and flipping on the light switch there. Soft illumination lit up the room, chasing away the dappled shadows that shifted along the floor, as well as the more sinister shadows of the past that had seemed to linger on after Neku's story had faded to silence.

He returned to the table and sat, facing Rose expectantly. He looked weary and sad, but seemed composed and ready to continue.

Rose took a deep breath. She was unsure how much more she could handle, but she needed to hear the rest. "So, what happened next? After the...failed Ceremony?"

Neku looked down at where his hands were folded on the table, fingers interlaced, pale blue against twisted black. "I held it together a little longer. Long enough to hide the seed and make sure it was protected. Then I...well. Honestly, I don't remember a lot after that. Mostly bits and pieces, like I was living in a dream and had a hard time knowing what was real and what wasn't. I was very confused and most of that time is pretty vague to me, even now.

"The devastation from the failed sacrifice was widespread. Much of what happened I didn't find out about until much later, but once I regained my senses, I found that we lost about thirty percent of the population in that initial blast, more in some cities. I was..." He paused and took a deep breath. "I was too afraid to leave the castle at the time, and I had to rely on newspapers and articles that came with my food deliveries to find out what happened." His voice had dropped to a whisper, and it was clear to Rose that he was ashamed of his cowardice. "Villages were razed, fields and forests were obliterated."

A choked sound escaped from Rose's throat.

"The Drani'shadara's sacrifice wasn't entirely in vain though," he continued. "Though the Rot was released back into the world, it didn't spread as fast as it had before, and I was able to cast a spell to further contain it. It's slower now, creeping forward instead of rushing."

"But still spreading," Rose said.

Neku nodded.

"And eventually it will destroy the world? There's nothing you can do to stop it?"

Neku hesitated, an unreadable expression crossing his face.

"What?"

His eyes met hers, pleading with her to understand. "After...what happened, I was a coward. I told myself I had to stay close to the gate, keep it safe and filter the magic that passes through, but really, I was afraid to leave. I was afraid to see what had happened to the world, afraid to see the damage I had caused."

Rose felt that Neku was taking more blame than he was strictly due, but she held her tongue, letting him talk.

"I've been here a long time now, trapped in a prison of my own making, and I've had a lot of time to think. I've looked at the problem from every angle, thought of every possible solution. Our worlds are linked, yours and this one, and without the Drani'shadara, eventually they will both die. Without the Drani'shadara, there can be no new magic created, no protection, and the Rot will spread, corrupting everything it touches. Already it begins to spread faster, and the magical failsafes I have put in place will not hold forever. It's only a matter of time until it passes through the gate and infects your world as well. Because of their link, when the Rot passes through, they will both die."

Rose felt the blood drain from her face. She was stunned. Neku's story, while tragic, had nevertheless felt like just that—a story, something removed from real life. She would do what she could to help, if there was anything she *could* do, and then she would return to her own world, to her own life, whatever that even meant for her now.

But with this statement, everything he had said became suddenly very real and very immediate. *Her* world would die? *Her* world would be corrupted by Rot? How was that even possible? There was no magic in her world!

She didn't realize she had spoken aloud until Neku gave her a sad smile. "There has always been magic in your world. The people there have just forgotten it. Surely you have stories there? Myths and legends of magic?"

"Yes, but that's all they are, myths and legends! *Stories.* They aren't real," Rose spluttered. Her cheeks felt hot and she could feel her heartbeat loud in her ears. "None of this is real. None of this makes any sense!" She stared at Neku where he sat across the table, his purple eyes looking steadily at her. Suddenly he seemed very far away, the table stretching miles between them. It was too much. Everything was too much, one thing after another, insanity piling on top of insanity. Her ears were ringing, and vaguely she began to recognize the signs of an impending panic attack. They had become familiar early in the spring, after she'd lost her family. She forced herself to take slow deep breaths, to stay in the present. She placed her hands flat on the table, using the hard, cool surface to ground herself.

"Enough." Neku's voice, as it echoed her thoughts, was

firm. "I'm sorry. I should not have piled all of this on you at once. That is enough for tonight."

"No, I—" she began to protest, but he cut her off. His gaze was steady and calm, calmer than it had been all night, and his voice was understanding.

"I have not been fair to you, throwing everything at you like this. You need time to process. I've had nearly ninety years, and you've only had hours." He reached across the table and took her hand in his. His touch immediately made her feel more grounded and centered. She closed her eyes, pulling in a deep breath and letting it out. He was right; she needed time to think, to figure out how she felt. Her emotions were all jumbled and she didn't even know how to react at this point.

She squeezed his hand tight, and after a moment, he released hers. She immediately felt the loss. He pushed his chair back and stood, the patterns shifting in his skin as he circled around the table to join her. Not wanting to stop and examine her motivation, she reclaimed his hand and he let her, seeming to understand her distress as she stood as well. She felt off balance still, her heartbeat felt louder than it should, but she forced herself to keep her breathing even.

"Let me show you back to your room," he said. "Get some sleep, and we can talk again when you are ready. Take as much time as you need." His voice was soft and soothing, and he pulled her gently toward the door.

Her mind raced as she followed his lead blindly, all of her attention focused inward. His words kept repeating in her mind.

"It's only a matter of time until it passes through the gate and infects your world as well. Because of their link, when the Rot passes through, they will both die."

She squeezed her eyes shut, trying to block out the

words, but they continued to echo in her ears, bouncing around in her skull. It was all absurd. Magic and mystical creatures. Dying planeswalkers. Rot. *Thirty percent of the population died in that initial blast.*

As they passed down the corridor toward the stairs, Rose could see the Rot in her mind's eye. The abandoned villages she'd seen from the Millipede. Creeping down the building in Trelissar mere feet away from where she'd sat huddled against the wall in the dark. Scar-like ridges of puckered black slashing through the skin on Ydenda's face. Tears began to leak out from between her heavy eyelids.

Rose could feel Neku's worried gaze on her as he led her up the stairs, but there was nothing she could do. She could feel her hand tremble in his grip as the tears began to spill faster, collecting on her lashes before overflowing to trace damp tracks down her cheeks. The emotions began to swell within her, everything she had suppressed over the last few days, shock and fear at the Ma'ar's attack, terror as she fled through the city, panic on the Mist Bridge, confusion and pain at Neku's story, they all swirled within her in a tempest of conflicting emotions, until she could do nothing but give in. Her breath caught, and like a flood, the emotions all boiled up and she began to cry in earnest, tears pouring down her face as ragged sobs tore from her chest.

They had arrived outside her room, and after only a split second of hesitation, Neku pulled her to his chest and wrapped his arms around her. She was too overwhelmed to be embarrassed as she cried into his chest, feeling her tears soak through his shirt, and she felt one of his hands smooth her hair as they stood together in a tight embrace.

He murmured softly against her hair, words in a language she didn't understand, but they were soothing nonetheless. Ever so slowly, her sobs began to quiet, her breathing slowing and growing calm as she continued to cling to him, hands fisted in his shirt. It seemed like it had been an age since she had just been held and comforted, and she hadn't even realized how much she missed simple human contact.

They stood there as time slowed and grew meaningless, until Rose's mind felt light and empty with the fatigue that followed the rush of intense emotion. Eventually her eyelids began to feel heavy and she let herself drift, feeling nothing other than the hard planes of his back under her hands as she held him, and the reassuring weight of his arms tight around her, and then exhaustion swallowed her and she felt nothing more until she awoke later in the dark, alone in the enormous bed.

25

ROSE

Rose had once taken a science class in college that had taught that a lot of processing of new concepts happened while you slept. The professor had jokingly suggested they should all study for exams right before bed, and then allow the information to cement in their brains while they were sleeping. She had taken the instructor's advice, and while she couldn't say it had definitively helped her on the exam, she did know that when she awoke fully the following morning, she felt much more calm and centered.

It may have been in large part due to the full night of sleep in an actual bed, or perhaps the hot meal the night before, but when she sat up in the huge bed and looked out the window at the colorful blues and greens of the leaves outside, she felt more like herself than she had in ages.

She was in the same room she had woken up in the day before, and while she didn't find Neku's unconscious body on the floor this time, it did still occur to her that this was likely *his* room. As far as she had seen in her exploration, no other bedrooms were functional after being shut up for ninety years, so she wondered where he had gone after he'd left her the night before.

At any rate, once she had showered and found her way down to the kitchen, he was already there, bent over the stove with a spatula in his hand, flipping over vibrant red pancakes that seemed distinctly similar to the ones Ydenda had served her. She grew sad for a moment at the thought of Ydenda. She'd felt more of a connection to the strange, scatterbrained woman in the Broken City than she currently did to anyone in her own world. She didn't yet know what her role was in this mess of a situation—if she could even contribute anything at all—but if possible, she would certainly do her part to save the people of this world—and her own—from the Rot.

Aside from the Ma'ar and his disturbing posse of brown-suited lackeys—and the Ragman in the windmill, she thought with a shudder—everyone she had met so far in this world had been warm, kind and generous. Ydenda had taken her in without a second thought. Anae at the hotel had helped her buy clothes and lent her jewelry. Neku himself had bandaged her hands and—well, what exactly *had* he done to her hands?

She'd taken the bandages off in the shower this morning, and the two cuts now resembled normal, healing wounds. Slightly scabbed, red, but not swollen or glowing or anything else unusual. They didn't hurt any more than normal wounds did, either. She looked down at the two cuts, one through her palm and the other across the back of her opposite hand. She needed more answers today. More explanations. She was ready.

Her footsteps must have alerted Neku of her presence, because he looked up when she entered the kitchen. When his deep purple gaze landed on her she found that she felt surprisingly nervous, unsure of how to react after his embrace the night before. She had been a complete wreck, and he had just been comforting her, yet she still felt awkward and a little shy.

When he shot her a tentative smile though, she found herself returning it and relaxing.

"Did you sleep well?" he asked.

She nodded. "I haven't slept that well in a long time. What about you? And I'm sorry; I'm pretty sure I made you give up your room. Where did you sleep?"

"No, don't apologize," he said, flipping a pancake. "In a castle this size, there's no excuse for me not to have more than one bedroom open. It's my own fault. I just never actually expected you to come."

This last was said more to himself than to her, but Rose let it pass for now. She would press him for more answers after breakfast.

"I slept on the couch in the foyer," he continued, and then, when Rose made to apologize again, he added, "It was quite comfortable, and honestly, it's not the first night I've spent there. I tend to wander when I can't sleep."

Neku used the spatula to slide the cooked pancakes onto a plate, then poured another dollop of the blood-red batter into the pan.

"Those look just like the pancakes Ydenda made me for breakfast a few days ago," she commented, watching the vibrant batter start to bubble and solidify around the edges. "If they're the same as what she made, they were delicious."

Neku raised an eyebrow at her. "Ydenda?"

"A lady I met in the forest after I left here. She took me in for the night and helped me get to Trelissar. She...well, actually she did a lot for me."

"Oh, yes, you mentioned her before. She was one of the people who called you a planeswalker, right?"

Rose nodded, surprised that he remembered. "Yes, she actually had..." she trailed off, glancing at his arm. The black marks were hidden under his long sleeve, but poked out at the bottom where they wrapped around his hand. "She had marks like you. From the Rot." She felt awkward, unsure how he would respond, but he didn't seem fazed.

"Yes, a lot of people do," he said. "Those who weren't killed outright still bear the scars. It doesn't progress quickly though. At least, not yet." He grimaced. "Well, when I'm not using magic, anyway. When I do that, it tends to spread more rapidly."

Rose leaned against the counter and asked softly, "Is that...is that what caused you to pass out? Both times? I saw that it spread."

Neku nodded, his expression sober as he flipped the pancakes. "Yes. I try to use it as seldom as possible, but sometimes it's unavoidable. I used magic to seal your wounds, and again when I carried you away from the Bridge."

"You can *fly*," Rose said suddenly, remembering. Her eyes widened in awe as she looked at him, and his cheeks grew slightly pink.

"You should see what I used to be able to do when I was at full power," he said wryly, before grimacing again. "My magic is weak now, tainted, and my spells don't last long. That's why the seal on the cut on your hand failed so quickly. There was a time when that spell would have lasted for years."

Rose looked down at her hands, trying to imagine what it would be like to be able to command power like that.

He followed her gaze and said, "I seem to recall you left

here with only one cut though. What happened to you out there?"

When she didn't immediately respond, he added, "If you're ready to tell me, that is. You don't have to; I promised you could take as long as you want."

"No," she said softly. "I'm ready. I want you to know."

As Neku slid the current batch of pancakes onto the plate, Rose boosted herself up to sit on the counter near the edge of the stove, and began her story. For all that it had seemed to take a year to live through, her whole adventure had only lasted four days, and it took a surprisingly short amount of time to recount.

He didn't say anything as she spoke, but his expressions were reaction enough. His brows raised in amusement as she described Ydenda and her trip into Trelissar, then began to lower and darken as she recounted her meeting with Gann and the invitation to the opera. The Ma'ar's subsequent attack earned her a gasp, and then his expression turned thunderous as she described her flight across the city, her terrifying trek across the Mist Bridge, and the mob that awaited her upon her return.

The pancakes were done by the time she was finished, and rather than push him for answers, she grabbed the plates and made her way to the table. Neku followed with the pancakes, and they both settled comfortably into the seats they had occupied the previous night. The strange eyeball-jelly was present again, and Rose wisely avoided it this time in favor of a more pleasantly textured jam with a sweet berry flavor. The pancakes were just as good as she'd remembered.

Neku seemed lost in thought as they ate, and Rose waited as long as she could, polishing off a sizeable stack of pancakes before she couldn't help herself any longer and the questions bubbled out of her.

"What did you do to my hand? And the Ma'ar—why did he attack me? What did he want?" Once the floodgates had opened, Rose couldn't hold back. "What *is* a planeswalker? And the King—the Mist Bridge—why—"

She broke off when she heard Neku chuckling and shot him a glare.

His smile faded and he looked at her, a cautious question in his eyes. "Are you sure you're ready? I meant what I said; you can take all the time you need."

She met his gaze evenly. "I'm ready. I need to know."

Neku took a deep breath. "I explained about planeswalkers, right? They—*you*—have magical properties in your blood that allow you to pass through the gate."

Rose nodded.

"The magic is unique to you. Only planeswalkers can pass through the gate."

Rose nodded again, waiting impatiently for him to come to his point, but he just looked at her.

"Or anyone who has access to you. Or your blood."

For a moment, Rose stared, uncomprehending, then slowly the gears in her mind began to turn and the links fell into place. She suddenly felt very cold.

"So, the Ma'ar, he...he was...he wanted my *blood*?"

"With your blood, or with you, he could pass through the gate. To your world. To safety."

Rose raised an eyebrow. "Safety? I thought you said the Rot would eventually spread and destroy both worlds." She was proud of the way her voice didn't tremble.

Neku grimaced but let that pass. "That's why I cast the spell on your hand before you left. I sealed your blood, so you wouldn't bleed if...well, if anyone hurt you."

Rose felt shaky. "Was it that likely? Did you know someone would try to hurt me? I mean...you didn't know I was even going to leave at that point."

Neku was quick to reassure her. "No. I didn't think anyone would even recognize you as a planeswalker. There's no way to tell, aside from your blood. It was just a precaution. I couldn't risk anything happening to you."

"How did he know then?"

"It's the Ma'ar," Neku said softly. "He's got his fingers in everything, and a far reach. He knows the trouble we're all in, and he would notice any strangers entering his city. For all I know he's got people watching my castle. I'd be surprised if he didn't."

Rose shivered. "Will he come here looking for me?"

Neku shook his head. "Not if you're with me." His expression wasn't altogether convincing.

"Will he go after another planeswalker then?"

Neku looked at her blankly for just a moment before his face registered surprise. "There are no other planeswalkers. There haven't been for over a century. You're the only one."

26

YDENDA

Ydenda had grown adept at noticing Rot. Creeping through the branches of a dying tree or winding along the eaves of an abandoned building, the blackness that was nearly invisible to an unobservant eye would draw hers like a glowing lantern in the night. She didn't know if it was some kind of affinity borne of the Rot she carried on and in herself, or if it was simply a byproduct of her watchful nature, but she had become quite accustomed to noticing the subtle signs of Rot that a quick glance from an untrained eye might overlook.

The moment she awoke in Trelissar, her head throbbing and the stones of the floor cold under her shivering body, she knew something was different about the Rot here. Some subtle difference in the magic, almost like a taste on the back of her tongue that she couldn't place.

Ydenda lay still on the hard floor, her body unmoving but her senses extended. Stone beneath her, smooth and cold. The darkness was thick and dense, but as she waited, her eyes began to adjust and she could make out a dim light coming from the far end of what appeared to be a long hallway. Large shapes rose from the ground in intervals down the hallway, their hulking forms casting shadows in the dim light. And there was a smell, too, faint but sickly sweet. That at least she recognized. Rot.

Eventually, the pounding in her skull faded to a dull ache, and Ydenda levered herself to her knees, then used the edge of one of the large shapes to pull herself the rest of the way to her feet. It took a moment of running her hands over the ridges of the stone shape before she could place it. A... tomb? Was she dead? No, that seemed unlikely. She was fairly confident that when she was actually dead there wouldn't be any question about it.

She was cautious as she moved down the hallway toward the light, but there didn't seem to be anyone else around. That was odd, too. Why would anyone go to the trouble of capturing her, and then not bother to guard her? Unless they already had what they were after. She quickly stuck her hand in the deep pocket of her skirt. No, the vial was still there. She breathed a sigh of relief. That didn't make sense anyway. *She* didn't even know what was in the vial; why would anyone else be after it?

At the end of the hallway, the light grew to illuminate a narrow set of stone steps that led up out of the darkness and into a small room with wide shelves set into the walls. The shelves were overflowing with dusty rows of books, the gold text embossed on their spines catching the light. Moving through the room, Ydenda exited through the only other door and found herself in a tall, open room, its ceiling arching high overhead. *The Trelissar Cathedral*, she realized with a start. *I must have been left down in the catacombs.* She had no memory of ever being here before, and chose not to think about how she had known this.

Shadows shifted in front of the heavy main doors, and

she realized that despite the illusion of freedom, she was still under guard.

Ignoring the shadowy figures, Ydenda surveyed the large space with wide eyes. It was impressive on two counts: the elaborate ornamentation was such that she could only imagine how the room must have looked before it had been allowed to fall into ruin. Even in its neglected state, the few remaining intact stained-glass windows were beautiful, their jeweled panes splintering the outside light into rainbows on the dusty floor. Chandeliers hung high overhead and the carved wooden altar must have once gleamed.

Even more impressive, however, was the sheer amount of Rot that had overtaken the Cathedral. It was everywhere. Wrapped around the columns, dripping down the leaded lines of the windows, thickly coating the ceiling and oozing down the walls. And yet, she'd been right: the Rot was different here. It was motionless, even more so than the Rot outside the city, which seemed to creep slightly and tremble when you weren't looking, as if it *wanted* to be moving but was prevented somehow. And it seemed...less real, if that was possible, without that same foreboding sense of *life* that she was used to.

She approached the closest wooden pew, the back of the seat arcing majestically under its thick tar-like coating of Rot, her hand extended. She stopped shy of actually touching it, but it was the closest she had come to the Rot since...well, since it had first started to appear. She wasn't actually sure when that was, or what had caused it. And yet the Rot didn't quiver at her nearness, as it might have outside the city. What had been done here? Had they found a way to stop the spread? Was there a spell at work?

Ydenda was still standing motionless, examining the Rot, when the voices finally registered.

"—lost our chance." It was a man's voice, echoing up from the same stairwell she had come through.

Another man's voice answered him, the words unintelligible, but the voice was a rich baritone, commanding and self-assured.

The men stepped through from the library, and she saw it was actually three men. Her head gave a painful twinge of recognition at the first one, the brown-suited man she had encountered on her flight to the Millipede station. He was immediately followed by a second man wearing a nearly identical brown suit, and for a brief second Ydenda was uncertain which of the men she had seen before. She wondered for a moment what had become of the similarly-clad man she'd left unconscious and perhaps dead on her floor.

Bringing up the rear was the third man, the one with the deep baritone voice, and instead of a brown suit, this one was dressed all in black, from his tall hat to his polished boots. Though monochromatic, his clothes were all expensively cut and expertly tailored to his tall frame. This must be the infamous Ma'ar she had been hearing of.

The men were unhurried, talking amongst themselves, but they stopped when they entered the huge cathedral and caught sight of Ydenda standing by the pew.

"Ah, there you are." It was the man in black that spoke, seemingly unsurprised to find her up in the main sanctuary. He approached her where she stood by the pew, and to her astonishment, he paid no mind to the thick globs of Rot that coated the wooden bench right in front of them. He removed his hat and gave her a wide smile.

"Ydenda, I believe? I am the Ma'ar. I'm so delighted to finally meet you."

Ydenda cocked her head to the side as she studied him,

waiting a beat too long before she deliberately extended her black, corrupted hand toward him. To his credit, he barely hesitated before accepting her hand in his, shaking it firmly but perfunctorily before releasing it and sliding his own hand into his pocket.

Interesting. So, he didn't fear the Rot, didn't recoil from it like so many people did.

Ydenda had never met the Ma'ar. In fact, she wasn't sure if she had ever been to Trelissar before or not. But his reputation preceded him; she imagined few people in the Province didn't know who he was. She decided straightforwardness was best with a man of his nature. He likely spent his days surrounded by sycophants.

"And to what do I owe the honor of being your hostage?"

The Ma'ar replaced his hat on his head and gave her what she assumed was meant to be a charming smile, though his show of teeth looked a little predatory to her. "I don't know that *hostage* is the word I would choose."

"Prisoner?"

"I was thinking more along the lines of *guest*."

"Do you always issue such violent invitations to your guests?" she asked, eyebrow raised over her sightless white eye.

The Ma'ar's devilish smile widened, his eyes creasing at the corners. "Only the ones I really want to see. Come, won't you join me in the library? I was hoping we could chat." He turned without waiting for a response and made his way back to the tiny book-filled room they had emerged from. The two brown-suited men wordlessly moved to flank Ydenda and guided her after the retreating black form.

She fell into step between them, feeling the heavy weight of the vial brushing against her leg through her skirts as she walked. The sensation was comforting, reminding her that her instincts had never failed her. She may not know what she was doing here or what they wanted from her, but she could play along. When the time came to act, surely she would know it.

The library was small and cramped, with shelves that stretched all the way to the ceiling lining every wall, but there was still room enough for a small table that dominated the center of the space, and two armchairs that sat under the intact stained-glass window.

The Ma'ar ignored the armchairs and took a seat at the table, gesturing for Ydenda to sit across from him. The two men in brown took up stations next to the two doors, one that led back into the sanctuary, and the other that led to the stairs descending down into the catacombs. Ydenda sat in her assigned seat and looked to the Ma'ar where he sat across from her, his expression imperious. She stifled a smirk. Clearly, he fancied himself an interrogator at her inquisition.

When the Ma'ar spoke, it was without preamble. "You met a girl in the forest. Rose."

Alarm bells sounded in Ydenda's head. She'd known the girl was important. But *why?* What did the Ma'ar know, and how? Ydenda was used to feeling as though she was missing information, but something was really wrong this time.

She schooled her face to hide her inner turmoil and waited in silence. Her unblinking red gaze had caused lesser men to quail in her presence, but the Ma'ar didn't flinch as he dropped his bombshell.

"She's a planeswalker. Did you know?" This was delivered in a conversational tone, but Ydenda could see the Ma'ar's eyes were fixed on her face. The two brown-suited men also had an alertness to them despite their bored expressions and relaxed postures.

Ydenda's mind spun as she tried to sort through her whirling thoughts. A planeswalker. Had she known that? Yes, she thought so, it seemed familiar. And more importantly, it felt *right*. But she was still missing something. The girl was a planeswalker, but what exactly did that *mean*? She felt as if all the pieces of a huge puzzle were swirling in her brain but she was unable to figure out how they fit together.

"I had a chance to speak briefly with the girl," the Ma'ar continued, "but unfortunately our conversation was cut short. I was hoping you might be able to assist me."

Ydenda kept the confusion out of her voice with an effort. "And what exactly do you think I can do?"

The Ma'ar didn't blink. "I was hoping that your...unique position...might give you some insight into the girl's motives. What she knows. Her plans. Her location, perhaps?"

Unique position. What was that supposed to mean? The Ma'ar clearly knew more than she did. If she was honest, perhaps he would give her something that would help her fit the pieces together. She said the most truthful thing she could. "I have no idea what you're talking about."

For the briefest of seconds, the Ma'ar's composed expression cracked, and Ydenda caught a glimpse of the ugliness beneath it. But the mask was back in place so fast she wasn't sure if she had imagined it. She shifted in her seat, suddenly feeling uncomfortable.

The Ma'ar removed his hat and set it on the table, then leaned back in his chair. He leveled an unblinking gaze at her. "I think you know exactly what I'm talking about. She flew off with the gatekeeper. Is she in his castle? Has she gone back through the gate?"

Gatekeeper. Gate. Planeswalker. The words swirled in Ydenda's head, words she hadn't heard in so long she'd practically forgotten they existed. And yet they struck something deep inside her, something she couldn't identify. They sounded so familiar, so important, but the scars inside her ran deep. She just couldn't make the connection. She remained silent, masking the turmoil inside her with a bland expression.

The Ma'ar leaned forward toward her, bracing his elbows on the table. His expression took on a menacing cast. "What about the gatekeeper? What does he know?"

What does the gatekeeper know? What does the Ma'ar know? What do I know?

The silence stretched.

In one abrupt motion, the Ma'ar shot to his feet and slammed his hands down on the table. His mask had slipped again, and the expression on his face made Ydenda shudder. She didn't see a signal, but without a word the two men in brown stepped away from their positions at the doors, moving around the table to stand on either side of her. Ydenda felt claustrophobic; their wordless presence at her back feeling more menacing than anything the Ma'ar had said.

When he spoke again, the veneer of civility was gone.

"I have left you alone for years." His words were hissed, his expression murderous. "I let you live your life, despite everything you've done. I convinced myself you'd already been punished enough for your actions." A sweeping gesture took in her ruined face, the creeping Rot that covered half her body.

Ydenda shrank back in her seat. *What actions? What had she done?*

"Besides, you were of no use to me," the Ma'ar continued with a sneer, leaning closer as she cowered away. "Not like this. But now, I'll be *damned* if I'm going to let you take this away from me. I *will* find that girl, and you *will* help me."

One of the men in brown casually dropped a hand on her shoulder, and Ydenda flinched. She could feel her heart pounding in her throat, and it took everything she had to hold back the tears that pricked behind her lids. Emotions buffeted her like a tempest, rising up and crashing within her until she couldn't separate them. Fear of the Ma'ar. Worry for Rose. Frustration at being unable to recall things that were so obviously important. Shame, dark and suffocating, from a source deep within her that she couldn't even identify.

The Ma'ar's face was inches away from hers now, his piercing eyes looking into hers as if he could see the emotions swirling inside her. With a glower of disgust he said to his men, "Throw her back in the catacombs, and stay with her this time."

Ydenda felt a hand grip each of her arms and haul her to her feet. She could feel her whole body tremble. The hands on her arms were tight and painful, but she wasn't sure she would be able to support her own weight without them. The two men yanked her toward the stairs, but before they cleared the threshold, the Ma'ar stepped into her path and leaned in close. She tried to shrink away from his looming presence, but the hands gripped her crushingly tight, rooting her to the spot.

"I have little time to wait, so I suggest you think hard, and try to remember something that may help me." She could feel his hot breath on her face, and despite her best efforts, the tears she had been struggling to hold back began to leak out.

The Ma'ar straightened and turned to the brown-suited men. "If she is unable to recall any useful information in the next hour, you have my leave to...assist her."

27

ROSE

After breakfast, Rose retreated back to her room to let her mind adjust to the overwhelming amount of new information that kept getting thrown at her. She had been prepared to keep going, to hear the rest, but Neku was insistent that they take a break. She thought he was just nervous about a potential repeat of the previous night, but now, standing in front of the window and looking out over the sprawling forest, she considered that he might have a point.

It was a lot to take in. She thought back to the day—a literal world away now—that she'd first gotten that phone call from the police. She remembered the way her mind had been blank as she'd sped recklessly to the hospital, the roil of emotions when she'd been forced to come to terms with losing her whole family in one blow. More than anything, what stayed with her was how she'd felt when she'd left the hospital. After sitting like a zombie as arrangements had been made, she'd brushed off the social worker she'd been assigned, and left. It had been a beautiful spring day, the sun bright and warm, and everything had seemed so *normal* as she walked out of the rotating hospital doors. Like she should just pick up where she'd left off and head back to the university so she didn't miss the graduation ceremony. It was like her brain was unable to process everything that had happened, so it was fully prepared to block it out instead and just move on with business as usual.

She could recognize the same feelings brewing inside her now. Everything was so big, so overwhelming, and she didn't know how to deal with it, so she could feel herself shutting down.

But this was different. Here, there was still something to fight for, a whole world of people with their lives ahead of them. They'd been living with this shadow over them for years and managed to survive, even to thrive. To be fair, Rose wasn't sure how many of the people here actually knew what had happened and exactly how dire their situation was. Come to think of it, Neku had said it was nearly ninety years ago that the resurrection failed. Rose wondered if there was anyone alive now who even remembered a time before the Rot. But at the same time, she reasoned, no one could look at the Rot and think anything good was in store.

Still, it wasn't over yet, and there had to be *something* they could do. Neku wouldn't have reacted the way he did to her presence here if everything was already hopeless. She clung to that thought as she looked out over the dense canopy of leaves.

A pillar of stone caught her eye where it jutted out from the side of the castle near the edge of her vision, and she leaned forward, pressing her face close to the glass. It seemed to be the support pillar for some kind of flat expanse of stone overhead—a balcony, maybe?—that curved around the wall out of her line of sight. She calculated the distance. Up two flights, maybe three, and down the hall toward the right.

Neku had said he was going to use this time to clear out a second bedroom for himself and launder more of Ysenderia's old clothes for Rose to wear, so she had time to kill. And he hadn't told her to stay in her room. If she was trapped alone with her thoughts for the time being, maybe she would explore a little. She had recovered from her trials in the city enough that fresh air was starting to sound appealing again.

Leaving the room and making her way to the stairwell at the end of the hallway, Rose started up toward the next level instead of following her usual route down to the kitchen. The floor above looked much like the one below—a long expanse of rich carpeting blanketed the stone floor, and the hallway was lined with closed doors on either side. It was obvious no one had been up here in a while, though. The wall sconces were dark, the only light filtering in from a small window halfway down the hall, and there was a musty odor of disuse that permeated the air. As she poked her head through the doors—the ones that were unlocked anyway—she could see that the furniture in the rooms was blanketed in thick layers of dust and cobwebs.

She found the balcony up two more flights of stairs, down a shorter hallway and behind a pair of large, arched French doors. The doors were locked, but with a small amount of force the lock grudgingly gave way with a loud creak of protest and the doors swung open on rusty hinges.

The balcony itself was large but secluded, and despite the chilly air it was protected from the wind by the way it was set into the concave curve of the wall. Thick stone pillars rose at the corners and a low stone railing curved around the exterior, offering protection from the treacherous drop to the stone courtyard far below.

The view was spectacular. The forest stretched out in

panorama, and from her position at the edge of the balcony, Rose could imagine she was floating in the air, the brilliant hues of the leaves encircling her on all sides and seemingly alive as they swayed in the breeze, casting their dappled shadows on the grass below.

A speck of darkness caught Rose's eye, and she squinted toward the west, trying to make out the blurry shape. It was a dead tree, its branches stark and black against the vivid purples and blues of the surrounding leaves. No...she looked closer. Not just dead. With a shock, she realized what she was seeing. The darkness wasn't just the bare wood of the trunk and branches poking through, it was the light-swallowing blackness of a tree that had been consumed by the Rot.

From this height, Rose could see the canopy of the forest spreading out away from the castle, and her eyes began to pick out other Rot-swallowed forms. A tall black shape—maybe a building or tower—far away to the northwest, a whole stand of twisted black skeletons not far from the edge of the forest to the north. Rose shivered, pulling the edges of her sweater closer around her. The leaves were so dense that the black forms blended almost invisibly into the surrounding trees, but now that she saw them, she couldn't stop picking them out. And there were a lot of them, spreading away into the distance.

She wondered how much more Rot was out there that she'd missed on her travels. And how fast was it moving? How long would the spell that held it off last? How much time did they really have?

Her reverie was broken by the sound of creaking hinges and a door closing softly behind her, and she turned to find Neku joining her at the edge of the balcony. He didn't look at her, his gaze instead focused out over the surrounding forest. It took him a moment to speak.

"You see it now." His voice was soft, his words a statement not a question.

Rose nodded. "It's everywhere. I keep seeing more, everywhere I look. Has it always been this bad?"

Neku let out a long breath. "It's getting worse. The spell is holding, but it's weakening. It's only a matter of time before it breaks and the Rot spreads like it did in the beginning. It's...it's really a miracle you came when you did."

Rose was silent for a moment, looking out over what was, on the surface, a scene of immense beauty, colorful leaves shifting in the sparkling sunlight. It would be so easy to pretend that the surface was all there was. Pretend there was no undercurrent of corruption and death lurking underneath. Just as it would have been easy to pretend that it was just a normal beautiful sunny spring afternoon when she'd walked out of the hospital. But denial hadn't changed reality then, and it wouldn't now.

Her voice was soft but steady as she turned to face Neku. "Tell me what I can do."

His deep purple eyes met hers, and he searched her expression. She didn't know what he was looking for, but he must have found it, because finally he nodded. Turning away, he led her back out of the windy uncovered area of the balcony, and toward a pair of wrought iron chairs that framed a small table standing to one side of the doors. The patterns in his skin shifted slowly as he moved. She took a seat in one and waited as he situated himself in the other.

When he spoke, Neku's attention was still focused out over the trees, his gaze abstracted. "Without the Drani'shadara, both worlds will die. The magic will continue to Rot until there is nothing left, and the worlds will crumble to dust." The eerie echo of his previous words made goosebumps rise on Rose's arms, and after a moment he finally turned to look at her. "If there is to be any hope of a future, of any kind, the Drani'shadara has to be resurrected."

Rose took a deep breath. "And that's where I come in, right? If I'm a planeswalker, as you all seem to think, then I can..." She struggled to remember how he had described it. "I can...perform the Ceremony? With my blood?"

He nodded. "That's right. You would use your blood to water the seed, so the Drani'shadara can be reborn."

Rose furrowed her brow. "That's right, the seed. That's what you left with after the Ceremony failed. What did you do with it?"

"There's a garden, not too far from here, to the south." Neku gestured vaguely. "It's called the Garden of Blue. It was one of the Drani'shadara's favorite places; it spent a lot of time there when it was alive. I took the seed there, hoping there would be enough residual magic left to assist me in protecting it. I cast the most powerful enchantment I could to seal the Garden and slow the spread of the Rot."

"What do you mean, seal the Garden?" Rose asked.

"I locked it so that only a planeswalker can enter. That way the Rot can't creep in, and no one can enter and inadvertently spread the Rot inside, either. Even I can't go in, since..." He gestured at his corrupted arm.

"You can't enter?" Rose said, surprised.

He shook his head. "Only a planeswalker. That's the only way to keep the seed safe from the Rot."

"And you said I was the only planeswalker in years."

Neku nodded in agreement.

"So before me there was...Ysenderia? And William?"

"That's right. But they're both dead now."

Rose raised an incredulous eyebrow. "So basically, when you sealed it, you made it so *no one* could enter. And you just *hoped* a new planeswalker would be born, and would show up before it was too late?"

His lips tilted upward, ever-so-slightly. "It worked, didn't it?"

Rose wasn't sure the joke was all that funny, or if it was simply a desperate act of hope, but she found it heartening that he still had the ability to smile after all that had happened.

"What if a planeswalker had been born in this world? Would that have worked?"

"Well, the enchantment I cast will admit any planeswalker. I couldn't make it more specific than that. But technically, no, that wouldn't work," Neku said. "There are traces of Rot in everyone here, even if it's not visible like it is on me, or your friend from the village. It's in the air, it's everywhere. Even if they don't know it or it doesn't really affect them, everyone here is corrupted. It has to be someone from your world."

"But if a planeswalker were born here, how would you keep them out?" Rose asked.

"I couldn't," Neku admitted. "But they wouldn't know the seed was there. They wouldn't know anything about it unless they heard it from me."

Rose thought hard, trying to keep it all straight. Suddenly something occurred to her. "If the Rot is everywhere, wouldn't that mean I would be corrupted too, just from being here?"

He shook his head patiently. "No, that's why I cast the spell on you before you left the castle. It sealed in your blood and protected you from the Ma'ar, but it also protected you from the Rot. You're safe here in the castle, but when we leave again, I'll have to recast it." He gave another half-smile. "You're the only uncorrupted person in the world."

Rose let that sink in for a moment. His reticence to explain the whole story up front was starting to make sense. How do you explain to a stranger that you're pinning the hopes of a whole world on their shoulders and expect them not to freak out?

Except she wasn't freaking out. Not anymore, anyway. She felt...useful. Needed. Like she finally had something to contribute, some modicum of control over something for the first time in months.

And as she looked across to Neku's now familiar face across the wrought iron table between them, where he eyed her with a combination of cautious hope and uncertainty, she thought that he wasn't a stranger. Maybe it was the magical tie between them, but she had felt a bond with him from the moment she'd first stepped into his castle, and it had only grown since then. How could he doubt that she would do what was needed to help him? To help everyone?

She reached across the table and gripped his hand where it lay, black tendrils creeping out from his sleeve to twine around his wrist. She gave it a squeeze and watched as his face relaxed minutely.

"So," she said, releasing his hand and sitting back in her chair, "you're telling me that we need to go to the Garden of Blue and retrieve the seed, so I can...uh...perform the Ceremony. Then the Drani'shadara can come back and...what then? Aren't we right back where we started? The Drani'shadara couldn't get rid of the Rot last time, so what do you think will be different this time?"

Neku, who had started to relax, immediately stiffened.

His face took on a guarded look. "This time," he said slowly, "I wasn't planning to try to get rid of the Rot."

Rose looked at him in confusion. "What do you mean?"

"I think it's too late for that. We can't get rid of the Rot. And if we couldn't do it ninety years ago, we certainly can't do it now, when it's gotten even worse."

"But it hasn't gotten worse," she protested. "It's not spreading now."

"Due to a temporary spell that is already beginning to fail. When we—*you*—remove the seed from the Garden, it will weaken the spell even further. And once it breaks, there will be nothing I can do."

"But if you don't get rid of the Rot, then you—the world can't...how..." she spluttered. Her feeling of optimistic usefulness drained away, replaced by foreboding.

With an effort, Neku took a breath and visibly steeled himself. "The plan is that you'll take the seed back to your world, and plant it there where the Drani'shadara can return uncorrupted. Once you're gone, I'll seal the gate. Permanently. Our worlds will separate. Then your world can continue on uncorrupted with the Drani'shadara's protection, and this world will..." He paused and took a breath. "Succumb to the Rot."

"*What?*" Rose didn't know where to start. "You—wait, how will you seal the gate?"

Neku looked at her, his eyes filled with sorrow. "I'll finish what William started."

His words dropped heavily into the space between them like stones cast into a pond. She almost imagined she could feel the ripples they made, washing over her, energy building inside her until she couldn't sit still. Pushing herself out of the wrought iron chair, she began to pace the length of the balcony. Neku's words swirled in her head. *Seal the gate. Finish what William started.*

He sat quietly, giving her space, and finally she whirled on him, hands on her hips. "So, let me get this straight. You're going to, what, *kill* yourself? To seal the gate? And let the whole world *die*?"

Neku looked sick, but he didn't look away. "I didn't say it was a great plan, but it's all we can do."

"*You* said that all worlds are linked in pairs. How do you even know my world can survive without a sister world? Maybe it'll just die anyway!"

Neku grimaced, but it was clear the thought had occurred to him before. "I don't know. I don't think that will happen, but I honestly don't know. Once this world is gone, and all the Rot is gone, maybe the Drani'shadara will know a way to fix it. Create a new world, or...bind it to another. I don't know. I just..." His eyes pleaded with her to understand. "I don't know what else to do."

Rose felt her anger begin to fade. She could see the strain this had put on him. The stress of constantly filtering the magic at the gate. The pain of losing people he loved and watching his world crumble around him. The weight of responsibility. It wasn't his fault.

With a sigh, she dropped back into her chair and fixed him with a pointed look.

"To be clear, I think this is a terrible idea. But tell me how it works."

28

THE MA'AR

The Ma'ar stood in his usual spot on the dais, using the podium in front of him to support his weight. Today the table at the base of the dais was bracketed by representatives of two caravans of Klistfolk, squabbling over some dispute that seemed to involve the large insect-like creatures that pulled their wagons. The Ma'ar's attention was wandering, and he thought he must have missed the part where they explained exactly what the issue was, and yet he did not have even the remotest interest in finding out what he had missed.

The high-pitched voices receded to the background of his attention yet again as his mind wandered back to the catacombs, where that infernal woman was still being detained. He gritted his teeth.

It had been two days now, and Ydenda had given him nothing. Not one useful word, not a hint of something he could use. It was fortunate that he didn't actually expect anything from her. He'd known she was a long shot from the start.

But still, he had to keep up the pretense, let the woman

think that his questions were piling up. Where was the girl? What was her plan? And more importantly: how to get her out of the gatekeeper's grip?

But honestly. He was the *Ma'ar*. He was the keeper of information, privy to other people's secrets. He knew damn well where the girl was: she was in the gatekeeper's castle; she had to be. And her plan wasn't too hard to figure out. If she hadn't already fled back to her own world, then the gatekeeper was certainly going to try to talk her into resurrecting the Drani'shadara. It was the third question that really mattered. How to get her out of the gatekeeper's grip. And into his own.

The Ma'ar knew he would be next to defenseless against the powers of the gatekeeper, and he stood no chance of getting to the girl if they were together. Besides, the Ma'ar's strengths had always lay in outwitting his foes, not overpowering them. He had to find another way to get to her. He didn't need much, just a drop of her blood would suffice. As for that, the Ma'ar had a plan.

It wasn't necessarily a good plan, but unfortunately it was the only plan he had.

The plan involved using Ydenda as bait to get to the girl, but in order to do that, he had to wait until they left the gatekeeper's castle, when Nekuthaedris would be weaker. And who knew when that would be. He had his men watching the castle and surrounding areas, but so far there had been no sign of the girl or the gatekeeper. So, until then he was waiting, biding his time. Which was not something the Ma'ar was particularly good at.

It really was unfortunate that he had to keep Ydenda...*occupied*...while he waited. He really did try not to harm people unless it was necessary. But in this case, the necessity was certain. And besides, he thought, leaning heavily against the podium, she hadn't been a total waste after all.

He'd been sure that she didn't actually know anything useful, especially when his hired goons—generally second to none in their ability to extract information from less-than-willing participants—were unable to get anything from the woman. And so, he would have been content to leave her alone, just keep her in custody and wait until the opportunity arose to go after Rose.

But then they'd found the glass vial. Tiny, with delicately carved vines encircling the top and holding the stopper in place, filled with a faintly iridescent liquid. He didn't know what it was. But he could feel the magic in it. It was the same power he felt from the bones he...*liberated*...from the Ossuary.

The woman claimed not to know what was in the vial, or where it came from, but of course that was ridiculous. He'd seen her face when his goons had handed it over. Her face had been thick with red welts and oozing wounds—honestly, it was practically an improvement over her usual unsettling appearance—but it hadn't been enough to hide her horrified expression when he'd taken the vial and tipped it toward the light.

She obviously knew more than she was saying. And he was going to find out exactly what that was. It was only a matter of time.

The squealing babble of voices rose higher than the Ma'ar's ability to block them out, and he found himself abruptly returned to the present. Rows of beady eyes glared up at him from behind the table, and he was suddenly tired —a deep weariness that seemed to permeate to the very core of his being. That feeling seemed to be creeping up on him more often lately. It was an ugly reminder that the magic was failing, that his body was not prepared to support over a hundred years of continuous existence without some magical assistance.

And that magical assistance was running perilously low. Two days prior, he had made a hasty trip to the Ossuary and removed the very last of the bones resting there. Once those were gone, there would be no more. For decades now, he had been using the magic in those bones to protect his city, and to extend his own life. But now that the end was in sight, unfortunately the city was no longer his priority.

Below him, one of the Klistfolk, a caravan leader by his appearance, stepped forward and raised his tiny chin. He opened his mouth to address the Ma'ar, but before the air could leave his lungs the Ma'ar banged his gavel loudly against the wood of the podium. The echoing noise effectively cut him off and startled the remaining Klistfolk and all the onlookers into silence. Despite his weariness, the Ma'ar smiled inwardly. It was the small pleasures in life.

The room was quiet, but he raised his voice anyway. "Due to unforeseen circumstances, all court proceedings have been canceled for the day. Please see the receptionist on your way out to reschedule. We apologize for the inconvenience."

With that, the Ma'ar turned and slid out the back door into the hallway that led to his office. He could hear the rising murmur of voices behind him, wondering what kind of "unforeseen circumstances" could have arisen in the last few seconds.

His office was cool and blissfully quiet, and the Ma'ar locked the door before removing his tall black hat and dropping unceremoniously into the chair behind the desk. After a moment, he reached into the hidden breast pocket on the inside of his vest and retrieved the small glass vial. He set it carefully on the desk and folded his hands, watching as the thick liquid swirled lazily inside.

His thoughts strayed back to the gatekeeper, considering. Aside from his little stunt at the bridge, whisking the girl away when the Ma'ar had been *so close*, the gatekeeper hadn't been seen in decades. Was it possible the man had really not left his castle at all in the intervening years? If that was the case, then it was possible the Ma'ar was actually the last person to speak with the gatekeeper after the...*incident*. And the man had been in no great shape then. If Nekuthaedris was still as mentally unstable as he had been at their last meeting, perhaps he didn't really pose as much of a threat as the Ma'ar feared.

He eyed the shimmering liquid. There was power in that vial, if only he knew what to do with it.

Well. He would continue to wait. For now. He still thought using Ydenda was his best shot at getting to the girl. But if there wasn't news from the castle soon, maybe it would be time to pay a visit to the gatekeeper after all.

29

THE MA'AR

87 YEARS EARLIER

The forest path was dark and ominous, the branches like living things twisting overhead. Being out here, alone after dark, was possibly one of the Ma'ar's stupider and more reckless actions, in a life filled with potentially stupid and reckless actions. But he hadn't gotten to where he was by taking the safe route. It wasn't every man who could claim such a high position in government by age twenty-seven. Even if the position was entirely made up.

Ma'ar.

It had a nice ring to it though.

He thought back to his last stupid and reckless action. That would have to be crossing the Mist Bridge to see the King, nearly two years ago. And that risk had surely paid off. A trip that local lore promised was so dangerous no one ever returned, across a bridge that was guaranteed to drive a person mad. And yet the Ma'ar had crossed, and imagine his surprise to find that not only did he return in one piece, and not any less sane than he had been at the start, but there actually hadn't been a King at the other end of the bridge at all.

Such useful information. He knew there must have been a King there at one point; he could remember the decrees coming into the city when he'd been a child. Laws had been passed, punishments meted out. He couldn't remember when that had stopped.

He'd wondered, at the time, what had happened. Wondered when the rumors of the dangerous journey had started—rumors he was more than happy to promote and improve upon. Wondered what the people would say if they knew their King was no longer there. Of course, they didn't really need to know. If Trelissar was in need of leadership, the Ma'ar was more than happy to step in and fill the void. It really hadn't been all that difficult to work his way up through the ranks of the Trelissar's poorly-run political system. And thus, less than a year later, a new governmental position had been born.

Besides, he couldn't have imagined a more perfect scenario. Second-in-command, of course, under the wise leadership of the non-existent King, the Ma'ar was able to have all the power but take none of the blame for any of the mistakes that were an unfortunate side-effect of running a city. And mistakes tended to happen when you took risks.

Yes, the Ma'ar took risks, but they frequently paid off. He hoped this current risk would also be worth it. Because at the moment, hurrying through the darkness, the path ahead of him lit by only a dim lantern and the trees looming threateningly on all sides, he wasn't feeling particularly good about the situation.

Especially considering the fact that it had been less than

two weeks since he had lost over a third of his citizens in a... what? An attack? Like the rest of Trelissar's inhabitants, the Ma'ar had no idea what had happened.

It had started slowly at first, so slowly that no one had realized the danger until it was too late. It began with nothing more than a shadow, a hazy darkness at the edge of one's vision. Over time it became denser, thicker, heavier. A blackness creeping into the city, seeping out of the ground itself, slowly spreading and lethal to touch. No one knew what it was, or where it had come from. Attempts to study it failed. Attempts to contain it failed. The reports were the same all over the Kingdom, all over the world.

Then, with an almost imperceptible shift, it started to grow, to spread faster. Welling up out of the earth, the blackness began to separate out into tendrils, creeping with an almost sentient purpose. Families were forced to relocate, property was abandoned. The Ma'ar was faced with his first real crisis of office, one that he hadn't the faintest idea how to deal with.

And then, nearly two weeks ago, it had all come quite catastrophically to a head.

The detonation had come out of nowhere. The blast was so intense it shook the very ground itself, and then...it was everywhere. Thick, viscous, twisting blackness, pouring over walls, bubbling out of drains. It swallowed people where they stood, engulfed entire houses and left only blackened husks and ruined bodies. There wasn't time to panic. A third of the population was wiped out in the span of about forty minutes.

And then...quite as suddenly as it had started, it had all stopped. Almost as if someone had hit pause on the destruction. The black substance, whatever it was, was still there, but it seemed frozen now, locked in stasis.

The Ma'ar had been asleep in his bed at the time, as were most sensible inhabitants of the city, and it was only sheer luck that his house had been spared from the oozing blackness. But when he'd hurriedly thrown on a dressing gown and left the building, when he'd heard the screams and sobs, and saw the enormity of the destruction, well, that was the last straw. He needed answers, and he needed them *now*.

Whatever the source of the destruction or the cause of its temporary suspension, magic was obviously involved. Which meant the most logical course of action was to seek out the one magical being that would have any idea what was going on and would know how he could protect his people: the Drani'shadara.

But after over a week of searching and casting his net of information as wide as possible, it had become apparent that no one seemed to have any idea where the Drani'shadara was. It was possible, of course, that the magical being was just in the sister world and out of reach, but something about the situation felt wrong to the Ma'ar. There was no way the Drani'shadara wasn't aware of the devastation that had occurred here, and if that was the case, why wasn't the creature here, helping to deal with the aftermath?

No, if the Drani'shadara wasn't here, there was a reason, and the next best source of information would be the gatekeeper. If he didn't know what was going on, then he would at least know how to find the Drani'shadara.

And that was why the Ma'ar now found himself trudging, in the dark, through what he prayed was not a Rot-infested forest, along the path that led to the gatekeeper's castle.

The Rot, while still ever-present in Trelissar, had not

moved in the two weeks since the incident, and the Ma'ar prayed that was the case here in this God-forsaken forest as well. It had been an endless day, with a long, cold Millipede ride and hours on foot through the dense trees so far. He was used to lavishly decorated offices with comfortable chairs upholstered in fine fabrics, not tromping through the underbrush at night. The last thing he wanted was to die in such an uncivilized manner.

The Ma'ar's foot caught a tree root that snaked across the path and he stumbled, cursing, his lantern swinging wildly. He could have waited for morning, true, probably *should* have, but once he'd finally arrived in the Broken City —a place that now sadly fit its name after the devastation— he'd been so impatient that he set off at once. He could be a patient man when necessary, especially when waiting for a carefully laid plan to pay off, but in this he was definitely reaching the end of his tether.

At any rate, he had to be getting close now. He'd been in this forest for hours already. He'd only been to the gatekeeper's castle once before, as a small child for a Rebirth Ceremony, but he didn't remember the trip taking *that* long.

That had been an amazing day though. He remembered little of the event itself beyond brief flashes of memory: sitting on his father's shoulders as the new Drani'shadara had ascended the steps amidst singing and cheering. Stuffing his face at the feast afterwards until his mother had taken away his plate. The Ceremony had been in the late evening, and he'd been allowed to stay up the entire night with the rest of the revelers, his first time ever doing so. He vaguely remembered the immense pride he'd taken in forcing himself to stay awake, boasting to his classmates afterwards about his accomplishment. They had seemed less than impressed, but even then, he had known that following through on a challenge you had set yourself was something to take pride in.

Another tree root upset his footing, and the Ma'ar was unable to stop himself from falling this time. Snarling, he went down in a heap, his lantern rolling to the side and managing against all odds to stay alight. He heaved himself to his feet and snatched up the lantern, angry at himself for allowing his thoughts to become so distracting that he couldn't watch where he was going.

Focusing on the path and stepping deliberately, it was barely a quarter-mile farther before the path opened into a large clearing. The sweeping vista of Nekuthaedris's castle, gleaming in the moonlight, stretched before him.

Finally.

~

The Ma'ar had been knocking on the heavy castle door for nearly ten minutes, his frustration growing steadily with each crash of the iron ring against the wood. He knew the gatekeeper was here. He *had* to be. The Ma'ar refused to even consider the possibility that he'd come all this way for nothing. Besides, he knew it took a large staff to run a castle of this size. Even if Nekuthaedris himself was asleep, or away, *someone* would be here to let him in and answer his questions.

He raised his hand to grasp the ring again—he'd stay here all night if he had to—when he heard the sound of a latch giving way and the door finally began to swing inwards. The Ma'ar nearly stumbled off balance, but regained his footing before arranging his features into his most competent, in-charge, you-want-to-answer-my-questions expression. He had been working hard to perfect that look of late, and it was a good mask to cover the panic that rose in him more and more often these days.

One glance at the man behind the door wiped the expression clean off his face. The Ma'ar had only seen Nekuthaedris a handful of times before in passing, but the gatekeeper had never, to his recollection, looked like *this*.

The man looked gaunt and frail, his body wasted away as if he hadn't eaten in two weeks. His clothing was dirty and scuffed, and it hung limply on his thin frame. The gatekeeper's normally shining white hair was greasy and unkempt, stained almost a yellowish-brown, and the pale blue of his skin had a gray cast that made him look sickly and almost...insubstantial. In the dim light from the moon and the Ma'ar's lantern, the man looked as though he might dissipate and fade away.

The Ma'ar was in no great shape himself, not after so many sleepless nights spent trying to protect his city, and he knew the stress and fear had taken a toll. But the gatekeeper was in another state altogether.

It was his eyes that were the most troublesome, though. Once a deep, piercing purple, they too seemed washed out and faded, and they were open wide, too wide, but seemed to have trouble focusing. Currently, they stared unseeing out past the Ma'ar into the gloom of the forest.

"I do apologize if I have awoken you," the Ma'ar began, a touch uncertainly, although he knew without a doubt the gatekeeper hadn't been sleeping. "I, erm," he cleared his throat and pulled himself together, standing straight and rearranging his expression. "I am the Ma'ar of Trelissar," he began in a stronger voice, "and I've come to ask some questions."

When the gatekeeper made no move to respond, he added, "I wonder if I might come in for a moment."

At that, the gatekeeper managed a nod, his eyes blinking rapidly before finding their focus on the Ma'ar's face, and he stepped back out of the way. Feeling unnerved, the Ma'ar stepped through to the foyer. He wasn't sure the man was quite all there.

The gatekeeper didn't follow him into the castle, and the Ma'ar was forced to awkwardly backtrack across the foyer. Only after he took a seat, uninvited, on a chaise near the door and overtly gestured for the man to join him did the gatekeeper close the door and sink into the adjacent chair.

Any plans the Ma'ar had to demand answers fled in the face of this wasted wreck of a man. Concerned despite himself, the Ma'ar leaned forward.

"Are you...quite alright?"

No answer. The Ma'ar wondered belatedly if the man was still capable of speech. He glanced around nervously. Come to think of it, where was everyone else? The castle had an air of abandonment to it. No lights were lit save his own lantern that now sat at his feet, casting up flickering shadows, and not another soul was to be seen inside the castle.

What had happened here?

Best to get right to the point then.

"Where is the Drani'shadara?" The Ma'ar's voice was low, but urgent. "I have been searching for weeks with no luck. And *what* is the black stuff? Folks in the city have started calling it *Rot*, but I know it has to be of magical origin. What is it and how do we stop it?"

The Ma'ar had spent so much time in charge, so much effort spent holding himself together to prevent further panic amongst his citizens, so much careful wording to cover the fact that he didn't know what to do, so many promises that he would fix this. And now, faced with someone who might actually possess the answers he needed, he found himself unable to stem the flow of questions. Despite his best efforts, his voice shook as the words tumbled out.

"What was the explosion? Why did the Rot stop moving? Will it start again? How do I keep my city safe? *Where is the Drani'shadara?*"

Nekuthaedris's eyes were wide and unseeing, fixed on the darkness of the night outside the window, and his voice, when it finally came, was a dry whisper like wind over bones.

"The Drani'shadara is dead."

The Ma'ar recoiled in horror. "*What?*"

Slowly, the story began to spill out, though the Ma'ar got the impression that the gatekeeper might not be fully aware of his presence there. The man spoke as if he was talking to himself, reliving horrible memories rather than holding a conversation. The story was convoluted and hard to follow, and Nekuthaedris repeated himself often, fixating on certain events while leaving out other important details. He ignored the Ma'ar's interrupted questions as though he didn't hear, his wide eyes unblinking as they stared unseeing out the window.

With much difficulty and increasing alarm, the Ma'ar began to piece together the story. It seemed they were all dead—the old male planeswalker from the sister world, the young female planeswalker, the Drani'shadara. Something had happened with the old planeswalker—he couldn't quite understand what—that had started the spread of the Rot. Decaying magic, he now understood, which explained its sudden appearance with no apparent source. Both the Drani'shadara and the woman had died in some attempt to stop the Rot, which had apparently also caused the explosion and surge of Rot that had killed so many people. The gatekeeper had done something with the Drani'shadara's seed—again, it was unclear what—and the spell of protection he'd cast had apparently also stopped the spread of the Rot. Or slowed it, at any rate. It seemed not to be a permanent fix.

The Ma'ar sat very still, his back stiff against the upright back of the chair as he took the information in. This was bad. As bad as it could get. If the Rot was, in fact, corrupted magic, spoiled and decaying, then there was absolutely nothing he could do. Nothing anyone could do, in reality, aside from the few beings in the world who actually possessed the ability to access magic. All of which were now dead aside from this vacant, shell-shocked creature in front of him.

Not for the first time in his life, the Ma'ar cursed his own misfortune at not being born a planeswalker. He could be the most ambitious, resourceful man alive, but without magical abilities, what good was he *really*? Especially faced with a catastrophe such as this?

On the chaise, Nekuthaedris had lapsed into silence. The Ma'ar turned over the gatekeeper's words, forcing his tired brain to work through them, looking for possibilities. He'd come here looking for answers, and though he'd found them, he felt even more frustrated and helpless than before. There had to be something he could do. Scowling, he turned back to the gatekeeper.

"What did you do with the seed?"

The man didn't seem to hear him, his unnerving wide-eyed gaze still blank and unmoving. "I failed." The gatekeeper's voice was barely audible, and very slowly, his head dropped forward to rest in his hands, elbows propped on his knees. "I failed them all."

With the movement, the torn cuff of his sleeve fell back, and suddenly the Ma'ar caught sight of the twisting black lines that encircled the gatekeeper's forearm. They were thick and shiny and stood out in bold relief against the contrast of the man's sallow blue skin. Shocked, the Ma'ar shot to his feet and stumbled back in alarm. The man had Rot...*on his skin?*

Quite suddenly, the Ma'ar became uncomfortably aware of just how close a call it had been. If the Rot had actually been on the man, *in* him when he cast the spell that halted its forward progress...well. Seconds later and it would have been too late. It was starting to look like they had been fortunate in losing only a third of the population.

The Ma'ar backed away from the wretched form of the gatekeeper, his lip curling unconsciously in a sneer. So much magic, so much potential in this husk of a man, all wasted. Imagine that much magic in the hands of someone with the right drive and ambition. Someone like him. *He* would not have failed his people like this. *He* would have found a way. He still would.

There was nothing else for him here. He retrieved his lantern and turned to the exit, a slight scowl on his face at the single door available to him there. Another planeswalker, that's what he needed. With planeswalker blood, he could leave this dying world behind. Sighing, he tamped down the envy that coiled within him. It was not a useful emotion. No use wasting energy on things that did not serve his goals. He would find a way through this, he told himself. He always did. The Ma'ar did not give up.

He swung the door open and stepped through without a glance back at the form on the chaise.

The night swallowed him whole, the cool air wrapping around him like a cloak as he made his way down the stairs to the path below. At the base of the stairs where the trail split, he paused, considering. After a moment he turned, following the smaller branch as it wound around the base of the castle to the high stone archway there.

The entrance to the Ossuary felt completely different than it had when he'd last been here as a child. No singing revelers, no bright lights, no cheers and laughter. The place was no less sacred now though, and the Ma'ar could still feel the same anticipation he had all those years ago as he made his way down the stone steps.

Just as before, his breath caught in wonder as he rounded the corner and stepped into the tall stone room. The cavern seemed unaffected by the magic that had taken place there not two weeks ago, all its splendor intact, from the altar with its ceremonial dagger suspended above, to the piles of gleaming bones scattered throughout the chamber. They glittered in the light from his lantern with a faint iridescence.

All this magic, just sitting here, bound up in useless bones. Just like the gatekeeper. Such a waste.

Sighing, the Ma'ar turned to leave, when suddenly a pile of bones in the corner by the stairs caught his eye, illuminated by his lantern. It was smaller than the others, older, the bones crumbling together as age turned them to dust. Kneeling, he picked up a handful of the bone dust, letting it run through his fingers like sand. How sacrilegious was this, he thought to himself, idly wondering if the magic was released back into the earth as the bones crumbled.

Suddenly his mind focused, latching onto that thought. He tipped his head close to his hand, watching the iridescent gleam as the dust ran through his fingers. Well. He had never been one to take the safe road. How could you know if a risk would pay off if you were too scared to take it?

He hesitated for a bare moment as he considered that he was about to desecrate a sacred site, then dismissed the thought and raised his hand to his mouth. Morals had no bearing at a time like this, and besides, nothing was really ever black and white anyway.

The dust was thick as it coated his throat, and he coughed, dust puffing from his lips even as he swallowed it down. He sat back on his heels for a moment, considering. Well, he didn't *feel* any different. But he would give it time.

He looked around, taking in the bones all around him. The *potential* all around him. If this worked, if magic could be released from the bones, then what else could he do with it? The possibilities were endless.

Not pausing to second-guess himself, the Ma'ar began to gather bones, filling his pockets to bursting. He focused on the older, crumbling bones, but took a few of the newer, brighter ones as well. It couldn't hurt to experiment. He would have to come back with a larger bag.

When he could hold no more, he rose, hoisting his lantern and making his way up the steps and back out into the dark night. When his feet hit the path into the forest, his steps were light, and he thought to himself that he might be feeling a bit stronger, a bit sharper. Or, it might be his imagination. But as he felt the sharp shapes in his pockets digging into his legs as he walked, he knew for certain that whatever the outcome, this had been a risk worth taking.

30

ROSE

Rose stood with Neku at the highest point of the castle—the keep, Neku had explained, from long ago when the castle had actually functioned defensively. The view from up here, peering out from between the crenellations, was astounding, with the forest extending thick and lush in every direction, a veritable wall of multicolored leaves, flat and endless to the north and breaking up into gently rolling hills toward the south. It made it seem as if they were the only two people in the world.

She was having a hard time appreciating the beauty of the scene, however, on account of the butterflies that had taken up unwelcome residence in her stomach. As amazing as the thought of flying was, she wasn't entirely sure she was ready to repeat the experience.

"You've done it before," Neku reminded her with smiling eyes. "And I won't drop you. I promise."

"How can you be sure?" she protested, shying back from the edge. "You said yourself the magic was failing. And you said you get weaker when you're away from the gate. What if your magic gives out and we both crash? What if the Rot overwhelms you and you pass out again? What if we can't make it to the garden? What if—"

He laughed out loud at her barrage of questions, and she shot him a glare.

"All perfectly reasonable concerns," she muttered under her breath.

And all concerns she had voiced before. They had been over this in depth, all through the previous evening and much of the morning as well—the risks, the dangers, weighing them against the benefits. She knew there was no other way. But she still didn't like it.

She had eventually conceded to go along with his plan, but secretly she hoped that another option would present itself. Maybe once she was in the garden, once she had the seed...maybe then she could find a way. To save the world. To save Neku.

She knew it was unlikely. Neku'd had the past ninety years to turn the problem over in his head, and if he hadn't come up with a better solution than this, then it was unlikely that a nobody, who had only a week ago been unaware that planeswalkers and magic even *existed,* would be able to come up with a better one.

And yet she couldn't stand the thought of the sacrifice he seemed determined to make. She had only known him for such a short time, but he seemed such a fundamental part of the world. Of *her* world too, for that matter. She couldn't imagine it without him. There had to be something else she could do. She kept these thoughts to herself though, not wanting to start another argument.

He came to stand by her, and Rose got the impression that he wanted to put an arm around her shoulders, but didn't quite dare.

"Look," he said soothingly, "when my magic fails, I can

feel it coming. If something happens, we'll have plenty of time to land and recover. I promise we won't crash."

"The last two times you've used your magic, the Rot in you has spread and you've passed out," she said, unable to keep her worry in check. "What do I do if that happens again? What if the Rot in you...spreads too much? What if you end up unconscious? Again?"

This time he did reach out and lay a hand on her arm, giving it a squeeze. His touch didn't erase her concerns, but it was reassuring nonetheless.

"I'll do my best," he said quietly. "I can't promise that using magic won't affect me, but I'll fight it. I was able to fly with you from the Mist Bridge back to the castle, and that's further than we need to go now. I'll be okay."

She met his eyes and saw his own worry that he was working hard to keep hidden beneath his reassuring exterior. Her stomach flipped.

"I have been using magic in small amounts here and there," he went on. "It doesn't always affect me so drastically. The Rot doesn't spread much each time, and I don't pass out every time I use it."

"How reassuring," Rose muttered sarcastically.

"Besides," he continued, "I have to cast a new sealing spell on you before we can leave, so we can consider it a trial run."

She'd forgotten about that. He had to seal her blood like before, so she wouldn't be corrupted by the magic of this world and bring the Rot with her back through the gateway.

Wordlessly, she held her hand out toward him. Fine. She would see if he could cast this spell without being overwhelmed. If not...well, they would have to fly anyway, but if he could perform this spell and remain unaffected, she would at least feel marginally better about the situation.

Neku took her proffered hand in his and turned so they were facing each other. He held it in his palm and raised his other hand to hover over hers.

"Wait!" Rose said, then gave him a tug, pulling them both away from the edge. "If you do pass out, I'd prefer it if you at least managed not to fall off the top of the castle."

Neku suppressed a smile, as if that wasn't a valid concern, then raised his hand over hers again. The spell this time was even more anticlimactic than before. Her cut from before was entirely healed at this point, and she had no open wounds, so there was no line of light, no cut to heal as he drew his finger down the length of her palm in a motion Rose thought was probably arbitrary. The tingling sensation was still there, but Rose wasn't quite sure if it was because of the magic or an effect of his finger against her skin.

"Is that it?" she asked dubiously, eyeing her hand.

"That's it."

His voice was a bit shaky and she looked up at him closely. "Are you okay?"

"Yes, I'm...fine."

He clearly wasn't entirely fine. He held himself very still and his eyes blinked rapidly, as if he were fighting a surge of dizziness or nausea, but he didn't look to be in danger of fainting. Rose gave him a moment to recover, watching carefully in case anything changed. The ropes of black on his wrist seemed to shiver slightly, but they didn't creep any further. After a moment he seemed to steady as he overcame whatever internal battle he fought, and the wide smile he directed at her seemed to contain a little more relief than reassurance.

She raised an eyebrow. "You still think you can fly?"

He nodded decisively. "Yes. Whenever you are ready."

Rose spared a last glance out over the expanse of trees,

then took a deep breath. "Let's get this over with. How should I...?" She raised her arms awkwardly.

"I'll carry you. Just hold on tight." Stepping close, Neku bent and in one smooth motion, swept her up into his arms, hooking one arm under her knees and the other tight around her back. She held his shoulders, then watched in awe as a pair of wings, nonexistent just a moment earlier, unfurled from Neku's shoulder blades. They were huge and dark, shaped almost like bat wings, but vaguely insubstantial as if they were formed out of mist. Thin tracings of silver glimmered faintly in the webbing.

What they were about to do seemed suddenly more real and immediate. She tried to remind herself that she'd done this before, but then again, she'd been largely unconscious for the majority of that trip. Rose drew in a sharp breath.

Neku glanced down one last time for confirmation, and at her tight nod he stepped smoothly to the edge of the crenellations and without a moment of hesitation, stepped off the edge.

Rose choked on a gasp and her hands left his shoulders to wrap tightly around his neck as they dropped in a sudden rush. Clamping her jaw shut to suppress a shriek, she buried her face against his chest, then peeked out to watch the massive wings billow and catch the air, bearing them back up until they were level with the edge of the keep they had just left.

They hovered there a moment, his wings beating the air with slow, heavy strokes, and he looked down at her.

"You alright?" he asked. Though they were mere inches apart he pitched his voice low to carry under the rush of wind churned up from his buffeting wings.

She nodded and looked up, intending to ask him the same question, but the look on his face was answer enough.

His eyes were alight like she'd never seen them; the smile that stretched his mouth was wide and entirely genuine. His face was just inches from hers, and for a brief second she forgot she was hanging, suspended in the air above a lethal fall, supported only by his arms and a pair of insubstantial magical wings. Her heart thumped hard in her chest.

"I used to do this all the time," he said, his eyes sparkling. She imagined this must be how he used to look, before he took the weight of the world on his shoulders. His face took on a mischievous cast, and he glanced down toward the ground far below. "Do you trust me?"

She abruptly remembered where she was, and narrowed her eyes at him. "I said I did once. Don't make me regret it."

He gave a laugh, a *real* laugh. "Hold on tight," he warned, barely giving her time to react before launching them into a sickening free fall.

This time, she did scream, long and loud, as he tucked his wings tight to his body and let them hurtle down toward the ground, and if the screeching was right next to his ear, well, it was his own fault. The fall didn't last long enough for her scream to morph into real fear before he unfurled the wings again, and their headlong dive turned into a wide looping arc, bringing them up at an angle to soar out over the forest.

Rose's breath caught as he brought them down to skim over the treetops on the edge of the clearing, so close she could have reached out a hand to feel the leaves sweeping past had she been able to relinquish her death grip on Neku's neck. Instead she simply watched in amazement as the multicolored leaves swayed on their branches, disturbed by the gust of air that marked their passage. It was *beautiful.*

She glanced up at Neku's face and caught him watching

her, his eyes sparkling at her obvious delight. She grinned back.

After another loop around the meadow, Neku turned them to face south, rising further above the trees so he could see where they were going. His dark, misty wings took on a stronger, more purposeful beat, bearing them toward the rolling hills to the south.

With that, Rose was reminded of their purpose. While she still relished the feeling of soaring weightless through the air—both terrifying and exhilarating in equal measure—and her eyes still drank in the spectacular view below, her smile faded as she thought ahead to what would happen when they landed.

Neku had been reluctant to put their plan into motion so soon, pushing for at least another day of rest and discussion before moving forward down this inevitable path. But Rose had rested enough, and their discussions were going nowhere. She was not particularly good at sitting still; if there was something to be done, she wanted to be doing it, not talking about it. Besides, the Ma'ar was still out there somewhere, a thought that made her distinctly uncomfortable.

Personally, she thought Neku believed she was rushing into this too fast, without enough consideration, and maybe he thought she didn't fully grasp the enormity of what they were about to do. But while she may not have had ninety years to mull over the idea as he had, she still could plainly see that bringing the Drani'shadara back, as soon as possible, was the important first step of whatever might happen next. Besides, she still held out hope that Neku's way was not the only way.

Gripping her hands tight around his neck, she leaned

into the warmth of his chest. She would take everything as it came, she thought, and try not to get ahead of herself.

As the rolling hills beneath them grew in size the forest began to thin, eventually giving way to a small, tidy village. The houses were set close together, and the peaked roofs were colorful from their vantage high above. She could see people moving in the streets below. Not abandoned, then, she thought with a sigh of relief.

Neku carried them over the village in the blink of an eye and continued south, their path eventually merging with the shining body of a river, which wound its way through the trees and fields like a sinuous glittering snake. He bent his head close to Rose's.

"That's the Trelis River, the same one that eventually passes by Trelissar if you keep heading south," he said in a low voice. His mouth was close to her ear so she could hear him over the rush of wind, and she shivered a little as she felt his breath stir her hair.

"How far does the river go?" she asked.

"It's a major tributary of the Alerris River. If you follow it for another two hundred miles or so, you can see where they join. Then if you keep going another thousand miles further, it empties into the Etlass Sea. Fortunately, we're not going that far."

She looked up at him. "Have you ever flown that far?"

He looked back at her, and she thought she could see a hint of sadness behind the smile he gave her. "Of course."

She looked back down over the huge expanse of water beneath them, resting her head against his chest. He'd lost so much. The whole world had. The wind mixed together the strands of their hair, hers dark as night and his bright and shining white in the sunlight. They flew on.

As the river swept by, the banks dotted with small towns

and oddly-shaped boats moving ponderously through the water, Rose began to lose track of time. She stared out toward the distant horizon, her gaze unfocused as her eyelids began to grow heavy.

Lulled by the rhythm of Neku's beating wings, it wasn't until she felt something startlingly cold on her toes that she realized they had dropped so low. The cold of the water soaking through her shoe as they skimmed the surface of the river jerked her to wakefulness, and she yelped in surprise. Abruptly, Neku pulled them back up, rising to a safe distance above the water. Rose twisted in his arms, turning to look up at him.

With one glance at his face, she could see he was struggling. A thin sheen of sweat covered his forehead, and his eyes were wide, fixed doggedly ahead under a brow creased in concentration.

Oh no. She hadn't been paying attention. How long had he been like this?

"Neku," she said, struggling to keep the anxiety out of her voice. "Should we land?"

He spared a quick glance down at her. "I'm fine. We're close." He was quiet for a moment, and she could see he was concentrating hard on keeping them above the water. She felt a tremble run through his arms where they supported her back and legs.

When he spoke again, his voice was low. "I'll get us to the entrance. If I...if something happens, go in anyway. Don't wait for me to wake up. We're not safe out in the open, and I don't know how long the spell on your blood will hold."

Rose shivered in alarm. She hadn't thought of that. She couldn't be outside his castle if the spell gave out.

"Get the seed," he went on, his voice shaking slightly.

They began to drop again, and Neku altered his course toward the shore. The area was wooded again, no sign of civilization on this stretch of the river. His wing beats were wobbly as they began to gain height, and she clenched her hands tighter where they clasped around his neck, feeling suddenly nauseous.

Rose squeezed her eyes shut, willing herself to stay calm. He'd said they were close. Suddenly they dipped alarmingly to one side, and her eyes flew open just in time to see them clear the bank, rising at an awkward angle above the trees that crowded close, their roots twisting down into the water. She stifled a scream, her heart galloping madly in her chest.

The ground tilted again as they dipped precariously, and she tried not to look down at where the trees rushed by just below them, jagged branches reaching out as if trying to snag their clothing. Instead, she focused on his face, but rather than the reassurance she sought, her panic grew. He was pale now, his blue skin tinged with gray, his breathing labored. His eyes were narrowed to slits and focused almost entirely inward.

"Neku!"

"It's...that clearing ahead..." His words came out in breathless pants. Rose swung her head around frantically and caught a glimpse of a clearing in the trees ahead. His wing beats were slow now, jarring and unbalanced, barely keeping them above the trees. "Get...the seed, and I'll...get us back to the castle."

"Neku, you can't—"

"I *will*," he growled, and then she felt the arm that supported her legs go slack. Lurching as her weight shifted, she flailed briefly before wrapping her legs around his waist to take the strain off her arms as they floundered in the air.

With a jolt of terror she suddenly realized they weren't going to make it.

"Put us down!" she screamed.

They dipped—intentionally or not, Rose couldn't tell—and her clothes caught on the branches.

"*Hold on.*" Neku's voice was inhuman.

They fell.

Rose ducked her head, burying it into Neku's chest as they dropped, branches tearing sharply at her clothes and skin. His wings beat hard, once, slowing their progress, and then again, jerking them up even as gravity pulled them down.

The fall seemed to both last a lifetime and be over in seconds, and by the time they crashed to the ground with bruising force, Rose had lost track of which way was up and which was down. She lost her grip on Neku as the impact sent her tumbling downhill, and the last thing she remembered was the force of her head coming into contact with the unforgiving trunk of a tree.

31

YDENDA

In the confines of the catacombs, deep underneath the Trelissar Cathedral, it was dark all the time. Even the flickering torches set into the walls didn't afford enough light to chase away all the shadows, and it wasn't long before Ydenda lost all track of time. It was impossible to tell night from day, and the schedule they chose to follow when providing her with food did nothing to help.

The men-in-brown had stopped by often enough in the beginning, encouraging her to provide answers she didn't have to questions she didn't understand. But as it had become more and more apparent that either their methods weren't effective or she didn't have anything useful to provide them, even their visits had become more infrequent.

She spent most of her time sleeping, if one could use that word to describe the fitful dozes she drifted in and out of. Strange dreams of twisted shadows danced on the back of her eyelids as she slept, and half-forgotten memories clouded her mind when she woke, until she could no longer tell which was which. Sometimes she thought she was losing what remained of her sanity, down in the darkness.

Ydenda was fairly sure she was awake now though, as she lay listlessly on her side in a now familiar alcove formed where the edge of a tomb met the stone wall. She felt safest there, with the wall blocking one side and the tomb another, and a slight overhang from the lip of the tomb above her head. It meant she could at least hear if someone was coming.

Not that she could go far, anyway. Her right ankle was secured by a heavy iron manacle, which was attached to a long chain that led to an iron spike driven deep into the wall. She did have a decent length of chain to work with, long enough to reach the makeshift privy they had set up for her. It was also long enough to reach to the other side of the catacombs, from which point she could just hear the voices of the men talking in the library above if she listened very hard. All attempts to remove the manacle had been entirely futile though, and the iron weight around her ankle was heavy and discouraged moving unless she needed to.

Still disoriented from sleep, she stretched weakly and, with great effort, hauled herself up to a sitting position. She had no idea how long it had been since she'd last seen another person. Long enough for the cuts on her face to stop hurting, though the abrasions on her back still throbbed. Some of the welts might still be oozing, she thought, since she still often woke to find her shirt stuck to the skin of her back in places.

Her shirt, like the rest of her clothing, was filthy. It was a miracle, she thought idly, that her wounds hadn't become infected. Though, considering the pain in her back, she supposed that might not be true. She wasn't sure she cared. It seemed the longer she'd been here, the more her normally positive outlook had begun to fade, and now she wasn't sure there was anything left.

Tiredly, she let herself slide back down to lay flat again. There was no reason to be awake. Maybe she would sleep through the next delivery of food. That was okay. Perhaps if she slept through enough meals, she could just quietly die down here.

She wasn't sure why the Ma'ar was keeping her alive anyway; clearly, she didn't know anything of use to him. And he'd already found the glass vial, so she didn't even have that to drive her anymore. Though she did still feel a slight pleasure at the fact that he didn't seem to know what it was any more than she did. She wished she'd been able to get the vial to Rose. Ydenda still felt that inexplicable drive, the instinctive knowledge that she was missing something important.

But none of that mattered now. She had failed in her task, whatever it was, and there was something surprisingly reassuring in the knowledge that there was nothing the Ma'ar or his men could do or say that would make her spill her secrets, since she had no idea what they were.

Time passed as she lay still, the cold floor pressing painfully against her wounded back, but the insistent pressure of her full bladder kept sleep at bay. She ignored it for a time, until the discomfort grew to the point that she groaned and slowly began to push herself upright again.

Her legs were unstable beneath her, and she used the tomb for support, leaning heavily against it until she regained her balance. The length of chain scraped loudly as she hobbled slowly across the floor; there was no stealth to be found down here.

After relieving herself in the bucket they had provided in an alcove set further down the hallway—though not quite far enough to contain the smell—she dragged herself wearily back toward her alcove. It was only as she stopped to lean against the wall and the clanking of the chain fell silent that she could suddenly hear the voices, faint from above.

She debated dragging herself back across the corridor as far as her chain would permit so she could hear more clearly, and had just decided she couldn't be bothered to care when a new, deeper voice joined the mix.

The Ma'ar.

She perked up, almost despite herself, and began to slowly make her way across the hallway.

The Ma'ar's lackeys were always up there; they seemed to have turned the small library into a makeshift headquarters, and she heard them conversing often enough. She wasn't sure how many of them there were. When they came down to interrogate her or provide food, they were always dressed immaculately in forgettable brown attire and their faces blurred together in her mind.

But visits from the Ma'ar were rare, or at least rarely overheard. And as much as she had convinced herself she'd given up, at the sound of his voice her feet still dragged her across the hall to better hear them. If there was any new information, any chance to retrieve her vial, she wanted to know.

She hobbled to the outer limits of her chain and the grinding links fell silent. With the voices above raised in agitation, she didn't have to strain this time to hear them, and she found herself holding her breath as she leaned against the far wall.

"—can't go in!"

It was one of the Ma'ar's lackeys, and Ydenda started. She had never before heard one of the men-in-brown raise his voice to the Ma'ar.

The Ma'ar's reply was a deep growl.

"We don't *need* to go in. We wait for her to come out and take her then."

"With the gatekeeper there? He'll never let you take her. He'll fly away with her like he did at the bridge."

Ydenda's breath caught. They could only be talking about Rose. She leaned as far forward as she could, cursing the shackle on her ankle and listening intently.

"He's weakened," the Ma'ar said dismissively. "I'm not sure he's even entirely sane. He can't protect her from *all* of us."

"He's still *magical,*" the other voice protested. "I say we stick to our original plan, and use the woman. We can't stand against the gatekeeper, unless you're prepared to sacrifice the whole crew."

The long pause following this statement was reply enough.

Where, Ydenda thought, mentally urging them to keep talking, *where is she?*

"Recovering the girl is non-negotiable, and worth any cost," the Ma'ar said after the pause, his tone dangerously calm. "You've known that from the beginning," he continued, his voice starting to rise. "Without her blood we can't cross through, and while *you* are welcome to stay here and rot with the rest of the world, *I* am going to the Garden of Blue, and I will be leaving this God-forsaken, Rot-infested death trap, one way or another!"

Ydenda's heart froze in her chest like a block of solid ice as the pieces fell into place. The voices from above continued to argue, but she was no longer listening.

Rose was a planeswalker, and in a rush of remembrance, Ydenda realized what exactly that *meant.* It meant the girl could cross between the worlds, and anyone with access to her blood could do the same. *That* was why the

Ma'ar wanted her. He was going to use her blood to cross over!

With a sharp exhale, Ydenda sank to her knees. But that wouldn't work, she realized with a sort of gasping laugh. How could he not realize that? The Rot was *in* him, it was in all of them. It was in the very air they breathed! He thought he was abandoning a sinking ship, but really he would just spread the Rot and doom the sister world as well. Her laugh broke on a sob. How had she not realized this before? It was so obvious. Why else would he want the girl?

Her mind was spinning, thoughts racing furiously, but somehow she felt more clear and lucid than she had in years. What had the Ma'ar said? The Garden of Blue. That must be where Rose would go, with the gatekeeper. Briefly, Ydenda wondered why, why the girl was even still here, in this world, if she had found her way back to the gate. There was still clearly more going on than she knew.

But it didn't matter. Ydenda had to get there. She had to warn them. She had to—the drive hit her more than ever— she had to get the vial. She racked her brain, her breath coming fast and sharp, but there was still nothing there. She couldn't remember what the vial was or where it had come from. But she knew it was important, *knew* it. She had to get out of here.

Suddenly, Ydenda became aware that the voices above had stopped. Silence reigned now, and her breath slowed as she slumped back against the wall. She glared down at her ankle, where the metal of the shackle gleamed in the flickering torchlight. Who was she kidding? There was no way out of this. The best she could do was hope that the gatekeeper was strong enough to defend Rose and protect her from the Ma'ar. That, and hope her instincts were wrong and the vial wasn't necessary to whatever they were doing.

Tiredly, Ydenda pushed off from the wall and dragged herself back to the relative safety of her tomb. She slid down the side, trying to keep the raw skin of her back from rubbing on the stone as she did so, and curled into a ball. She wondered what the gatekeeper was like. She'd never met him, at least, not that she remembered, although she knew his castle wasn't that far from her village. The Ma'ar had suggested that he wasn't entirely sane. She wondered if that was related to whatever had set off the Rot in the first place, and she desperately hoped he was stable enough to protect Rose from the Ma'ar and get her back to her own world.

As her brain began to grow foggy with sleep again, Ydenda wondered idly why she cared what happened. The Rot was spreading, any fool could see that, and if her world collapsed, she would die with it, and willingly. There was no escape for her.

She was moments away from oblivion when the sound of footsteps on the stairs roused her again. *It's just food*, she reassured herself as the vestiges of sleep fled, but her body stiffened anyway, her shoulders hunched against the pain in her back.

The steps grew louder as they reached the bottom of the stairs and echoed through the corridor. Ydenda didn't realize how tightly her whole body had been clenched until a pair of shiny brown shoes stopped in front of her and a metal tray was deposited on the stone floor by her face. Drawing in a deep breath and trying to still her shaking hands, she pushed up to sit, then hauled herself up to stand.

Without a word of acknowledgment, the man in brown turned to leave, and the words were out of her mouth before she had the conscious thought to speak.

"What's in the Garden of Blue?"

Immediately she cringed, wishing she could pull the words back, but the damage had already been done. The man turned back toward her, his face expressionless.

"You were listening." His voice was as blank and emotionless as his face, and Ydenda found this almost more frightening than if he had looked angry. She shrank back, flattening herself against the side of the tomb.

The man cocked his head to study her, his empty gaze taking her in from her disheveled hair, down her torn, stained clothing, and ending on her shackled ankle.

"No matter," he said, raising his gaze back to meet her eyes. "I don't think we have use of you any longer anyway."

"What do you mean?" Ydenda's voice came out in a whisper.

The man ignored her question and leaned closer. Some nameless emotion flickered in the depths of his eyes, and Ydenda tried to lean away but there was nowhere to go. When he spoke again, it was as though he was talking to himself.

"I'd dispose of you now, but he hasn't given the order yet. And you know how he gets..." He leaned back and gave her a mocking smile. "But I'm sure I'll be seeing you again soon." He turned away again, and before Ydenda could think her hand shot out and grabbed hold of his wrist.

"Wait—" she gasped, and then it happened.

He turned toward her again, his face twisted in a snarl, and without conscious thought Ydenda reached down inside herself, into the well of terror and fear and hatred that resided there, and she drew it up, and she *pushed* it out. And before her horrified eyes, the deep black ropes of Rot that twisted around her arm began to move. It came alive, swelling and expanding like a living thing, before twisting, writhing across her skin until it crossed over where her grasping fingers clung to his wrist. It happened so fast, wrapping around his arm in a viscous black mass, disappearing under his clothes only to reappear moments later, twining around his neck, and when his mouth opened on a scream the tendrils plunged forward and disappeared down his throat in a nightmarish frenzy. The scream stopped abruptly on a choking gurgle, and Ydenda stared in horror as the brown irises of the man's eyes turned black. His skin began to shrivel and blacken, as if all the moisture had been leached out, and then he collapsed, as if there had never been any life in him at all.

Ydenda snatched her hand away as he fell, landing heavily in her forgotten tray of food. The contents splattered everywhere, but she didn't notice, instead staring in disbelief at her own hand, which looked exactly the way it always had, ropy black marks set motionless into her skin. She wouldn't have believed it was real if it weren't for the lifeless body sprawled in front of her, its skin darkened and withered.

It took Ydenda a moment to realize the sharp, panicked sounds she heard were her own breaths, and then she forced herself into action, searching frantically in the man's pocket for the keys, fumbling them one after another into the lock with shaking hands until the manacle gave way, then staggering down the hallway without a backward glance. Up the stairs, through the empty library, and out the door into the cold night air.

32

ROSE

When Rose cracked open her eyes, the edges of the world were blurry and her vision seemed to pulse in time with the pounding in her head. Quickly, she closed them again, much preferring darkness to the piercing light.

She hurt all over. What had happened? She laid as still as possible, piecing together recent events—talking to Neku on the balcony, standing on top of the keep with the forest spread out below them, the thrilling flight—*oh no*. Her eyes flew open as it all came crashing back, and she jerked herself upright, bracing against a surge of nausea. Forcing it down and squinting, she scanned the surrounding forest. They'd been separated in the crash—where was he?

Glancing around as her vision began to clear and her stomach settled, she realized that the light wasn't piercing after all. It was actually rather dim here on the forest floor; the sunlight that spilled through the canopy to light her surroundings was soft and diffuse. Late afternoon, maybe?

Later than it should be, either way. Neku had said it wasn't safe out here. Did he mean the Ma'ar? Or the Rot? Or something even worse?

There was no doubt the Ma'ar would have been watching the castle. When they left, would he have known where they were going? How long would it take him or his men in brown to show up?

She searched the surrounding trees, suddenly uncomfortably aware of just how vulnerable and exposed she was without Neku's protection. Not that he was particularly useful if he was unconscious.

God, she *hated* feeling like some kind of damsel in distress. She had always been perfectly capable of taking care of herself in the past. *Not that I ever expected to be faced with knife-wielding politicians*, she thought ruefully. Besides, if the Ma'ar showed up, it probably wouldn't be on his own, and she didn't think any preparation or training would enable her to stand up to a group of them. She needed magic. She needed Neku.

The tree she had been laying against sat at the base of an incline, and Rose turned and began to trudge up the gentle slope, hoping against hope that she hadn't fallen far. As she moved, her joints popped and her sore muscles protested. Everything hurt. She must be bruised and scratched all over.

With that thought, she looked down at her hands in alarm. No blood, she thought with a mixture of relief and curious appraisal. They were scratched, there was no doubt about that, but the marks were all sealed white lines, glowing faintly with an iridescent gleam where the blood should have been oozing out. She touched her face carefully and felt the same thing. Slightly raised lines crossing her cheeks, a rough patch from an abrasion, but dry, no sign of blood. She breathed a sigh of relief. The spell still held. There was still time.

Where *was* he?

Using a low branch to pull herself up, Rose crested the

top of the slope and stopped dead. The tree directly in front of her was withered and twisted, its trunk so black it seemed to pull the surrounding light into itself. She skittered back a few paces, nearly falling back down the slope before catching herself on a branch.

It was a whole stand of trees, she saw, at least a half dozen standing in a semicircle that had succumbed to the Rot. They stood, twisted and dead, with their bare blackened branches reaching toward the sky. Rose took a deep breath and carefully sidestepped them. She wondered what would happen if she touched the Rot directly. Would the spell still protect her even then?

Above the ridge and away from the Rotted trees, Neku wasn't hard to find, with his shining white hair spread around his head. It looked like a halo against the dark leaves that blanketed the forest floor, and Rose's relief when she saw it was palpable.

Unfortunately, he was still out cold.

She dropped to her knees beside him and carefully cleared the twigs and leaf debris from his hair and face. His breathing was even, at least, and his heartbeat strong and steady. He looked no worse for wear than the last two times she'd seen him like this.

Gingerly, Rose pulled Neku's hair away from his collar and examined the spot where the Rot protruded from his clothes to creep up his neck. Just as she had feared—it had definitely spread. It now climbed the entire column of his neck and ran behind his ear, disappearing into his hair. She swore softly, then lifted his hand where it lay by his side to examine it. The Rot had spread there as well, engulfing his wrist and creeping down his fingers.

Rose laid Neku's hand gently back on the ground by his side and rocked back on her heels. What should she do?

She could feel her anxiety rising as she considered her options.

On one hand, she didn't want to leave him alone in the forest. What if the Ma'ar showed up while she was gone? But on the other hand, he'd been adamant that she should enter the Garden right away. Surely that was the best thing she could do for him, for both of them.

Leaning over, Rose straightened Neku's clothes and his hair. She prayed he would wake up soon. Her decision was made, but she still hated the thought of leaving him here.

Briefly, she considered moving him to the Garden entrance, but quickly dismissed that thought. She had no way of moving him, short of dragging him, which seemed like a colossally bad idea. He would be fine where he was. He *would*, she told herself again, before rising to her feet and turning in a circle.

The realization came to her quite suddenly that she didn't know where to go. Panic rose sharply in her as she imagined wandering lost through the woods with no one to guide her, before she forced herself to take a breath and calm down. She pictured flying down the river, and seeing the Garden as they flew over the bank. She was pretty sure it had been to the east—or at least, they'd been facing that way when she'd seen the clearing through the trees. Her sense of direction was disoriented by the fall, but she was able to see the slant of the afternoon sun through the thick trees.

With a quick, nervous backward glance at Neku's motionless form, she took a deep breath and started through the trees to the east, one eye carefully watching for Rot as she maneuvered through the underbrush.

∽

In the end, it took Rose longer to find the Garden than she had anticipated. The Rot was thicker here than she had seen in the forest surrounding Neku's castle, and she had to take a confusing and circuitous route around clusters of decaying black trees to keep moving east. It was only when she was starting to think in earnest that she wouldn't be able to find the place—or at least, not before dark, when she certainly didn't want to be blundering about in a Rot-infested forest—that the trees gave way to a large, grassy clearing.

Relief flooded into her, as tangible as a living thing.

Finally.

Without pause, Rose headed into the clearing.

About a hundred feet into the tall grass stood a massive stone wall, which curved around in an unbroken line out of sight. Over the top of the wall spilled a profusion of vines and leaves, dotted with thick clusters of flowers in all shapes and sizes. The only thing the masses of foliage had in common was that they were all different shades of blue.

Trust everything in this world to be literal, Rose thought to herself with a smile.

But while the interior of the Garden spilled over the wall in a seemingly lush celebration of life, when she grew closer Rose could see that quite the opposite was true of the Garden's exterior. The large stones were pocked with Rot, light-swallowing splotches marring the wall like splatters of tar, thick and black.

Rose shuddered as she skirted the outside wall, moving around as it curved toward the south. It seemed like she'd trekked nearly a mile by the time the tall grass slowly transitioned to gravel, which in turn gave way to a path of large flagstones. She had to be getting somewhere.

Indeed she was, for only moments later the entrance rose into sight, a great, spiked wrought-iron gate that loomed over the path like the entrance to a haunted mansion. *This* was one of the Drani'shadara's favorite places? Perhaps she didn't have such a clear impression of the creature as she thought.

The gate, too, was choked with cascading blue ivy. It appeared to be free of Rot, though it was no less intimidating for it. The flagstones here formed a path that led straight out from the gate back toward what was likely a road. That, Rose assumed, was probably the way normal people reached the Garden, not crashing through the trees like paratroopers.

Pausing in front of the gate, Rose looked back toward the forest. She knew now she would never be able to find Neku where she'd left him in the woods, especially not once full dark fell. She could only hope that he would regain consciousness soon and come find her here.

Heaving a sigh, she looked toward the gate again. Now that she'd actually arrived, she felt oddly reluctant to go in. It almost felt like if she entered the Garden, she was accepting her role as planeswalker, like it would become more real somehow. There was something...momentous about entering the Garden. Something intangible, that Rose couldn't define but could feel in her bones. Or maybe in her blood.

With a deep breath, Rose reached out and caught hold of the heavy iron latch that secured the gate. She lifted it and gave a tug, and with a creak, the gate swung out. Forcing her feet into action, she stepped across the threshold, into the Garden of Blue.

And that's when everything changed.

33

ROSE

Rose wasn't sure what she had expected, but this wasn't it. One step into the Garden of Blue and it was like she'd entered another world. Again. The darkening twilight that had been descending like a blanket outside the wall disappeared between one step and the next, the sky brightening into a cloudless expanse of blue.

The Garden itself was a sight to behold. It had clearly at one point been filled with perfectly manicured beds, charming walking trails, and labeled displays featuring educational information on the many varieties of plant life. But now, untouched for over eighty years, it resembled more of a wild jungle than anything else.

Most of the beds were still in place, the raised borders barely visible beneath the profusion of plants that grew up and around the worn signs. The labels were still surprisingly bright and clear despite their age, yet still unreadable to Rose, written in the strange, symbolic language of this world. Generations of trees from young saplings to towering giants grew in random places, their trunks entwined with creeping exotic vines. Leaves of all shapes and sizes sprouted from weeds that choked the walking paths nearly beyond recognition, and an abundance of blooming flowers covered every available surface.

The cold air from outside the wall had vanished as well, replaced by a comfortable temperate breeze, the air heavily scented by an ever-changing parade of floral scents.

Rose stood and stared, her senses overwhelmed.

Between the temperature and the light, it was obvious that magic was still at work here, preserving and protecting the Garden, despite its overgrown and neglected appearance. And yet Rose wasn't sure if the Garden's most obvious and bizarre feature—its color—was magically enhanced or just a strange design choice made by its long-banished gardeners. Everything was blue.

Everything.

Every leaf, every branch, every tree and flower and paving stone and blade of grass. The array of different hues was astonishing—there were blooms ranging from the darkest of midnight blues to the faintest periwinkles, so pale they were nearly white. Bright, vivid cobalt leaves the size of dinner plates; thick gnarled trunks the color of faded denim. It was astounding.

When Rose bent down to look closely at a cluster of flowers scarcely larger than the dots on a pair of dice, her own clothing caught her eye and she froze in astonishment. Her pants, which she was pretty sure had previously been black, were now a dark navy blue; her green sweater was now the color of a ripe blueberry. Well, that certainly answered her question about the extent of magical enhancement.

She was so fascinated by her clothing that it took her a moment to realize that even her skin had changed. It was now a pale sky blue, reminiscent of Neku's skin.

Neku. Rose suddenly wished he was here to see this. Wished he was able to enter the Garden at all.

Quite suddenly, it occurred to her that this must be what the whole world had been like before the Rot. Because it wasn't just a visual change. The Garden *felt* different than the world outside. It was like a heaviness had been lifted, a vague oppressive feeling she hadn't even noticed was there until it was suddenly gone.

She'd seen the Rot, seen the way it swallowed trees and engulfed whole buildings, but she hadn't really understood the way it poisoned the very essence of the world. Her task suddenly seemed much more urgent.

Rising to her feet, Rose brushed the thin layer of blue dirt from her knees and turned to look around. Neku hadn't mentioned where exactly in the Garden he had left the seed, and she hadn't thought to ask. That suddenly seemed like a grave oversight. Though she hadn't imagined the place would be quite as large as it appeared.

Rose turned in a circle, then began to walk, slowly picking her way through the remnants of the overgrown trail. Or at least, where she thought the trail had been. As she walked, she tried to put herself in Neku's shoes. Where would he have put the seed?

He hadn't been in his right mind at the time, overcome with grief and loss and overwhelmed by Rot, his only thought focused on securing and protecting the seed. And yet, the spell he'd cast made it so no one could enter the Garden except for a planeswalker. He'd said that even he was unable to enter. So, would he have tried to hide the seed somewhere safe? Or would he have left it somewhere obvious, where it could be quickly found when the time was right?

Rose tilted her head back as she walked, taking in the

mass of blue foliage that towered overhead and pushed close on either side. Anything that might have been obvious eighty-seven years ago was surely overgrown now, swallowed whole by this blue jungle. And she wasn't even from this world. How could she possibly know what to look for?

And yet, the magic of this place was palpable. Between the warmly scented breeze, the bright light of day, and the colorful press of life on all sides, it was obvious that the seed was still here; its magic still intact. Despite the stress of the situation, and all the concerns and worries that had been accumulating over the past week, not to mention whatever might await her on the other side of the Garden's gate, Rose was finding it hard to hold on to those stresses here. Any doubts she may have had about why the Drani'shadara loved this place had vanished.

With each step she took deeper into the Garden, her mood lightened, and she wished even harder that Neku could be here to experience it with her. She wished her *family* could be here to experience it with her.

She pushed a branch out of her way, bright azure blossoms dripping in clusters from the tip. Blue had been her sister's favorite color. What would Lily have said about a garden like this? Before now, she couldn't have imagined her parents' response to any of her journey. Would they have focused on the danger? Would they have been awed by the majesty of the forests in this world? But here, in the Garden...she could picture it easily. She could imagine her mother wandering along the path, stopping every few feet to exclaim over a new species of flower she couldn't identify. Her father would have made corny blue jokes.

And if Neku were here with her, he would have understood the power of the magic in the air, and even though he'd been here before, probably countless times, he would have held her hand, and smiled at her in shared amazement.

Neku would have liked her family. And once they got past his bizarre appearance, she thought they would have liked him too.

The thought made her feel sad, as thinking of her family always did, but this time the melancholy wasn't bone deep, wasn't as debilitating as it had been. She wasn't sure how that made her feel. Did it mean she was forgetting her family? Moving on without them? Or was it perhaps the first sign that she was healing, maybe even finding a new purpose?

Rose's footsteps crunched on the layer of fallen blue leaves as she picked her way down the old path. The remains of an old decorative stone border were visible in random intervals in the brush to either side, and she followed the path where she could see it. It curved around in a gentle arc, which Rose thought must follow the outer wall that was no longer visible through the thick foliage. If she was just looping around the outside, would she eventually end up back at the gate where she'd started?

She supposed she'd find out.

Following the path, one eye taking in the amazing array of different flowers and plants surrounding her, the other watching out for anything seemingly out of the ordinary, her mind wandering and feeling fully relaxed and at peace for the first time in ages, Rose didn't notice anything out of the ordinary until the first piece of glass crunched underfoot.

She stopped, startled at the sound, then checked the bottom of her foot. To her relief, the shard hadn't pierced the thin sole of the slipper-like shoes she had borrowed from Ysenderia's closet in Neku's castle. Picking her way carefully through the thick weeds that choked the path, she caught sight of the next piece of glass before she could step on it. This one was a huge pane, pale translucent blue with thick veins of lead running through it, jagged on the edges and glittering in the light. It was impossible to tell how large it was, as the encroaching foliage had swallowed the majority of the pane, but from the edges that caught the light through the leaves, it looked easily the size of a car.

Rose glanced around, then looked up.

Rising out of the ground a little ways ahead of her was the thick wall of a curved building she hadn't even noticed through the overgrown foliage. And rising from the top of the wall, arcing up through the air in a majestic curve, rose the remains of the roof—a huge geodesic glass dome, fashioned out of hundreds of interlocking hexagonal panes, sealed together with thick lines of lead. Even in its current state—the majority of the panes broken or cracked, leading dull and pitted, trees pushing through the gaps to seek the sun—it was a sight to behold. Rose assumed it was originally some kind of climate-controlled greenhouse, and as she gazed up at the wreckage of glass and overgrown jungle that was clearly once the focal point of the entire Garden, she realized the huge building likely stood right in the center. If she had been the gatekeeper, looking for the perfect place to leave the Drani'shadara's seed to make sure it could be easily found, that would be the ideal spot.

Her tentative optimism at finding the seed's hopeful location turned to dismay as she looked down at the ground. While she could see the gaping hole in the wall of the greenhouse that must have once held a door, the path between her and the entrance was littered with broken glass and debris. It would be like navigating a minefield. Especially wearing thin-soled slippers. Rose groaned aloud.

She wondered what on earth could have happened here. With the glass strewn over the ground so far from where the dome had originally stood, it almost looked like some kind of explosion had taken place.

Reaching up, she caught hold of a branch and slowly began to maneuver her way forward. Passing herself along, hand over hand on low branches and trailing vines, she tested her balance as she skirted around vast piles of smashed glass.

By the time she reached the missing door, Rose's legs were shaking with the stress of forging a precarious trail through the debris. Her relief at reaching the entrance was short lived, as the smashed glass continued on inside the structure as well, and what was more, whatever paths may have at one point existed inside the domed building had been completely lost to time. It was just a huge hill covered by a solid mass of blue jungle.

Rose searched through the chaos for some kind of order, and a moment later her eyes lighted on a glint of crumbling stone. Picking her way forward gingerly, she found a flight of wide stone steps, almost entirely engulfed by a thick carpet of blue moss and leafy vines, that rose up and away toward what must be the center of the greenhouse.

She found the mossy edge of one stair and started to ascend, moving slowly to watch for glass and slippery patches. There was no railing, nothing to hold on to, and the stairs were only visible here and there, crumbling in other areas where the growing roots had undermined their integrity.

At long last, Rose crested the last of the stairs and the ground leveled out. Up here the trail was still visible, and it led away from the stairs, winding around a series of very strange looking blue cactus-like plants, with bulbous bodies and long, deadly-looking spines.

She had to be close to the center now, and she began to get a little nervous, the anticipation growing as she closed in on her goal. The stone walkway was almost entirely clear up here, since the bulbous plants seemed content not to spread, just growing large and fat in their blue sandy spaces. There was no broken glass here either, having all fallen down the hill or been washed away in the—did it rain in the Garden? Rose didn't know. What she *did* know was that she had to be getting close.

Up until now, she'd been able to *see* the effects of magic around her—the way her blood had shimmered when Neku cast his spell; the dark, mist-like wings that rose like an apparition from between his shoulder blades; the way the Garden shone in the daylight despite the falling dusk outside. And yet she'd never been able to *feel* the magic, not the way she realized she could now—like a deep wordless vibration in her bones, a hum of power deep within the earth itself. It was a strange, reassuring feeling.

The path wound around in a wandering, circuitous loop, clearly carefully designed so one could see the strange plants to their best advantage. Rounding a display of large soft-looking plants with long pointy spikes that rather resembled giant vicious pale-blue marshmallows, the center of the dome came quite suddenly into view.

Rose stopped, her mouth falling open.

Because there, standing quite still with her back to Rose stood a tall, thin woman with long tangles of wild hair, blue so dark it was almost black.

Rose's voice, when she found it, was shaky and uncertain.

"Ydenda?"

34

ROSE

Rose's mind was racing, thoughts tumbling over each other, even before the woman turned slowly to face her. Why was she here? *How* did she get here? And the fact that she was here at all must mean—

Was she a *planeswalker*? Could that be possible? Neku had said—

All thoughts flew from Rose's head when the woman turned fully and Rose saw her face. Ydenda looked *terrible*. She was covered in dark bruises, angry abrasions marking her cheek, the shine of unshed tears glimmering in the woman's mismatched eyes. Her dark hair was matted with blood. Rose stifled a gasp, wanting to reach out, but forcing herself to remain where she was, unsure how the other woman would react to her presence.

As it turned out, there was no reason to worry. With a sob, Ydenda threw herself at Rose, wrapping the younger woman in a crushing embrace, and with a surge of relief, Rose returned the hug just as tightly.

"You made it," Ydenda said, pulling her back to hold at

arm's length. Her voice was scratchy. "You're safe. I've been so worried."

What? Rose scarcely knew where to start. "Why are you here? Do you—how did you—" She stopped and took a breath. "What happened to you? Are you *okay?*"

A shadow darkened Ydenda's eyes. "I'm okay." Her voice was soft. "I'll be okay."

"Why are you here? Not that I'm not thrilled to see you," Rose amended quickly, "but I—"

She broke off abruptly when the tears filling the other woman's eyes spilled over, leaving tracks through the dirt and blood that stained her face. "I don't *know!*" Her wail was plaintive, and Rose could see fear in her eyes, an expression that looked out of place on a face that had always seemed to be smiling. Before she could respond, Ydenda took her hand and pulled her forward, and for the first time Rose noticed what had been previously hidden from view behind the woman's body.

"I don't *know* why I'm here," she repeated. "I came for you. What *is* this?"

Rose stared, completely overwhelmed, her gaze transfixed on the sight before her.

The path spread out in front of her in a large circle, with multiple other paths continuing off down the hill on the other side. In the middle of the circular walkway was what appeared to be a large stone sundial, built of thick solid stone. Its crumbling edges and faded paint were the only signs of age; the markings around the edges of the dial were still vaguely visible and the heavy base still looked solid. But on top of the thick round plate, where the shadow-casting pointer must have at one time sat, instead there laid an enormous, oblong *something.*

Any concern Rose may have had about not recognizing

the seed when she saw it suddenly struck her as absurd. There was nothing else like this in the world, in either world, and she knew this immediately and with certainty.

The seed was large, bigger even than an ostrich egg, and oval rather than round. At first glance it appeared to be carved with intricate swirling patterns, but when she leaned in closer she could see the designs were moving, swirling slowly like the patterns that showed in Neku's skin when he moved. It was *beautiful*.

It took Rose a moment before she realized that it was the first thing she'd seen since entering the Garden that wasn't blue. Even Ydenda was blue, her piercing red eye now a blindingly bright cobalt and the unmarred skin of her face the same pale blue as Rose's. Though now that she noticed it, the thick black Rot that bisected her face was still solid black, not a hint of color visible.

But the seed...it was filled with color. Its body was a pale shimmering green, and the slowly eddying swirls shifted colors as they moved—from soft pale lavender to dark forest green to rusty orange before shifting back. She'd never seen anything like it. And the power that emanated from it was so dense, so *present*, that she felt like she could feel it vibrating in her bones.

Rose tore her eyes from the hypnotizing swirl of colors in the seed and looked at Ydenda, who was also staring, transfixed. Her expression was heart-wrenching—a mixture of awe and confusion and sadness and loss. It was an expression Rose had never seen on the woman's face.

With a sudden jerk of alarm, Rose remembered what Neku had said about the Garden and the spell that protected it. There weren't supposed to *be* any planeswalkers in this world.

"You haven't touched it, have you?" she asked Ydenda,

looking at the seed in horror. What if she was too late, and the seed had been corrupted before she'd even gotten there?

Ydenda shook her head, confused, and Rose let out a slow breath.

"I haven't touched anything. What is it?" the woman asked again, her voice a whisper.

"It's the Drani'shadara's seed," Rose said hesitantly, unsure if her words would mean anything.

Ydenda's expression grew alarmed, and she took a step back. "The *seed?* What is it doing here? Why has no one resurrected the Drani'shadara?" Her alarm faded a second later, replaced with confusion, as if her own words didn't make sense to her.

Rose blew out a breath. "It's a long story. You'd better come with me." She tilted her head as she looked at the other woman. "How did you get here?"

Ydenda furrowed her brow. "I came from Trelissar. I took a Millipede. It's not far."

"No, I mean the Garden. How did you get in?"

"What do you mean? I just walked through the gate. I was looking for you."

It was true then. Uncertainly, Rose said, "Did you...did you know you were a planeswalker?"

Ydenda's baffled and confused expression answered her question quite clearly before she even responded.

"What?"

Rose shook her head. "There's too much to explain. We need to go. Neku—the gatekeeper—should be waiting for us outside the gate. He'll explain everything. He'll know what to do."

He'd better, she thought. Just when things were starting to make sense, everything got turned on its head again. She should have known it wouldn't be as simple as she'd have liked.

And yet, even if she had no idea what was going on, Rose couldn't deny that she was beyond thrilled to see her friend again. Even if Ydenda seemed to know even less than she did. Reaching out, she gripped the woman's hand again and pulled her forward into another embrace.

"I'm really, really, *really* happy to see you," she said.

Ydenda smiled, the expression erasing the shadows from her eyes and giving Rose a glimpse of the woman who had been so kind to her what seemed like an age ago. Her voice, when she spoke, was warm and musical. "You have no idea."

∽

If being reunited with her friend wasn't joy enough, Ydenda led Rose back down the hill on a path that was blissfully free of broken glass. The dome on this side was largely intact, and therefore the stairs, while still largely overgrown with moss, were at least free of dangerous debris.

Rose had rolled up the hem of her oversized sweater and wrapped the seed to the best of her ability in the excess fabric. The seed wasn't entirely covered, but with Ydenda avoiding it as if it were a bomb that would detonate with her touch, it was the best she could do. She gripped it tightly in both hands as they descended. Where the seed wasn't covered by her shirt, it felt smooth and hard in her hands, slightly warm to the touch, and the swirling designs pulled at her attention until she had to force herself to look down at the stairs to keep from falling. Ydenda's uncorrupted arm was threaded through hers as they descended together, lending support and reassurance that Rose was pretty sure went both ways.

They didn't talk as they went. Rose's attention was divided between the seed and the treacherous path, but the questions were again piling up in her head. How had Ydenda not known she was a planeswalker? Yet the woman had been able to identify *Rose* as a planeswalker when they'd first met. And it was clear from Ydenda's bleeding wounds and the Rot that covered much of her visible body that she had no spell protecting her.

Besides, Ydenda hadn't recognized the seed for what it was, and yet she'd come looking for Rose. How had she known to look here? Why was she looking in the first place?

Rose kept her questions to herself. Every time she glanced sideways at Ydenda's face she glimpsed the woman's furrowed brow and introspective look. It looked like Ydenda was having as much trouble processing the situation as Rose was. They would talk again when they were safely back at Neku's castle, seed in hand. There would be time to talk then, to figure out a new strategy. Besides, Rose thought with a sudden burst of hope, with *two* planeswalkers, surely they could figure out a better plan, a way to keep Neku from sacrificing himself. Between the three of them, they would find a solution. They just had to get back to the castle.

Lost in her thoughts, Rose almost didn't notice they were off the stairs and back into the minefield of broken glass that framed the entrance to the domed building until Ydenda gave her arm a tug. She stumbled slightly to the left, narrowly missing the shard of glass protruding from the ground where she'd been about to step.

She regained her balance and they proceeded slowly, attention focused on their feet as they stepped carefully, helping each other through the debris. Rose had grown so accustomed to the silence between them that she was surprised when Ydenda spoke.

The other woman reached out and gently touched an abrasion on Rose's cheek. "What happened to you? You look...different than the last time I saw you."

Rose suspected she didn't just mean the cuts and bruises. She gave a slight shrug and smiled wryly. "I...*we*... fell out of the sky." She gave a shaky laugh at the other woman's confused expression. "A lot has happened since I left you."

Before she could stop herself, the story seemed to pour out, or at least as much of it as she could tell. She left out Neku's story, and his plan with the seed—that could wait until they were back at the castle—but she told Ydenda about her trip to Trelissar, her run-in with the Ma'ar, and all that had happened since then, ending with their flight and terrifying crash in the forest.

Ydenda didn't interrupt as she talked, and Rose could see from her expression that the woman was trying hard to absorb the new information and piece it together with what she knew.

When the tale eventually slowed to a halt, Ydenda turned to Rose, sorrow on her face. "I'm so sorry," she said sadly. "I should never have let you leave. I shouldn't have told you to seek out the King. I just..." She blew out her breath. Rose had never seen the woman look so uncertain. "I just...have feelings about things sometimes, you know? I can't always remember...things I think I'm supposed to. And I got used to following my gut. I was wrong this time."

Rose was shaking her head. "No, none of this was your fault. And there was no way to know what the Ma'ar was really after."

The color seemed to drain out of Ydenda's face. "I forgot to tell you. He knows you're here. That's why I came. He knows you were coming here, and he wants your blood, to cross the gate, and—"

"I know," Rose said soothingly. "I know." She had never seen Ydenda so agitated. She seemed much more serious and less self-assured than Rose remembered. What had happened to the unfailingly positive, irreverent woman she had left in the Broken City?

Come to think of it, why had Ydenda left the Broken City in the first place? If she was trailing Rose, and had followed her to Trelissar...

"What happened to you in Trelissar?" Rose asked, not sure she wanted to hear the answer to her question.

Ydenda looked down at the ground, then took Rose's arm and started walking again, pulling her along. They had passed the broken glass from the ruined dome by now and strolled together along the path that led back toward the gate.

They walked in silence for a minute, and Rose didn't push her, but eventually Ydenda began to talk. Her story was jumbled and confusing, much like Ydenda herself, but Rose got the gist. Her hands clenched around the seed as Ydenda described her time in the city. Her description was vague, but the marks on her face spoke volumes, and from the way she walked, stiffly and carefully as if her clothes rubbed painfully on her skin, Rose got the impression there was plenty more evidence from her time with the Ma'ar that wasn't visible.

Ydenda glossed over her escape, and Rose had the feeling that something important was missing there as well, but she spoke at length about a missing vial that had apparently been confiscated by the Ma'ar. Rose wasn't sure what she was referring to, and Ydenda herself didn't seem clear on this, but she was insistent that it was important.

Rose hoped Neku would know what she was talking about.

She gritted her teeth through Ydenda's story, but when the woman stopped talking Rose swallowed her irate anger and simply said, "I'm so sorry." From Ydenda's stiff posture she could tell that neither pity nor sympathy would be welcomed, so she contented herself with a tight squeeze of the woman's arm, which was promptly returned with a grateful glance.

They fell into silence again as the path curved along toward the gate, and Rose's anxiety began to mount again as she thought about what awaited them outside. Would the Ma'ar be there? Would Neku? Was he alright? *Please let him be alright.* Come to think of it, how was he going to be able to get them both back to the castle? Rose didn't think he would be able to fly with both of them—she wasn't even sure he would be able to fly with just her—and she certainly wasn't willing to leave her friend behind now. There had to be a way she could save them both. There *had* to be.

∽

At long last, the gate drew into sight in the distance, its heavy iron bars a threatening contrast to the peaceful magic of the Garden. Rose's nerves were stretched thin with worry, and she gripped tight to the seed, both she and Ydenda leaning on each other for support.

In the distance, through the thick bars, Rose could see that full dark had fallen—how long had she been in here, anyway? A shadowed figure was visible through the bars, but his features were unrecognizable in the dark. Rose tensed. Was it Neku? The Ma'ar?

They drew closer, their footsteps slow and silent on the

thick blue mat of undergrowth, traces of stone peeking through the dense foliage. Rose held her breath, her eyes fixed on the shadowed figure, her hands tight on the seed.

One step, then another, and then—there! Was that a glint of white? Between one step and the next, Neku's familiar face came into view, his curtain of white hair gleaming in the blue light that spilled from the Garden to cast a pool of dim illumination through the bars of the gate. She saw his eyes light up when he caught sight of her.

Relief crashed over her in a wave. He was *here*. He was *okay*. She picked up her pace, tears pricking her eyes as the fear and worry melted away. She had made it half a dozen steps toward the gate when she suddenly realized that Ydenda was no longer at her side.

Pulling up short, Rose turned to look back.

Ydenda was frozen a few paces back, her eyes wide and fixed on the figure behind the gate. Her mouth opened, then closed, then opened again on a voice that was tremulous and shaky like Rose had never heard it.

"Nekuthaedris?"

Rose turned to look at Neku, mere steps away through the gate, and found him staring past her at Ydenda. His face was frozen in shock, and his hands where they gripped the bars of the gate were white-knuckled and trembling.

Rose looked back and forth between the two uncertainly. "Neku?" she asked softly.

His eyes strayed to hers for just a moment, the bewilderment and confusion clear in the second before his gaze locked back on Ydenda. His voice, when he spoke, was hoarse with disbelief.

"*Ysenderia?*"

35

ROSE

At the sound of the familiar name, Rose nearly lost her grip on the seed. She spun around to face Ydenda. "*Ysenderia?*"

The woman's eyes were huge, and Rose could see the moment that understanding began to dawn on her face.

"That...that was my name...wasn't it?" Her voice was barely above a whisper. Her eyes were fixed on Neku and the mixture of hope and desperation in her eyes was painful to watch.

She took a small step forward. "I know you," she began slowly. "I *know* I do...but I can't *remember.*" Ydenda's voice broke on the word and Rose's heart went out to her.

So many pieces were falling into place for Rose—Ydenda's memory loss and confusion, her cryptic comments that even she didn't seem to understand, the harsh lines of Rot that bisected her features. And yet even now, the pieces were missing for Ydenda—*Ysenderia*—she corrected herself. The night of the failed Ceremony had affected her irreparably. Rose looked to Neku and shivered, thinking of how close he had come to suffering the same fate. By the look on his face, it was clear his thoughts were running along similar lines. His hands were gripping the bars of the gate so hard his knuckles were white, as if he wanted to pull them apart and rush in.

A choked sob sounded behind her, and she swung back to face her friend again. "*Why* can't I remember?" the woman asked, her voice pleading.

Rose moved then, shifting the bulk of the seed to one hand and holding it out to the side so she could put an arm around her friend.

"He's the gatekeeper," she said softly, "You used to be close friends. You're a planeswalker, and there was an accident." She hesitated, unsure of how much to say, but she could feel Ydenda holding very still, listening to her. "It was many years ago; you and Neku were trying to contain the Rot, and the Drani'shadara died and you couldn't resurrect it. He—Neku—hid the seed here and cast a spell to protect it, and that's why I'm here, to take the seed and resurrect the Drani'shadara."

She squeezed her friend tighter, her voice breaking. "That's why you know this place. You've been here before, and that's why you know Neku. He was your friend." She pulled back to look into Ydenda's face. Tears streamed down the woman's cheeks, but Rose could see that she still didn't remember.

"He thought you were dead," she said softly. Ydenda's expression was a study in frustration and anguish, but it was still clear as she looked at Neku that she remembered *something*, however vague. Rose gave her a gentle push toward the gate, and Ydenda started to move forward hesitantly.

Rose could see the shine of tears on Neku's face too, and when Ydenda reached the gate he put his hands through the bars and held them out. Ydenda put her hands in his, linking together two pale blue hands and two twisted with black Rot.

"It really *is* you," Neku said in wonder. "I had no idea."

Ydenda didn't respond, just stood still as tears continued to spill down her cheeks.

Rose shifted the seed back into the safety of a two-handed grip, and Neku's eyes caught the movement, shifting to focus on the seed. His expression grew serious as he seemed to realize where they were and what they were doing.

"You got it," he breathed. Then his eyes widened in alarm, just as Rose's had, and he darted a quick look at Ydenda before looking back at Rose. She gave her head a quick shake. *It's safe. Safe as it can be.*

He turned to Ydenda again, his eyes pleading. "Come with us, back to the castle, and I'll tell you everything. I'll help you remember."

Neku looked to Rose, and she nodded. She wasn't letting Ydenda out of her sight, not after whatever the Ma'ar had done to her.

"Will you come with us?" she asked, and Ydenda nodded, smiling tremulously. Neku gave her hands a squeeze before releasing them, then stepped back to give them space to open the gate.

Rose turned back one last time to take in the beauty of the Garden. She tried desperately to fix it in her memory. She didn't ever want to forget this place, its beauty and magic. Though she supposed she was taking the magic with her, she thought, gripping the seed tightly. Even still, magic had been flowing through the roots of this place for nearly ninety years now. It would take more than removing the seed to take that away.

Taking a deep breath to steel herself, she gave Ydenda's

arm a squeeze before reaching for the latch of the gate. The heavy iron swung open smoothly despite the creak of the hinges, and the two women exchanged a glance before moving forward together to where Neku stood waiting on the other side.

It came like an audible *snap,* only felt rather than heard, reverberating in Rose's bones as if she'd been slapped. All the breath fled from her lungs, and she saw Neku's eyes widen in alarm. In the same moment, she felt a searing heat on her palms and looked down to see the colors on the seed swirling faster and brighter, heat radiating out from it into her hands. She nearly dropped it, but in the next moment the heat faded abruptly as if it had never been there.

"*No!*" The shout came from Ydenda, and Rose pulled her attention away from the seed and followed her friend's shocked gaze toward the Garden. Her mouth opened on an audible gasp. The Rot that had been thick on the pocked exterior wall of the Garden had come to life, moving like Rose had never seen it. It twisted, pulsing and shifting, separating into thick, ropy strands before reforming, crawling over the pitted stones at an alarming rate.

Rose stumbled back away from the wall, pulling Ydenda with her. Neku lunged forward as she tripped, grabbing them both before they fell.

"The spell," he gasped, his voice hoarse and panicked. "It's broken!"

In a shuddering rush, the Rot breached the gate and flooded into the Garden, swallowing everything in its path. Horrified, Rose turned to face Neku, and the faint movement of writhing shadows caught her eye from behind him in the darkness of the forest.

"The trees," she gasped, clinging tightly to the seed with one hand and Neku with the other. "The Rot is everywhere."

"It's alive again," Ydenda choked out. "It's spreading."

"The spell is broken," Neku repeated. "We have to get back to the castle *now*."

And at that moment, the first pulse of a dull, throbbing pain spread through Rose, lighting up every cut and scrape she had sustained in the crash. Alarm followed quickly on the heels of the pain.

Oh, no. Her spell was failing, too.

36

THE MA'AR

The concussive pulse of power hit the Ma'ar so hard his knees buckled and he nearly lost his balance. Grasping at the heavy table in the Cathedral library to keep himself upright, he looked around in alarm.

What the hell was that?

It had felt like a physical impact, like someone had struck him with a massive, overtight rubber band, snapping it against his bones. But there was no one else here. Glancing around to assure himself that he was still alone, he returned the mysterious vial he had been examining yet again to his pocket and stuck his head out of the library door into the main sanctuary of the Cathedral.

His posse of hired goons was split at the moment—one contingent was supposed to be en route to the Garden of Blue while a second force was watching the gatekeeper's castle and surrounding area. There shouldn't be anyone else here, but he certainly hadn't imagined that snapping sensation.

"Is anyone—"

The words died on his lips. The Rot that coated the

Cathedral, unmoving for decades, was still no longer. Patches of shiny black that coated the walls between the broken window panes were creeping downward, seeking blindly, sending out tendrils that, meeting with the sides of the blackened pews nearby, joined together into one seething black mass.

The Ma'ar jerked his head back into the library, his pulse pounding wildly. *The spell has been broken.*

What *happened?* Had the gatekeeper removed the spell that had slowed the progress of decay for nearly the past century? Why would he do that? Or was it something else? Had the spell failed naturally? It couldn't last forever.

Or did it have something to do with the girl, Rose? Had she resurrected the Drani'shadara? Or—no. Had she returned to her own world with the seed? Was he too late?

Angrily, the Ma'ar shook his head. It didn't matter. It was time to go. He had done his best here, done his best for his people, but if the spell was broken, it was too late for them. If he was honest, it had been too late for them for years. The gatekeeper's spell had been a temporary fix. The Ma'ar's burned bones had been a temporary fix. Besides, there was only a handful of bones left, and those were *his*. It was time to stop wasting resources on a lost cause, and time to stop relying on his lackeys to do his job.

Grabbing his long black coat off the chair where he'd been sitting, he threw the heavy wool over his shoulders where it settled like a piece of armor. His hat was next, then the black gloves, and with each piece he felt like he was layering on a piece of himself, his confidence and determination restored. He was the *Ma'ar*. It wasn't too late.

Striding purposefully, he made his way down the stairs into the dimly lit confines of the catacombs. His lip curled in a sneer as he passed the open manacle and withered husk of a body that had been left there to rot. He thought the body had once belonged to Gann, but only because he hadn't seen the man around since the incident. The body he strode past, pointedly ignoring, was unrecognizable, blackened and withered. It looked as if it would crumble to dust if he touched it, but he didn't pause to find out.

Further down the hallway, he arrived at the alcove that housed the nameless tomb containing his most prized possessions and he set his feet and heaved the heavy lid aside, revealing the small cache of bones.

There weren't many left now, only a few dozen, all that had remained in the Ossuary. They certainly weren't the best, all deeply yellowed and pitted with age, but it was all there was. And he would need them, to take with him and continue his preservation in the sister world. There would be no point crossing over if he would just die there.

He did have the vial, he reminded himself. Its contents were clearly magical, and drinking it was an option, but he didn't know what they *were*. For all he knew it might kill him faster. Better to keep that as a last resort.

Leaning over the lip of the tomb, he grasped a handful and gently lifted them out. Despite his careful handling, the bones immediately began to crumble at his touch. Cursing, he hastily laid them back down. He didn't remember them being this fragile when he'd taken them. Had the broken spell affected them too?

He tried again with the same result, the bones disintegrating at his touch into a cloud of dust.

Dammit! He didn't have *time* for this. If the Rot sealed the entryway before he could leave, he would be trapped down here. He cursed again, frantically trying to weigh his options. But he didn't have any. He had no choice. He would have to consume these here and now.

This would change his plans though, he thought angrily. Now he no longer simply needed the girl's blood to cross the gate. Now he needed her, too. He needed to make sure she made it through and resurrected the Drani'shadara. He would need a new supply of bones on the other side of the gate. Even if the contents of the vial worked, they wouldn't last forever.

Reaching in, the Ma'ar ground his palm down on the crumbling pile of bones, and watched them disintegrate before him. It was a surprisingly pitiful amount of dust left when he lifted his hand, even from so many bones.

Over the years he had discovered that the bones went down easier when mixed into his food or drink, but there was no time for that. Scooping up as much as he could, he stuffed the dust into his mouth, coughing and spluttering as he forced himself to swallow.

There. That would have to do.

Moving around to the other side of the tomb, he heaved the lid back into place. He knew it was an unnecessary waste of precious time, but after nearly a century of treating these bones with the utmost care and respect—well, other than burning and consuming them, but that was beside the point—it felt sacrilegious to leave them open and unprotected.

Dusting his hands off on his pants, the Ma'ar turned and strode off down the long hallway, breaking into a jog as the light from the stairwell came into view. He hurried up the stairs. The small library was still free from Rot, but when he exited into the Cathedral his heart leaped into his throat.

What had once been a vast, ornate masterpiece of design that had held on to vestiges of its beauty despite the shattered windows, crumbling stone, and insidious presence of Rot, was now a wreckage that held no trace of its former grandeur. The interior of the large room was nearly entirely black, swallowed by thick ropes of tar-like Rot.

His mind turned frantically, assessing and planning. He had to get to the castle, as fast as possible. He hadn't used his own personal transport in ages, but it would be significantly faster than the Millipede. Which he doubted was even still running at this point. He couldn't afford to lose another second.

A stream of invective escaped the Ma'ar's mouth as he plunged into the wreckage of the Cathedral, careful not to touch any of the creeping Rot as he leaped between the few remaining untouched patches of floor between the library and the main entrance. He didn't know if it was pure luck or some lingering protection born of the ingested bones, but his feet flew over the stones, nimbly avoiding the Rot despite his bulk, until he finally reached the door. He shoved it open with his shoulder and was out and away without a backward glance.

37

INTERLUDE

The Maiden's Voyage was an old cruising catamaran that had found its second life as a fishing vessel. When Gellis had rescued the decrepit old boat on its way to the junkyard and vowed to overhaul the entire craft and make it seaworthy again, his wife had been concerned that he'd been affected by the Rot.

But Gellis had found retirement to be less of the long vacation he had imagined and more an endless stretch of boredom, so he'd decided to take his wife's pre-retirement appeal—"Just think, honey, you can spend your time doing anything you want!"—at face value. It was a suggestion he now rather imagined she regretted, but he was fairly sure her appeal had just been a ploy to get him to agree to move to the shore anyway. And since she had succeeded, he thought it was only fair of him to buy a boat.

Fortunately, her complaints had faded once he actually *had* restored the old boat, and even more so once he had started to use it to bring in a small income. Plus, it gave him the perfect excuse to spend his days out on the water, away from his wife. Away from everyone, really. Just him, and the sea, and the salt breeze.

It was early morning out on the shore of the Western Provinces. Gellis doubted Jana was even out of bed yet. It had still been dark, the sun just starting to peek over the horizon when he'd left her wrapped in their blankets, snoring contentedly, and made his way down to the wharf, a steaming mug of Corlis root tea in one hand and the newspaper in the other. It was the best way to spend the morning. Out on the water, strong tea, the morning news, and silence all around.

He could take his time, relax, catch a handful of grousefish as the tide came in, and make it home for an early lunch after Jana was done meeting with her book club.

The tiny red-speckled fish weren't biting today though. Most of the larger fishing boats ignored the grousefish since they were hard to preserve and started to smell distinctly unappetizing well before they could make their way inland to the larger markets, so Gellis usually had no trouble collecting enough to sell at the local market. Plus, they tasted amazing if you ate them the same day, and Jana made a mean grousefish stew. But today he hadn't had a single nibble on the line.

He tipped his head back and drained the last dregs of the Corlis root tea, before sitting the mug down and leaning over the edge of the bridgedeck that connected the two hulls to peer into the water. The surface of the water shone a bright blue-green in the morning sun, but beneath it Gellis couldn't make out any of the telltale glinting red spots that would indicate a school of grousefish. Usually he couldn't spit in any direction without hitting a patch of red.

Sighing, Gellis began to reel in his line. Maybe if he took the boat up north a ways he would have better luck.

It was at that moment he noticed something dark moving in the water beneath the bow of the boat. Leaning over to catch a better look, he squinted, holding up a sun-darkened hand to shield his eyes from the glare. It looked huge, larger than a blue dornfish, and he didn't even know there *were* fish bigger than that this close to shore.

The shadow moved closer to the surface, writhing and twisting back on itself, the water churning to a froth. The boat bobbed on the waves, and Gellis gripped the railing, pulling himself back up to stand.

Feeling nauseous and disgruntled at that fact—Gellis hadn't been seasick a day in his life—he dropped the fishing pole onto the deck behind him and put both hands on the railing to steady himself.

The sea beneath him was dark, the water roiling, and before Gellis could even get his feet beneath him, the black shape broke the surface, questing tendrils separating from the mass and reaching out to wind around the hull.

Rot!

Gellis' heart spasmed in shock, his mouth opening to let loose a scream of pure terror. But all he got out was a choked gurgle before the Rot was on him too, and then it was over in the blink of an eye.

The coiling mass of Rot spread toward the shore in a vast oil-slick wave, leaving it its wake the torn wreckage of a fishing catamaran, bobbing gently on the coal-black waves. The desiccated corpse that had once been Gellis lay on the bridgedeck, a blackened husk, still clutching the railing with both hands.

Back on the shore it was silent. Nothing moved except the pulsing darkness of Rot as it crept out of the tenebrous gloom of the ocean to engulf the sleepy seaside village. In Gellis's house, Jana looked out the window as a shadow blotted out the light from the sun. Moments later, six withered corpses lay on the carpeted floor of the living room, books still clutched in blackened hands.

∽

The wooden shack stood empty in the forest far to the south of Trelissar, moss heavy on two of its three remaining sides. The third side had thin tendrils of Rot filling the spaces between the poorly constructed planks, almost like caulk, put there intentionally to seal the gaps. The Rot was the reason the shack had been abandoned in the first place—no longer a convenient location for illicit alcohol production—but this Rot was old, frozen motionless by the spell that had halted its progress throughout the world.

Decades later, the shack stood there still, one wall long since lost to the elements, trees growing up through the foundation. A family of large, squirrel-like rodents was currently making its home under the rotting floorboards, their thick greenish fur helping them blend seamlessly in amongst the abundant clumps of moss.

Much of the long-abandoned distillery equipment was still in place, though it too had mostly been absorbed into the forest. A heavy copper still lay on its side in the corner, a lovely green patina showing through the vines that grew over the surface. Broken pipes and gaskets littered the floor under a thick layer of decaying leaves and brush.

The Rot had scared away any human occupants, but the animals had eventually returned. The crumbling roof offered shelter from the elements, and as long as one avoided the one Rot-tainted wall, the shack made quite a cozy home.

The nearest village was three miles away via a long overgrown path, and this far removed from any human presence, the forest surrounding the shack was alive with sounds. The droning hum of insects filled the air, overlaid with the melodious trilling of a variety of birds. A cool breeze rustled through the trees, setting branches to creaking and leaves to fluttering. Most of the larger denizens of the wood were fast asleep in their dens and warrens, but the rustling sounds of any number of diurnal creatures could be heard, collecting food and building nests.

It began with a shift, an almost imperceptible change in air pressure, like a sound played just outside of the range of hearing. It was something sensed on a base, instinctual level; an unidentifiable feeling of wrongness. Silence fell like a shroud, blanketing the forest as even the wind seemed to still and the trees held their breath.

Then the Rot came like a wave, swallowing everything in its path. It was a huge, writhing mass of coal-black darkness, questing tendrils reaching ahead of the main body, engulfing and devouring as it came. Anything with the power to flee did so, crashing ahead of the wave in a frantic stampede, but panic-fueled muscles were no match for the destructive power of rotting magic, and the surging wall of death claimed every life, every breath, as it rolled inexorably onward.

In the end, all that remained of the forest was a misshapen sea of twisted, lifeless shapes, the hulking husks of trees reaching their blackened limbs to the sky. The withered carcasses of innumerable creatures littered the forest floor. The air was still now, no hint of a breeze, and the oppressive silence had a finality to it that was utterly absolute. The entire effect would have been devastating had there been anyone left to see it.

ROSE

Rose didn't know what to do. Panic welled up in her throat like bile, leaving an acrid taste on her tongue. Everything was coming to a head all at once, and she had no idea how they were going to deal with it. Neku couldn't fly with both of them; hell, she didn't think he was in any shape to fly at all, and with the spell broken and the Rot spreading again, they *needed* him.

And spreading it was, at an alarming rate. The moon was nearly full over the forest, casting its yellow light over the landscape. She could see the sinuous shadows creeping through the woods ahead, and the entrance to the Garden of Blue was growing choked with Rot. She didn't look back, afraid her panic would turn to despair if she watched the destruction of the Garden, but she could see her own horror reflected on Ydenda's face as the other woman stared transfixed at the encroaching Rot.

At this rate it would box them in entirely before much longer. What would happen when it reached them?

She clutched the seed to her chest, wrapping her body around it in a protective stance, and tried not to wince when another lance of pain seared through her cuts and scrapes. Neku noticed the movement anyway, and his gaze zeroed in on her.

"Your spell," he said in a harsh voice, "is it failing?"

It was obvious that he knew the answer, but she nodded anyway. "I don't know how long it'll last."

Neku's expression turned determined, his face set like stone. "Then we have to go, right now. Last time it started to fade when you were on the Mist Bridge, right? And lasted long enough to get us back to the castle?"

She nodded again, uncertainly.

"Well, we're a little closer now than we were then. It'll have to last until we get back. It'll just have to." There was a note of desperate finality in his voice, and he took her free hand and opened his other arm toward Ydenda. "Come on, let's go."

Rose gawked at him. "What are you thinking? You can't *fly!* You barely made it here with just me; you can't hold two of us, and we can't afford for you to lose control when we get there. Or before!"

Neku's eyes were anguished when they met hers. "We have no other choice. We have to get back to the castle. You have the seed, and I *will* get you through that gate!"

"But you—"

Rose had no chance to finish her sentence before she felt a pair of hands shove against her back hard, sending her tumbling into Neku. He stumbled back, gripping her shoulders to keep them both upright, and Rose turned in shock just in time to see Ydenda fall where they had just been standing, a thick tendril of Rot coiled around her ankle.

"Go!" Ydenda yelled, her face contorted in agony.

"No!" Rose screamed, releasing Neku to reach toward her friend.

"We're not leaving you." Neku's voice was a fierce growl, and he reached down in one swift motion. When his hand met with Ydenda's shoulder there was a burst of light, bright as lightning. Rose blinked in the afterimage as the tendril of Rot recoiled, releasing Ydenda's leg with a horrible sucking sound. Ydenda screamed, and Rose let out a gasp. *More* magic? It had worked, but at what cost?

The Rot recovered quickly, tentatively questing out again, but Neku hauled Ydenda up, pulling her in and wrapping an arm around each of them.

"Hold on," he growled, and didn't give them time to react before the misty wings billowed to life. Rose had just enough time to adjust the seed so it was fully covered by her shirt and secure in her grip before the trio began to rise with a mighty beat of Neku's insubstantial wings.

They rose steadily in an awkward huddle, Neku's arms locked around them like a vice, and Rose's stomach roiled as they tilted to avoid the trees and started toward the river at an angle. In the dark of the night the water appeared black, moonlight glinting on the tips of the waves. With her arms clamped around both Neku and the seed and her legs dangling awkwardly, she felt much less secure and stable than she had on their flight downriver.

Ydenda held tight to Neku with both arms, but her eyes were squeezed shut and a low keening sound came from her lips, an agonized wail audible under the buffeting wind.

"Will she be alright?" Rose asked Neku breathlessly, raising her voice to be heard even though his head was only inches away. "Did the Rot hurt her badly?"

"It wasn't the Rot," Neku responded. A sheen of sweat was already visible on his brow as they soared out over the river and turned northward, and Rose's stomach clenched.

"What?"

"It wasn't the Rot," he repeated through gritted teeth. "It was me. The Rot is painless. But the magic I used to repel it would have felt like fire on her leg, and on all the Rot already in her body." After a pause, he added, as if to himself, "There was no other way."

With the arm clenched around his neck, Rose gave him a squeeze, but remained silent. Her skin throbbed all down her arms and on her face where the scrapes from their crash landing had cut into her. She gritted her teeth against the pain of the fading spell, willing it to hold a little longer. Looking down over the river as they flew unerringly northward, following the dark, sinuous shape of the water, she could see the Rot now. Even in the darkness of the night it was clearly visible, blacker than black, swallowing the moonlight instead of reflecting it. Every patch of Rot they flew past was moving now, writhing like it was waking from a deep sleep.

She hoped Ydenda would be alright. She hoped they would make it back to the castle before the spell protecting her blood faded entirely. She hoped they would make it back to the castle *at all*. She hoped she would be able to make it back through the gate without sacrificing either Neku or Ydenda in the process. She hoped she would be able to resurrect the Drani'shadara on the other side, and that the newborn creature would know what to do. She *hoped*.

But at the same time, she could hear Ydenda's low, pained keening. And they were less than a mile up the river and already she could feel Neku's muscles quivering under the strain. And she could see the Rot on the riverbank below, swelling and reaching out, searching and spreading. And if she was completely honest with herself, she didn't think any of her hopes had a chance in hell of coming true.

∼

Rose wasn't sure how long the journey down to the Garden had taken, but she estimated they were little more than halfway back when they began slowly but surely to lose altitude, and Neku began issuing instructions in a low voice. Ydenda had stopped her keening some time ago and had fallen into silence, but the woman hung limply in Neku's arms and Rose had no idea if she was listening, or even aware of her surroundings at all.

"If we don't make it all the way, you have to leave me," he said quietly. "Get back to the castle any way you can."

Rose could see Neku's hand where it wrapped around Ydenda's shoulder, and his knuckles were white. The patterns that moved through his skin, an echo of those she'd seen on the seed, were sluggish and faint.

"How?" she asked simply, forcing herself to pay attention despite the pain from her fading spell.

"You have the seed. Show it to anyone, and they will be bound to help you. Anyone in this world will recognize it, and will aid you. If they are able."

Rose didn't have to see his expression to know he was as doubtful of his last words as she was. Would anyone be able to help her? Would there be anyone left to do so? And would her spell last that long?

"You must get back to the gate. When you do, use your blood, and the doors will open for you. Go into the foyer, and exit through the other door. You'll know which one. When you are back in your world, bury the seed in the forest, and water it with your blood."

"That's it? That's all that's needed for the Ceremony?"

"That's it. Just water the seed, and then...when the

Drani'shadara is reborn, tell it...tell it I am sorry." His voice cracked, and Rose drew in a breath.

"Tell it...I did my best, we all did, and I'm so sorry."

A tear formed in the corner of his eye and hovered there for a moment before spilling out and tracing a damp trail down his pale cheek. Rose had no idea what to say, and so she leaned in, and Neku bowed his head and rested his forehead against hers.

His skin was hot against hers, feverish, and she could feel his trembling through the arm he had around her.

"I'm going to put you down in the next town we cross," he said quietly. "I don't want to crash again."

She wanted to protest, wanted to exclaim that she couldn't leave him; this couldn't be the last time she saw him. But instead she kept silent and nodded against his chest, ducking her head so he wouldn't see her own tears fall.

They had veered away from the river and Rose remembered they had flown over a small village on the way down, situated on the edge of the forest. That must be where he was heading. She hoped the village was still there, that it was still safe.

By the time the rooftops drew into view in the distance, no more than the size of pinheads, Neku's breathing was ragged and his wing beats unstable. Rose squeezed her eyes shut and buried her face in his neck, praying he could at least make it to the ground before he lost control.

"Rose," he gasped as they wove an erratic path through the air toward the houses, "remember what I said. Go as fast as you can. Ysenderia," he addressed the woman for the first time since rescuing her from the Rot, "Help her. Get her to the castle. Help her get the seed—"

Ydenda jerked her head up, almost unbalancing them,

and Neku broke off while he beat his wings with an effort to keep them steady. The shifting patterns in his skin were barely visible now.

"The seed!" Ydenda's eyes, which had been closed for the majority of the journey as she hung limply in Neku's grip, now opened wide and fixed on his face with an intensity that alarmed Rose.

"Use the seed," she said urgently. "You can draw on its magic and use it to fly."

Rose eyes flew from Ydenda's face to Neku's. He could do that?

But he was shaking his head, despair on his pale, sweat-sheened face. "I can't," he protested. "If I drain the magic from the seed, then the Drani'shadara can't be resurrected. I *can't* steal that magic."

Rose's heart sank. But Ydenda's look became even more urgent. "You *can*. There's a way."

"What way?" Neku's wingbeats were starting to slow, jolting them erratically through the air.

Ydenda's face twisted in agonized uncertainty. "I...I don't know! I can't remember. But there is a way. Draw the magic from the seed. If you land, she will never make it back. *Trust me.*"

Rose looked between the two of them, uncertain what she thought they should do, but she could see that Neku didn't have time to consider his actions. He was at the end of his abilities.

And so, with a last, desperate glance down at Ydenda, he closed his eyes. Rose didn't sense anything, but she felt the seed heat up where it rested against her skin, growing warm the same way it had when the spell had been broken. As she watched where it peeked through her shirt, the swirling colors on the seed dimmed slightly. When the colors stabilized, they still shifted, swirling and changing, but they were slightly paler and less vibrant.

But the benefits to Neku were immediately obvious. His wingbeats stabilized, his trembling subsided, and his labored breathing eased. They gained altitude again, soaring over the village and turning toward the forest. His brow was still creased though, as he looked down at the two women he held tightly. "I hope you know what you're doing."

Ydenda kept her features smooth, but Rose caught a glint of worry in the woman's eyes as she turned her head, and she thought Ydenda might be hoping the same thing.

∾

The voyage over the forest was long and nerve-wracking, and Rose could tell each of the three of them was struggling in their own way.

Neku didn't say anything, but Rose felt the seed grow hot twice more, the shifting colors dimming further each time. She could tell it pained him terribly to draw power from the seed, and she prayed Ydenda had some solution to ensure the seed would still be viable, though she couldn't imagine what that solution might be.

Ydenda didn't seem to notice as Neku drew additional power from the seed. She had retreated inward again, holding tight to Neku but otherwise hanging motionless, eyes closed and brow furrowed. Rose watched her friend closely. She was not the cheerful woman Rose had first encountered with her bag of heads in the forest, and she wondered again what exactly had happened in the intervening days, and more importantly, if the damage was irreparable.

For her part, as the flight dragged on Rose continued to grit her teeth against the rising pain from the fading spell, trying to focus on other things to keep from getting overwhelmed. The only other things to focus on, however, were the increasing Rot in the forest below them, and whatever awaited them back at the castle. And judging from the state of the forest below, it wouldn't be good.

She hadn't imagined the Rot could spread so rapidly. What had been barely discernible clumps of black on the flight down to the Garden had now morphed into a seething, spreading sea of darkness. More trees were affected now than not, and Rose prayed Neku's power would hold and they would not have to land in the forest, because she knew without a doubt that if they landed, they would not survive.

They kept their height though, flying well out of reach of the expanses of dead forest, the tar-black Rot that coated the trees sending its questing tendrils out in all directions, devouring whatever lay in its path. Rose didn't know if maybe she preferred the physical pain that kept her distracted from the horror below them.

Neku kept his gaze fixed straight ahead as they flew, but Rose knew he was well aware of what was happening below, for his stoic expression was belied by the slow drip of tears down his cheeks. She felt like her heart was breaking for him, for them all.

It seemed an age had passed by the time the highest turrets of the castle appeared in the distance. The first rays of sunlight were peeking up beyond the trees to the east, but the light seemed weak, hazy, like it was being swallowed by the intense darkness of the Rot. In the dim light of the sun, the devastation of the forest below was even more stark, and Rose's heart sank.

Her skin still burned, and the relief she felt from making it back before the spell disappeared completely was tempered by the reality of the situation she was faced with.

There was no time left. No time to come up with a new plan, to talk Neku out of his sacrifice. No time to help Ydenda remember what she'd lost. No time to slow down, to *think* before she had to flee through the gate. A sob lodged in her throat, and she clutched Neku tightly to her, feeling his hair brush her cheek in the wind. No time to say goodbye.

As if he could read her thoughts, Neku squeezed the arm he had around her, before shifting slightly.

"Ysenderia, are you...with us?" His voice was low.

"I am here." She responded without opening her eyes.

"I had hoped we would have time together before we were forced to act. Time to explain, time to talk." His voice was tinged with regret as he looked down at them both. "But we are well out of time. We have to move forward with the plan immediately."

Ydenda's eyes opened. "I understand," she said simply. Rose marveled at how easily they had both fallen back into their roles of gatekeeper and planeswalker, their first concern always with the gate and the Drani'shadara, despite their years apart and all that had happened.

"We are going to land at the Ossuary," Neku continued. "I will use the ceremonial dagger there to sacrifice myself. It is my hope that the magic it holds will be enough to destroy me, thus sealing the gate forever. With the gate sealed, the Rot will not be able to pass, and this world will die with me." His words came out without emotion, a clinical description of the events to come, and a shiver traced down Rose's spine. "Rose is going to take the seed through the gate and plant it on the other side, in hopes that the Drani'shadara will know what to do once it is reborn."

Rose flinched at his words, her heart twisting, but Ydenda did not question him, despite the distress visible on her face.

Neku's next words, however, were soft and tentative. "You...cannot cross with her."

"I know." Ydenda's voice was still even.

Neku continued, "I tried to take as little magic from the seed as possible, but I will need to draw a little more to keep the Rot at bay once we land. You said there was a way to ensure the seed is still viable. What is it?"

Ydenda's words were hesitant, and Rose had the unsettling impression that the woman wasn't entirely sure what she was going to say until the words came out of her mouth. "We need...to replenish the magic that was used. If the...if Rose takes the bones from the Ossuary and...buries them with the seed, there should be enough magic there to ensure the Drani'shadara will be reborn."

Neku had begun nodding before she was finished. "Of course," he said, but he seemed uncertain.

Rose made a questioning noise, and he looked at her. "Not many of the bones remain in the Ossuary, and the ones that do remain are very old," he said. "Many are...missing. But there should still enough left for this."

Ydenda drew in a sharp breath. "Missing? Someone has taken the Drani'shadara's *bones?*"

Neku opened his mouth to reply, but at that moment the castle loomed before them, and in one swift beat of insubstantial wings, he altered his course and brought them soaring out over the meadow.

While the trees they had been passing over were thick with Rot, the meadow was still clear, and the sunlit grass was a stark contrast to the ruination of the adjacent forest. Rose felt Neku release an audible sigh of relief, and she wondered if the magic of the gate was keeping the Rot at bay, and if so, how long it would last. Not long, she thought. Not long at all.

"Ysenderia, I want you to help Rose gather the bones. I will retrieve the dagger, and then everyone must retreat into the castle, as quickly as possible."

Neku's voice was harsh with command, and both women nodded.

He aimed them toward the side of the castle where the high stone archway of the Ossuary entrance was visible, and they dropped toward the ground in a sickening rush. The moment they landed the three took off toward the archway at a run.

Rose stumbled a little, feeling lightheaded from the pain of the receding spell. The pain itself seemed to be fading, and she wasn't sure if that was a good thing or not. She clutched the seed tightly to her chest as she regained her footing and, clearing the archway, pelted down the stone stairs after Ydenda, Neku close behind.

She was so preoccupied—with her own pain, with fear, with the urgency of the situation and the task to come—that she didn't even notice that the lanterns lining the stone stairs were lit. It was only when she crashed into Ydenda's back where her friend had frozen at the bottom of the steps and sent them both stumbling, only when she heard Neku's panicked shout from behind them at the top of the stairs, that she realized something was wrong.

She grabbed hold of Ydenda with her free arm to keep from falling, and looked up to see what had caused her to stop so abruptly.

The main chamber of the Ossuary was completely

barren. Not a single bone remained, not a speck of dust on floor or altar. And in the center of the room, his form backlit by the flickering lanterns set into their alcoves on the wall, stood a tall, dark figure in a long black coat and tall hat.

"Well, it's about time you showed up," said the Ma'ar.

39

ROSE

The Ma'ar looked both exactly the same as Rose remembered and entirely different. In the split second that she stood with Ydenda, frozen in shock and fear, her mind took in the details. He wore the same style of clothing that she had last seen him in, at the opera what seemed like a lifetime ago. A long black brocade coat, a tall black hat, fine gloves, all perfectly tailored and impeccably styled. But the coat was stained with mud and leaf debris, a gaping hole rending the fine fabric across the left breast, a split seam along the right shoulder. The rest of his clothing was in similar disrepair, but it was the look on his face that disturbed Rose the most.

He wore a wide smile that twisted his features almost jovially, like they were old friends reunited, but the light in his eyes was manic and unhinged, and Rose almost took a step back. She could feel Ydenda trembling against her, and she reached out with her free hand, wrapping an arm around her friend in an act of...what? Support? Protection? Rose wasn't sure she had either of those to give.

The moment seemed to stretch, but it was only the space

of a few heartbeats before there came the sound of a scuffle on the stairs and Rose felt a push from behind. She staggered into the dank confines of the Ossuary, pulling Ydenda with her, as Neku entered as well, his arms held tight in the grip of a pair of the Ma'ar's brown-suited lackeys. More of the Ma'ar's men followed behind, crowding into the cavern.

No...

Rose clutched the seed tightly, her fingers white against the dim swirl of colors, and pressed herself back against the wall next to Ydenda, keeping as far as she could from both the Ma'ar and his men. She felt claustrophobic and light-headed, sick with the fear and adrenaline that coursed through her system.

She took in the scene in front of her: the Ma'ar stood to the right, near the altar, and eight of the Ma'ar's minions crowded the entryway to her left—six humans and two of the strange Frankenmice creatures she'd seen in the forest and again on the Mist Bridge.

How on earth had they gotten here? She'd seen the Rot outside; there was no way anyone could have passed through the forest and survived. And while the Ma'ar at least looked as if he'd done battle with the forest, his men appeared unscathed, their clothes clean and unmarked.

They were already here, she realized. *Waiting for us.*

Neku stood in the middle of the group, his arms in the grip of two of the humans, and Rose could see his shock at the clean-swept chamber, not a bone in sight. As he took in the Ma'ar's presence, his expression changed, a confusing combination of emotions crossing his face. He seemed exhausted and wary, but his features were also suffused with a dark determination. Rose couldn't imagine that he had the strength or the magic left to fight, and she spared a glance down at the seed, taking in its muted colors and sluggish movement. How much magic did it have left to give? With the bones gone, was it already too late to resurrect the Drani'shadara?

To her right, the Ma'ar took a step forward, and Rose glanced up quickly, only to see him watching her intently, his eyes slightly unfocused.

"I had a speech prepared for when I saw you again," he said, the manic cast to his eyes reflected in his deep voice. "I was going to explain how your blood is not your own; as a planeswalker, you belong to all of us. The greater good and all that. This is bigger than you."

A moment later, the light in the cavern dimmed just a fraction. One of the lanterns at the top of the stairs had gone out.

"Boss..." one of the men-in-brown murmured as the others began to shift nervously.

"But it's obviously too late for that," the Ma'ar continued, his face twisting into a sneer. He took a step toward her, and a whimper escaped from Ydenda. His voice began to rise. "I saw the forest. This world won't last 'til sundown. And after everything I've done, all the *work* I've put in, all the *risks* I've taken..."

Another light from the stairs went out, and Rose could feel the almost palpable rise of tension in the cavern. The flickering lantern light danced upon the Ma'ar's face, casting shadows under his eyes like a skeleton.

In the next second, everything happened at once. A third light went out, and Rose saw a thin tendril of Rot reach around the corner from the stairs. She sucked in a breath, ready to yell—she wasn't even sure what—and then the Ma'ar lunged.

Just as it had been at the opera, Rose was shocked by his speed. He came at her quick as a viper, and his hand locked around her arm like a vice as he growled in her ear, "I will *not* be left behind."

Someone let out a shriek—was it her or Ydenda?—and as her heart leaped into her throat, she heard a scuffle by the stairs. There was a burst of light from Neku; one of the men holding his arms was blown backwards and landed heavily against the wall—right where the questing tendril of Rot was snaking around the corner.

The Rot was moving much slower than it had been in the forest, perhaps due to the magic that still lingered here, but still it happened fast enough. The man-in-brown only had time for a quick, panicked indrawn breath, and then the Rot was on him, in him, pulling out his life force like water being wrung out of a sponge. Rose was frozen in horror, staring as the man went from a real, live person to a blackened husk in the space of a heartbeat.

She took an involuntary step back away from the scene in front of her. Her back came up against the stone of the wall, and in doing so she realized the Ma'ar no longer had a grip on her arm.

He too had paused to watch his man fall, and in that brief moment, Ydenda had attacked, pulling the Ma'ar away from her with a savage yell and shoving him against the wall. During the struggle, the Ma'ar had somehow found the time to draw a knife, the long blade gleaming wickedly sharp in the flickering light, and he held it aloft in one gloved hand, angled to strike at Ydenda's chest. His other hand was bent behind him, trapped between his body and the wall where Ydenda had pushed him. She was pressing him back with all her weight, and both her hands were raised to grip his arm that held the knife, pressing it back and away.

Rose couldn't imagine how Ydenda was holding him at

bay with her slight form, her weight negligible against his solid bulk. Rose pushed off the wall, rushing toward them and preparing to grab at the Ma'ar's arm with her free hand, to help, somehow, but Ydenda saw her coming and screamed at her, "No! Stay back!"

She halted, confused.

Though the Ma'ar struggled against her, the knife remained aloft, his body pinned, and then Rose saw Ydenda's face. An expression of intense, desperate concentration suffused her features, as if she was fighting some immense internal battle. And then Rose saw the Rot, the old, shiny ridges of black that covered half Ydenda's face and spiraled around her arm, she saw it *move,* creeping forward, inching down her arm and toward the Ma'ar.

A choked sound escaped her throat, and she took an involuntary step back. What was *happening?*

Neku was shouting behind her, and she could see flashes of light and hear screams coming from the entryway, but she stood transfixed, staring at the Ma'ar and Ydenda and feeling panicked and helpless, unsure what she could possibly do, and—

"Rose!" Neku's roar broke through and she whirled toward his voice. "*Get back to the castle!*"

Two more of the Ma'ar's men had been consumed by the Rot, their bodies lying shriveled at odd angles across the entryway. The remaining five had all drawn knives—long deadly-looking things with curved blades, and had Neku backed into a corner, where the Rot was slowly spreading along the wall. There was a wicked cut across Neku's cheek that was oozing thick, dark red blood.

Rose hesitated. It seemed cowardly to flee like this, leaving Ydenda and Neku alone here to...what? Die at the hands of the Ma'ar and his men? Succumb to the Rot? And yet she knew they were fighting for her, fighting to give her a chance to get away. Would she waste the opportunity they were buying her?

But was there even anything left of their plan that would work? If Neku couldn't kill himself with the magical dagger on the wall, the gate wouldn't seal properly and Rose's world would be doomed just as this one was. And with the bones all gone, and the magic of the seed so diminished...what were they fighting for at this point anyway?

"*GO!*" Neku roared again, breaking through her indecision, and she began to move toward the stairs, holding the seed tightly in both hands.

The Ma'ar's head snapped up at Neku's shout, and he turned his head away from where he still struggled with Ydenda to yell toward his men. "Don't let her get away! If she goes, you all die!"

Two of the Ma'ar's men broke away and turned their knives on Rose, and in the pause, Neku lunged forward, breaking through the semicircle of men that surrounded him to sprint toward the back of the cavern where the altar lay. Rose gasped as his efforts earned him a long gash along his left arm, and more blood, a red so dark it was nearly black, began to well thickly from the cut and run down his arm. But still he pushed forward, leaping onto the altar and grabbing the ornately decorated dagger from its setting on the wall. He nearly fumbled the weapon as he dropped down off the altar, but caught it and turned back toward the melee, brandishing the dagger before him.

"Get away from her," he ordered.

One of the men-in-brown grabbed Rose's arm and pulled her roughly against him, wrapping an arm around her from behind and setting the edge of his weapon against her throat.

The whole of Rose's attention narrowed down to that single point of focus, that razor-thin slice of metal pushing against the skin of her throat. She forgot how to breathe, how to move, all her muscles locked in place.

"Don't kill her, you idiot," roared the Ma'ar. "Just hold her until I'm done here."

Rose felt the blade leave her throat, but it stayed near, his arm still hovering too close, and then the man pulled her back, away from the Rot and the other struggling men. He pressed his back against the wall and held her against his chest, his arm still locked around her. She took a shallow breath, angrily cursing her own stupidity for not leaving when she had the chance.

The look Neku shot her was desperate, but she dared not struggle, not with the blade still so close. From this vantage, though, she could see the rest of the scene as it unfolded. The Rot was gaining traction, still slow moving, but thick now where it flowed down the wall, tendrils reaching and questing. The two Frankenmice had fallen to it now as well, their small, oddly shaped forms even more disturbing than the others as they lay, devoid of life, piled atop the others. The remaining three men had moved forward to meet Neku in the center of the room, and the air was filled with grunts and groans and the harsh sounds of metal scraping against metal.

He wasn't using magic, Rose saw, so she assumed his powers were depleted, and she cringed at the sight of him up against three men. He couldn't turn the knife on himself while she was still here, and she was still trapped, unable to do anything to help either of them.

A grunt from further down the wall caught her attention, and she kept her head perfectly still while swiveling her eyes to look toward Ydenda and the Ma'ar. They still stood, locked together, the Ma'ar's knife raised and her arms holding his arm in place, but the pair didn't struggle. They had reversed positions at some point, and Ydenda's back was to the wall now, both of the Ma'ar's hands on the hilt of the knife. But it was like they had both somehow forgotten the blade. He didn't press and she didn't resist as they both seemed entirely consumed by an internal battle. The Rot on Ydenda's arm had crept forward, and now coated the Ma'ar's hand where it grasped the knife, but it remained there, quivering slightly, rather than moving to consume him as it had his minions by the door. Each of the pair was drenched in sweat, eyes wild yet staring sightlessly as each struggled for control, Ydenda trying to push the Rot forward and the Ma'ar trying to somehow hold it back.

Rose had no idea either action was even possible. She assumed Ydenda's control was somehow tied to her being a planeswalker, but what uncanny abilities did the Ma'ar possess, and how?

A shrill scream sounded from the center of the room, and Rose looked back in time to see one of the Ma'ar's men fall in a pool of blood, his hands clenched tight over his stomach. Bile rose in her throat and she tried not to retch.

Neku was heavily wounded as well, viscous blood oozing from gashes that seem to cover his body, but he still stood, dagger in hand, eyes feral and hair wild and matted. The swirling patterns in his skin were all but gone, but still he pressed forward, slashing with the ceremonial dagger as he held his two remaining opponents at bay.

Suddenly, a deep rumbling sound met her ears, low and immense, as if the entire castle was shifting on its foundation. Everyone froze, feeling the ominous rumbling, and then there was a gasp and a gurgle, and the brown-clad arm holding her in place dropped, the knife clattering to the floor. Rose spun around, and screamed.

Rot, thick and black, was seeping out of the very wall behind her, as if the stone was as porous as a sponge. Rose stumbled back away from the body as the wall seemed to bubble and turn black, swallowing the brown-suited man as if he were sinking into a pit of tar, his body disappearing slowly until nothing remained but his withered limbs.

And then, everything happened at once. The Ma'ar's two remaining men, who had turned at her scream, were dispatched efficiently by Neku's blade, falling in a heap atop their friend. Ydenda, whose back was pressed against the same wall as Rose's assailant, gave a great gasp, and as if in slow motion, both she and the Ma'ar moved as one. Ydenda seemed to draw the Rot at her back into her body, but instead of succumbing she pushed it *through* herself, and out into the Ma'ar. At the same moment, the Ma'ar, with an audible grunt, pushed his knife down, and in, until it pierced Ydenda's breast.

"NO!"

Rose's voice melded with Neku's as they both surged toward the pair, but it was too late. Ydenda and the Ma'ar crumpled together, sagging to the ground. Slowly, so much slower than his companions, the Rot consumed the Ma'ar. His eyes rolled back as his head lolled to one side, lifeless against the stone floor.

Ydenda slumped atop him, blood pouring from the wound in her chest, Rot coating her back where she'd been pressed against the wall.

Rose reached the pair a step ahead of Neku and fell to her knees, tears streaming from her eyes.

"Don't touch them." Neku's voice came from just behind her, and he didn't pause, just reached down to take her hand gently in his own. "Come on, we have to go." Tears mixed with the blood that coated his own cheeks as he pulled her to her feet.

Rose took a shuddering breath and was about to turn away to follow Neku when something caught her eye.

"Wait! Look—"

Ydenda's hand, which had been lying limp on the Ma'ar's chest, was moving, sliding bonelessly forward, fingertips ducking under the shredded remains of the Ma'ar's coat to grasp at his vest.

"What—is she—" Rose knelt again, heedless of the pool of blood spreading across the floor. She pulled Neku down beside her, and the pair watched as Ydenda's hand reappeared from inside the Ma'ar's vest, a thin glass vial clutched in her fingers.

Neku drew in a long, shuddering breath, then, releasing her hand, reached down and carefully removed the vial from Ydenda's limp grasp. A moment later, the Rot engulfed her.

Their eyes met for the briefest of moments, but Rose thought the anguish she saw in Neku's gaze would swallow her before she looked away, rising and pulling him up too. He held the bloodstained dagger in one hand, the vial he clutched protectively in the other. Rose gripped the seed to her with one hand and took Neku's arm with the other, and together they fled, stepping over withered bodies and creeping Rot to ascend the stairs, clutching tightly to each other as they headed for the castle.

40

ROSE

The race back up to the castle was silent and fraught with danger. There was only a narrow strip of stone on the stairs that wasn't covered with twisting black tendrils. The steps were dimly lit from above by the weak sunlight and from below by the two remaining lit lanterns, but the light from below was extinguished while they still climbed, carefully leaping from step to step, avoiding the Rot. When they finally cleared the top step and passed under the archway and into the meadow, it was no better. Rot was thick on the castle walls, swallowing the windows and climbing the turrets, and not a single live tree was left on the edge of the forest.

Rose didn't have time to stop and stare, Neku urging her forward as fast as they could go toward the steps that led up to the front door, but she managed to take it all in anyway. The shock and grief lodged in her chest like a stone weight, dragging her down. The world was eerily silent as they ran, no chirping birds, not even the rustle of leaves or the breeze in the grass. It was like the world had been blanketed in death. Rose wondered in passing if the two of them were the only two living creatures left in the world.

She stumbled up the stairs behind Neku, her hand clamped around his elbow, warm blood from his wounds running down her hand. He panted ahead of her, staggering as he climbed on shaking legs. Rose felt no better.

Tendrils of Rot stretched across the heavy wood of the door, but Neku pulled it open anyway, grasping the heavy handle and wrenching it toward him. The Rot stretched and broke, splattering thick droplets onto his hand, but he didn't pause, stepping back to push her ahead of him into the foyer and slamming the door behind him. The shock of it closing reverberated throughout the castle.

The second the door was shut, Neku crumpled, sagging against the wood before sliding down to slump on the floor. Blood dripped from a dozen wounds, staining the marble floor beneath him. In the light of the foyer Rose could see how bad he looked—skin gray and sallow, no sign of shifting patterns, hair matted and dirty, clothes torn and stained. Worse was the Rot. Sometime since their frantic flight it had spread, black marks protruding from under his shirt to snake around his neck, more reaching down from under his hairline to spider across his cheek.

Rose dropped to her knees beside him, her heart in her throat, and tentatively reached out a hand toward his face, stopping short before her fingers made contact.

"Rose..." His voice was hoarse, barely audible. Leaving the dagger on the floor by his side, he raised a hand and captured hers, pulling their clasped hands against his chest.

Rose looked down at their interlaced fingers, hers pale, his spattered with Rot. "Is this okay?" she asked in a whisper. "The spell is gone..."

He shook his head in a weak motion. "I renewed it, when

we landed and I saw the Ma'ar's men. You were protected the whole time."

Rose blinked in surprise. She hadn't even noticed when the pain had disappeared. "I didn't realize…"

"I'll have to remove it now, before you go through the gate." He coughed, and released her hand, raising his other hand and depositing the contents into her palm. The little glass vial glittered, and Rose raised it toward the light, watching the colors shift and swirl, an iridescent glimmer to the liquid inside.

"What is it?" she asked softly.

"The Drani'shadara's tears," Neku responded quietly. "Years ago, the Drani'shadara would always attend opening night at the opera in Trelissar. They would try to outdo themselves each year, putting on the most magnificent spectacle they could." He sighed. "I've been a time or two myself, over the years. Anyway, sometimes the spectacle was enough that it would move the Drani'shadara to tears. They would collect the tears with its blessing, and use them to make paint. They were imbued with magic, so they could make paint with colors that would shift and change on the canvas. The greatest artists of all time lived in Trelissar then, and they had galleries that people would travel from all over the world to see." He looked down at Rose again, longing in his eyes. "I wish you could have seen it."

Looking at the iridescent liquid in the vial, Rose could imagine what masterpieces could be made from such a substance. "Where did this come from, then?" she asked.

Neku shrugged with an effort. "I don't know. No new paintings have been made since the Rot came. The tears used to be stored in the now abandoned city museum in Trelissar. I never considered what happened to them after the Drani'shadara died."

"Ydenda told me in the Garden of Blue that she'd had a vial." Rose said. "She said the Ma'ar had taken it from her."

Neku nodded slowly. "She must have gone back for it at some point after the Rot came. Part of her must have remembered." He heaved a sigh, his tone wistful. "Ysenderia. I can't believe she was there the whole time. I wonder if she even knew what it was."

Rose held the vial carefully, reverently. "It still has its magic, then?"

Neku nodded. "It will replenish the magic I stole from the seed. Mix it with your blood."

Rose looked at the vial a moment longer, before tucking it carefully into the pocket of her pants.

Suddenly the light in the room changed, darkening as Rot crept across the outside of the window, blotting out the dim light from the sun.

"You have to go now," Neku said quietly.

Tears filled Rose's eyes again, but she nodded.

"I'm going to release the spell on you. You can't touch me after that. Go through the other door."

"Then what?" Rose whispered, though she already knew the answer.

"Plant the seed. And I'll use the dagger."

Her tears spilled over, cascading down her cheeks.

"Are you ready?"

Rose nodded, her eyes on Neku, her throat too thick to speak.

Neku took her free hand, the one that didn't hold the seed, and clutched it in both of his, meeting her eyes. She saw him hesitate for a fraction of a second, then he gave her hand a light tug, and pulled her toward him.

Rose's breath caught, and her eyes closed the instant

before his lips met hers. The kiss was gentle, lovely, a promise of all the things that could have been, if only...

His lips were soft, his skin warm, and after a time he broke the kiss and pulled back, leaning his forehead against hers. A second later he pulled her back in. The second kiss was rough, urgent, and she could taste the salt of both their tears on her tongue in the moment before he released her.

Their eyes met in a look that said everything neither of them had the words to say, before Neku released her hands.

"*Go,*" he said, and released the spell. Her cuts and scrapes began to bleed again.

Her heart splintering in her chest, Rose went.

41

NEKUTHAEDRIS

The door closed behind Rose with a resounding thud, reverberating the air around him like the tolling of a great bell. There was a finality to the sound, and Neku let his eyelids grow heavy as his head fell back against the wood of the door.

His thoughts drifted. Impressions danced before his closed eyes, long remembered images, thoughts, feelings. He was in Trelissar, sitting next to the Drani'shadara at the opening night of the opera season. It was a comedy about a bird in a cage that granted wishes that always went awry. He wore a tall blue hat that matched his suit, and laughed until his sides hurt.

The head chef at the castle, Juni, had just given birth to triplets, and the entire staff had gathered around, despite her protestations, to exclaim in hushed voices over the tiny sleeping faces.

He was in New York City, on the Fourth of July, watching fireworks burst in colorful streaks against the night sky.

It was snowing. He hid, crouching out of sight on the balcony above the castle door, waiting as Ysenderia came up the path. The snowball caught her right on the top of the head, and her outrage made him laugh so hard he nearly fell off the balcony.

Wings spread, Neku soared out over the open waters of the Etlass Sea on a star-studded night.

Rose, her lips soft and warm, pressed against his.

Thousands of days, millions of moments, filled with wonder, and beauty, and friendship, and life.

He could still feel the pressure of her lips on his, still smell the scent of her all around him, when he picked up the magically-imbued dagger from the floor by his side. He didn't open his eyes. Didn't look down at the crust of blood that marred the decorative filigree as he raised the blade to his chest, tucking the tip under the bottom edge of his rib and angling it upward.

He let his thoughts flow, reveling in the memories, the sights and sounds and tastes, and there was the faintest of smiles on his face when he used all of his remaining strength to drive the dagger home.

42

ROSE

The trip back through the gate happened between one step and the next. One second Rose was standing in the grand foyer of the castle, Neku's broken, bleeding, beloved face looking at her from where he sat slumped against the thick wood of the door they'd entered through. The next second she had wrenched open the identical door that fitted seamlessly into the wall next to the first. She stepped through, closed it, and found herself back in a clearing that looked so utterly familiar and yet so utterly foreign at the same time that she fell to her knees, struggling for breath.

Behind her, the small cozy cottage she had entered what seemed like a lifetime ago sat quietly nestled amidst the wildflowers. Across the meadow towered a forest filled with oaks, maples, and pines, their branches thick with standard green leaves. Familiar birdsong filled the woods and the grass was teeming with the sound of buzzing insects. A hot, sticky summer wind blew lightly through the meadow, and the mid-afternoon sun was bright overhead.

If she hadn't still been clutching the seed in her arms,

she would have thought it was all a dream. But the seed was there, its muted colors swirling together, and she could feel the glass vial digging into her leg through her pants. And, more than anything else, she could still feel the press of Neku's lips on her own.

It was all real. She knew she shouldn't be wasting time, kneeling here, staring off into space. But her mind was overflowing, struggling to process everything she had been through. As the adrenaline and fear drained out of her system, it left room for the pain and loss to take hold, and they seemed to fill a space inside her that was as vast and deep as the ocean.

Rising to her feet long enough to move away from the cottage and out into the meadow, Rose lay down on her back in the tall grass, pillowed her head on her arms, and just let herself breathe. She could feel the tickle of grass on her skin, and she focused on the feeling, letting her emotions bubble up inside her and overflow, silent tears streaming down her cheeks.

She looked up at the cottage, at the steeply pitched roof, and the wisteria that climbed the trellises that framed the door. She looked at the simple wooden entry and thought about how easy it would be to walk back across the meadow, through that door, and back into the world that had, in less than a month, come to feel like home.

But she knew there wouldn't be anything on the other side of that door that she could return to.

A minute later, as she watched, the entire house shivered slightly, trembled and began to grow transparent. A moment stretched when she could see the outline of the far trees through the wavering walls, and then it faded into nothingness. Where the cottage had once stood, nothing remained, not even flattened grass to prove it had once existed. And

Rose knew it was over. The gate was closed, and her memories were all that remained of an entire world.

She lay silent in the grass, her cheeks drying in the warm breeze.

There was a time, after the accident, when Rose thought she would never feel as lost and alone as she had then. Never before faced with a tragedy so great as losing her entire family in one stroke, she was unable to imagine a pain greater than that. And now, lying alone in the grass, she slowly came to realize that she had been right. Because while the loss of an entire world was surely objectively worse, while the loss of Neku and Ydenda felt like her heart had been ripped out and trampled, still, these feelings of loss and pain were no longer new and foreign. The deep ache of loss had become familiar, and Rose realized that while the pain now felt fresh and overwhelming, the kind of pain you didn't know if you could live through, couldn't imagine recovering from, she had been through it before. And she *had* lived through it. She *had* recovered from it.

And she would again.

A long moment passed as Rose lay in the grass, mind blank as she watched the clouds move slowly through the sky and listened to the sound of the birds in the trees. Then she rolled onto her side, and then onto her knees, where she pushed back to sit. Grabbing a fistful of grass, she yanked it out by the roots, then grabbed another handful and did the same. Slowly, she cleared a small circle, pulling out the roots and brushing the loose pebbles aside. Then she pushed her fingers down into the rich, loamy soil, and dug out a small trench. More, digging deeper, until her fingers were black with dirt and she had a cavity just the right size. Gently, reverently, she laid the seed into the hole she'd made, then carefully covered it back up, pushing the dirt back in around it and gently tamping down the mound.

Sitting back on her haunches, Rose retrieved the vial from her pocket. The liquid still glittered behind the glass, swirling thickly as she held it up. She pried the stopper off the top with a fingernail, then poured the viscous liquid over the mounded soil where she'd buried the seed. It seeped into the earth and disappeared.

She placed the empty vial on the ground, closed her hand tightly, and brought the side of her fist down on the delicate glass. It shattered, splinters of glass skittering away, two larger fragments lodging deep in the skin on the side of her palm.

Drawing in a sharp breath, Rose braced herself and pulled the glass free with her other hand. Blood welled up from the wounds, thick and red, spilling down the side of her hand in a slow, dripping stream. Rose held her hand close over the mound of earth, and watched as her blood saturated the soil. She sat there, silently watching, until the blood began to clot and the wound stopped oozing.

Then she sat back on her heels, and waited.

~

Rose waited for hours, sitting quietly by the mound of dirt, keeping vigil. She had no idea how long Rebirth ceremonies usually took, or if they varied on opposite sides of the gate, or if she had done it correctly, or if the magic would work at all. But she waited, patiently at first, then impatiently, then patiently again, until the sun began to drop behind the trees and she knew she had to leave.

Walking home in the dark wasn't an option, she knew; that was what had started her down this path in the first place, and with the sun beginning to set, she had maybe an hour before it would be full dark in the forest.

She didn't want to go, couldn't bear the thought of leaving the meadow and returning to the life that no longer felt like hers, but she was bone weary, fatigued and exhausted both physically and emotionally, not to mention starving. She tried to remember when she'd last slept or eaten, or showered and changed her clothes even, and couldn't summon the memory. It was time to go.

She made the trek through the woods on autopilot. The trees here were too small, too green. The smells of the forest were wrong. But her feet led her unerringly back along the narrow deer path, then onto the main trail, and eventually she came out behind the dumpsters in the corner of the parking lot of her apartment complex.

The door to her apartment was locked, as she'd left it, the keys long gone in a pair of pants or a backpack somewhere during her journey. Stooping, Rose found a loose brick laying amidst the trash lining the wall of the building. Without a pause to think or care, she hurled it through the window of her first floor apartment. The glass shattered and rained down, and after knocking out the remaining shards, Rose hauled herself through the now empty frame, carefully avoiding the broken glass that now lay scattered all over her couch.

Inside the apartment she sat in the dark for a moment, trying to find the strength to push on a little further. Eventually, she rose and found the light switch, flooding the small space with artificial light.

A warm breeze blew in through the broken window. She would have to fix that, or at least report it. If she stayed here. She already knew she wasn't going to. She wondered where she might go, what she might do. But those were thoughts for tomorrow. Or the next day.

She went into the kitchen and found her phone sitting just where she'd left it on the table, waiting for her as if she'd been gone no more than an hour. The light flashed when she turned it on. One missed call, one new voicemail. Only one call, in all this time.

The message was from her job. She didn't listen to it, just left the phone on the table and went to the fridge. There was fruit there, a bag of apples. She ate one standing over the sink, remembering the apple she'd eaten in Neku's kitchen, how delighted she'd been to find something familiar. This apple tasted like sawdust in her mouth. She finished it, then ate another.

When she was full enough she showered, washing herself clean of blood and dirt and whatever else was stuck in her hair and dried on her skin. She washed her hair with citrus-scented shampoo that smelled nothing like bogberry or borlus root. Then she dried off, bandaged her hand and treated her other cuts and scrapes, and put on the most comfortable clothes she could find—the softest pants, the stretchiest tank top.

For some reason she couldn't quite identify, she couldn't bear the thought of sleeping alone in her bed. Back in the living room, she swept the glass off the couch and lay down there. The breeze was still warm and soothing, but sleep felt like it was a million miles away. She propped her hands under her head and turned toward the back of the couch, under the empty window frame. She looked up at the night sky. Without the glass divider, it looked so close, yet also so far away. She felt like she could fall up, into the sky, and drift there forever. The summer night was studded with stars, bright and flickering over the darkness of the nearby forest. Her eyes automatically picked out familiar constellations, drilled into her head through countless camping trips with her parents.

She wondered idly if the stars had been the same in the sister world. She'd never thought to look up and see. Staring up at the familiar light of the stars, Rose thought sleep would never come.

But eventually, it did.

43

ROSE

When Rose woke, it was still pitch black, and the only indication that time had passed at all was that the constellations above had moved across the sky. She had no idea what time it was or how long she'd been asleep, only that dawn was still a long way off.

She closed her eyes again, trying to relax, but sleep wouldn't come, and after a time she opened her eyes and sat up, throwing off the light blanket she'd pulled over her in the night.

It was quiet, the way it is at nighttime near a forest, which is to say not quiet at all. Through the broken window, the buzzing of insects was loud. She could hear the sound of frogs from somewhere nearby—chorus frogs from the sound of it, with their strange song that sounded like a finger stroking down the edge of a comb. The bark of someone's dog from somewhere else in the complex.

Rose pushed to her feet and stood there for a moment, listening to the sounds of the night, considering. Then, without stopping to think, she grabbed a light cardigan from the back of a kitchen chair and a flashlight from the drawer.

She left her phone on the table, slid on her shoes, and headed out the door, not bothering to lock it behind her.

Even with the broken window, the air outside was slightly cooler, and Rose shrugged into the sweater. The sky was clear, the stars still visible, and the moon was bright as she made her way across the parking lot. The second she stepped off the asphalt and onto the forest path though, the moonlight dimmed, swallowed by the dense foliage overhead. Rose switched on the flashlight, letting the beam guide her into the trees and down the trail.

She wasn't sure what she was doing. There was nothing there for her. Just an empty clearing and painful memories. But the night air felt soothing after the claustrophobia of her apartment, and she somehow felt less alone out here.

Her mind wandered as she walked through the forest, and she let it go where it would. She thought about the first time she'd seen Ydenda in the forest, and how alarming she'd looked with her piercing red eye and milky white one, face bisected by lines of Rot. She remembered the delicious red pancakes both Ydenda and Neku had made her. She remembered how fancy she'd felt when Anae had helped dress her for the opera, lending her jewelry and fussing over her hair. She thought too about her shock when the Ma'ar had pulled a knife on her at the opera. She remembered the terror she'd felt on the Mist Bridge, passing that shadowy figure time and time again. She thought about how skittish Neku had been when she'd first met him, and how much he'd changed in the short time she'd known him.

She was so lost in her thoughts that she missed the turn off to the deer path, and had to backtrack when she realized she had gone too far. Coming back from the other direction, the narrow beam of her flashlight lighting the trail in an unfamiliar way, she almost missed it again, but her attention was caught by a dim light through the trees right where the turn off was.

Surprised, she looked up. Had she lost track of time and dawn was coming already? But no, the stars were still visible through the gaps in the leaves overhead. The sky hadn't lightened at all. Looking back down the path, she saw the light again.

Her heart sped up, and she clicked off her flashlight. She wasn't ready to encounter another person, wasn't sure she could deal with talking to someone who had their life in order, who hadn't been through what she had over the past week. Besides, what kind of person was wandering around in the forest in the early hours of the morning on a—Rose suddenly realized she had no idea what day it was. Was it even still August?

She stood still. She wanted to move off the trail into the trees, but she didn't want to make any noise and call attention to herself.

Peering through the blackness that surrounded her, Rose was uncomfortably reminded of the Rot in the forests of the sister world, and she had to remind herself that it wasn't here, that she was safe. And suddenly there it was again—a pale light through the trees. It was low to the ground, and moving. The beam from a flashlight? No, it didn't look quite right. She stayed motionless, holding her breath as it moved slowly closer. It was on the deer path with her, she realized, coming toward her. Her muscles tensed, and she debated whether to run.

But before she could take a step, could convince her muscles to move, a strange feeling came over her, something she had never felt before. It was almost like an image formed in her mind, not something she had thought, but more like a thought that had been put there by someone else, some*thing* else.

Her shock was so profound, she completely missed the actual content of the thought. She was still processing the feeling, almost starting to convince herself that she'd imagined it, when it came again. It was a question, an impression of something curious and inquisitive.

Planeswalker?

Rose's flashlight slipped from nerveless fingers, and with one gasping breath, she began to run. She tripped, stumbling over roots in the dark, but she aimed for the light she could still see moving in the trees. And she could see it more clearly now, colored lights, shifting and swirling together in lazy spirals, and as she grew closer the lights became clearer, and took on the shape of a creature. The most amazing, bizarre, and beautiful creature she had ever seen or could ever imagine.

It was small, no higher than her waist, with a shaggy coat of pale green, and it gave off a pearlescent glow as it walked, lighting the woods around it with shifting arcs of color. Thin vines and tiny budding flowers twined through its coat, and life sprouted where it walked, plants growing, blooming, fading, in a trail behind it as it moved. Small, ridged, curling horns grew from the sides of its head.

Rose ran, stumbling through the forest, and when she finally grew close enough she fell on the creature with a sob, wrapping her arms tight around the small body, threading her fingers into the thick fur and burying her face in the creature's warm neck, heedless of the flowers being crushed under the force of her embrace.

The sending that she received then was both amused and compassionate, and she pulled back, feeling slightly embarrassed.

Do not be embarrassed. The sending contained words this time, forming in her thoughts. It seemed like it should have felt intrusive, but somehow it didn't. It felt normal, like a way of communicating that she'd always been able to do, but had just never known it.

"You must be the Drani'shadara," she said, the words feeling foolish and obvious on her tongue.

And you are Rose. It is my greatest honor to meet a new planeswalker.

Sitting back on the dry leaves of the forest floor, Rose felt a pang, joy and sorrow warring in her heart.

"You—there is so much I have to tell you," she began. "So much has happened since you've been gone, and I don't even know half of it. But Nekuthaedris...the gate is closed. Maybe it's gone, I don't know how it works, and he said to tell you he's so sorry—and you—we—" The words spilled out, tumbling over each other as they gained momentum, and Rose didn't know what to say first, didn't know how to start or how to explain.

The sending that filled her mind then, stemming the flow of words, was one of peace, calm and understanding.

I know. I know what has happened.

Looking at the creature, Rose felt like she could fall into the depths of its eyes and drown there.

"But how? I—"

The memories are in the magic. I have seen it all.

Rose was quiet then, unsure of what to say.

It is a great sacrifice you have made. You have shown great courage, every step of the way.

Rose's voice was soft, hesitant. "Neku said he didn't know what would happen when he closed the gate. He didn't know if this world could survive on its own, without a gate, without a...gatekeeper." Her voice cracked on the word.

The sorrow was clear in the sending she received. *It cannot. All worlds must be bound in pairs.*

Her breath caught. "So, this world will die too, then? Everything we've done...was too late?"

The Drani'shadara didn't answer, just leveled its unfathomable gaze on her for a long moment. Then it rose to its feet, turned, and started down the path, moving slowly toward the clearing.

Come, planeswalker. It is time for you to see what we have created.

Rising, Rose followed the Drani'shadara down the path, using the swirls of light it emitted to see where to step. *Created? What did* that *mean?*

She trailed after the creature, watching the tiny plants grow and die in its wake as it walked, and felt...well, she wasn't even sure how she felt. Overwhelmed, she supposed. Despite Neku's description, the Drani'shadara wasn't anything like she'd expected. It was...*more*.

Together, they walked down the deer path, and the further they went, the more tense Rose grew. The Drani'shadara must have sensed her agitation, because it paused once, looking back over its shoulder.

Be calm, planeswalker. It is not an ending you have brought. It is a beginning.

And with that, for the first time, Rose felt the faintest stirrings of hope.

They continued on, moving slowly and carefully in the dark of the forest, and it seemed like ages before the break in the trees loomed ahead.

Rose's heartbeat sped up, like a hummingbird fluttering its wings in her chest, and she forced herself to breathe, slowly, evenly. She held tight rein on the hope in her chest, letting it burn like the flame of a small candle, but not grow.

And then the trees ended, the meadow opening up before them, the stars and the bright moon shining down to light the clearing with a soft glow. Rose's breath caught in her throat, and she felt as if her heart had stopped beating.

There, in the center of the tall grass, stood a tall, rambling farmhouse. It was a two story structure paneled in wide planks of clapboard siding, with lots of large windows and a huge covered wraparound porch supported by decorative columns. Bright green shutters framed the windows and flowers grew in profusion from the window boxes on either side of the bright red door.

It looked nothing like the cottage that had once stood there, and nothing like Neku's castle, but Rose didn't care. She knew it was home. The flickering candle flame of hope within her bloomed into a forest fire, engulfing her, but rather than destroying, it rebuilt her, from her soul outward.

She bounded up onto the porch in two steps and reached for the handle of the door. It was locked.

"Of course," she muttered, "I need blood to pass through."

Allow me, came the sending, and the Drani'shadara lowered its head and gently nudged the door open with a push from one of its horns. Together, they stepped through.

It wasn't Neku's castle, and for a moment, Rose felt dread rising within her. But no, she thought, no matter what had been created here, that world, the sister world, was gone, and the castle with it. The house on her side was new, of course this one would be as well. A new house and a new world.

The new house may not have been a castle, but it certainly still seemed impressive enough. With its warm wood floors, high ceiling with a low-hanging chandelier, and elaborate fireplace, it put her in mind of a manor house on a European lord's estate. Long hallways stretched out to either side of the grand foyer, but Rose had no desire to explore right now. The Drani'shadara seemed to know where to go, and Rose followed.

She turned around, and followed it right back out the door set into the wall adjacent to the one they had entered through. And outside this door, Rose stopped, her breath catching in her throat.

It was daytime again here, bright puffy clouds drifting through a blue sky. They were not in a meadow, surrounded by forest, as she had half expected. Instead, the house seemed to be perched at the edge of a sheer cliff, jagged ridges of rock giving way to nothing but an endless sea of sparkling water that stretched all the way to the far horizon. Turning in a slow circle, Rose could see behind the house to where mountains rose in the distance, their white peaks stretching toward the sky.

The door had let them out onto a porch, with steps leading down and away from the house to the right, but to the left there was nothing but a tall railing and beyond that the endless stretch of sea and sky.

And also to the left, at the edge of the railing, with his back to Rose and his face toward the sea, stood a tall, familiar form, with shining white hair blowing softly in the ocean breeze.

"Nekuthaedris."

He turned at her voice, and the smile that stretched across his face was wide, and real, and just for her. There was not a trace of Rot to be seen on him. His slanted eyes were the deepest purple, his skin pale blue and healthy, with faint lines of filigree etched through it that moved when he opened his arms.

She was in them between one breath and the next, and

he folded her into him and held her tightly. The Drani'shadara was there, then, trailing flowers in its wake as it stepped to the railing beside them and looked out over the sea so far below. Rose didn't have to look up at Neku's face to know that a silent conversation had already taken place between the two of them, apologies and forgiveness, sorrow and regret, and the joy of being reunited.

After a time, he released her, and she stepped back, and they stood together at the railing, the three of them.

Rose turned and looked up at the house, and the mountains beyond. "It looks more like my world than I expected," she mused. "What are the people like? What is the world like?"

Neku smiled down at her and took her hand in his, lacing their fingers together. "I don't know. I haven't even left the house yet."

She looked at him in surprise, but he only smiled.

"I was waiting for you."

EPILOGUE

There was more work to be done than Rose could ever have imagined. It ranged from small things—like exploring the area around the house, meeting local people, finding out where to buy food—to bigger things—like breaking ground on the construction of a new Ossuary, set into the cliff by the house. There was so much to discover: new modes of transportation, new types of technology to learn. Sometimes Rose felt like she could scarcely take it all in, but by and large this world, like the other world, was very similar to Rose's own in many fundamental ways. Besides, the people were on the whole very friendly and welcoming, which made a world of difference.

Rose was confused about how exactly the details worked.

"So, did this world exist before the other one died? Or did it just kind of pop into existence at the moment it was needed?" she had asked Neku one day as they walked down the winding path that led to the nearest town, one that Rose had been delighted to find was within walking distance.

Neku had shrugged. "That's possible."

"But then, what about the people here? They all have memories; they have history! Where did that come from?"

Neku had laughed and swung his arm around her shoulders. "I don't know. Maybe this one was paired with another one that was lost."

"Well, then what happened to *their* gatekeeper?"

He had sobered at that. "I don't know. I don't think there's any way to know. We just have to take care of what we've been given."

Rose had been quiet for a minute then, turning the possibilities over in her head. Eventually she'd asked, "Do you think the Drani'shadara knows?"

"Oh, I'm sure of it," he'd replied.

Rose, thinking of the swirling depths of unfathomable knowledge in the Drani'shadara's eye, was sure of it too.

∼

It had not been smooth sailing on all fronts, however. The magic that Neku had taken from the seed had not been entirely restored from the vial of tears Rose had poured over it, and as a consequence, the Drani'shadara appeared to be aging much faster than usual. According to Neku, the length of the Drani'shadara's life was wildly variable, with Rebirth ceremonies taking place anywhere from every few decades to more than a century stretching between them.

But this time, little more than two years had passed before it became apparent that the time for a Ceremony was drawing near. The Drani'shadara was enormous, rising high above Rose's shoulder, and its coat had deepened to a dark, forest green. The flowers that bloomed from the vines that wreathed it were starting to wilt, and the plants that sprouted from the ground in each step grew slower and shriveled faster. Its glow had dimmed, and it moved slower as well.

They had rushed to finish the Ossuary in time, and sent out notices all over the world, inviting anyone who wished to attend, encouraging those who couldn't to celebrate the occasion with friends and family in their own cities and towns. Determined to return the Ceremony to the happy celebration it was meant to be, Rose and Neku had gone all out. And it had taken six months of planning, organizing and decorating, but at last the day had come.

Chefs had come from the village, bringing enough food to create a feast for a small city, and were currently laying it out on the lawn in front of the house. The house itself had been decorated from top to bottom with flowers, and beautiful patterned lanterns lined the path from the house down to the Ossuary, just waiting for it to grow dark.

Rose, for her part, was unaccountably nervous. As far as either of them knew, she was still the only planeswalker alive in either world, but Neku assured her that more would show up eventually.

"But how will they know to come here? How will they know what they are?" Rose was upstairs in the expansive bathroom, brushing out her hair to keep from fidgeting with her dress.

"They'll come eventually. They always do," Neku assured her, shrugging into the embroidered coat he would be wearing for the festivities. "You came, didn't you? The gate found you."

Rose raised an eyebrow, wondering, not for the first time, about the chain of events that brought her to where she was today.

"Besides," Neku continued, "I don't know why you're so nervous. You've performed the Ceremony before."

"Not with people watching!" she protested. "What if I mess it up?"

Neku stepped close and dropped a kiss on the top of her head. "You won't."

~

The sun began to set, dropping slowly behind the sea to the west, and before Rose knew it, it was time for the Ceremony to start. Guests had been arriving all throughout the day, trickling in in twos and threes, so it never looked like all that many people, but when she descended the stairs and went out onto the lawn, the number of people who had come was shocking.

Nearly the entirety of the nearby village was in attendance, and the village as a whole had thrown open its doors to provide lodging for anyone who had traveled from farther away, of whom there were plenty. A sizeable group was in attendance from Colandris, the capital city of the region, and there were even a handful of travelers from as far as Sewerd, on the other side of the sea. There were people speaking in languages she couldn't identify, dressed in strange, foreign clothes. Rose supposed an event like this, that might not happen again in one's lifetime, was not to be missed.

The sea of people filled the lawn and stretched up toward the hill in the distance that led to the village. Groups of musicians were scattered throughout the lawn, but when Rose and Neku walked through the door, through the gate and into the world, somehow, they all knew to stop playing at once. Neku raised his voice, magically augmenting it so it could be heard by everyone in attendance.

"Welcome, welcome everyone! We are so glad you could all be here today. We have gathered to celebrate..."

Rose stopped paying attention as she caught sight of the Drani'shadara emerging through the crowd. Her breath caught, as it did every time. The creature looked no less magnificent now, nearing the end of its life, than it had the first moment she had seen it in the woods. Its darkened coat was still thick and healthy; its massive curved horns were burnished and gleaming.

Its ponderous footsteps were slow as it wove through the crowd, stopping in intervals to communicate with the villagers, or to let a child pick a flower from its coat, or pet its fur, and each person it passed appeared just as awestruck as Rose herself felt.

Finally, it reached the front steps of the house, and Rose realized Neku had stopped talking. People began to move, some groups forming up into rows that lined the stone walkway that led down to the Ossuary, others forming a procession that would follow them down the path.

The musicians began to play again as Rose slid her hand through the crook of Neku's elbow, and the two of them followed the Drani'shadara's slow steps off the porch.

The Ossuary was set deep into the rock of the cliff upon which the house had been built—or appeared, or however that worked—and in many ways it resembled the one Rose had known from Neku's former castle. The path curved around a steep, tight curve, with the rock face of the cliff on one side and nothing on the other but a sturdy railing and a drop to the sea. It was dark enough now that the lanterns had all been lit, their lights shining through intricately carved iron holders to cast beautiful patterns across the stone as they descended. Revelers lined the walkway, and as they passed, hands reached out to touch the Drani'shadara's shaggy coat, to touch her and Neku's shoulders, and grasp their hands for luck.

At the bottom of the path was a high stone arch. The word "Ossuary" had been carved into it in the strange, curling writing of the world that no longer existed, a reminder of the importance of their task. Rose closed her eyes briefly as they passed under the arch, the image of a face forming in her thoughts. A beloved but terrifying face, with thick tangled black hair, a piercing red eye and a milky white one peering out through black streaks of Rot. She missed Ydenda, and wished desperately that her friend could be here, could know that her sacrifice was not in vain. She thought Ydenda would have been very happy here, and would be proud of what they had accomplished.

When she opened her eyes, she saw Neku was looking at her, his eyes shining in the light from the lanterns. She could tell he had been thinking similar thoughts, and she squeezed his arm tightly, leaning into him.

The interior of the cavern was familiar: all stone, with an altar set into the far wall and alcoves with lanterns lining the remaining walls. No bones though, not yet, and Rose looked forward to a time when the cavern was filled with bones and the hum of magic could be felt in the air.

The feast and revelry would last all night, but the Ceremony itself was short and simple. The revelers remained outside as the three of them entered. The Drani'shadara strode to the far side of the cavern, and heaved its mass up onto the altar, where it turned to face them before lying down and curling into a comfortable position, its head propped on its forelegs, long tail wrapped around its body.

Releasing her arm, Neku reached into the deep pockets of his embroidered coat and procured a long-bladed dagger, its hilt intricately carved with swirling patterns. It was an ordinary dagger, not yet magically imbued or attuned to the Drani'shadara, and it had been forged only a month before by an ancient blacksmith down in the village. He handed the blade to Rose, hilt first, and she took it gingerly, feeling the weight of the cool metal in her hands.

The Drani'shadara looked up at Rose expectantly, and for a brief moment, she froze in horror.

"I don't...I don't have to *kill* it or something, do I?" she whispered out of the side of her mouth. "You didn't mention that part!"

Neku snorted with poorly-suppressed laughter, and a sending from the Drani'shadara told Rose that the creature was equally amused.

"No," Neku assured her. "I told you once that if the Drani'shadara is at the end of its life, it can trigger the Rebirth Ceremony itself. It was only because of...extenuating circumstances that we did it differently before."

Rose blew out a breath.

A sending came to her, filling her mind.

Are you ready?

Rose nodded, a little jerkily.

All will be well.

And then it happened. The Drani'shadara closed its eyes and released a deep, long breath, the air flowing out in a slow, steady stream. It relaxed, all its muscles going limp, and there was just a brief moment where it looked as if it was simply sleeping, before it started to change. Gradually, its dark green coat began to brown at the edges, growing coarse and brittle before seeming to dry out, like leather left too long in the sun. The vines encircling it turned brown and began to decay, the flowers wilting, the horns drooping. It appeared to Rose, who watched with a measure of both fascination and alarm, like the natural process of decay, only sped up, the skin eventually turning to dust and blowing away, until nothing remained on the altar except a pile of heavy white bones, and a bright, swirling seed nestled in the hollow they formed.

Rose let out the breath she didn't realize she'd been holding, and turned to Neku, who gave her a broad smile and a nod.

She lifted the dagger. Taking a deep breath, she placed the sharp edge of the blade against the back of her forearm, well away from any major veins or arteries, and with a sharp jerk, pulled the blade through her skin.

She gave a small gasp, and the blood welled thick and fast, running down her arm in a stream, and dripping bright red droplets onto the surface of the seed. Neku had assured her that they didn't need to bury the seed in the soil—that had simply been a precaution in case the transformation wasn't instantaneous and she'd needed to leave the meadow. It was fascinating this time to see the effects of the blood up close. It was like the etched spirals of color on the surface of the seed soaked the blood in, drinking it up, and it began to glow even brighter.

After a moment the blood stopped flowing, and Rose stepped back to let Neku wrap a bandage around her arm. But the glowing spirals on the surface of the seed continued to grow brighter, light emanating from the designs until they began to break apart, the light spilling out from the swirls almost too bright to look at as the seed began to change shape.

Rose watched in awe as the seed slowly morphed, and she was amazed to see that it really was like a seed, growing to form a plant, rather than hatching like an egg as she'd half expected. The Drani'shadara wasn't contained inside the seed; it *was* the seed, and slowly the seed grew larger, legs forming and pushing out, a head appearing with protruding horns. Fur grew, the palest green, and flowers sprouted and began to bloom, and finally, when the creature was about the size Rose had first seen in the forest, it slowed, and stopped, and opened its eyes.

The body was small, and new, but the twisting vortex of color was the same, and Rose felt Neku's hand slip into hers as a smile stretched across her face.

"Welcome back," she said softly, and the sending she received in response was filled with joy and happiness.

Neku retrieved the dagger and set it onto the shelf above the altar that had been fashioned for that reason, and, linking arms, they crossed the cavern and passed together under the archway.

The cry that went up amongst the onlookers when the Drani'shadara reemerged was instantaneous and deafening, and Rose couldn't keep from laughing. As they climbed the stone path, retracing their steps up toward the lawn, bright patterned light from the lanterns illuminated the smiling faces on both sides. Green plants and flowers bloomed ahead of them in the wake of the Drani'shadara's footsteps, and Rose looked out over the night-dark waters of the sea and felt the deep, enveloping contentment of someone who had finally found her place.

∼

Keep reading for an exclusive sneak peek of *Season of Embers,* Book One of *The Bonded Trilogy,* the debut collaboration from Rachael Vaughn and Wendi Williams. Told in alternating perspectives, this thrilling young adult novel uncovers a town's hidden secrets, exposing the lengths it, and its citizens, will go to in order to preserve their way of life.

Sofi and Darja may seem like average teenagers, but they're anything but. After all, one of them is alive...and one of them is not. The bond that joins them sets them on a collision course with the Vaikesti, a people dedicated to the old ways, the old beliefs...and an ancient magic.

But when a stranger starts poking around in the darkest corners of the town's history, Sofi and Darja must decide if he's friend or foe, and if he can help solve the riddle of an archaic and mysterious text—before the whole town ends in ashes.

CHAPTER 1

SOFI

"Sofi, hold *still!*"

My sister Arina's voice was shrill as she yanked my head back into position. My eyes watered as she tied another ribbon into place around a lock of my pale blond hair, tucking bright blue cornflowers around the plaited strands as she went. My mother made a sound of dissatisfaction from behind Arina, and in the mirror I could see her reach over my oldest sister's shoulder to adjust a stray tendril of hair that had snaked free from one of my elaborate braids.

A second later my mother's reflection disappeared as I caught a flash of flaxen hair out of the corner of my vision.

"Marten, no!"

A crash sounded from the kitchen, and my mother sprinted out of my bedroom after my two-year-old nephew. My middle sister, Hanna, was hot on her heels. The house was filled near to bursting, with my mother, grandmother, two aunts, three cousins, two sisters, and five children between them. It was bedlam.

It was always like this on Spring Day, when all the men

of the house disappeared and left the women to prepare for the Ceremony. I capitalized it in my mind, the importance of the event clear even though I knew barely anything about what would happen. Normally I disliked the chaos of this day, much preferring peace and quiet to the insanity that came of having my whole family gathered in one place. But today I didn't mind it, because it took at least some of the focus off me. Because today was *my* Spring Day, just a few weeks after my eighteenth birthday. And while I disliked noise and groups of people, I *hated* being the center of attention.

A cry came from the kitchen, and my head turned at the sound, but Arina gave my hair a vicious tug and I quickly straightened, stifling a groan.

"Don't pull all my hair out!" My voice came out in a whine. My nerves were showing. I'd spent most of my life looking forward to today with a stomach-twisting mixture of curiosity, dread, and excitement, and now that it was actually *here*, I was surprised I'd been able to keep from throwing up.

"There!" With a final eye-watering twist, Arina fastened the last ribbon into place and turned me to face my reflection in the mirror. I had to admit, she'd done an amazing job. The front part of my hair was caught back in a series of elaborate braids, all twined with satiny white ribbons. The rest was left to fall free in soft white-blond waves. Cascades of cornflowers, the very first of the season, were also woven through, seemingly held in place by magic. Against the dark brown of my eyes and my pale skin, the effect made me feel stunning—not a word I would have ever used to describe myself. I hardly recognized the face in the mirror.

A second shrill cry echoed down the hallway, and Arina looked up sharply at the sound of her own child, five-year-old Mia. She flashed a quick smile at me in the mirror. "You look beautiful. Don't worry, you'll do fine."

Uh-oh, I must not have hidden my nerves that well after all. Bending down, she gave me a quick hug. "I wish I could be there with you," she said. Her voice was wistful, but the look in her eyes was unreadable. Worried, maybe? Before I could puzzle it out, she left the room to deal with the escalating cries coming down the hall from the kitchen. Since only women over eighteen were able to attend the Ceremony tonight, Arina had volunteered to stay at home with the children. Looking at the stranger in the mirror, I half-wished I could take her place.

And yet despite my dislike of attention, I had to admit I was *curious*. So much of the Ceremony was shrouded in secrecy, I had only been able to glean the basics over the years.

Spring Day itself was a widely cherished event that our town had been celebrating ever since my great-grandfather and the small contingent of other immigrants had left our small, Eastern European homeland in the late nineteenth century, fleeing foreign occupation and establishing our little community of Vaikesti here in the midwestern United States. Not everyone in town was descended from the immigrant population, but a large majority was, and we kept to the old traditions, which included Spring Day. The bulk of the festivities would take place tomorrow, on the first of May, including singing, dancing, and plenty of food. And while every child in town looked forward to the carnival-like atmosphere of Spring Day, it was the events of tonight that made my stomach twist with nerves.

I knew the Ceremony took place at midnight. I knew only women were permitted to attend. I knew it would honor every girl who had turned eighteen since last Spring

Day. And I knew I had to participate in a secret ritual. But that was all I knew. My mother had explained that the ritual was intended to welcome me as an adult member of the community and honor the bond we all shared with our ancestors and the earth. But I had no idea what that really *meant*. The women of the community were notoriously tight-lipped, and even my sisters had been unwilling to share more.

My thoughts were interrupted as my mother reentered the room.

Her dark eyes, normally tired, were sparkling in her lined face, and she held in her arms a beautiful white dress I'd never seen before.

"Are you ready?" she asked, laying the dress out on the foot of my bed. I raised an eyebrow as I took in the yards of white fabric woven through with white ribbons and seed pearls, lace netting around the hem and scooped neck.

"Is it Spring Day or am I getting married?" I asked, half joking, but my mother didn't smile.

"Both of your sisters wore this dress on their Spring Day ceremonies," she answered. "Besides, it's tradition."

I knew better than to argue with that. "It's tradition," was the answer to pretty much any question I'd asked since I was old enough to ask questions. Besides, the dress *was* beautiful. Shrugging, I got to my feet and pulled off my t-shirt, then wriggled out of my jeans. My mother helped me step into the dress and maneuver it into place, doing up the hidden zipper in the back. She fluffed my hair out around my shoulders and turned me to face the mirror.

I really *did* look like I was going to a wedding. My own. I sucked in a breath. My mother was getting teary-eyed behind me. What the hell was going to happen tonight?

Hanna stuck her head around the door frame. She gave

me an approving smile before addressing my mother. "Arina's getting the kids ready for bed. Then it should be about time to go. Are you two ready?"

I had no idea if I was ready, so I didn't answer, but my mother gave a nod. "Make sure your *Vanaemake* is awake and ready. We'll be there in a minute."

Hanna nodded and left to find my grandmother. My mother turned me to face her.

"Do you remember all your words?"

"I think so," I said nervously. Each of the girls participating in the Ceremony had a series of lines to recite as part of the ritual. I'd been practicing my phrases, and while every kid raised in Vaikesti had more than a passing familiarity with the traditional language of our ancestors, the phrases were meant to be sung, and I'd have been lying if I said I wasn't afraid I'd mess up and make a fool of myself in front of my friends and family.

My mother sat on the edge of my bed and patted the quilt next to her. I joined her, perching awkwardly in my dress. Her face was serious as she looked me over, and my heart sped up. Was I *finally* going to find out what the night had in store for me?

"Sofi," she began. "Tonight is a very special night, you know that."

I didn't know anything, so I kept still and didn't interrupt.

"I don't know what your sisters may have told you, but I don't want you to worry."

What was *that* supposed to mean? They hadn't told me anything. I immediately began to worry.

"The rituals are old," she went on, "but the binding is symbolic. Maybe a long time ago the magic really worked, I don't know, but —"

She broke off when Hanna poked her head around the door again. I could have strangled my sister. Binding? *Magic?*

"We're ready when you are," my sister announced.

My mother made no effort to finish what she'd been saying; she just leaned in and gave me a quick kiss on the cheek. "I'm proud of you, *kallike,*" she whispered, then rose and left the room. I didn't miss the meaningful glance she shared with my sister on her way out.

Hanna must have seen the panicked expression on my face, because she gave me an understanding smile. "Don't worry," she said quietly as she ushered me out of the room, fussing over the trailing ribbons from my dress. Her lips were close to my ear. "The binding isn't real. I think they always hope it will be, but the words never work."

Before I had a chance to react, my aunts and older cousins joined the procession, my grandmother bringing up the rear, and I was herded out the door and into the cool night air. Whatever questions I might have had, it was too late. The Spring Day Ceremony was here.

CHAPTER 2
DARJA

I was floating. Weightless and untethered, blood thrummed in my fingertips and buzzed beneath my lips. My eyes were open, but everything around me was pleasantly out-of-focus. Velvet darkness hovered at the edges of my vision. I blinked, then blinked again, longer this time, gently coaxed by the siren song of unconsciousness.

But, no. It was important that I stay awake. I couldn't think why, but I knew it mattered. I sucked in a deep breath and felt my lungs fill with cool, antiseptic-scented air. Another breath. This one I held until I saw spots dance in front of my vision.

Slightly more alert, I focused my gaze on my surroundings, curious about what was causing this delicious lightness, like my whole body had been inflated with helium. I looked down my arm and saw something resembling a plastic butterfly perched on the back of my hand, and I smiled, delighted. It occurred to me only in a fleeting moment of clarity that "delighted" was not a word I would have used to describe my life before this place—this feeling—but I shook it off.

From the butterfly, a plastic tube snaked its way up a crisp white sheet, looped over a bed rail, and then twined around a metal pole like a hungry vine before disappearing into a plump bag filled with clear liquid. This, I was mostly sure, was the source of my current state of zen.

"Thank you," I mumbled incoherently in the general direction of the bag. My voice sounded thick and far away, not-quite-connected to the rest of me. The rest of me, meanwhile, pulsed with a thrilling numbness, like a foot fallen asleep, tingling and warm.

"What was that?"

The voice sounded as equally distant as my own, and for a moment, I thought it must have been me. But then a presence materialized at my side, a slim figure in a red polo and khaki pants. *Ms. Kross.* I tried to smirk, but couldn't get my face to cooperate. I had gotten in trouble for telling her all the *tajas* looked like they ran cash registers at Target. It felt like ages ago, but couldn't have been more than a few weeks.

It had been a sound beating, but nothing less than I deserved, as *Mama Taja* reminded me throughout. I'd laughed at her afterward, was struck again, then sent to Ms. Kross, who'd been stone silent as she bandaged my backside. Had I blushed? I couldn't remember now, but I didn't think so.

I looked at Ms. Kross now, her heart-shaped face stern. She'd told me once that looking mean made her seem older, and that made the girls respect her. I hadn't told her that at night, in our rooms, we frowned as hard as we could, seeing who could come closest to looking like "Kross the Boss."

I snorted at the thought, louder than I'd expected in the quiet room, nearly frightening myself out of my still-tingling skin.

"Is something funny?" she said, moving closer to check

the tubing attached to my happy little butterfly. "Does it hurt?"

"Yes," I said, answering the first question. Then, to the second, "And, no. Nothing hurts. Everything feels wonderful."

She cleared her throat. "Yes, well. That's the medication doing its job. It should last until..." She faltered, cleared her throat again, then busied herself clicking a small dial near the bag that hung above me.

"Until...?"

"The Ceremony. You remember, of course?"

I did. No amount of happy juice could cloud those memories. Naturally, I'd never attended one, but it was seemingly all we learned about, all we talked about, and sometimes, all we dreamed about. The Ceremony was our reason for existing, or so we were told. We wouldn't all be Chosen, but we were meant to act like we were. Because eventually, when we turned eighteen, one of us would be selected for the honor of representing the *koolis* at the Ceremony. It was a hard path, *Mama Taja* seemed to enjoy telling us, but whoever was Chosen would be rewarded beyond her wildest imaginings.

Was this my wildest imagining? The buzz was great, sure, but had I been dreaming of celebrating my eighteenth birthday shivering naked under a sheet in a hospital bed, too stoned to move?

"What's going to happen?" I asked, feeling suddenly breathless. The plastic butterfly seemed to have migrated to my belly, where it unfurled and beat its wings, sending my heart pounding into my throat.

"All shall be revealed," Ms. Kross said softly, the tired words sounding even more exhausted than usual.

"And the spirit shall be fulfilled," I responded, as I had

done every morning in *eksam*. I used to think if I just moved my lips without vocalizing the words, it wouldn't count. I didn't know why it had even bothered me, but it had, so I'd continued my silent protest until Helena Tamm went to *Mama Taja* and told her I refused to receive the spirit. I couldn't sit for a week.

"Good girl," Ms. Kross said, patting my arm with a cold hand that sent a chill crawling up my skin, leaving a trail of goosebumps in its wake. "Are you able to move?" she asked, crossing to a wardrobe in the corner and opening its doors to peer inside.

I tried to lift my arm, but only managed a couple fingers. "Not really," I said, attempting a shrug.

Ms. Kross sighed. "I'll need to find someone to help dress you." She turned away from the wardrobe, holding a long white dress over her arm, lace spilling nearly to the ground in a frothy cascade.

I swallowed, hard, feeling some emotion at seeing the dress, but not understanding what any of it meant. It was gorgeous, that much was obvious. The kind of dress I would have said I hated, but would have secretly wanted to crawl into, feeling the soft, handmade lace shift and slide against my skin.

I realized then what Ms. Kross had said. "Not *Mama Taja*," I said, hoping my face looked as pleading as I wanted it to.

"Darja," she said warningly, draping the dress over a chair and walking closer.

"Please," I said, meeting her eyes. Her icy blue gaze was piercing, but I didn't look away. I never had.

Finally, she relented. "Fine," she said tightly. "I'll go find Ms. Luts."

"Thank you," I said, but the door closed on my words, and she was gone.

Alone, I gathered whatever wits the drugs hadn't dulled, and looked around the room. We were in the *koolis*, I thought, but it wasn't a room I had ever been in before. Aside from the hospital bed and the wardrobe in the corner, the furnishings were sparse. Two chairs, one now hung with my white dress, sat near a shuttered window. Next to the door, a cabinet with a sink was attached to the wall. Above it hung a metal medicine chest. There were no mirrors. No pictures, no linens or curtains anywhere. It may as well have been an actual hospital room, as sterile as it was. The only indication of where I was hung over the medicine chest—a tapestry woven with two trees, heavy with spring blooms. Between them, a bonfire burned in red and orange threads. At the bottom, the words "*Tasakaalus, harmoonia*," were inscribed. In balance, harmony.

I didn't know what was coming. I didn't know if I was afraid, or excited, or just ready to get it over with. There hadn't been a day in the last eighteen years that I hadn't wondered what the hell The Ceremony was all about, and why no one could ever talk about it until they'd been to one. And even then, only to the other women in Vaikesti who'd attended. I'd seen the glances exchanged. The hushed whispers after another one of the *koolis* girls had her ceremony.

I wasn't sure what happened after. The girls were integrated back into Vaikesti when The Ceremony was over. We weren't told more than that; just that the girls had fulfilled their Great Command, and were free to return.

Return to what? I'd often wondered, but even at my most rebellious, I'd never had the courage to ask. I was raised at the *koolis* and though we had one day of classes each week at the county school, and one day a month to shop or socialize the next town over, we mostly kept to ourselves. The Vaikesti kids all knew us by the blue shift dresses we wore, and largely refused to interact with us. *Mama Taja* said it was because they resented our status, our opportunity to be selected as the Chosen, but the looks they gave us didn't convey jealousy; they were fearful, disgusted, even pitying. The county kids just thought we were weirdos and steered clear.

I was pulled from my confused and foggy thoughts by the sound of the door opening. Ms. Kross walked in with Ms. Luts in tow, holding a handful of vivid blue cornflowers. Ms. Luts was all round softness to Ms. Kross' sharp angles, and she was one of the few *tajas* that actually deigned to smile on occasion.

"Well," she said with a forced cheerfulness, bustling over to the bed and fiddling around with the same dial Ms. Kross had adjusted. "Are we ready to begin?"

"Begin wha—" I started to say, but the words were lost in a tidal wave of unimaginable bliss. Heat shot through my hand and up my arm, dispersing a warm glow throughout my extremities. I couldn't breathe, and I didn't much care. My eyelids fluttered, seemingly the only body part still capable of movement.

"That should do it," I heard Ms. Luts say. I felt the bed sink as she sat down at my feet and began pulling off the sheet, exposing my naked body to the chill air. "Let's get her dressed."

"Evelin," Ms. Kross said, sounding chastising, but already, their voices were fading. I didn't care about my nakedness. Didn't care that I was being pulled and tucked into my dress like an uncooperative toddler. Didn't even care when Ms. Luts pulled a brush through my long blond hair, hitting every snag along the way.

I was floating. Drifting. Disappearing. It was Ceremony time, and even though I couldn't muster the energy to care, I knew with some sort of sixth sense, ESP bullshit feeling that everything was totally, irrevocably about to change.

CHAPTER 3
SOFI

It was pitch black under the canopy of the forest. We parked the cars in the gravel lot at the edge of town behind the Rebane's house, where Merili and Lea Rebane joined us, and went the rest of the way on foot. The sense of anticipation I had been feeling all day seemed to blanket our group as soon as we reached the trees, and a hush fell over us, the only sounds the swish of our dresses and the crunch of leaves underfoot. I felt a surreal sense of disassociation as we followed the narrow trail through the trees, our path lit only by the sweeping beams of the flashlights. My anxiety, which had been building all day, had finally settled into a sort of nervous excitement.

Now that I was finally here, on my way through the woods surrounded by my family, my mother's and sister's words from the house faded into the background. I was surrounded by women who had participated in this very same ceremony on their own Spring Day, and no matter what the secrets may be or how many cryptic comments were made, each of these women had all made it through no worse for wear. I could do this too. I could become a real member of our community.

I'd never been to the old country, but I'd been told more than half the land there was blanketed with forests. And so, it was forests the immigrants had sought here as well, looking for any opportunity they could find to hold onto the old traditions. I couldn't imagine the trees here were anything like those back in that place the elders still called *Sünnipaik*, "home," but this was the only home I'd ever known. These woods were familiar to me, safe and comforting, the source of a thousand games of hide-and-seek. And after a minute I began to recognize where we were going—the Old Bonfire Grounds, where the whole town would gather to celebrate Midsummer Night in the summer and *Jõulud* in the winter.

This was probably just a bonfire and some ceremonial words. Just like all of our rituals. I tried to let this thought comfort me, and mentally chastised myself for getting so wound up. It almost worked.

I caught sight of another cluster of flashlight beams through the trees, and just a little further down the path we met up with Marta Kask and her family. Marta had been in my class at school since we were kids, until we'd graduated just two weeks ago. We weren't exactly close, but she was also newly eighteen, and seeing a familiar face in her own flowing white gown made me blow out a breath I didn't know I'd been holding. She looked like a ghost, her dress glowing pale as it seemed to float above the ground. If I remembered correctly, there should be two more girls here tonight. That is, assuming there weren't any girls from the *koolis* participating tonight. I thought there might be a girl or two my age over there, but we only saw them once a week at school, and like everyone else, I tried to steer clear.

Marta met my eyes and I could see my relief reflected back at me. I wondered if her family had told her any more than mine had. I doubted it. I directed what I hoped was a confident smile her way, and was met with a grimace that likely mirrored what was actually on my face.

Our two groups joined seamlessly and silently into one and we continued on toward the Old Bonfire Grounds. It wasn't far, less than a quarter mile, before I could see the flickering light of the fire in the distance. The wind rustled through the trees and I shivered in my thin dress. The weather was still temperamental this early in the spring, and the night air was chilly. Wishing I had a sweater, or at least long sleeves, I stepped faster, eager to feel the warmth of the fire on my skin. I supposed I should at least be glad it wasn't raining.

The trees began to thin gradually before giving way entirely to reveal a large clearing, and then suddenly we were there, the Old Bonfire Grounds, and my heart began to pick up again. The clearing was packed with people. It seemed we were the last ones there, and I didn't know where to look, my eyes jumping from the blinding light of the bonfire to the crowd, lighting on familiar faces and away as I tried to pick out other white dresses.

The crowd parted, making space for our two families. I felt my mother's hand on my arm, gently guiding me, and then when I didn't respond, grabbing my hand and dragging me around to the far side of the circle. I stumbled slightly before hurrying to catch up.

There were murmurs of greeting as we took our places, but the crowd was largely quiet, the sound of the crackling fire and thrumming of insects louder than the voices of what seemed to be nearly a hundred women. The same sense of silent anticipation that had settled over my family during our walk through the forest hung over the crowd like a cloud. I began to feel a bit queasy.

To my relief, we didn't have to wait long. We had just settled into place when the Ceremony began.

I wasn't surprised to see Eliise Tamm step forward. She leaned heavily on her cane as she turned her back to the fire and faced the gathered women. Eliise was my best friend Nora's great grandmother, and the oldest woman in Vaikesti by nearly a decade. Elders held a place of high esteem in our town, and her great-grandmother often presided over town events. Nora herself was still a few months shy of her eighteenth birthday though, and so had another year to wait before her own Spring Day Ceremony.

When Eliise opened her mouth to speak, the already quiet crowd fell as silent as death. Her body may have been frail, her back bent with age, but her voice was clear and strong in the silence of the clearing.

"Welcome to Spring Day!" A murmur of response echoed through the clearing. "We gather here tonight to welcome another generation of girls to Vaikesti adulthood. Tomorrow we celebrate the changing of the seasons and the synergy of our relationship with the earth. But tonight..." She glanced around the circle, her eyes lingering as she picked out the white dresses in the crowd. "Tonight we celebrate *you*."

A shiver ran up my spine. Eliise paused to clear her throat, then raised her voice again. "Marta Kask, please step forward."

I looked to Marta. Her eyes were as huge and round as dinner plates, but she joined Eliise by the fire.

"Elisabeth Koppel, please step forward."

Liz's dark head bobbed through the crowd and joined Marta at the front.

"Anna Saar, please step forward."

There was a pause, then another white dress materialized as the crowd across the way parted and let Anna through. She caught my eye as she took her place and winked. I held my breath.

"Sofia Ilves, please step forward."

My breath released in a whoosh, and I felt a nudge from Hanna behind me, and then I was moving, my feet carrying me forward to join the row of girls by the fire. I turned to face the crowd of silent women, faces I'd known since birth. The dancing flames reflected in their eyes, turning them into strangers. Or maybe I was the stranger. But only a little longer. After tonight, I would belong.

There was a moment of silence as we all stood in a line in front of the fire. I cast my eyes down, not wanting to meet all the expectant gazes looking back at me. Then, softly at first, Eliise began to sing. Her voice was lovely, high and haunting as it spiraled away into the darkness. A moment later, voices from around the circle picked up the melody, and soon the whole crowd had joined in, a harmony rising above the main melody in the words of the old country. I felt myself relax minutely at the sound, and after a moment, joined in. A festival in Vaikesti was never complete without music, and the familiarity was comforting.

I heard the other girls join in as well, and after a moment I felt Anna's hand slip into my own. I looked down and saw that she had linked hands with Liz on the other side as well, and I gave her fingers a squeeze.

The song ended the way it began, the voices dropping out one by one, until the chorus came back around again and only Eliise was singing, her voice fading softly as the last note stretched out into silence. We all stood for a moment, quiet and expectant, and then Eliise spoke again.

"Darja Kallas, please step forward."

I blinked in surprise, and felt Anna's hand tighten in mine, as the crowd parted and another girl stepped through. I hadn't seen her at first, standing as she was back by the trees, but she was wearing the same style of flowing white gown as the rest of us. Cornflowers were caught up in her dark blond hair.

I was momentarily confused. Was it her Spring Day Ceremony as well? Were there actually five girls? But if that was the case, why wasn't she called up here earlier with the rest of us? I slid a glance over to Anna, who gave me the barest shrug.

When the girl started through the crowd, her face caught the light and I realized I recognized her. I'd never seen her out of the blue dress she'd worn when she joined our class at school once a week, but she was one of the *koolis* girls. Of course. The *koolis* girls were kept apart from us in almost everything they did. Why not the Ceremony as well?

The girl—Darja, Eliise had called her—was flanked by two women as she walked, both wearing the recognizable khaki and red uniform of the *tajas*. They each had a shoulder under her arms, guiding her forward, and the crowd parted as they passed, giving them slightly more room than strictly necessary. I felt myself also moving aside without thought, making space for the girl.

Then the procession passed the crowd and I realized something was wrong. The *tajas* weren't *guiding* the girl, they were *carrying* her. She hung limply between them, her head lolling to the side, her feet dragging in the dust. What—?

The girl's eyes were alert though, and when she drew close her gaze met mine and I stepped back involuntarily, dropping Anna's hand in the process. Darja's pupils were dilated, the black orbs swallowing her eyes, and they locked on mine with an intensity that made me shudder. What was *wrong* with her?

Before I had time to react further, Eliise was speaking again, raising her voice to address the crowd.

"It is time. Time to welcome the Spring. Time to welcome five new members of our community. We have all watched these girls grow from children into women, and today they will earn their place with us as full members of Vaikesti, sworn to uphold the traditions we hold dear. Henceforth they will be bound to us, as we are all bound together, in life as in death, a circle of renewal that has no beginning and no end."

I tried to focus on her words, but I was acutely aware of the girl by my side, propped upright between the two *tajas*.

Eliise turned from the crowd to address the four—now five—of us, pitching her voice so everyone could still hear.

"From the earth we were born, and to it we return. We are bound to the earth in life, as we are bound in death. Tonight, we gather to strengthen those bonds, linking together each new member of our community with an *ohverdus,* so she may experience the bonds that connect us all."

I knew that word. *Ohverdus.* Sacrifice. I felt a shiver run down my spine, despite the heat from the fire that blazed behind me.

Eliise went on, looking at each of us in turn.

"The bonds we forge here tonight are permanent and real, and will guide you through the rest of your days. Will the *ohverdus* please step forward."

She looked expectantly at Darja, and the two *tajas* moved forward a step, hauling the girl with them. I looked uncomfortably between Eliise and Darja.

The old woman reached a withered hand into the deep

pocket of her pants, and came out holding a wickedly-sharp looking pair of scissors, the blades glinting in the firelight. I caught my breath as she leaned on her cane and hobbled a step toward Marta, who looked on with wide eyes.

A whispered word passed between the two, then Marta leaned down, letting Eliise tug a thick lock of her hair free from its elaborate styling. Raising the shears, Eliise snipped off a hank of Marta's golden hair, and I heard an involuntary sound of protest escape Marta before she could stop herself. Eliise had pulled the lock from underneath, where it wouldn't show, but I still winced in sympathy as Marta raised a hand to touch the blunt ends of her hair.

Without pause, Eliise moved down the line, removing a tress from Liz's dark hair and then one from Anna's loose curls before coming to stand in front of me. Obediently, I lowered my head as the other girls had, and the old woman separated a handful of strands from underneath my loose waves. The metal of the shears was icy cold where it brushed my neck, and I shivered as the blades sliced through.

Holding the four locks of hair deftly between the fingers of her gnarled hand, Eliise turned to stand before Darja, who stared back, unblinking. I'd expected the woman to remove a lock of Darja's hair as well, but instead, to my surprise, she replaced the scissors in her pocket. She let her cane fall by her feet and gestured at the *tajas*, who turned the girl around, so her back was to Eliise and the crowd. I watched, fascinated, as Eliise separated out a lock of Darja's dark blond hair with surprising dexterity and began to weave an intricate five-part braid, twining all of our stolen hair together. I could barely follow as her fingers flew through the strands, weaving us all together.

This must be the binding Mom and Hanna were talking

about, I thought with relief. I wasn't sure what exactly was supposed to happen here, but my mother's words echoed through my head. *"The binding is symbolic."* I shifted my weight from foot to foot. I was starting to get uncomfortable from standing so long. So far, the Ceremony had been rather underwhelming—singing and braiding hair? This is what I'd been so worked up about?

And yet I could still feel the presence of the *koolis* girl next to me, still as a statue. What was *wrong* with her?

Eliise finished her braiding and tied off the ends, then stepped back. "It is time for the *usutalitus* song."

I'd nearly forgotten.

"Marta, you may begin."

There was a long pause before Marta started. Her voice wavered and she took it slowly, carefully pronouncing the words. I glanced down the line and saw her eyes were closed, her cheeks pink as she sang.

In no time at all it was Liz's turn, and she picked up right where Marta left off, repeating the melody, her voice strong and firm. She looked out over the crowd as she sang, and I envied her poise, wishing I had half the confidence she did.

Anna's voice was soft and slightly off-key when she picked up the refrain from Liz. She stumbled over a few of the trickier words, and I felt a little better.

My heart was beating fast when she neared the end of her lines, but I started in where I was supposed to. My eyes picked out my mom and Hanna in the crowd, and I kept my focus on them, trying to pretend no one else was listening. The relief that washed over me as I ended my refrain was palpable, and I was so glad I'd gotten all my words right I didn't even care how many wrong notes I'd hit.

I trailed off my last note, expecting Darja to pick it up and keep the song going, but my note trailed into silence. I glanced over, and caught the *taja* on the side closest to me shifting uncomfortably under the weight of the girl. My relief dissipated, my unease returning in the silence that followed. Could the girl even talk?

Eliise stepped forward again, a smile on her lined face. "That was beautiful, girls," she said warmly. Turning to the crowd again, she raised her voice. "It is time for the *sidumine*, the binding, the last part of our ritual." She turned to Darja then, and raised a withered hand to lay against the girl's brow. She spoke rapidly, words in the old language, too fast for me to follow. When she was finished she stepped back and nodded at the two *tajas*. "You may proceed."

It happened so fast, I didn't have time to react. I don't know how I would have even if I'd been able. With a soft grunt of effort, the two women hoisted Darja between them, and stepped toward the fire. There was a plank there that I hadn't noticed, set into the bonfire at an angle. Flames lapped at its base, and without pause the two *tajas* moved the girl into position at the base of the plank, then let her arms go. The girl, already limp, fell back against the thick wooden plank, flames licking at the lace of her skirts even before the *tajas* had moved back out of the fire's reach.

What?!

I tried to say something, but the words caught in my throat, and before I could move, before I could *think*, Eliise was there, a small container in her hand, and she dropped it at the base of the plank. The fire plumed upward, billowing up around the girl.

Eliise's voice was loud in my ears, "*Vaim on täidetud.*"

And the voices of the crowd even louder, "*Tasakaalus, harmoonia.*" But the crowd, the other girls, everything else had ceased to exist as my focus narrowed down to Darja, where she lay motionless against the wooden plank, her body consumed by fire. Her eyes, though. They were still alert, dilated but aware, and they locked on mine, horror and agony clear in her gaze even though she was silent and still. My heartbeat thundered in my ears. Was this a trick? It couldn't be real.

Suddenly a flash of light caught my eye and I tore my gaze away from hers. It was her hair, the braid where Eliise had joined our locks together. It gleamed, flaring more brightly than the blinding light of the fire, for just a second, then faded. Had I imagined it? Was I imagining all of this?

That was when the screaming started.

∾

Want more *Season of Embers*? Sign up for our mailing list at https://www.rachaelvaughn.com/signup and as a first-time subscriber exclusive, you'll get the next chapter in Sofi and Darja's story, plus reminders about pre-orders and updates on the May 1st, 2020 release.

ACKNOWLEDGMENTS

Blood Rose was first conceived of nearly a decade before it was written, in the days when story ideas were plentiful, but the idea of actually writing books had never crossed our minds. It started out as an idea for a graphic novel, and we went so far as to write and illustrate about ten pages before everything ground to a halt. The birth of our daughter, coupled with the realization that we don't even remotely enjoy illustrating graphic novels, meant that this project was abandoned for years.

Then, after our first book was written and on its way to publication, and we were trying to decide what came next, we dug up the old outlines and found that the idea that Rose's story might actually get told was too exciting to pass up. So here we are.

I, Laura (Rachael), could never have done any of this without Trent (Vaughn), so thank you forever for all the work you put into this with me.

Wendi Williams, editor extraordinaire, and wearer of ALL THE HATS, you are everything. Thank you from the bottom of my heart.

Thank you to my daughter Seva, for understanding that I often come home from work and then keep on working, and for being awesome in all the ways.

Mom and Dad, and Mom and Dad, thanks to each of you for supporting us in our writing, and also in every other way. We would not be who we are without you.

Thanks to the gang at Firefly for your encouragement, and to Johnny in particular, for delivering cover art beyond my imagining.

Thanks to JCalebDesign for the cover design.

And last, but never least, all the gratitude in the world to our readers. I hope you love this book as much as we love you.

ALSO BY RACHAEL VAUGHN

The Last Culling

ABOUT THE AUTHOR

Rachael Vaughn is the creative brainchild of husband-and-wife writing duo, Laura Rachael Black and Trenton Vaughn Hockersmith.

Laura is the wordsmith of the pair, and a bona fide dabbler. With interests in everything from mosaics to wood carving and playing the hammered dulcimer, there isn't much that doesn't appeal to her insatiable need to create. When she isn't writing, Laura stays busy as the co-owner of Firefly Tattoo—one of Indianapolis's premier tattoo studios—where she is also a full-time artist. You can check out her professional tattoo gallery at https://www.fireflytattoo.com/f88479627.

Trent acts as the bookends of the writing process. He serves as the team's world-builder and plot developer on the front end, and acts as an editor and proofreader (plus the ultimate voice of reason) on the backside. His educational background in English and psychology help him craft vibrant worldscapes and compelling, authentic characters. When not mired in the trenches of world-building, Trent enjoys reading, playing video games, and practicing jiu-jitsu and tai-chi.

The team shares more than a pen name. Their home outside Indianapolis is also inhabited by their daughter, Seva, and Helena, the world's fluffiest cat.

Connect with Rachael Vaughn

∾

Mailing List:
https://www.rachaelvaughn.com/signup

Website:
www.rachaelvaughn.com

Facebook Page:
www.facebook.com/rachaelvaughnauthor

Instagram:
@rachaelvaughnauthor

Publisher:
www.glasswingpress.com